Advance praise for *In the Event of*

"Full of swoony steam, heartfelt charm, and laugh-out-loud moments, *In the Event of Love* is exactly the slow-burn, second-chance, friends-to-lovers romance I was craving. Treat yourself to the beautiful magic of Courtney Kae's writing!"
—Ali Hazelwood, *New York Times* bestselling author of *The Love Hypothesis*

"With its charming small town, snowy mountaintop kisses, and dreamy lesbian lumberjane, *In the Event of Love* is perfect for the holidays!" —Helen Hoang, *New York Times* bestselling author of *The Kiss Quotient*

"Courtney Kae's *In the Event of Love* is the small-town winter romance of my dreams; sparkling, pine-scented, and as beautifully atmospheric as the season itself. The Sapphic slow-burn love story is both gorgeously soft and steamy, the feelings will wreck you, and the laugh-out-loud moments will make you want to text entire paragraphs to your best friend. A completely charming read for any time of year."
—Lana Harper, *New York Times* bestselling author of *Payback's a Witch*

"*In the Event of Love* is ultra cozy, heart-meltingly sweet, and full of warm wit. Courtney Kae shines with a fresh, bright voice and supremely relatable characters including a dreamy lumberjane who instantly stole my heart!"
—Rosie Danan, author of *The Roommate*

"Wintry perfection, a cozy flannel blanket of a book that wraps its reader in the warmest hug, full of wish-they-were-real characters and off-the-charts sexual tension. [*In The Event of Love*] made me laugh, weep, and believe in the fairy-lit magic of second chances." —Rachel Lynn Solomon, bestselling author of *The Ex Talk*

"With the delicious small-town reunion tension of *Sweet Home Alabama* and the deeply romantic childhood friends-to-lovers arc of *Love & Other Words*, *In the Event of Love* is about finding your way home in every sense of the word. This is a joyful, cathartic story to savor . . . if, unlike me, you can keep yourself from devouring it in one go." —**Ashley Winstead, author of *Fool Me Once* and *In My Dreams I Hold a Knife***

"*In the Event of Love* is a holly jolly delight! Courtney Kae's debut is a cinematic second-chance romance that sparkles like a Christmas tree [. . .] you'll fall in love with the small town of Fern Falls just as much as you fall in love with Morgan and Rachel." —**Timothy Janovsky, author of *Never Been Kissed***

"*In the Event of Love* reads like a Hallmark Christmas movie and goes down like a mug of peppermint hot chocolate. Cozy, comforting, and surprisingly steamy— this is the queer Christmas story we deserve!" —**Alison Cochrun, author of *The Charm Offensive***

"The heartwarming romance we've been waiting for that delivers on our favorite holiday tropes. Courtney Kae is my new autobuy!" —**Saranna DeWylde, author of the Fairy Godmothers, Inc. series**

"Sweet as a cup of hot cocoa (with some spice mixed in), *In the Event of Love* is the feel-good, queer, second-chance holiday romance we've all been waiting for. With a charming, layered cast of characters, it will have you wanting to escape to quaint-yet-progressive Fern Falls alongside Morgan, Rachel, and the rest of the gang for a stroll through the trees and a treat from Peak Perk Cafe." —**Anita Kelly, author of *Love & Other Disasters***

In The Event of Love

COURTNEY KAE

KENSINGTON
PUBLISHING CORP.

www.kensingtonbooks.com

KENSINGTON BOOKS are published by
Kensington Publishing Corp.
119 West 40th Street
New York, NY 10018

All Kensington titles, imprints, and distributed lines are available at special quantity discounts for bulk purchases for sales promotion, premiums, fund-raising, educational, or institutional use.

This book is a work of fiction. Names, characters, businesses, organizations, places, events, and incidents either are the product of the author's imagination or are used fictitiously. Any resemblance to actual persons, living or dead, events, or locales is entirely coincidental.

To the extent that the image or images on the cover of this book depict a person or persons, such person or persons are merely models, and are not intended to portray any character or characters featured in the book.

Special book excerpts or customized printings can also be created to fit specific needs. For details, write or phone the office of the Kensington Sales Manager: Kensington Publishing Corp., 119 West 40th Street, New York, NY 10018. Attn. Sales Department. Phone: 1-800-221-2647.

The K logo is a trademark of Kensington Publishing Corp.

ISBN: 978-1-4967-3896-7 (ebook)

ISBN: 978-1-4967-3895-0

First Kensington Trade Paperback Printing: September 2022

10 9 8 7 6 5 4 3 2 1

Printed in the United States of America

For Michael. You make writing about true love easy.
For Aisley. You make love too small of a word.
For readers who are here to see themselves: Welcome home.

Fundraiser Quote

November 25, 9:15 p.m.

From: management@peakperk.com

Dear Morgan,

We apologize for the late notice, as we're sure you must be completely booked at this point, but we hope you might consider heading a last-minute fundraiser in Fern Falls this December? Your events at the inn were always so memorable, and your dad talks about you often. You would be the best person for this job with your knowledge of the area and history here. Even though you haven't been back in a while, we hope you'll reply for more information. It'd be great to have you around again.

Thank you so much for your time.

Warmly,

Peak Perk Café

CHAPTER 1

I jab my purple mani at "archive email" and hope management @peakperk feels the sting of Lilac Lover through the interwebs.

Fern Falls. Like some café could lure me home after seven years. Funny how Dad talks about me when he can't be bothered to send more than a text every other week. The five-hour drive between that minuscule mountain town and Santa Monica is a freedom I won't surrender, and I'm booked at least through bridal season 2088.

"If it isn't Morgan Ross," a voice booms above the roar of the bar. A collar of white chest hair peeks out from Frank's Big Wave Daddy tank top as he leans across the counter to swipe at a glob of something that might be salsa.

I should have had a second glass of wine prior to coming here. Bartender Frank is a buzzkill. I banish my cursed Android to my pocket before it summons more ghosts from my past. "Frank." I tilt back, praying to the core workout goddess I don't topple off this bamboo stool. "What's it been? A year?"

Wish it'd been longer, but my co-worker Sonia loves Five-

Dollar Margarita Fridays—and I've exhausted my cancellation passes. The Sand Bar is between our apartments, making it tough to skip when she knows my plans for tonight (chilling with my succulents).

Tomorrow, we'll tie up final details for our biggest wedding yet, and then I'll be too busy to visit this charming place with all the noise, the people, the sticky-syrup smell, the people, the literal sand piled along the molding, the peop—

"Thought I'd only get to see your face in the *Times*, but here she is, in the flesh! And in my bar!" Frank smacks the counter so enthusiastically, I jostle, gripping the stool for dear life.

Wearing Manolos to a bar with a beach complex was a terrible idea. As far as I'm concerned, the floor is actually lava. "Ha. Thanks, Frank. That was no big deal."

It was a *huge* deal, and I still love being reminded of it, even six months later. The *LA Times* article flashes in my mind with the pastel photo of the puppy tea party I ran for a local influencer celebrity. It brought so much buzz to The Barnes Events Company, Johanna put me on the McTannum and Sparks wedding, our top-tier celebrity clients. Well, Lexi Sparks is A-list. Chad McTannum was a child soap opera star, and now he just parties so hard and so often that even the tabloids stopped caring. But if all goes well, I'll be promoted to launch our sister site in New York come January. As far away from my hometown as I can get in this country and closer to running my own business, something that's all mine, that no one can pull out from under me. Take that, management@peakperk.

"So, tell me. Whatchya drinkin'?" There's zero counter space, just Frank, as he sprawls closer and whisper-yells, "And is Spum really dishing out a mil for the bachelorette party?"

I nearly choke on my own saliva. I hope whoever gave my clients that god-awful couple name is only referenced by explicit innuendos for the rest of their existence. I give Frank my best *Don't Fuck with Me* grin. "So, Big Wave Daddy's big into gossip mags, is he?"

Frank stands up (thank god) and raises his hands in faux innocence. "Hey, just thought they might consider the most happening dive on the strip is all."

If my mouth weren't already dry, I'd choke on my spit again. I'm done with the sweet part of *Don't Fuck with Me*. I spread my palms on the counter (regretting it instantly) and look Frank square in the eyes. "Lexi Sparks wouldn't consider holding her bachelorette party at your bar if—"

"If it didn't come so highly recommended!"

I snap my gaze to Sonia as she sidles up beside me, all overly cheery as always, brown skin glowing, brown curls flying, a margarita glass that could qualify as a small country in each hand.

I sigh. No one can stay mad around Sonia. It's sorcery, really. And why we make the best team. I bust the vendor's balls, and she makes them smile while they comply. Frank's doing it now.

"Nah, Sonia. You're too kind." He's literally blushing. I didn't think his face could get more "hopped off a tanning bed like this." He's sunburning as we speak.

"We're considering lots of places, but we'll add The Sand Bar to the list, okay?" she chirps, as she hoists onto a bamboo contraption and slides my marga-pitcher before me.

"Those are on me," he says to Sonia and winks, like we should sing praises of his ten-dollar generosity; then, hallelujah, he gets called to the other side of the bar.

My shoulders relax the slightest bit now that we're Frank-free. "Why are you nice to him?"

"Girl, he's harmless."

"He's gross."

"True, but the nontoxic kind. Which you'd know if you ever met me here anymore! I miss our weekly drink nights!" Sonia sips her sunrise-colored slush, and guilt brews in my gut. She really does try to be friends with me, so of course, I started keeping her at a distance once drinks turned into deeper conversations. Fern Falls ruined friendship for me. Specifically, Rachel

Reed ruined friendship—and romance—for me. And I will not dwell on something that happened over seven years ago. *It'd be great to have you around again.* Yeah. Real great to relive the most humiliating and painful moments of my youth, thanks so much, random café manager.

"Gross nontoxic isn't really selling the whole socializing thing, Sonia," I chide as I take a long drink of mango-rita . . . and, okay. I taste what she sees in this place and hate that it's absolutely delicious. I suck down another strawful. Or five. Thanks to the rosé I deemed as necessary prep for The Sand Bar, this liquor shoots straight to my head, replenishing the buzz that Frank dampened and then some.

She serves up some major side-eye, dark curls falling over her orange tank-top strap.

"Don't look at me in that tone," I say, lips wrapped around my sugared tequila injection.

Sonia narrows her eyes. "What's going on, Morgan?"

"Black roses." I slug another gulp and ignore the fact that half my pitcher-glass is drained, and I can't really taste the alcohol anymore . . .

"Morgaaan."

That dragged-out *a* means business. I mean to fully avoid all questions of a personal nature. "Lexi won't budge. Will we need to get them imported, or can a local florist come through?"

"Imported. Definitely. But don't change the subject. I've only seen you drain a drink that fast one time before, and . . ."

I clutch my glass, drink faster, throw caution to the brain freeze. Damn Sonia and her attention to detail. Getting an email from Fern Falls is not the same as my two-year-old breakup with Josh Taylor. I hate that she witnessed me that night in all my martinied glory, and there's no way I'm about to unpack my Fern Falls–fucked past in The Sand Bar. No way I'm going to let one stupid email and the stupid memories of the stupid people it's chained to take me down. Instead, I inhale the rest of my drink and say something so horrifying, my Manolos already despise me for it: "Let's dance."

Sonia peers at me like I just suggested an evening of sledding down Third Street Promenade.

I laugh and tug her through the tight crowd onto the dance floor . . . or the part of the floor mostly cleared of sand, where people bump along to some sort of electronic beat. There's another version of myself, the regular one, standing in the corner with her arms crossed and her blond hair pulled back in a bun, planning an extra-horrific hangover so I'll never attempt this again. Screw it. I want to forget that email. I want to forget Dad and how we haven't had a true more-than-surface conversation in years. I want to forget his terrible ex, Christy, who was the cause of our family's implosion. And I definitely want to forget goddamn Rachel Reed, like I'd been forgetting her every day until that email bombed my in-box. I want to be free again.

I shake out my hair and relish how it sways against my shoulders. Sonia beams, and the serotonin jolt of her high-wattage smile hits so hard, I actually start dancing.

She squeals. "Look at you go, girl! Get it! I haven't seen you like this since the Rodriguez wedding!"

Fair. The last time I dragged Sonia onto a dance floor was at her cousin Marco's wedding, the first event we pulled off without a single hitch. We partied until two a.m. Well, it's almost ten now, and we've got an upcoming event we're gonna ace again, and that's worth dancing for. Good things are coming, and no email can stop that.

"Listen," I yell above the noise, "we are badass and we're gonna knock this freaking Spum wedding out of the park, okay? We are moving to NYC to be our own boss bitches!" I don't even care that I embraced *Spum* or that my words slur or that this place smells like tropical sunscreen in the dead of fall. I just want to ride this awesome buzz (okay, more on the drunk end of the buzz spectrum, thanks to my pre-gaming) and let all the worries fall away.

Sonia tilts her head back and laughs. "Yeah! Those positions belong to us!"

I grit my teeth, shake my ass, and let that worry bounce off, too. There's no way Johanna's gonna pass me up for that promotion. I've been her top planner for years, helped her build this business from the ground up. Soon, I'll be in a new city, an even bigger place to get lost in. It'll be me, a fresh roster of A-list clients, and a chic apartment with closets packed full of designer clothes I buy with cash.

That'll be it.

Then I'll be something.

"NYC has nothing on me," I yell, then shake faster. Free, free, free.

A sly smirk creeps across Sonia's face. "The hottie at your back looks like he wants to be on you."

As she finishes saying it, a sultry voice wafts on the pineapple-laced air. "Hey, wanna dance?"

Some rainbow-hued disco ball flashes, making me squint as I glimpse his profile. He has a dark hoodie pulled low on his brow, so I can't even see his eyes, but his razor-sharp stubbled jawline summons my insta-reply. "Yes," I breathe.

Then the corner of his lip tilts up into a crooked smile, and R.I.P. me. R.I.P. me into the goddamn ground.

Thank the Sweet Lord Jesus for blessing me with bisexuality.

I start to sway against him but glance at Sonia with a raised brow. She beams, a true wingman, and whispers, "You know I'm dancing off a broken heart, friend. Let's go." Then she throws her hands up and bops her head to her own beat.

My chest aches. Sonia has reason to hurt. Her girlfriend of two years just moved to the UK, and long distance is tough on them. What reason do I have? This pain was supposed to be over when I left home, when I took what little planning experience I had to LA, got an internship with Johanna, and threw myself into her business. I'm independent now, far from that small mountain town that crushed me, and all it takes is one email to feel the stab of all those broken pieces again? Fuck. That.

So with true dignity and swagger, I grind my ass into the beautiful stranger's groin.

"Shit, girl." He chuckles low in his throat and stumbles back, wrapping his fingers around my hips. "You've got moves."

My heart squeezes again.

Whether it's that damn email or my damn subconscious, I'm seventeen again and at my high school graduation party, right back beneath those twinkling lights, among soft music. Rachel's lips meet mine. Right before we never speak again. The worst part is that I don't blame her for cutting me out of her life. Watching Christy break Dad's heart, break our family in front of the whole town that same night, made me want to break something, too. Rachel happened to be the closest thing. Collateral damage. And even after a lifetime of friendship, a glimpse of more, I wasn't worth hearing out, forgiving. I wasn't worth it.

For the second time tonight, I rebel. Push the pain back down where it belongs. The regular version of me storms out, promising hexes atop hangovers as I reach over my shoulder and press a bold finger to Beautiful Stranger's lips. "No talking," I whisper in a husky voice that belongs to no form of myself whatsoever.

He smiles, revealing a flash of white teeth, and my thoughts stop in their tracks. My body acts of its own accord as I turn into his neck and run a hand over his chest. His solid, well-formed chest. He slides his palms around my back and pulls me against him, hot, hard, encompassing everything.

There is no other version of me but the one here, now, in this gorgeous man's arms, my insides bursting to life with lust and thrill and thoughtlessness.

I want more of it and run my hands higher, dig my nails into the soft cotton of his sweatshirt. Strobe lights skew each movement, stroke, touch.

This won't hurt a thing.

Free, free.

The music crescendos, and he crushes his lips to mine.

Free.

Nothing else exists but his firm, sweet mouth, his tongue coaxing mine. I push back his hood and trail my fingers through his lush, silky hair.

My knees go weak, my blood buzzes, my brain's a black hole of bliss.

This is the whole wide world and it is so, so good.

Then the real world invades. Lights flash, and I pull away, blinking.

The music spikes, but the crowd is frozen around us.

"Morgan." Sonia's voice materializes beside me, jarring with its urgency.

"What's wrong?" I ask groggily.

Her face is all screwed up, like it was that time a birthday clown showed up wasted and pantless. Everyone in the crowd is holding up phones. My gut lurches into my throat. They're all pointed directly at me.

I pat my clothes. Shit. This was not the night to wear tight white slacks. Did I tear them while dancing? It's the end of the month, but did I start my period again? Great. I'm gonna go viral for being that girl with torn, bloody pants kissing a hot-ass guy. Oh my fucking god. I look up at Hot-Ass Guy, and whatever buzz I was riding screeches to a halt. The hood of his sweatshirt slaps his back as he runs for the exit, flocked by his friends.

Sonia takes my hand and tries to do the same with me, but my legs are heavy and everything is thick and bright, like swimming through piña colada pudding. People crowd too close with flashing phones and yell things like, "What's your name?" and

"How long have you two been hooking up?" I'm sweaty-cold-can't-breathe as I stumble with Sonia out the door.

I gulp fresh air to fill my too-tight lungs, run my clammy palms along my thighs. My heart's running sprints. "What—happened—"

Sonia braces me with a steady hand on my lower back.

She bends down and shows me her phone. Instagram fills the screen.

It's me. The photos. They're all of me. My body snaked with that guy's, plastered in an infinite, multi-filtered grid.

I barely hear her say, "I'm so sorry, Morgan. I had no idea with the hoodie and the lights," before I hurl mango margarita into the gutter, splattering my precious Manolos.

For once, I don't give a shit about shoes.

That wasn't just some guy. It was the very guy whose face was once on covers of *BuzzWhir News* for running stark naked out of The Viper Room. And I am the biggest idiot in the motherfucking USA, which says a lot.

I dissolve onto the concrete, swiping the back of my hand across my mouth, reckoning with what I've done.

That guy was Chad McTannum.

One half of Spum.

The whole of my career is over.

CHAPTER 2

Curse the asshole who invented windows.

I scramble to draw the curtains, and rushing out of bed does not bode well for me. I trip on the shameful remnants of last night: white slacks, gray blouse, and those damn dirty Manolos, puddled upon my vintage rug as evidence that it all was not, in fact, a terrible nightmare. Shoes never looked so guilty. I throw them across the room, where they slam into the side of the hamper. Traitors.

My life cannot be so fragile that one night—one minute—changes everything. The memory of that kiss makes me rush to the bathroom, where I hurl more evidence of my demise into the toilet. Fucking Chad McTannum. How could I have been so dense? What event planner doesn't recognize the face of her own client's fiancé?

I flush and slump to the side, cold tile against bare legs, and run a mental scan of the one in-person meeting I had with Lexi Sparks.

It was back in March, with Johanna and Sonia in the main

conference room at The Barnes. She came along to confirm her assistant hadn't booked her with an actual barn. Half her face was veiled in Dolce & Gabbana sunglasses, and her whole six-foot-one entourage was adorned with black suits, dark eyewear, and Bluetooth earpieces. It was like that scene straight out of her reality show when bodyguards followed her so closely, she accidentally kissed one of them instead of her date. Tiffany, her petite, blond, bubbly-to-mask-paranoia assistant, did all the talking—talking that grew progressively higher-pitched the longer the meeting lasted. Which, now that I recall, couldn't have been more than ten minutes.

Tiffany tapped on her tablet and set a date between Ms. Sparks' modeling, acting, social, and spa commitments. Lexi did an over-the-glasses scan of us with every ounce of Hollywood producer's daughter attitude she possessed, pushed them back up her pale pinprick of a nose, nodded at Tiffany, then sauntered out the door with a trail of suits at her heels.

Tiffany blustered up the handbag and full Starbucks tray she toted (because "Ms. Sparks might want a soy macchiato or hibiscus refresher at any given point"), said she'd be in touch (yet didn't say that meant a minimum of four times daily), then tripped through the door.

So, no. Unless Chad was disguised as a security guard, I'd never actually met him. Until last night.

I groan and melt onto the tile.

Too much pre-bar wine, a margarita that could flatten Lexi's guest list, and email-induced rage are my only excuses. Otherwise, I would have had to notice him. Even with the lights and that stupid hoodie, he reeked of the white cis male privilege that's enabled his decades-long, washed-up actor mantrum.

I rest my head against the wall and zone out at the view of my apartment through the frame of my bathroom door. I am this: clean lines and surfaces, pale neutrals swathed in filtered light, houseplants in favor of pets and picture frames, fridge stocked with cold brew and mail-delivery meals, expiry labels face-out.

I am not the girl I was last night.

I am not the girl I am now, moping on herringbone-patterned marble.

And I am definitely not the girl I was in Fern Falls.

I am Morgan Ann Ross. Planner to the stars. Near-future promotee to The Barnes, NYC, running the show and my own damn life. Cool, collected, in fucking charge.

I peel myself off the floor and splash cold water on my face; take in the girl in the mirror.

Maybe she's dehydrated and the only Californian in need of Vitamin D, but her balayage is well-blended, and her brows are on point. I'll slap some concealer beneath my eyes to highlight the blue part of the gray, march down to The Barnes, and work this whole thing out with Johanna. Drink some water and cold brew and fix this shit.

Good morning, Morgan.

I freeze as Google announces my fate.

It's seven a.m. on Saturday, November twenty-sixth. Currently, in Santa Monica, the weather is sixty-five degrees and sunny. Your commute to work is twenty minutes by foot, one hour by car. Your horoscope for today says beware of trouble with work, sex, love, social life, self, routine, thinking, and creativity. You have one hundred three notifications. Have a great day.

I hold my breath as Do Not Disturb shuts off and my purse transforms into a vibrator, nearly launching off the armchair.

I run across the room and scramble for my phone, clutching it like an anchor as I sink onto the edge of my bed. Each ping and flash across the screen swaps my self-affirmations for a splitting headache as I read the first cancellation:

Hey, Morgan. Sorry to do this in a text but Hedges and Stones can't afford to associate with this kind of press. We've got an album dropping with Sony and have to look our best. Good luck finding a band to perform if the wedding's still on. Peace.

The cancellations roll in—one text, email, DM, tweet after another. Caterer, lighting, venue, some favor company I haven't used in five years.

I skip right over the text from Dad checking in about the holidays. No sense in replying now, as my plans consist of self-imploding.

Time dissolves into doom as I scan and scan and scan.

Then the most dreaded one lands the final blow and I fall into the pillows, flimsy pep talk armor shot to shreds.

A tweet from the blue-checkmarked avant-garde avatar that is Lexi Sparks, to her 2M followers:

> Morgan Ross is a whore. Can't believe I trusted The Barnes. She'll never work in LA again. Fired, obv. #VictimizedForMyFame #MorTheWhore

I lurch off the bed to make a beeline for the toilet when my phone rings. It's Johanna's ringtone. The one that sounds like a fire alarm.

"Hello," I choke out as I freeze mid-lunge and swallow stomach acid.

I brace for a yell but shouldn't. Even in the worst-case event scenarios, I've watched her calmly pull someone to the side for making a disastrous mistake, then seen that same vendor sobbing in the bathroom ten minutes later. Johanna Barnes doesn't need to yell.

"Be in my office by eight." She hangs up.

It's seven-thirty.

Looks like I'm heading to my annihilation by foot.

I make it to hell with three minutes to spare.

Dread has turned my life into The Upside Down. Entering the charming boutique-style storefront of The Barnes used to feel like walking into a living dream, but today, the door carves me out as I push through it.

I stand in the entrance, clutching my purse in one hand and my chest with the other, taking in everything I stand to lose if this meeting ends in heartache. The business has evolved so much since we moved in, since Johanna hired me at eighteen straight out of Fern Falls. We've evolved, too. From mentor/mentee to boss/employee, but the heart in this place still beats strong. I tread slowly. My flats tap on the glossy concrete, then sink into the plush rugs I helped pick out. Blues and greens to set a calming tone. I run my fingers over the smooth back of a wooden chair and take in one of the four white tables placed throughout the room, a succulent terrarium in the center of each. Will I ever be able to hold a client meeting here again? Sit with them and reference our past events and current vendors, browse fabrics, florals, caterers, cakes, music, photographers, body paint, dog dresses—anything imaginable to make each event perfect, from the basic to the flamboyant? Goddamn, my gut hollows out. Before clients like Spum, the events were more simple, sincere. I loved that high of working with people, honoring major milestones in their lives, being the one they trusted to make their celebration worthy of all the time and work and love that led to that moment.

It's why Johanna's trusted me all these years. Maybe I'm not worthy of being that person anymore, of being trusted at all.

A clicking sound snaps my gaze to the coffee bar in the corner . . . where my nemesis, Miles Knocks, leans against the wall and glares over while pressing BREW on the Keurig. I'm usually out of the office, running my own events, on Saturdays. I'd work a milk-chug contest at a frat party right now if it meant avoiding him.

I fix my eyes on the lovely fiddle-leaf fig beside Miles, because I'd like to keep down the protein bar that I scarfed on my sprint here. Miles has worked at The Barnes for a third of the time I have, and has tried to steal my clients since day one. For a while, he got into the office before anyone else and went through my upcoming events. If there was a task on my list for that week, he was sure to bring it up in front of my client to make it sound like I was falling behind ("Oh, Morgan, you'd better move on that hotel block before the massage convention comes through"). There was no massage convention, and the event was ten months out, but I still spent two hours convincing Mr. Reynolds that his meditation retreat wasn't doomed. The only way I got Miles off my back that time was to be in the office before him. He surrendered when our arrival battle reached three-thirty a.m.

He waves like he's on a parade float, the sleeve of his gray blazer riding up to flaunt a neon-orange watch that makes his white skin look fluorescent.

Even in my hangover chic black slacks and beige cardigan, I hold my own against him any day.

He's sporting his trademark look: garishly bright slacks he calls "fashionably edgy." Today, they're ketchup red, just a few shades bolder than his hair.

"You know, Morgan, I'm disappointed," he says, as the coffee machine warms water with a growl.

I cross my arms. "That you don't have better fashion sense? Understandable."

He snorts. I don't look at him directly.

"I thought getting that promotion to spearhead the East Coast branch would be a fun challenge. I was looking forward to seeing you at least try to beat me. It would have made the work day entertaining."

I school my features and meet his bland, beady eyes. "It was never your challenge, Miles, because you were never in the running."

He sneers as the machine hisses and spits out his coffee. "Tell that to Johanna. And your new nickname. Which is trending, by the way."

Before I can recover enough to bark a retort, Johanna's office door creaks open.

Hashtag Mor the Whore vanishes from my mind as Sonia strides out, eyes red, cheeks blotchy.

Shit. Shit, shit, shit. "You okay?"

She raises her chin. "I will be."

Godammit. I understand disciplinary measures coming my way, but Sonia's? What the hell did *she* do wrong? If I get fired, she'll have to assist Miles, and holy hell, that would be a universe of hurt she doesn't deserve. The weight of responsibility bears down on my chest. I was supposed to be the one leading the fresh team in New York. My eye catches on Johanna's placard beside her door: JOHANNA BARNES: C.E.O., THE BARNES EVENTS COMPANY. I've imagined my own placard at the future New York office more times than I can count. MORGAN ROSS: DIRECTOR, THE BARNES EVENTS COMPANY, EAST COAST BRANCH. My plan was to promote Sonia to Head Events Planner, giving her a bump up while I got mine. My eyes burn, forcing me to clear my throat. I've done so much to get here. Proven myself through years of flawlessly executed events. I wanted this to be it. I wanted to finally be enough.

"Are you doing okay?" she asks, voice cracking.

I blink fast, her face coming back into focus. "Fine," I lie, keeping my features smooth, brave. "Thank you for being there for me last night."

"Always. I'm so sorry I didn't realize it was Chad sooner."

"Sonia, this is not your fault."

"I know. But I'm still sorry about all of it. And you know it's not yours, either, right? It's not your fault, Morgan." She rubs her arms and holds my gaze.

Her words hit like ice water.

I've berated myself all morning, and she's . . . right.

I was upset. I drank and danced at a bar. Isn't that pretty standard bar behavior? But Chad McTannum asked me to dance while incognito and engaged, and come to think of it, without a trace of alcohol on his lips. Not that intoxication would have excused his behavior; it just proves how willful it was. He went into The Sand Bar with a motive, and I was the victim who happened to be there—and the one taking the brunt of the fallout.

Where's the Chad the Cheater hashtag? He'd love a scummy fifteen minutes of Twitter fame.

Righteous anger heats me into a living, breathing, burning man. I won't only fight to keep my job; I'll make sure Sonia retains hers, too.

"Let me know if you need anything," I say, straining to keep any rage from my tone.

"You, too." She places a hand on my arm, then walks out, sniffling.

I face the gaping maw of Johanna's office door, grip my purse strap, and charge into the mouth of the beast, fully ignoring a dark chuckle that comes from the coffee bar. If Johanna is going to let Sonia and me go for this, she isn't the person I thought she was.

The woman herself sits in a dusky pink desk chair, typing away, the soft glow from her computer doing nothing to ease the frustration on her face.

Her brows knit together, dark eyes scanning the screen as she taps at her keyboard. Even under stress, she's the epitome of elegance. Her dark curls are piled high on her head, effortlessly stylish, and both her silk lavender blouse and berry lips pop against her dark brown skin. She waves a perfectly manicured hand toward a chair facing her desk and puts the other up to her earpiece. "Listen, Tom. I'm fully abreast of our contract terms, and we are well within the window to cancel without penalty and with a full refund. I expect to see the deposit reimbursed by day's end, or the next call you get will be from my lawyer."

My stomach sinks as I sit. Thomas is our contact at the Beverly Hills Hotel, where Lexi wanted her rehearsal dinner.

My boiling rage lowers to a simmer.

All of this is so messed up, and Johanna has to deal with it because of me. After all we've been through, this is new: this feeling of letting Johanna down. It makes my limbs leaden, and my neck flushes hot. Maybe it's for the best if she lets me go. If leaving is what it takes to save The Barnes's reputation, to not let her down again, I'll accept that. I won't let anyone suffer because of my mistake.

She takes off her earpiece and gives me her full attention. "Morgan—"

"Johanna." I shuffle in my seat, straightening as much as my tense muscles allow. "You need to give Sonia her job back." My voice is firm, confident. Like someone who feels those things. Like the Director of The Barnes Events Company, East Coast Branch.

Her features twist in confusion. Then she stands, rounds the front of her desk, and sits in the chair opposite me. She leans forward, resting both elbows on her navy slacks. "That's really what you think of me?" she asks, making direct eye contact.

I cradle my purse in my lap and swallow the brick in my throat. "No. I saw her leave upset, and I don't want anyone to suffer because of my error in judgment."

"Ah," Johanna says as she reaches for a to-go cup from her desk. It's from Violet's, our favorite café around the corner. She hands me the cup, purple flower logo face-out. I wrap my fingers around the warmth of it, and the lavender scent makes me go the slightest bit languid. All the memories of late-night planning sessions hit me right in the feels. Before she hired Sonia and Miles, it was her and me and hustle and grit and lattes from Violet's. We were close back then, grabbing drinks after work. She still invites me to her daughter Brynn's birthday parties, but now we don't call each other just to catch up as often. The thought of not having her in my life anymore twists my stomach into knots. I couldn't drink this coffee if I tried.

"Figured you could use one as much as me." She raises her own cup in salute.

My palm sweats against the cardboard sleeve. "Please tell me straight. Is this a 'let go' latte?" Lexi's tweet flashes in my mind: *Fired, obv.* Great. I can never have a latte again.

"Morgan. I'm not letting you go."

Instant relief washes through me. I should have known

Johanna would have my back. I wince for second-guessing that, then tense all over again. "What about Sonia?"

"Sonia is going to the UK," she says calmly.

My face scrunches. "Why?"

"She wants to work things out with Bridget, and is taking a month off to do so."

I take a slow sip of my drink. Rich floral notes focus my mind. Why would she leave right now? How could a long-distance relationship be more important than her own career, her income? Even with the wedding canceled, there's so much more work to do. We have to get right back on our feet, not let Miles or Mc-Tannum or any other prick win.

Johanna catches my gaze. "And I want you to do the same."

My neck stiffens in surprise. I search her face for the punch line, but it's deadpan. "Johanna, I don't have a girlfriend overseas." Wish I did, though. Then I wouldn't be kissing asshole actors in disguise.

Johanna sets her cup on the desk, leans back in her chair, and crosses her arms like a parental figure. I fidget in my seat. By the time I left home, Dad and I hardly spoke at all. I moved five hours away to escape that loneliness. The kind that comes from being cohabitants instead of family, each unspoken word burrowing deeper and deeper until apologies are too far down to reach and better left buried.

"I want you to take December off." Her tone is as firm as her stare.

"No." The word flies from my mouth.

"Morgan." She leans forward, lacing her fingers together like she's strapping in for a long ride, shimmery rose gels on display. "I'd like to think we're a family here. I know your character and how devoted you are to your clients, so I know what you did was unintentional, and I fully blame Chad. You have a backlog of unused vacation time, and I'm making you take it. I want you to rest and recover."

I sigh and stare at my cup. Run my thumb over the corn plastic lid. Unfortunately, Johanna makes perfect sense. This scandal will be history after the holidays, replaced with the buzz and plans of a brand-new year. Stepping back for a bit would be the smart thing to do. I squirm. Taking a month-long break, though, could be detrimental to my career. Miles will use every moment I'm gone to get a leg up on that promotion, while I'm stuck at home with jade plants and *Schitt's Creek*. As much as I love David and Patrick, the Spum wedding filled my holiday plans. There is only so much TV a girl can take before she paints a face on her couch and tells it her deepest secrets. I don't want a Wilson in my living room. "Johanna. I want to head my own team at the new site. I'm not going to step down and let McTannum ruin that for me."

I already let the drama with Christy, Dad, and Rachel strain my high school career. I won't let this jerk mess up my actual job.

"Morgan," Johanna says, and sighs. "I haven't seen you take so much as a coffee break in months. You don't know how to operate on anything other than stress."

"That's not true." But even as I say it, my knee bounces and my free hand itches to check the notifications on my phone, although I know they're a trash fire. I'm programmed to be on high alert for the next X factor. I have to tackle a new event. It's the only way to move forward, to show that my past can't control me. To prove I'm not the pushover I was in Fern Falls, the Morgan who felt worthless and had no idea who she was.

Johanna's tone is gentle as she continues, "Christmas is in four weeks. Our biggest wedding of the season is canceled. Miles and I can handle the smaller events. Go take time off, and when you return, we'll talk about that position."

I stand so fast I nearly drop my coffee. "Talk? I thought it was a done deal. Are you seriously considering Miles?"

Visions of high-rises and cocktail parties, Broadway tickets and Met visits stutter and fracture, replaced with the image of Miles's ear glued to Johanna's door. I can practically hear him breathing from here.

"Morgan. I want what's best for you, not only my company. We just confirmed the lease for the space in New York, and hiring will begin after the first of the year. There's a lot ahead, and a fresh team and cross-country move is going to increase your stress. I'm not saying no; I'm saying take some time. Discover things that matter to you besides work and other people's celebrations. Find something of your own to celebrate. Take a vacation. Visit home. Care for yourself, and then we'll talk about you caring for a team and starting the new year off fresh."

I place my coffee on the desk and sit back down, heart rate returning closer to normal. She's right. I know it in my bones and hate it with my soul. Four weeks of nothing but time and loneliness stretch before me. I can't even try to be a real friend to Sonia, because she's gone, and who knows if she'll come home.

Home. Johanna said to visit home. The room brightens, my mind fog clears, and Miles Knocks can one hundred percent suck it. I'm fixing this if it costs me every shred of pride to do so, and how much of that do I have left, anyway? What I do still have is one shot at that promotion, to prove I can handle whatever stress comes my way. To truly start over and reach the level of success I've only ever dreamed of. To finally prove myself. "What if I told you I have an event that could fix everything?"

Johanna raises a brow and sweeps her hand in the air for me to proceed.

I grow supercharged as the details string together. "I got a request to run a fundraiser in Fern Falls. Where I grew up." My voice pitches higher at the mention of my hometown, and I shiver at the thought of going back, the possibility of facing people from my past after seven years away.

"So you'd be working still?" Johanna asks. "I'm not sure that's a good idea."

No. I can't lose this chance. "Think about it." I lean forward. "City girl returns home after a scandal, runs a charity event. I get the slowed-down holiday you want for me, and if you send reporters to the event, The Barnes will get press coverage, associating us with a wholesome, small-town occasion. It's Hallmark-level perfection."

No need to confess my holiday home will be an Airbnb where I can hole up and avoid anyone and anything to do with my childhood. I'll still be working and lapping Miles for this promotion; that's all that matters.

Johanna rubs her chin.

She's considering this. My knee bounces harder.

"It's a good idea," she says cautiously. "Is this really what you want?"

"Yes," I holler, bursting from my chair. *Yes* to winning back my career, *no* to being home. But it's a small price to pay for the future of my dreams. A little fundraiser, a few weeks tops. How hard could it be?

"Okay," she says, steepling her fingers. "Go for it. Keep me posted on what you need and when you want a press release sent out. I'll put Miles on administration."

All at once, The Upside Down turns right side up. PR solved, career saved, Miles my bitch.

I reach out my hand to shake on it, but she raises a finger. "On one condition."

My insides freeze.

Her brows perk up her forehead. "You take time off while you're up there, Morgan. I mean it. Text me photos of snow or something. Show me you've rested and recharged."

Sure, snap some pictures of myself in a puffy coat, drinking cocoa, putting my feet up in a rented cabin. Easy as a small café fundraiser.

I grin like I've been given a second chance at life. "Deal."

We shake on it, and I head to the door.

"And Morgan?"

I peer over my shoulder.

"Happy holidays." She smiles, replaces her earpiece, and settles back in front of her computer.

"You, too, Johanna." The season will most definitely be

happy now. Brimming with that joy, I retrieve the archived email on my phone, head down, spirits high, as I exit her office.

"Went that bad, huh?" Miles asks without feeling, leaning against the wall beside Johanna's door.

I don't look up as I type out a quick reply to the Peak Perk Café:

My contract is attached and I charge travel expenses. I'll send you my housing invoice in advance. See you this coming Monday to begin planning.

I'm gonna take these hometown jerks for all they're worth, no regrets.

But first, to deal with *this* jerk.

He stands before me, arms crossed.

"Miles?" I say, my voice achingly sweet.

He smirks like he's about to receive all the respect he deserves, which he is.

"Go fuck a pair of plaid capris."

His mouth falls open.

I smirk and stride out the door, the world righted and laid out before me. Just a little hometown detour, and everything I want will be mine.

Free, free, free.

CHAPTER 3

The twists and turns into Fern Falls do not scream a friendly, "Welcome home, Morgan Ann." My ass is numb from the nearly five-hour drive, and my knuckles could crack in half from gripping the steering wheel so hard. Clearly, LA traffic wiped my memory of driving on icy mountain roads. I pray to not fly off this cliff, and grapple for the address I scribbled on a gas receipt before I lost reception. The "Cozy & Clean Cottage in the Pines" profile said cell service was spotty—not that it was nonexistent. I thought they'd have better coverage up here by now. My phone's zero bars mock me: *You should have planned better. You should have remembered this.* Stop judging me, zero bars. I've spent seven years trying to forget all about Fern Falls, and my brain prefers to continue that pattern of self-preservation, thanks so much.

Down the road, treetops pierce the gray sky, and my chest tightens. I'm really back. I crack the window and let fresh air soothe me. All that's left is to get in and out of this town as fast as I can. Run the fundraiser, show Johanna I can handle stress, get good press for The Barnes, some R&R for me—done.

I round a bend and cough on cold air. The old inn where I had my first job planning events in high school stands high on the hill, a haven of rich, honey-stained cedar. Massive logs bolster its fog-wreathed roof, and buttery light frames the endless windows, all poised to feature breathtaking views of the town and forest and mountains beyond. So many rooms and hallways, gardens and pathways. And the courtyard that haunts me still.

But what lies beneath the inn makes my stomach cinch like it's setting off an emergency siren: the sprawling acreage of plush, hunter-green pines that is the Reed Family Tree Farm.

I lose my breath as memories break free from their time-sealed vault.

Rachel and I playing tag through a weave of tree trunks, using walkie-talkies like a forest game of Marco Polo. The fairy garden we built throughout the farm. The cigarettes we snuck into the hayloft and never smoked. How I ruined everything, and how she never spoke to me again. No matter how many times I called or texted or tried to catch her eye around town during my last summer here. My cheeks tingle, a prelude to tears, but the urge to cry is shocked from my system.

My tires lose traction on a patch of ice.

Air streams in as I start to spin out of control, grasping uselessly at the steering wheel. I narrow my gaze to see something—anything—beyond the swirling green that devours the road, reciting the rule for driving on ice: pump the brakes, don't slam. Nothing helps. My gut punches into my throat. I'm going to crash. I should have put on chains. My tires skid and slide to prove the point. A scream echoes through my window. My seat belt tightens as the car squeals to a stop off the side of the road, to the sound of splitting wood.

I blink rapidly. Needle pricks surge through my veins.

Gasping, I pat down my blush peacoat, gray pants, feel for any bloodied or broken skin. One glance in the rearview proves my hair isn't soaked with red, skin unscathed. Thank god I wasn't driving faster, due to gawking at the hill. Everything besides the side of my car and a smattering of wood splinters in the muddy snow is fine. "I'm fine." *You're fine. You're fine. You're fine.*

"Are you okay?" someone hollers from outside my open window.

Off the side of the road and into the trees, a down-clad mother clutches a bundle of snow gear to her chest. A child must be inside, because the purple legs of the puffy pants kick.

My throat feels coated in dust, so I nod in response to her question.

Her expression morphs, and she stares me down like I'm Effie Trinket on Reaping Day. "Good! Now learn to drive before you kill somebody!"

There's the Fern Falls I remember.

"Sorry," I rasp.

What if I had hit someone instead of a hunk of wood?

Oh my god. Holy shit. Get. It. Together.

I take in what I ran over, and my lungs lose breath again. Two wooden beams stick up from the snow, a piece of crushed wood barely hanging on between them. Directly beneath is a smattering of jagged splinters, a puzzle of red-painted words I piece together with what's left of the sign: REED FAMILY TREE FARM, A FERN FALLS TRADITION!

I crashed right into the Reeds' sign.

Rachel's sign.

I force myself to breathe through the panic and take in more of my surroundings.

Beyond the crushed wood, slushy snow slopes into thick, green forest. Candy cane–striped caution tape blocks off the foremost section of trees, and a small red hut that resembles

Buddy the Elf's handiwork stands right before the border. Just how I remember it.

Unbidden emotion springs to my eyes. Jesus. So much for slipping through this place unnoticed. Now I'll be lucky if the entire town doesn't know about my crash-landing by noon.

I take a deep breath. Maybe Rachel moved away, like me. The last time I heard from her (and only time) was in an Instagram message two years ago, saying she was in LA. I try not to think about how that message messed me up so much, I never replied, let alone viewed her profile. How seeing her face-to-face would undo me. But no, she can't be here. This place must still belong to her parents. Rachel and her brother Adam must have moved away by now.

I open the door and step into icy mud, knee-high boots sinking in as I dodge broken pieces of the sign. I'll go right up to that little shack and speak with an employee, sort this all out.

There's a rush of color at the edge of my vision. Someone runs out of the trees—wielding an ax? I take two startled steps, and my Fendis betray me. I slip and fall face-first into freezing mud.

The wet cold shocks my nerves, and I make a graceful grunt as I push up, swiping filth from my eyes.

"Are you okay?" asks a deep, feminine voice that must belong to the ax-wielder who ran through the trees. Probably an employee. Great, now I can pay for the damages, deal with the insurance shit, and be on my way before having to face a Reed.

"I'm fine," I sputter as I scramble to catch my footing, eyes burning. Then my damn fashion betrays me again and I sprawl forward—straight into flannel-clad arms.

She's strong and holds me up with ease. I push my forearms between us, trying and failing to keep the mud to myself. I've splattered her with it, and as I follow my trail of dirt to her face, my stomach nosedives to the flaming core of Earth.

Her long brown hair is slung in a braid that trails from a

white beanie, pulled low on her brow. Those molten brown eyes, rimmed with lashes that never needed mascara. Her sun-kissed cheeks are flushed beneath a light smattering of freckles that fans from the bridge of her nose. I once wanted to count every one, sweet little spots that softened her edges. I take a shuddering breath. She smells like the goddamn forest.

"Morgan?" Her voice pulls at my bones, and I will every ounce of balance and dignity I possess to keep me upright as I jerk back.

Rachel Reed stares at me, and I can't blink. She's here. She caught my fall. I covered her in sludge. Those melted chocolate eyes are transfixed on my face like I'm a ghost. We don't budge until a car door slams, jolting us from our silent shock.

"Is everyone okay?" a male voice calls.

I turn toward the newcomer, the weight of Rachel's stare on my back. Oh, god. No. Getting every awkward encounter out of the way, right, Universe? Is that what you're up to? "Heeeeey, Ben," I say.

Ben Parrish stops in his tracks. The only resemblance to the lanky white teen who was my very best friend is the black-framed glasses he always pushed up his nose, and the big blue eyes that revealed every emotion. Now, he's much taller than me and filled out with lean muscle. He runs a hand through his dark blond hair, eyes as wide as his lenses. "Morgan?"

Is my first name all anyone can say around here? He glances at Rachel, and that lights a fire in my gut. It used to be him, me, Rachel, and her older brother Adam, the closest group through our childhood and early teens. Now here I am, the outsider. Just like the last months after high school, what was supposed to be our best summer together. I never asked to be pitted against them. I never asked to see them at all. Especially not while looking like a swamp monster. "Listen," I say, turning back to Rachel, "I'm really sorry about the sign. I promise I'll pay for it."

Her lips part, and my gaze catches on them. Pouty and perfect and red. Lips I kissed. Whom does she kiss now?

Ben's voice sounds, wiping Rachel's lips from my mind, thank god. "Looks like the first thing we need to do is get your car towed, yeah? I'll call Adam," he says, running toward the red kiosk. Great, he'll probably get a photo, too, and here comes my car on the front page of *The Fern Falls Gazette.*

"Do you want to go through insurance?" I glance back at Rachel, but she's already a good distance away, following Ben. Like a slap in the face, all those moments flood back. When my graduation party was everything I wanted, because Rachel Reed was kissing me. Then, how my whole world shifted and went to hell when Christy rejected Dad's public proposal. How I said things to Rachel days later that I couldn't take back. She cut me out of her life after that, like all our years of friendship—and the new feelings we shared—meant nothing at all, weren't worth working things out for. She left me without a word, without a second chance, just like she's leaving now. Despite appearances, people here don't change. That fires me up, and I charge after her, because I have changed. I'm bigger than this now. "Rachel," I demand as I march to the red shack where she stands behind the cash register. "How do you want to handle this?"

I slam my palms on the counter, which makes the register rattle. Ben's eyes go wide, a corded phone pressed to his ear. My cheeks heat, but I won't say sorry. She's the one who should apologize for shunning me all those years ago. Rachel looks up slowly, like she's dealing with a loose cannon. My face flames.

"Morgan. This is a lot right now. Why don't you make sure you're physically okay first, get your car taken care of, then we'll handle the sign." She's so logical and cool and reserved and I'm literally standing here screaming, covered in mud. This was not the plan. Not in my worst nightmare.

"I want to pay for it."

She nods slowly, then turns away. Walks straight out of the booth like I'm not worth her time. Like she said her piece, and I have no say at all.

I don't want to handle the sign later. I want to take care of this now, never to return to this farm again. "Rachel!" I call after her.

She picks up her ax, slings it over a shoulder, and disappears into the trees. Fine. Maybe she just lives in a fucking tree now.

"Hey. Are you okay?" Ben appears beside me, making me flinch. "The tow truck will be here in a few."

Of course it will. Driving across town takes five minutes, and they'll make it in three to witness this train wreck.

"Thanks," I say, because I'm too flustered to utter anything else, and I haven't spoken to Ben Parrish in years. And who knows, he probably despises me, too, for the way I left. And the mess I made before I did.

"I'm sure this isn't how you wanted to come back to town," he says quietly, "but it's really good to see you, Mor."

His surprising kindness seeps warmth into my stiff limbs. I take him in. His big, genuine smile, little crinkles beside his eyes. We were the best of friends, and after that awful graduation party, just kind of grew apart. Not a wrenching separation like what happened with Rachel and me; something more gradual. Texts between us that went days, then weeks, without replies. No more frantic calls to discuss *Pretty Little Liars* plot twists or to catch up on how his last summer break at his grandmother's beach house went. A slow drain of friendship that one day dried up completely. "You, too," I say, without a note of bitterness.

After a few moments of awkward silence, a tow truck blares around the corner. My stomach seizes as it approaches and parks, revealing the person behind the windshield. God forbid Fern Falls should have more than one Adam.

Rachel's brother jumps down from the driver's side, an uncharacteristic frown where his beaming smile once was. His dark brown hair is mussed, cheeks ruddy, brown eyes cold when they land on me. But maybe I'm imagining it.

"Wow. Morgan. I didn't expect to see you again." He runs a hand through his hair and glances at Ben awkwardly. Okay, nope. His new icy demeanor must have everything to do with me, and how I treated his sister. The worst part is, I can't even blame him for hating me. I kind of hate myself a little bit, too. I hate all of this. I scrub my cheek, forgetting the mud drying on my skin. Some dirt flakes off. "I didn't expect to be back for a while, either." Or ever.

He glances around the property like he'd rather be anywhere but here, and I mean, same.

"You don't work at the farm anymore?" I ask, to fill the silence.

"Adam has his own auto shop," Ben says with a bit of a stammer. "He's won tons of accolades, voted best on the mountain." His cheeks turn red.

"It's not all that." Adam scrubs at the side of his neck, then turns toward my car and lets out a low whistle. He walks over and circles it, studying the very physical evidence of how together my life is right now. "It looks like mostly surface damage, although I can't say as much for the sign," he diagnoses, hands on hips, most likely adding this catastrophe to his list of Reasons to Resent Morgan Ross. "I guess I can tow it, if you want." His tone sounds like he'd rather lend me his toothbrush to wash my face with.

"I can give you a ride, Morgan," Ben offers. Thank god for one person here who doesn't hate me.

I'm exhausted and don't want to think about driving on that road again, so I grab my luggage from the (thankfully still intact) trunk.

Adam gives me his card before driving off, saying he'll call once he gets a closer look. I thank him, even though I'd rather scream. I want to get out of here well before the allotted time Johanna gave me.

I don't know when the fundraiser is scheduled for, but I do have an appointment at Peak Perk Café tomorrow morning to sort out the details. Details I hope will have me heading back to Santa Monica ASAP.

I load my luggage into the back of Ben's red Subaru as he waves goodbye to Adam, watching the tow truck well after it's farther down the road. I remember them having crushes on each other in high school before Adam graduated a year before us. Apparently, one of them still does. I have an urge to ask about it when we get in the car but bite my tongue. That's none of my business. Not anymore and not for a long time now.

As we buckle in and he backs out, I glare at the little red shack and the trees beyond it that Rachel slipped into. The nerve of her. If I was anyone else, she would have figured this out with me right here, right now. But no, she still has it out for me. She never gave me the second chance I would have given her. Why would seven years change that?

I laugh aloud at the thought, because being here makes me feel like a teen again. Awkward and awful and hated by all.

"Wow, that look could start a forest fire."

I startle, snapping out of my daydream—day*mare*. "Thanks for the drive," I say to change the subject.

He clears his throat. "So. You're really back, huh?"

"Not for long."

He sits up straighter. "How are things with you?"

My entire life is falling apart, just like the day I left. This town is a real special place. "So busy I can't believe I had time to come help out with an event up here, honestly. Working with a lot of celebrities and high-profile execs."

I'm already coating his upholstery with dirt. He doesn't need to see me as any more of a disaster.

Ben's throat bobs before he says, "A lot of really important stuff keeping you from coming home to say hey to old friends and family, yeah?"

I angle away from him, my face screwing up in disgust.

Who the hell does he think he is? So what if we were best friends in high school? He wasn't there for me when I needed him most, just like everyone else who I thought cared about me in this town. There's no point in holding back now. "You really gave those evergreens a run for their money pining after Adam Reed."

He clears his throat about twenty times. His knuckles whiten, and he grows extra-focused on the road. "It's not like that."

"Why not? Didn't it used to be?"

"Some things change, Morgan Ann, unlike your coldness with Rachel."

A thousand retorts sizzle on my tongue, but all I can huff out is, "You don't know the half of it."

"Neither do you," he mumbles.

Before I can fire back a reply, the car comes to a stop. Panic flares in my chest. I can't bring myself to look out the window. I didn't grab the directions to the rental cabin, which means we must be at Dad's house. The space we filled up with so much silence and pain after Christy left us. I swallow hard. They didn't date that long, maybe a year, but he let her in. Into our home, our lives; he hoped for more with her. And when that didn't happen, it was like he didn't stop wanting more. Life back with just the two of us was no longer enough. I hold my breath as I turn. There's the charming little cottage, identical to its Airbnb profile picture. What the hell? "How do you know where I'm staying?"

He winces. "Eh, sorry. I know as much as makes it around town, you know?"

Ugh. The invoice I sent to management@peakperk. Makes sense the whole town would know every detail by now.

I follow him out of the car and steady my steps before I get the chance to fall again. I don't need anyone else from my past catching me today. "How long have you known I was coming?"

He puts my luggage at the front of the cobblestone pathway that leads to the house. "Listen. What matters is that I'm sorry we got off on the wrong foot. I shouldn't have brought up old shit. I want to get to know you now, this Morgan. She seems really interesting and I'm sure has good reasons for being gone so long."

My muscles relax the slightest bit. A fresh start sounds good. I won't have to deal with these people after the fundraiser is over, and it's not like I'll be working with Ben or anything. I can suck it up for a minute to end this in a peaceful way. For karma, or whatever.

I shake his outstretched hand and force my best congenial expression. "To the new versions of us. And thank you for the ride."

"You holler if you need anything, okay?" His bright smile is full-on charm. What the hell is Adam waiting for?

"I don't have your new number?"

"The new Ben Parrish isn't that new." He chuckles. "I'm still at the same number, just like I'm still in the same old house down the hill from here."

I picture the A-frame cabin with purple eaves, which he lived in with his mom. It had a small storefront she ran a naturals shop out of, Mountaintop Mystic. It always smelled like freshly picked herbs and something delicious baking in the oven.

A woman's face pulls me from my reverie. Her pale nose is pressed up against the windowpane of the adjacent cabin as she stares unabashedly between Ben and me.

"It looks like we have an audience."

Ben chuckles and shakes his head. "Oh, that's Ms. Holloway. She moved to town a couple years ago. You know how it is up here. Hermits and busybodies. No one in between."

I huff out a laugh and give Ms. Holloway an elaborate wave.

The red-checkered curtains snap closed, and her salt-and-pepper hair disappears behind them. I give it five minutes before all of Fern Falls knows I'm here, if they don't already. Time to get inside and close my own curtains. God forbid any of my new social media followers find me up here, or worse, paparazzi. "Thanks, Ben," I say, picking up my bags.

He waves as he rounds the car, gets in, drives off.

I let my shoulders relax as I take in this little cutie of a cottage.

A porch wraps the perimeter of the log home, pines feathering the edges. A boxwood wreath charms the red Dutch door and garland loops the railings. A string of simple lights runs along the edge of the low, snow-dusted roof, and a vintage sled leans against the steps. Sweet reminders that the holidays are near, and suddenly, I'm grateful I won't have to spend this time alone in my apartment again, reheating leftovers and fighting the urge to drive up and see Dad, break our face-to-face stalemate for the first time in years. At least this cottage is a good kind of welcome, finally. Just me and 22456 Holly Lane at the top of the world, where everything is snowy-fresh and beautiful.

How can five hours from Los Angeles feel like another planet? I forgot how stunning this place is.

I shake my head at the irony of walking into this adorable home while covered in mud and traumatized from past demons.

If twenty-one was for legal cocktails, twenty-five is for full-blown breakdowns. I sigh at the winter wonderland spread before me. At least this breakdown comes with a breathtaking view.

Tomorrow will be better. I'll meet with the owner of Peak Perk, free from Ben and Rachel, one day closer to leaving this place. Tomorrow, I'll be myself again.

CHAPTER 4

The view from the cottage is even prettier in soft morning light. Somehow, I'll find a way to ruin this day. Slam my lips into someone else's? Crash my car into a beloved landmark? Fall into the arms of another person I've tried to forget for seven years?

Amazing how you can spend so much time crafting the perfect image, and over one weekend, it's all flung to hell. Never thought I'd actually love a Monday.

At least I've got sensible boots on, I won't be driving anywhere, and my lips are frozen. I curl my fingers around the warmth of a mug I pulled from the pantry, playing a serious game of how much cheap coffee does it take to replace central heating? Pretty soon I'll have to break down and build a fire in the potbelly stove I know isn't just for aesthetics. But toughing out the cold means I won't settle in. Getting comfortable will only open up more chances to run into Dad, Ben, or Rachel. I only have to see Adam one more time, and just to get my car back and leave this place once this little café fundraiser is over. That's how it's gonna stay.

The clock on the microwave shows nine a.m., finally. Peak Perk doesn't open until ten, so with our appointed nine-thirty meeting time, I should steer clear of more uncomfortable encounters.

It's gonna take at least twenty minutes to descend the hill into town. I place my mug on the counter and sigh. If only I could settle in beside it. Pulling my sweater on tight, I head out the door, where Ms. Holloway is already out on her front porch, rocking in her chair and writing in some notebook.

"Morning." I salute more than wave.

She peers over the top of her glasses and strokes the ball of tortoiseshell fur in her lap. Ben was wrong. There's a third kind of person in Fern Falls: the hermit–busybody hybrid.

I clear my throat and close the door behind me, praying I don't create a catastrophe before it even shuts.

Twenty minutes was a stretch. Thirty minutes is, too, because these "sensible" boots prove they're made for city sidewalks and not mountain inclines. I owe Ms. Holloway a thank-you card for serving as an initiation for the multitude of awkward stares my solitary parade ushers from cabin windows.

Eyes forward, I keep sliding to town, way behind schedule (first catastrophe of the day).

The purr of an engine pulls up beside me. And, yep, okay, they're stopping. *Keep inching forward. Don't make eye contact.*

The window squeaks down.

"You want a ride?"

I speed my steps. I'd remember that voice anywhere. It haunted my dreams all night. "Nope," I reply, and keep walk-sliding.

"I'm going into town. Are you headed there?" Her tires crunch snow at the same rate my boots do, emphasizing how very late I am and how it's still gonna take me at least twenty minutes if I continue like this.

I stop and sigh. What choice do I have? The meeting's in ten minutes, and the whole point of taking this job is to make a comeback, prove I can do something right. Arriving late won't show anything except that I can't function in these boots and I'm a poor planner. And I am anything but a poor planner. Despite these last few days.

I huff a foggy breath and turn toward Rachel. Her fingers hang loosely on the steering wheel, and her arm drapes out the window of her old red pickup with the farm's name on the door. She looks completely casual. A few strands of dark hair stray from beneath that same white beanie, if only to emphasize how cool and collected she is.

"Okay, thanks," I force out. My insides pummel me as I round the truck to the passenger side. I wobble on some ice. Thankfully, the door handle is there to help me save face. Barely.

Launching myself into the cab with too much force, the whole thing jolts more than my stomach. My cold fingers fumble for the seat belt, and I try to buckle it as smoothly as possible.

"Where are you headed?" she asks as she continues down the road.

How many awkward car rides must I endure? I stare out the window instead of answering her right away. Snowy mounds wink off evergreen branches. Little cottages hide between the trees, smoke lacing from their chimneys. The whole scene is charming, I hate to admit. And I definitely won't admit my plans to Rachel Reed, who made me feel like shit as a teen and is still holding that up pretty damn well, based off yesterday. "Into town," I say. That's all she needs to know.

The corner of her lip tilts up, like she realizes I'm being intentionally vague. It's awful, and so is that dimple beside her mouth. How it makes a few rogue freckles dance higher up her perfectly arched cheekbone. I turn toward a cabin with a snowman in the front yard. A few children run around it, building a snow dog. Cool. They're more productive and capable than this grown-ass adult, who couldn't even make it to her own meeting without the help of her teen frenemy.

"Listen," Rachel starts, her tone tentative. "I'm . . . really sorry for how I acted yesterday."

I stare at her, snowman and dog forgotten. She squeezes the steering wheel like a makeshift stress ball. Are her insides twisting like mine? Is this just as hard for her? No. I will not feel empathy for Rachel. Bitterness is better, a balm for the tangled feelings beneath that I never want to explore.

"Yeah," I say, because it's not okay, but I don't want to be a complete dick all out in the open.

"It's just that, um, it was a real surprise to see you?"

"No shit," I blurt.

She laughs, and *ouch*, a thread of pain pulses beneath that bitterness. The sound is low and velvety-smooth, and how corny to compare it to music, but damn. I missed it so much, long before I moved away. Rachel's laugh does something warm and gooey to my heart, spreads it like melted chocolate across my whole chest. It always has. Fuck.

"So, you're back. For how long?" She still strangles the hell out of her steering wheel.

"As long as it takes to get my car back." Which is not a full-on lie. There's no reason she needs to hear about the fundraiser. No reason I need to share anything with her at all.

"Okay, then." She nods like she knows this is a closed deal.

Maybe I am a dick. She's obviously trying to extend some sort of olive branch, and all I can do is push her away. But why shouldn't I? She cut me out in the past, and years between last seeing each other doesn't mean I can forget that. I owe her nothing. Oh. Except a new sign. "Like I said, I'll pay you for the damage I caused on the farm as soon as you let me know how you want to handle it." There. I'm not completely terrible.

"Noted. Thanks."

Guess she can play the vague game, too.

We roll into the center of town, which is two parallel rows of log buildings with different business names painted on windows to distinguish each store from the next. Melting snow makes the caramel-colored facades gleam. The reflection of the lights from each strewn wreath and garland dances atop the wet street, so the whole strip sparkles in holiday hues. I remember the greasy-good pepperoni slices from Guy's Pies and candy runs to the Fern Falls General Store, but there are other names like Rainbow Reading and Tea and Tarot that are new to me. My stomach cinches at the sight of Dad's office: Ross Real Estate. I'll have to check in with him before I leave here. But that's a problem for another hour.

Rachel parks, gets out, shuts the door. No way is she walking away again. She can't stall this payment for the sign repair any longer. I've already dealt with her two times too many. "Hey, Reed," I call as I exit the truck. She heads up to a storefront and pulls open a hunter-green door. I cross my arms like this is some sort of standoff. "You need to let me know how much to pay you for the sign. I'm gonna cover it. I don't want to owe you anything."

Maybe I imagine it, but a flicker of something crosses her face—hurt?—before it vanishes and she says, "They have the best coffee here. Have you tried it yet?"

How dare she distract me with something so dear to my heart. I stomp through the door like the full-grown woman I am. "Don't change the subject."

"Vanilla lattes." She shrugs, approaching the counter. "They're my favorite, and no one makes them better than Ben."

I begin to sputter something to regain any hold on this conversation when a wrecking ball of dread slams me in the gut. I trail my gaze back to the light blue script on the window.

No. Absolutely not.

Peak Perk is scrawled on the glass. Of course, there can only be one café in this town, and one Adam, and I bet my failures of boots there's only one Ben.

I breathe through burning rage. "Ben Parrish?" I ask with all the charm of toxic waste.

"Yeah." Rachel tilts her head like this is something as unquestionable as the shape of our planet. "He took over Mary Sue's Café when she moved, changed the name, updated it. Looks great, right?"

I clench my fists and take in the space, casting daggers at its offensive cuteness. It used to be all overbaked breads in a smudged case, dark wood paneling, and vinyl tablecloths topped with faded silk floral centerpieces. Now, unlike the standard pine exterior, soft neutrals and pastels fill the room. White walls and beige hardwood floors serve as a soothing backdrop to round tables painted in light aquas and yellows with mismatched metal chairs draped with cozy throw pillows and blankets. A brick fireplace fills the far wall and crackles with a low burning flame. Soft music plays, the place smells like brown sugar, and this is a personal attack. I steel my senses against the shabby-chic charm that is so perfectly Ben.

I should have known this had Parrish written all over it from how he knew where I was staying. Why did I have it in my head that he still worked with his mom at the naturals shop? And why did he fail to mention that he was my client? Bottom line, what the actual fuck?

The man himself walks out from the kitchen and takes his place behind the counter, which is a massive, repurposed light pink dresser. I glare at him despite his pressed white apron, pale blue dress shirt, and wide, innocent eyes. Why the hell would he keep this a secret? I almost ask it outright when Rachel says, "Hey, Parrish. Two vanilla lattes, please? Ross here needs to taste coffee that isn't crafted from corporate greed."

I serve her a solid glare. "I support small businesses, thank you very much." A quick scan of the hand-lettered chalkboard menu that spans the entire wall behind the counter definitely has me curious, though.

Ben gives a high-pitched laugh and gets busy with the espresso machine, a whir of nervous energy. I stare at him, and yep, he avoids looking at me completely, and his cheeks are flushed, so you know what? I'm gonna put it out there. "I'm good on the latte, just here for our scheduled meeting."

"Meeting?" Rachel asks without missing a beat, while Ben almost drops the metal pitcher he's pouring milk into.

I clench my jaw and don't spare her another glance. I'll mail her a check or settle it with Adam, and she can just deal. And I won't have to deal with her again.

Ben blurts a sharp spike of a laugh and places two cups in front of us. "Drink first, okay? Coffee makes everything better."

Even Rachel seems suspicious now, and I don't love sharing this with her. I grab my coffee first to beat her to it, take a sip, and—Oh, My Ever Loving Latte Goddess. It's smooth and not too sweet and tastes like every holiday I've ever loved.

Ben clears his throat and nudges his glasses up the bridge of his nose. "Now that I have you both here, you should know it's for your own good."

I force my mood to stay bristly, despite this magical concoction. "What are you talking about, Ben?"

Rachel, on the other hand, looks exactly how she did when she stared at me yesterday. Like some unwelcome spirit entered the room.

"Come? Sit?" he squeaks, motioning to two oversized armchairs flanking the fireplace.

My leg twitches, and I remind myself I need this job because I need my promotion, and that is why I'm gonna sit. Not because Ben asked me to.

I approach the closest chair and perch on its edge, casting Rachel a look that dares her to do the same.

She strides over, and why do I notice the sway of her hips? Her jeans ride low enough that each step makes her red flannel pull up a fraction of an inch, revealing a slice of skin that makes me want to crush this coffee cup. I settle into the chair, shaking my limbs loose. She needs an urgent memo that high-waisted jeans are actually quite in fashion now. What is this, 2002? I pull at the collar of my coat. The fireplace gives off way too much heat. Like the warmth of being caught up in her arms yesterday. She passes me, and my eyelids shutter at her heady scent of pine, and something richer, deeper, smokier. This is ridiculous. The whole place is made of pine, and there's a goddamn fire a foot away from my face. Rachel Reed is nothing special. She takes a seat across from me, and those few loose strands of hair graze her cheek. I close my eyes to savor my latte, and not to stop myself from staring at where her hair brushes the corner of her lip.

I scan the space, skipping over Rachel's general direction. A gallery of local photography covers the walls. Spring meadows, woodland creatures, and snowy peaks star in yellow frames. A blue jay perches on the windowsill outside, lucky little bastard. A patinated metal wall clock above the door ticks by, and hopefully the morning rush will start soon. I snort. What would that crowd even look like in this town? Ten people?

Rachel peers up from her cup, and I focus on mine. Very hard. A+ for focus.

Finally, Ben comes over with a plate of muffins (that unfortunately, look as wonderful as this drink in my mouth) and an expression that would qualify him as the eighth companion of Snow White: Guilty.

He sets the muffins on the knee-high hearth and pulls up a white metal chair, sits, slings an ankle over one knee.

I set down my coffee and cross my arms. "Spill it, Parrish."

"Okay, so, I meant to tell you sooner, Rach, I really did," he mumbles while examining his laced fingers.

Rach? What am I? Don't I matter in this equation? "I believe I'm the person you hired and whom you should be explaining this meeting to?"

Ben pulls at his collar. I will not feel sorry for him.

Rachel leans forward. "And I'm the person you told you had a major holiday event planned for, and whom you should be explaining this meeting to?" When she says *whom*, she does this frilly thing with her fingers, and I glare at her blatant mocking of me. Then, what she said registers.

"Ben," I say, voice sharp. "What exactly is for our own good?"

I know it in my gut before he says it aloud, and I've already made up my mind. He will not convince me to work with Rachel, no matter how good his lattes are. No matter how her hips sway.

He holds out his hands, placating. "Morgan, you're the best. I have followed The Barnes on Instagram for a long time, and your events are truly spectacular. No one could do a better job saving the farm."

I was not expecting that flattery. My cheeks burn, and I reach for my cup and take another drink to hide my blush. Then the last thing he said sinks in, just as Rachel leans forward and says, "Really, Morgan? You offered to do that?" Her drown-in-me brown eyes are so full of hope, my heart lurches.

"I . . ." I take an extra-long sip of my latte. Holy hell. Here I was, assuming I wouldn't run into Rachel again, and she's my goddamn client. No wonder Ben was so hush-hush about this. He set us up on some blind business date.

They both stare, waiting. But I ran from here to protect my heart. I was never good enough for these people, even though they were supposed to be my safety net. And I'm not here to feel that way again.

It's time to admit defeat. This is where the perseverance ends, where I set my limits. I will not work with Rachel Reed.

I don't meet her eyes when I force out, "I can't. I'm sorry."

Silence.

"There's no event, then." She stands abruptly and saunters toward the door. Not that I notice any sort of purposeful saunter. Maybe she's just good at walking, okay?

"This isn't my fault," I say, giving Ben the side-eye of the century.

"All right, Ross." Rachel turns and brushes past Ben, bend-ing low to get up in my space. "What are you so scared of? If no one could do a better job saving the farm, what are you running from? You just arrived, and you've already decided you're too good for this place?" She straightens. Runs a hand over her braid. When she speaks again, her voice is tired. "You've been back for a day, so it's about time you leave without any explanation or goodbye, right? That's your style."

I don't back down for a second. I rise, making my muscles stretch so my eyes at least meet her nose. "Why would you care about a goodbye, when you didn't care about me while I was here?"

She squints. "That's what you thought?"

Oh, we're doing this. "You didn't speak to me for months. Why does it matter to you that I left?"

Rachel squeezes the back of her neck and goes silent. Like I knew she would. She never cared if I was here or not.

"So . . . this is progress. This is something, yeah? Communication is good," Ben says.

We glare at him.

"Communication is something you need to learn," I say.

He gets up and joins the showdown. "Would you have come to this meeting if I'd revealed this sooner?" he asks, glancing between us.

I press my lips together, because I know my answer. I would have dealt with a million pantless birthday clowns before agreeing to meet with this girl.

"And Rachel," he continues, "you can't let a corporation buy out the farm. You can't give up on land that belongs to your family, to this town. Morgan knows her shit about throwing an event. At least give this some thought in order to raise funds, to fight back." He pushes at his glasses.

His pleading will not soften my resolve. Not a chance.

Rachel bites her bottom lip (I'm definitely not looking) and sighs, shaking her head as though arguing with herself now, too. "No."

I arch a brow and cross my arms. "So I'm not the only one turning this down?"

She deflates, shoulders falling, like how she acted yesterday when I approached her at the kiosk. "I would never want to make someone stay against their will," she says, then stalks out the door, cold air trailing in her pine-laced wake.

I growl at Ben. "Is that what you wanted? A Ross and Reed showdown?"

He shrugs and points to the plate on the hearth, full of untouched pastries. "Muffin?"

I glare at him. "I'm taking all of these." I swipe up the plate and stomp toward the door.

Ben doesn't move.

"What are you waiting for?" I ask. "I'm taking a ride from you, too. To Adam's Auto."

He twists his lips. "I'll need to make a delivery along the way."

"Fine." As long as I can leave this place.

Ben retreats behind the counter and grabs two large bakery boxes. Then he flips the sign on the window to CLOSED (which answers my morning rush question) and follows me out, a brown sugar scent wafting from the pink cardboard boxes in his arms.

"Can't stay mad at a guy carrying cinnamon rolls," he sing-songs as we step into the cold.

I follow him to the car, making sure he sees my death stare over the roof.

He puts the boxes in the back while I strap into the passenger seat like this red Subaru is about to blast me ever farther into the deep space of my past.

CHAPTER 5

I bite into my second lemon-poppy muffin, and yes, they are the literal best, and no, I will never tell Ben. The snowbanks grow taller alongside the road the higher up we drive, and I cough on crumbs when I realize where we're headed. Oh, hell no. "Ben," I say, barking his name like an admonishment.

"Hmm?" His brow kicks up, while his eyes stay firmly fixed on the road.

When did he become such a conniving scoundrel? "Absolutely not."

"I don't know what you're talking about." He rolls his shoulder like he's working out a knot.

"Yeah?" I press. "Like you mysteriously knew where my Airbnb was?"

He sighs dramatically. "Mrs. Hart really wanted to see you when you came to town."

The image of my first boss flashes in my mind. The way her full cheeks pushed her narrow glasses up to her brows when she laughed. I can't help but grin. And feel a stab of guilt that I didn't think of coming to visit her first. "So she's still running the inn?"

"She'll run that place from the grave; you know that."

I place the muffin back in the console and clutch my seat belt. I got my work ethic from her and look forward to seeing her again, despite the memories that place holds.

We pull up to the inn, HART'S HOME B&B emblazoned in a deep hunter green on a pinewood sign out front, and it's like someone pulled a picture from teen Morgan's memory scrapbook.

Each December, Mrs. Hart made it her personal mission to decorate every square inch of the property, and from the look of things, she got started early this year. Life-sized deer made of woven willow branches sparkle with lights and traipse among the boxwood shrubs at the base of the wraparound porch. Giant wreaths with red velvet bows crown each roof gable. Anything that can be framed with lights or wrapped with garland most certainly is, and bedazzled twin evergreens flank the double doors at the top of the porch steps, promising the warmest welcome waiting inside.

Ben parks. I reach for my belt buckle and freeze, knuckles whitening. I hope she's not upset that I quit. I know I gave more than enough notice and left on good terms with her offer of referrals, but time can change feelings. I swallow hard at the image of Rachel storming out of the café doors. Time can cement old hurts.

"You want to come inside?" he asks as he pulls the boxes of cinnamon buns from the back seat.

I unbuckle. Rachel Reed won't stop me from doing a damn thing. "Yes," I say, somehow sounding like my confidence isn't made of wrapping paper.

My feet don't even slip when I step out of the car. Great. Just when I've gotten my equilibrium up here, it's time to leave.

I follow Ben up the porch and into the lobby. The smells of pine and cinnamon bring back memories of working here, helping to plan as many events as I could to stay busy my senior year, then even more that following summer, free of Dad and all the silence that filled our home once Christy left. I couldn't face the painful contrast of the joy we shared before she entered our life with the sullen, reserved man he became after she rejected his proposal.

A giant jar of candy canes sits on the shiny pine counter, and the front of the check-in station is draped with holiday garlands, alternating between red and green holly berries and blue and silver dreidels.

"Morning, Mrs. Hart!" Ben calls as he walks in. "Your daily delivery for the continental breakfast."

The door closes behind me, and a voice I'll never forget greets us from the counter. "Ben, you sweetie, thank you!" Then her eyes catch on me, and she positively beams. My whole heart might burst from my chest. "Oh my word, is that you, Morgan Ann?"

Jane Hart peers atop her spectacles, low on the bridge of her nose. Her hair is fully white now, in short tight curls, but her eyes still twinkle. Her cheeks are the same rosy red as the sequined poinsettias on her sweater. She was always warm and friendly, and seeing her the same creates this strange sense of time morphing. Being back in here, her greeting me as I enter, has me feeling seventeen again.

Ben and his pink boxes head toward the side room off the main lobby, where a fireplace glows and a table of food attracts a line of guests.

"Mrs. Hart, wow, how are you?" I ask, tucking my hair behind my ears as I approach.

Instead of replying, she runs around the counter and pulls me into a hearty hug against her wide frame. Something in my soul sighs in relief, a band unwinding the slightest bit. I sink into her shoulder; then, she pulls back, holding both of mine. "Look at you, fully grown! How is LA treating you, dear?" Her tone is bright and warm. I had nothing to worry about.

"It's been good to me. Thank you so much." Good up until a few days ago, but no one here needs to know about that. The thought of returning to the city, to nothing except an empty apartment and canceled events, makes my stomach clench.

"Don't you be modest, now! Your father certainly hasn't been. You should hear how he goes on about your success." She reaches over and casually straightens some of the decorative garland like she hasn't dropped an info bomb.

"Really?" The same man who has barely texted in weeks or ever mentioned my events? Who shut me out once Christy left, making it clear our family of two was no longer enough for him—I wasn't enough for him.

She nods. "He is so proud of you! Comes in with the latest articles you've been featured in. We're all so proud! I knew there were big things in store for you, Morgan."

"Thank you so much," I reply, then face away to school my features. Let this info soak in however it can. Too much rain on compact soil. Ben's at the head of the buffet table, chatting it up with some family, probably meddling in their personal lives, too. When I turn back, a guest approaches the counter.

"One minute, dear?" Mrs. Hart asks me.

"Of course." I walk to the edge of the entry space.

A young woman heaves a mint-green diaper bag onto the counter and tucks a wisp of pale hair into her messy bun. "I'm so sorry," she starts, voice small. "We need to check out early."

"Oh? I thought you all planned to go sledding today? And you'll miss our holiday reading tonight."

I smile to myself. Of course, her response has nothing to do with cancellation fees. We're not in LA anymore.

"Yes," the woman says, worrying at an *I love Mommy* keychain on her bag, "we just, well, funds are tight, and we did some excursions that the kids were excited about and—"

Mrs. Hart holds up a hand. "You'll stay," she says in that tone that not a soul would dare disagree with. "No one is leaving my inn without experiencing everything Fern Falls has to offer. This is on me. We'll call it a . . . tourism promo, yep." She punches her keyboard, entering something into her computer, problem solved.

"Oh my gosh, no, I couldn't possibly—"

My former boss fixes that over-the-glasses gaze on her. "Nonsense. Bill is so set on reading *The Polar Express* to the kids tonight that if the room isn't packed, he'll be moping. Trust me. You're doing me a favor. He's been rehearsing his narrator voice for weeks now."

The woman looses a shuddering sigh. "I don't know how to thank you."

Mrs. Hart sweeps an arm toward the buffet. "By enjoying breakfast. Best pastries in town."

My smile widens. There's the hard stuff here in Fern Falls, but my memories of the Harts are only good. Even before she became my employer, she was a family friend. She and Bill would come to the house every Sunday during warmer weeks for the fresh lemonade Dad made, with Meyer lemons picked straight from his tree in the yard.

We sat on the front porch, where the conversation always turned to memories of Mom. I cradled my chin in my hands, listening to Jane Hart recount the tales of their failed crafting attempts, how they once tried to knit hats, but the final products wound up being so large and misshapen that they were donated to the Harts' dogs: Kona (a spunky Shiba Inu) and Murray (a peppy Jack Russell), for their beloved blanket collection. How I wished I had my own stories to tell of Mom. Wished I had her in my life long enough to remember more than the sound of her laugh. But I was grateful still. At least cancer didn't steal that memory.

"Now then, Morgan Ann. You come with me." Mrs. Hart's voice gently pulls me from my thoughts. She rounds the counter and heads toward the room where Ben lingers at the breakfast display, along with the family now enjoying their cinnamon rolls. She walks straight to a full armchair beside the fireplace, and I don't dare refuse to follow.

I pass over the glossy wood floor and step onto the carpet with a pattern that can only be described as one thing: if all the holidays threw a messy party. It's red and green and gray and blue with no actual definition between the colors.

I cross between green-red and blue-gray until I land in the seat facing her. The firelight illuminates her face, and woodsmoke singes the air as the glowing logs crackle. The fireplace is open on the other side and framed with river rock that reaches to the ceiling. Through the gap, Ben peeks over. I can't be too mad at him for bringing me here. It's the nicest home has felt in a long time.

"So. How have you really been, dear?" she asks without subtlety.

I strain to keep any signs of distress off my face. "What do you mean?"

True to form, she doesn't give any ground and keeps her stare fixed on me. "Ben said you'd be up here, to keep an eye on you, make sure you're taking care of yourself after the whole social media mess."

My cheeks heat, and I glance at Ben. He knew about the Spum scandal and still wanted me up here to run the fundraiser? All those cancellation texts flash in my mind. Longtime clients who wrote me off without a second thought, and here's Ben, giving me a second chance.

And I can't even give one to Rachel, just like she never gave one to me. Maybe I'm not any better than her.

I swallow hard. "I'm doing fine. Truly." Because what else do I say? That my next stop is to get my car and get the hell out of here?

"Good." She nods. "If you need anything at all, I'm here for you. You will always belong here."

The sentiment hits me right in the chest, and I wasn't prepared for it. I try to catch my breath to respond with some kind of thanks, when the doors of the lobby sweep wide open.

My stomach falls through the seat at the sight of the woman who enters.

A tall, lithe, incredibly put-together blond strolls inside and scans the space like it owes her. I'd recognize that gait anywhere. That sharp nose and chin.

Christy Vaughn. My breaths halt. The last time I saw her was here, at this inn, in the courtyard beyond the back patio. She stood beneath a canopy of string lights and rejected my father's proposal after nearly a year of posing as the girlfriend who wanted marriage—who wanted to be my stepmom. Afternoon outings to restaurants with place settings that made me unsure of what utensil to grab first. Picnics at the lake when she'd let Dad choose. Planning that graduation party with me and promising there'd be many more, only to break that promise hours later, along with Dad's heart.

He chose her, with status and wealth we'd never had before, like he wanted to level us up, experience more of the world. Then she rejected us, publicly, brutally.

We weren't the same after her, Dad and I. Our simple life was no longer enough for him. He crumbled inward, and I lashed out, breaking everything and everyone in my path until I got out of here to make a name for myself, to be successful. To be enough again. Without Christy.

Hell of a job I've done.

She perches her sunglasses atop her head and spots Mrs. Hart, who sighs and stands.

"Ah, Jane. So happy you took my meeting reque—"

She stops cold when she sees me. Her face goes a bit more pale as she pulls in her lips and nods. So much for sinking into the upholstery. "Wow. Morgan? Is that you? I haven't seen you since . . . in a very long time."

I clear my throat and get up, stretching as tall as my five-foot-two frame allows. "I could say the same to you," I huff, like I didn't leave Fern Falls shortly after she did. Like her sudden departure didn't destroy my family.

She smirks. "How is your father doing?"

My blood turns acidic. I should know the answer. I should know more than she does about my own dad. "He's fine," I guess boldly. "What are you doing here?"

"We have a meeting, actually," Mrs. Hart says, the chipperness in her tone gone.

"That's right," agrees Christy, placing her hand on her hip. "Vaughn Enterprises is creating some exciting opportunities in Fern Falls, and I wanted our lovely Hart's Home B and B to be one of the first to know about them."

Prickles run along my arms. Vaughn Enterprises is her family's business that franchised the ski resort in Snow Hill, the neighboring mountain community. It changed the town from the quirky, charming place I visited as a kid into something glossy, aloof, and way overpriced for locals to thrive in. "What do you want with the inn? It's not like there's a ski run you can suck the soul out of here." I don't care that my words and tone are sharp. I don't want her anywhere near this inn.

Mrs. Hart crosses her arms, awaiting the answer.

Christy's tight smile falters for a fraction of a second. "I was planning on sharing this in private . . . Vaughn Enterprises wants to start a close relationship with the very capable owners of this inn, as well as the tree farm below it. Fern Falls is a lovely place worthy of all the support my family business has to give."

My stomach fills with lead. "You want to acquire the tree farm, too?"

"Morgan," Christy says sharply. "What I want is to begin a working relationship, which is why I'm here. Jane? Shall we?"

Her tone makes me feel eight years younger. Like she still has any say over my life.

"Christy. I'll be right with you in the reading room." My old boss points her toward the open space past the check-in counter. The cozy room is filled with more armchairs and round tables.

Bookshelves wrap the perimeter, covering the walls with well-loved spines from floor to ceiling.

"Morgan. You take care now," Christy says, then walks away.

Mrs. Hart's face is creased with concern.

I place a hand on her arm. "Is the inn struggling?"

She shakes her head. "Don't you worry. I've got this covered. You make Rachel's fundraiser as successful as you can. I know she's in the best hands with you."

My eyes sting. Of course, Ben told her about the fundraiser. If she only knew how I reacted to the news not an hour ago.

Now my one reason for turning down the job seems so trivial compared to what's at stake. If working with Rachel stops Vaughn Enterprises from sinking its claws into the inn, the farm, and all of Fern Falls, it would be worth it.

I give her a hug. "It's so good to see you again."

"You too, sweetheart," she says, patting my back. "Come say hi again while you're here. And I mean it, don't worry about the inn." Then she crosses to the other side of the room.

Ben's voice echoes off the wooden ceiling beams as he talks happily to the family that Mrs. Hart just helped. These kinds of things would never happen if Christy came in and turned this personal experience into a corporate one. There wouldn't be "tourism promos" to help out struggling families, overdone holiday decor to brighten spirits, bakers gifting cinnamon rolls for the breakfast buffet.

There wouldn't be any soul.

Before I can change my mind, I project loud enough so Christy hears me, "You may not have known I'm in town to run a fundraiser for the tree farm, and in turn, this inn. And I'm the best in the business."

Christy stares from her armchair, her expression blank. "I wish you all the best, then. This lovely town deserves every support." She nods sharply and smiles. It doesn't reach her ice-blue eyes.

Mrs. Hart winks as she pulls the library doors shut.

Before I know it, Ben's arms are around my shoulders. When was the last time I was appreciated like this by any client? Any friend? I can't help but hug him back.

"Welcome home, Mor," he says. Then he loops his arm through mine, and we exit the front doors.

Cold air fills my lungs with a sense of expansion, strength. Nothing and no one can stop me now.

Ben opens the passenger door for me. "Okay, you mountain-town vigilante. Let's pick up your car so you can get to Rachel's and convince her to let you run that fundraiser."

No one could stop me except goddamn Rachel Reed.

CHAPTER 6

The Universe is pulling some real shit. Despite all my plans to avoid Rachel, here I am, back at the farm, ready to beg for her business. This place has some magnetic force that should be investigated.

If only convincing her to work with me were as easy as getting my car back from Adam. Of course, he was more than happy to see me leave and get as far away from his sister as possible. I'm sure he'll be thrilled that I'm trying to stay (cue sarcasm). He said my sedan had some surface scratches and dents he fixed in record time. It's as good as new now.

I exit my car and take a deep breath, willing myself to not slip or glance at the remnants of the ruined sign.

A few families mill around the tree lot, but there's no line at the kiosk yet. I use the moment to go straight to the counter, where an employee is working. Rachel may have the ball in her court, but that doesn't mean I can't play.

The girl at the cash register seems around my age, maybe a year or so younger. She has short platinum pigtails with blue tips and wears a purple sweater with a little pin in the shape of an ax that says THWACK THE PATRIARCHY. It's not a stretch to offer a genuine smile. "Hey"—I read her name tag—"Whitney. My name is Morgan Ross. I'm a professional event planner and am interested in working with the farm."

"Oh, hi. Hey." She peers to the left and right, like she was warned to be on the lookout for a wild blond. Like I'll somehow tear down the shack with my bare hands in a matter of seconds.

I shrug it off and refocus on the long game. "You seem really experienced here. I was hoping you might be able to tell me a bit more about this tree farm?"

I hold my breath, hoping for intel that will help me show Rachel I'm invested, convince her to work with me.

She smiles tightly. "What do you want to know?"

"What's your busiest time like? What's involved with running this place? What's the size of your typical holiday crowd?"

Whitney stares, wide-eyed. Dammit. Too much too fast.

She chews on her bottom lip. "Well, Rachel handles the labor-intensive stuff, like caring for the trees and making sure they're free of disease, chopping down the ones that are dead or preventing further growth."

The image of Rachel bursting from the forest with an ax over her shoulder flashes through my mind, and I flush, clear my throat. "Has disease been an issue lately?" Focus on the farm, Morgan. Not the way that flannel was rolled up, exposing her toned forearms. The way the calluses on her fingers scraped your neck when she caught you, sending a shiver straight to—

"Not too much," Whitney replies. "Some from summer drought, but better than previous years, and we've had a wet winter so far." She pauses. Brushes some pine needles off the counter. "Honestly, the biggest threat right now is that we're behind on payments with the bank. I help manage the books here and at my second job, too, and there's a similar story everywhere in town."

Worry pinches my throat. "What's going on? Is there a reason for the fall in business?"

She shakes her head in a helpless way. "Over the past few years, the resort in Snow Hill has attracted more tourism, and this year especially, after previous slow seasons, Fern Falls can't keep up. It's hard to compete with day spas and ski slopes when all you have to offer is some simple holiday charm, you know?"

Any boldness I had from my run-in with Christy fizzles and dies. When I replied to Ben's email, I expected a minor-level fundraiser. This is . . . not that. This is beyond a gala or silent auction. This is more than one business. The Reed Family Tree Farm and Hart's Home B&B are only the beginning. If Christy gets the land they share, that's it, she'll have the foothold she needs to take the rest of the town and morph it into Snow Hill 2.0. Not only does the farm need to raise a crap-ton of money to settle back payments, they'll need funds to keep corporate lawyers at bay. We need something big and grand to stave off Vaughn Enterprises, and we're gonna need it fast. "Exactly how long do you have?" My voice trembles at the massive task ahead. At the thought of failing Rachel. Again.

"A little over a month." Her voice is thick as she busies herself with a notepad on the counter.

The air thickens, and my sight drifts to the pictures on the back wall of the little shack. Maps of the area, local awards, certificates, stunning landscape shots like the ones at the café, holiday cards from loyal clients—and right in the middle: an old framed photo of Rachel and me, arms around each other, bundled in winter scarves and smiling before a backdrop of evergreens.

My chest tightens. She kept that picture, kept me up on the wall. All this time. "What's Rachel going to do?" I wonder aloud, the weight of it all sinking in. This is her livelihood. Where are her parents, and why aren't they supporting her? Why isn't Adam helping? When did all of this become her responsibility?

As if omnipresent, Rachel's voice sounds, "I can figure that out for myself."

I whirl to find her directly behind me.

It's the influx of information settling in my brain, throwing me off guard. That's the only reason I flush hot all over. A slight sheen of sweat glistens on her brow and down her chest to where the top buttons of her flannel fall open. I keep my eyes focused on her face, physically restraining my gaze from trailing lower. Strands of dark hair sweep loose from her braid and cling to her neck, and when she bends to rest her ax against the counter, I get a front-row show to how well she fills out those jeans. My heartbeat fills my ears. I step back, putting more space between us. I should not be noticing any of this.

"What are you doing back here, Morgan?" she asks, straightening, hands on her hips. "You should be long gone by now."

I shift my stance so my feet are planted firmly on the ground. "I'm here to help." I force the words to be clear.

Rachel folds her arms, making her cleavage perk up, making my gaze move higher, and leans against the counter. "You're only here because Ben tricked you into this. You don't owe me anything."

I stiffen. "You were just as thrilled to work together when you stomped out that door."

She looks me square in the eyes. "This has nothing to do with you. Ben promised me a holiday event, which I thought would be great for the community. I never wanted to do a fundraiser."

"Why?" I blurt. Doesn't she care about this place?

"Yeah, Rach, why? Don't you want to try to save the farm?" Whitney asks, eyes wide.

Rachel's face softens. She stuffs a hand in her pocket, and it bulges like she's curling her fingers into a fist. She used to do that when she was stressed. I . . . remember that. I stare at the toes of my boots. I never wanted to be someone who made her feel that way. But why wouldn't she want to keep land that belongs to her, this town? "Why aren't you fighting for this?"

She fixes me with a serious stare. "It isn't that simple. And maybe I need to realize when it's time to let things go."

I press my arms to my stomach. The way she looks at me . . . like she's talking about more than the farm.

She pushes off the counter, grabs her ax, and heads back toward the trees.

Heat surges up my neck. This can't be over like that. "And now is that time?" I call after her. "You're going to give up that easily?"

She whirls around like I've pulled her by the arm. "You think this is easy for me? You've got this all figured out?"

I breathe in deep, morphing my lungs into armor. "I care about this."

Her eyes narrow. I smooth my features, making my expression as open and honest as possible. Yes, I care about my job, but I also don't want to see this place go under. If a fundraiser could help both of us and the whole freaking town by keeping Vaughn Enterprises at bay, why wouldn't I work for that? The fifteen-year-old version of me in that photo would want me to help if I could. And I can.

Rachel closes in, fists tightening around the arm of her ax, her gaze so intense, I take a breath to ground myself. "I don't believe you," she says, tone flat. Then she turns and marches into the forest.

I stare after her. My arms hang uselessly at my sides, and my mouth opens and shuts like some inspired, problem-solving phrase might spontaneously pop out.

Whitney clears her throat, and I turn just as she snaps her head down and scribbles on that notepad.

If Rachel keeps walking away, maybe I should let her go. I could work around her, right? Ben might have some ideas.

I pace back and forth in front of the kiosk, carving a trench in the snow. My phone buzzes, a sound so completely out of place up here that I whip it from my pocket. Ha. One bar. Guess angry pacing's good for something. I pull up a new text from Johanna:

Hi, Morgan! Hope you're settling in okay and ready to recharge! Send me photos!

I groan and hammer out:

Going great! Send pics soon!

Then I shove the piece-of-hell technology back in my pocket. I have to make this work with Rachel, or the only thing I'll have for Johanna is a resignation.

I push up my jacket sleeves like I'm about to perform physical labor or get into a fist fight—either of which could theoretically occur right now—and stomp toward the trees. "Any clue where she went off to?" I ask Whitney as I pass the kiosk.

She smiles, her whole face brightening, as she yells, "She goes to the chopping stump when she's upset!"

Waving a thank-you, I head into the pines without looking back. I can't let Johanna down. I can't let Christy win. I can't let Rachel cut me out again.

My stomps slow as the forest thickens. Branches brush my coat with the heady scent of pine. Being back on this land must reconnect neural pathways, because memories flood back in waves of pins and needles. Rach and I running through this place, playing hide and seek. Staring up at the stars. Helping out when the holiday season boomed. That time, days before our kiss, when she grazed my hand, and I blushed so hard my cheeks spelled out a neon: *You're more than a friend to me.*

My heart aches. Things were so easy when I believed the people I cared about cared for me. Before I knew they'd hurt me the most.

The snow-dusted path widens, and this—I remember this, too. The chopping stump was where Rachel went when she was fired up, especially after fights with her dad. She never told me about them, never wanted to talk much about her relationship with her father. All she wanted to do was pummel a hunk of wood with an ax. The same old *thwack* sounds from a few feet ahead.

Boot tracks lead to where the path spills into a small clearing. I don't mean to freeze. I don't mean to stare. I don't mean to tingle in the deepest parts of my body when I see her. But my body doesn't care what I came here for. There is only Rachel.

Her hair is loose, long and wild and flecked with snow. It sways across her shoulder blades as she raises and lowers her ax, over and over and over. Each swing showcases the defined muscles and glistening skin exposed by her tight tank top, her flannel slung on a nearby tree limb. I grip a branch myself. Those jeans were made for her ass, and I bite my lip as she bends forward, one boot braced on the stump.

Rachel was always so goddamn stunning, and time has only intensified that. Fuck you, Time.

She hurls the ax down, and the log splits. The *crack* snaps me from the lusty haze I should've never indulged in the first place. I clear my throat.

Slowly, she props her ax against the side of the stump. She doesn't turn, just stands there, motionless but for the rise and fall of her shoulders.

I force myself to speak. "I was at the inn today, and Christy Vaughn came to meet with Mrs. Hart. Has she met with you, too?" I grimace. Not the smoothest start, but honest at least. And it's a distraction from Rachel's skill at chopping wood. An angry heat roils beneath my skin at the thought of Christy taking everything over.

She drags her fingers through her hair. "Yeah. About a week ago."

"You're not gonna sell to her, right? That's what she wants, for her corporation to take over Fern Falls like it took over Snow Hill, I guarantee it."

She snaps her gaze to me, eyes filled with fire. "And suddenly you care about this, Morgan? You show up out of nowhere, after being gone for years, and now you have a heart for this place and know how to solve all our problems? You have no idea how hard things have been, so don't you dare judge me for considering her offer." She turns back toward the stump.

My heart lurches. "You're right," I say. "I don't know what it's been like. But I'm here now, and I can help. I want to help. Let me prove it to you." She doesn't have to know how badly I need this, too.

Her hair frames her profile. "How?"

I worry at the hem of my pocket. "A lot is new in town. Why don't you reintroduce me to Fern Falls? Show me how it's changed since I left." Did I really utter those words? Willingly offer to trudge back down a painful memory lane with someone who drives in the knife? I have to. She needs to see that I'm committed, and I need to familiarize myself with the market, find the best way to beat Christy.

She turns. "You . . . really want this?" Her eyes are pleading as she steps forward, and some ridiculous, masochistic part of me feels she's talking about more than the fundraiser.

A chill creeps through my core. Am I really prepared to face the hurt of my past with her head on? I've barely survived the past twenty-four hours.

She comes closer, her warmth radiating in the tight space between us.

"I need this," I breathe. That, at least, is the truth. So much for keeping it to myself.

Her thumbs hook through her belt loops. "Okay," she says, rocking back on her heels. "We could start tomorrow. Meet me back here in the morning?"

She's really going to give me a chance. "Wow, okay. Um, thank you." I nod and turn back down the path before she can see my stupid, unbidden smile.

After a few steps, I come to a stop and look at the trees. It's early afternoon. The hours until I meet Rachel will only be filled with doom-scrolling my ever-so-popular hashtag and crying into too many cups of coffee. I sure as hell can't send Johanna a selfie of that hot mess.

But if we started the tour sooner . . .

I turn slowly. My breath hitches when I find Rachel still staring after me, arms crossed. I hope my ass looked okay. What? No. Stop. "So . . ." I say, twisting the hem of my jacket in my fingers. "If one were to visit a place in town say, tonight, where would one start?"

Rachel's lips quirk up and she adjusts her stance. "A few of us are heading to the bar at eight. You're welcome to join. If you want."

I purse my lips to keep the warm rush that fills my chest from splitting my face into a giddy grin. "See you there." I cough and turn, start walking away.

"See you tonight," she calls after me. "It'll be our first official reintroduction."

I pause. She has to be talking about us, right? Not just the town? Maybe that other side of me isn't so ridiculous after all. But masochistic, definitely, because this partnership with Rachel Reed already has me wanting to glance back and check if she's watching me leave again.

I wait until I pass Whitney at the kiosk to let my grin loose. She gives me a thumbs-up, and I feel a small sense of triumph.

But I can only hope that tonight's bar experience will be leaps and bounds better than my last.

CHAPTER 7

Just because I changed my outfit ten times does not mean I care about how I look for Rachel. Not at all. The scarf was too scratchy. The pants were too long. The blouse was too . . . *blah*. This sweater and jeans, and these sturdy boots, aren't perfect, but they are perfectly comfortable, so I'm already doing better than my last night out.

When I finally get my comfy ass out the door, it's eight p.m., and the fact that I'm late does nothing to quell my nerves. What if tonight's worse than Friday? What if I run into everyone from my past and can't escape? What if someone recognizes me from the Internet? What if they all still see me as that stupid girl in a gaudy dress floundering in a courtyard? What if Rachel felt obligated to invite me and doesn't want me there at all?

By the time I park, I'm a jumble of self-destructive what-ifs. I sit, stare at the building, and try to breathe in some courage.

This is not the neon-lit, rotted-logs-patched-with-plywood bar I remember passing as a teen. A beautiful handcrafted sign claims the space above the gem-green doors as THE STACKS. It's the only business all lit up besides the pizza shop a few doors down, and it looks like a damn Thomas Kinkade painting. White lights frame the windows and gleam off the varnished exterior, making the whole building shine, the snow around it glow. People file in, clad in cozy attire, lured by soft, sweet music.

Everyone greets each other with hugs, and I might throw up. There's no one at the door to meet me.

Best case, I walk in unnoticed. Grab a drink and a dark corner, take two sips of beer, get a photo for Johanna, then duck out. Tell Rachel tomorrow that I couldn't find her. I can hide in a corner for five minutes, right? That's trying.

Something knocks on my window, and I startle. Ben waves with the same enthusiasm he had when I announced I was staying, and I can't deny that seeing him makes me a bit lighter, makes entering The Stacks less intimidating.

I open the door and step out. Despite my comfortable outfit, it's still cold AF, so we actually need to go inside. Dammit.

"You're here!" He beams like I'm a superhero answering his signal.

"Hey," I say.

Before I know it, his arms are around me. "I'm so glad you're in Fern Falls again." He pulls back. "This is going to be amazing, you know."

I can't help but smile . . . and hope he's right. Hope Rachel decides to work with me. "Let's get through tonight first, okay?" My voice wavers as more people heap inside.

Just as Ben and I are about to join them, my name comes out of nowhere.

"Morgan."

I turn, and Dad stands before me, hands in his pockets, squinting like I might be a figment of his imagination. He clears his throat. "How are you?" His voice is soft, a little far away.

My muscles brace against the greeting. "I—I'm good, Dad. How are you?" The sight of the man before me clashes with past images of him still stuck in my mind. He rubs his scruffy jawline with one hand. His once clean-shaven face was bright with anticipation when he got on one knee in front of the whole town to ask Christy to marry him. There's so much gray in his hair now. I'll never forget how he dragged his fingers through it when Christy said no; how his knuckles turned white, and I worried he might tear it out at the roots. His eyes are lined with deep wrinkles. They were bloodshot for weeks after she left. And it didn't matter how I tried to comfort him, that I made his favorite meals. Nothing mattered. There was a Christy-sized hole in our home, and I hated her for it. Hated myself for not being enough to fill it in. He's still in blue jeans and a Dodgers sweatshirt pushed up to his elbows. That hasn't changed, just like the tension between us.

"I'm good. Just closed up the office." He nods to his business a few doors down, like I might have forgotten where it's located. "How long are you in town for?" he asks in a rush.

There was a time, a few years back, when I drove up for his birthday. I brought cupcakes, and we went to the lake, but after a quiet, uncomfortable evening, I left and avoided coming back since. So I didn't have to feel seventeen all over again. "A little while." That feels too cold, and I add, "I'll stop by soon, yeah?"

"Sounds great," he says with a small smile. "Have fun tonight. You too, Ben."

"Good to see you, Mr. Ross." Ben waves.

We stand there awkwardly for a second; then, he leans in for a hug. I return it stiffly, too many emotions clinging to me like hardened clay. I didn't want to run into him like this, by chance. I should have gone and seen him when I first arrived. Now my offer to get together seems like an afterthought.

I swallow past a burning sensation in my throat as he pulls away and walks toward the parking lot. He was never an afterthought to me . . . like I was to him.

I take a minute to steady myself. I survived the first surprise of the night, and I'm still here, still standing; the ground hasn't swallowed me whole.

"C'mon." Ben loops his arm through mine and leads me into The Stacks.

I hold my breath, like stepping over the threshold is plunging beneath water. Then my lungs relax in a sigh of relief. This is not The Sand Bar. This is spacious and clean—and cozy?

Groups of people huddle near a small stage up front that's topped with old rugs. Others sit at tables spaced across the floor, polished tops reflecting the soft glow of pendant lights. The chairs are made of worn leather and strewn with emerald throw pillows, a few with yellow-gold blankets slung over their backs. The bar takes up the whole left side of the room, and the wall behind it is made entirely of built-in shelving. I gasp. Instead of just holding liquor, hundreds of beautiful old books crowd the shelves, gem-toned spines between sparkling glass bottles. The whole space feels like a bar that wishes it were a library. A li-bar-y, ha.

"It's pretty great, right?" Bens asks, his eyes twinkling as he takes it all in.

"It's fantastic." And just the kind of happy ambience I need to shake off the funk of seeing Dad.

He motions to a young man behind the counter with tousled blond hair, a swoon-worthy smile, and not-so-lean muscles defined through a white T-shirt. Ben squeezes my arm. "Tanner moved here from LA a few years back. Loved the town so much, he stayed, bought and renovated this bar, and now it's become a big gathering place for friends and charity events. Like tonight."

Charity events? Rachel didn't mention anything about that. "Looks like he might love more than the town?" I nudge my head toward a barstool, where Whitney, the employee from the tree farm, sits reading. Her blue-fringed hair peeks out beneath a pale pink beanie. Tanner keeps glancing over at her between taking orders.

"Oh," he sighs. "They've had a thing for months."

"Yeah?"

He snorts. "Yeah. A thing where Tanner smiles at her, and she completely ignores him."

That girl just gained even more of my respect.

"What are you drinking?" Ben asks.

"Oh, um, a lager? With lime?" Definitely not a margarita.

Ben points toward the back of the room. "Want to grab a table, and I'll grab drinks?"

"You sure? I can—"

He gives me a slanted gaze. "I owe you a lot more. This is on me."

I laugh and stop reaching into my bag. He's not wrong. "Thank you," I say, then head to the spot he indicated, grateful for some sort of direction, like he knew I felt lost.

I keep my head down and settle in at a pub table against the back wall. It doesn't have the cozy feel of the lower seats in front, but with two chairs and three open sides, there's less of a chance for people to pass by. And the whole wall is made of more bookshelves. So worst-case, I can grab a classic to bury my nose in if anyone notices me.

I peel off my jacket and sling it over the chair, along with my purse. The furniture is made of pine, and is it possible to sink into a wooden barstool? I didn't think so until this moment.

Leaning back, I let the live music soothe me. But that's not just any musician on stage. Adam Reed strums lovely chords on his guitar, while a girl sings. It's calm and sort of indie and nothing like the kind of music he used to play with a group of dudes in his garage. Then my gaze wanders to an unlit tree beside the stage. It's grand and tall, adorned with ornaments, nearly brushing one of the exposed beams in the ceiling.

A flannel pattern I'd recognize anywhere moves before the darkened branches. Rachel stands beside the stage, and—how long has she been looking at me? My cheeks heat as I offer a small wave. She smiles, like she was trying to get my attention, and waves back. My sweater is suddenly too hot. *You came*, she mouths, her whole face open and bright. I nod and grin, somehow functioning despite the warmth flooding my body.

A beer clinks down on the table before me, full and frothy with a bright green lime slice balanced on the rim. I wrap my hands around the chilled glass and drink too fast, cold carbonation bringing my body heat closer to normal. I put it back down and force my gaze to Ben. He settles across from me with a beer of his own, dark as chocolate syrup. He takes a sip, and some foam sticks to his lip. I smile. "Thanks so much."

"Like I said, I owe you a lot more than a beer."

"Not at all." I take another gulp, involuntarily sneaking a peek at Rachel over the rim of my glass. My teeth clench, and I set my drink down. She's talking to Tanner. The adorable literature-loving bar owner who uses his unique space to host charity events. No big deal. He touches her arm and makes her laugh that deep, soothing sound I love so much. Maybe he flirts with everyone in this town. Something acrid settles in my stomach. I glare at him like eyeballs can hex, then practically chug my beer, hoping Ben didn't catch what must have been pure evil flash across my face. I have no business with jealousy. I have no business with anything here except actual business.

But Ben is transfixed by something behind me. I follow his line of sight to find Adam waving and heading our way. He . . . can't be waving at me? An instrumental score plays from the speakers overhead, replacing the live music.

I wave anyway and glance at Ben, whose face glows like the sun's just risen.

"Hey, you two. Good to see you here."

Uh, really? He's glad to see me, as well? Didn't see that coming.

"Hey-oh!" Ben blurts.

Adam's lips tilt up. I bury my smile in another sip of beer.

"So how's your car running?" he asks, shifting his attention to me. His smile is tight, but I'll take it.

"Great, really, thank you so much."

He nods. "Thank you for helping my sister out. If there's anything you need while you're here, you let us know, okay?"

Us. He obviously didn't run that offer by Rachel. "Thanks. A lot." My whole chest expands at his gesture. I can tell it took a lot for him to extend this offer. I don't want to let him down. Not again.

Something brushes my hand. The checks I gave him (because of course, he didn't have Venmo and didn't take card) slide beneath my fingers.

"And it's on me." He raises a hand before I can protest. "Rachel and I are really grateful for the help. So one check returned because fixing your car is the least I can do, and the second check because there's no way I'm handling the sign situation for Rachel. She'll want to take care of that herself."

"No, it's—" Before I can give the checks back, the same girl who sang with him onstage appears at his side. She places a drink in his hand and a kiss on his cheek. A wave of sympathy for Ben hits me in the gut. She's adorable, with two long red pigtails trailing from a mint-green beanie. Her cheeks almost match her hair as she presses into Adam's side.

I can't even glance at Ben. He must be aching.

"This is Vanessa. My uh, bandmate," Adam says as he wraps an arm around her shoulders, and I don't imagine the cursory glance he gives Ben. It only lasts a beat, but it's so full of heat and regret that I sip my beer just to cool down. What happened between them? Why do they dance around each other like this?

"Hi!" She raises her bottle in greeting, and when she smiles, a little dimple forms beside her eye.

I have to grip my glass to keep from reaching over and giving my friend a comforting pat on the arm, no matter how Adam might look at him.

"We'll see you two later?" Adam says, glancing between us. Longer at Ben.

"See you," I say, somehow the one out of our pity party of two who can think of any response.

Adam and Vanessa walk back toward the stage and Rachel and Tanner. I force my eyes away from the laughing lumberjane and the librarian-barkeeper to check on Ben.

He stares into his beer as if he'd like to drown in it.

"What happened between you two?" I ask, shoving the checks into my purse. Somehow, someway, I will make a Reed accept my money.

"I have a confession to make," Ben says, not looking up from his beer abyss.

I press my elbows onto the tabletop and wrap my hands around my glass. "What's up?" I ask, trying to sound casual.

"I really do love your work, and I've followed it online for a while—not in a creepy way—just admiring, it's awesome—"

"Ben, breathe." The boy is practically turning blue.

He takes a shuddering breath and meets my eyes. "I shouldn't have tricked you and Rachel. I'm sorry for that. But I hope you can save the farm for another reason, too."

"Okay." I brace for whatever catastrophe this trip has in store for me next.

"If Rachel sells or loses the farm, she'll leave." He looks back down at his drink. "Then Adam will, too. His business could do a lot better in a big city, and with his family gone for good, he won't have anyone else keeping him here. It's not like he'd stay for me."

Ah. There it is. "So this isn't purely altruistic?" I take a pull of my beer.

His eyes go wide as he looks up. Light glints off his lenses. "I'm a horrible, thirsty asshole."

I sputter and swipe my chin. "Ben, have you ever told him how you feel?"

He shakes his head. "I came close once, I really did. In high school. Then he graduated, and I stopped seeing him every day, and even in this small town, we grew apart. And when I finished senior year, we were both starting our jobs, then taking over our own businesses, and the time is never right because of my nerves and his . . . Vanessas." He winces. "Have you ever loved someone for so long that if you had to tell them how much you care, you'd be scared to even begin and that you may never stop talking once you start?" He lets out a shuddering breath. "And worst of all, that they wouldn't feel the same? It's easier to walk around a little bit broken and still have hope, than to know you don't stand a chance at all."

It's my turn to peer into my drink. To hide any answers in my eyes from Ben. To stop myself from staring at Rachel. "There's no perfect time. You just have to go for it. Whenever you choose to tell him will be the right moment." Then, brave again, I glance up and say, "You should see how he looks at you."

His eyes widen. "No. Really?"

I nod. "Even with his Vanessas."

Ben blushes crimson. "It's good to have you back, Mor."

I try to take the compliment. I want to be wanted. I raise my glass. "Happy to assist in the mission to quench your undying thirst."

He laughs big and loud as we clink our glasses.

But the joy is tainted. There's an issue I need to get off my chest, too. "There's actually something I want to talk with you about, too."

His brows crease like he knows what's coming. "Morgan, you don't have to—"

"No, I do." I grip my glass. "I'm so sorry that I pushed you away that summer after my graduation party. I was ashamed. I felt like I wasn't good enough. It didn't have anything to do with you. You were always kind to me. I didn't know how to be myself after that moment, to feel like me anymore. I'm sorry."

He puts his hand over mine. "I know you are. And I'm sorry I didn't try harder to push past that tough exterior you put up."

"It's not like I made it easy for you. I stopped answering your phone calls and everything. Especially when Rachel wouldn't talk to me anymore, I didn't know how to span that gap, how to stay a part of our group when so much had changed between us."

"Well, you just did. And believe me, it's water under the bridge. We are older now. That was a hard time." I don't miss how his gaze slips to Rachel. "For all of us."

Questions rattle my brain. What could he be referencing? Did something happen to Rachel that I'm not aware of? Before I get the chance to ask, we're interrupted by Vanessa's melodic voice crooning through the mic. "Hey, everyone. Thanks for coming out." The crowd quiets down. "And thank you, Tanner, for hosting this event."

I almost roll my eyes on instinct as the bar owner's face splits into a grin and the crowd cheers. He still stands by the tree, close to Rachel. Too close. "Doesn't he have drinks to pour or something?" Shit. I said that out loud.

Ben snorts. "Welcome to my life."

Vanessa continues, "Ten percent of all drink purchases goes toward the Fern Falls Memorial Hospital."

More cheers, more high-beam Tanner smiles. Whatever, Tanner. You could have donated twenty percent, asshole. The cheapskate takes the mic. "We also want to take a moment to remind you about the annual Fern Falls Holiday Festival. You all turned up in a big way for our Pride Parade and Oktoberfest, and we anticipate this festival to be just as successful. Especially because we've received donations from a generous sponsor, and ten percent of all booth proceeds will also be going to charity. Make sure you mark your calendars!" He steps down, and everyone claps. I pat my palms together to at least appear polite.

"And another big thanks," Vanessa goes on, "to Rachel Reed of the Reed Family Tree Farm, for donating the gorgeous evergreen for our lighting tonight that will be brought to the hospital lobby tomorrow morning for all the patients, families, and staff to enjoy."

My face flushes when Rachel walks onto the stage. Everyone

stares, so it gives me an excuse to do the same. Her hair is in its typical side braid, and her red flannel is unbuttoned at the top. I clench and release my fist at an image from earlier today: her untamed hair, white tank top, perfect curves. How my skin charged with electricity when she came close.

I catch Ben eyeing me from the corner of my vision and take a sip of my drink. Thank god for cold beer. I'm going to be through this thing in one more gulp if this keeps up.

Rachel takes the mic. "Thanks, everyone, for being here." As she speaks, the lights dim, and I couldn't tear my eyes from her if I tried. I should try. The way her hair shines and her skin glows and her lips glisten when she smiles. That dimple on the right side of her mouth. She's blushing and glances down like she's shy. That does something swoopy to my stomach, and I don't love how my body keeps betraying me. This girl is not mine. She doesn't want to be. She never did.

I clear my throat and drink again, taking extreme caution to not look at Ben.

Rachel continues, "I'm in charge of picking the person to light our tree, and tonight, I have someone specific in mind."

A guitar strums, and when I look up, she's the one playing.

Like she used to in high school. When it was just her and me in the hayloft in her barn. That was the only place she'd play back then, too shy in front of others. But she trusted me. A sense of pride fills me up at seeing her bring this secret part of herself out into the open. And a sense of loss, too, at no longer having those moments with her, all to ourselves. Damn their musical family.

"Someone who recently came back into my life in a really . . . sudden way." She chuckles.

My stomach tightens. Please don't—

"Morgan? Would you do us the honors this year?" Rachel finds me, and the whole room turns to look.

"There's no perfect time. You have to go for it," Ben whispers, throwing my words back at me.

I glare at him, and he smiles innocently.

"Come on up, Morgan," Rachel coaxes.

There's no way out of this.

With all eyes on me, I take a deep breath and stand. I edge around the crowd, ever aware of Rachel's gaze in a way that keeps me grounded.

For some reason, she wants to involve me in this. I don't want her to regret it.

I reach the tree, and it's even prettier up close.

A garland of crystal teardrops weaves through the greenery, and tiny fairy ornaments grace each and every branch. Hundreds of figurines with shimmery wings in pastel colors. I gulp. Even though I was too young to remember many details of Mom's final stay in the hospital, I think maybe she would have loved this. I swallow against guilt at not knowing for sure and brush a fragile sculpture with my fingertips. When I turned five, Dad and I started hanging a new ornament in her memory each year. So many whimsical monuments to her life decorated our tree by the time I left home.

"Here you go, Morgan."

I blink and find Tanner at my side, handing me the plug to the string of lights.

His smile is so reassuring that sadly, I don't think I hate him at all.

I locate the outlet on the wall and look back at Rachel. She grins and keeps strumming.

I bend down and plug it in. The whole room gasps.

When I stand back up, I do too.

It's gorgeous. Thousands of tiny white lights hit the crystals like prisms, winking rainbows off every surface.

Rachel strums the chords to a slowed-down version of "Wonderful Christmastime," and joy fills the room with a presence all its own. Some patrons get up and slow dance beside their tables. The air is made of hope, a tingle of something big and bright and new ahead.

Before this feeling fades and I change my mind, I approach the stage where Rachel plays. Her gaze holds steady on mine, transforming my insides into winged things.

Tanner's stare must be pinned to my back, and that makes me braver. I have history with Rachel, and that's got to mean more than a library bar. Not that I care.

I know where I want to go with her tomorrow to continue our town tour, and don't want to chicken out. I bend close to the collar of her shirt. Her eyes go wide, and she clutches her guitar like it's tethering her to the earth.

Then I whisper in her ear, tell her where I want to meet in the morning, and pull back before being so near her becomes any more intoxicating, sucking the courage right out of me.

Her lips creep up, and she nods. "See you there, Ross."

The way she says my last name makes my toes curl, and I thank the holiday spirits that I took my shot when I did.

I turn back to Ben, and I must be the picture of helplessness, because he rushes up and loops his arm through mine. We walk through the crowd the same way we entered.

"You know she's watching you leave, right?" he says in a hushed tone.

I hold my breath and keep my legs moving through the door, a stupid grin splitting my face, butterflies jamming up my throat.

Maybe this bar experience will end in vomit like my last, for entirely different reasons.

CHAPTER 8

I'm an utter fool for asking Rachel to meet me here.

Fern Falls Peak is made for romance. Outside of winter, the trail is tame enough to drive on, and I always heard tales by the lockers of classmates who went up over the weekend and came back down experienced, in love, or heartbroken. Romance is fun like that.

Now, taking this place in, I get it. It's truly stunning and feels made of promise, like love itself. Snow-dappled trees fleck the hill as far as it slopes to a dark, liquid snake of a stream. Then it's wide open, snow-white ranchland reaching straight to where the waking sun blushes the horizon. Hopefully, Rachel will be here soon. Hopefully, she forgot any memories associated with this spot, because here's why I'm an idiot: This is where we were when I was fifteen and fell in love with her.

I shiver. It was warmer then. To escape the pressing heat, we drove up the mountain. The air was cooler at the lookout. We parked at the end of a long line of cars—then flamed with embarrassment at all the fogged-up windows. I pulled my ball cap low, trying to hide my heated cheeks. Rachel turned on the truck radio. Pop music played softly. "Up for a game?" she asked, moonlight winking off her eyes. I nodded. "Every groan or make-out sound that makes us cringe earns one volume dial up."

I giggled. The car beside us squeaked. I cranked the dial. That's how it went until Gaga blared, and we bounced Rachel's Dodge for very different reasons than the other vehicles bounced. People yelled at us in husky voices, demanding we turn it down, but we danced and sang so loudly, we barely heard them. And god, her laugh. It melted into me like early morning warmth. So distinguishable from the cold sleep of the rest of the world, filled with hope for good things to come.

I shake my head, returning to the present. If I'm going to do this event for Rachel, work with her, I need to go all in, face every cobweb of my past so nothing can jump out and surprise me. That's why I chose Fern Falls Peak. That's the only reason.

Before I can forget, I pull out my phone and take a photo of the stunning view, then text it to Johanna and write:

Early morning hike. No filter.

I bury my phone and hands in my pockets. My breath mingles with the fog, and I dare Fern Falls Peak to give me its best shot. I'm a new person now, and this Morgan doesn't fall in love with girls at scenic lookouts.

I distract myself from the weight of this moment by remembering what this place is named after. Back in the beginning of Fern Falls, Blake and Lucinda Strutt took a swim in the waterfall up the hill from here. A swim sans clothes. It was the first reported case of skinny-dipping, and the "criminal" couple used some of the area's plentiful ferns to hide from law enforcement, but the sheriff swiped their apparel off the bank to draw them out. An event infamous around here as The Bare-Ass Standoff. I crack up, and the sound echoes off the trees.

"Sorry to intrude on your big diabolical laughter moment."

Snorting at the surprise of Rachel's voice, I spin to find her cresting the trail. Her mouth quirks up at one corner, and mine does the same in response. She strides over in her boots and jeans, long dark hair bunched up between the bottom of her gray beanie and the collar of her Carhartt jacket. Her nose and cheeks are pink from her hike, and her eyes straight-up sparkle.

"Hey," I say, like the suave ass I am.

She reaches me and smiles. "I mean, if I didn't already wake at dawn and trudge through snow on the daily, this meeting might actually be villainous of you. Especially without coffee."

I dive more than reach into the tote bag at my feet and retrieve the thermos and mugs I scrounged from a kitchen cabinet in the rental cabin. I hold them up like a peace offering. "As if I'd forget coffee. Am I redeemable now?"

Her brow kicks up. "I don't know. That evil cackle was pretty realistic." She winks and settles onto a fallen log at the edge of the lookout like she didn't just make every cell in my body catch fire. Is she flirting with me? I shake my head and keep my hands from doing the same as I pour our hazelnut coffee and breathe in the buttery scent. I place Rachel's cup beside her and take a seat, too. Apart from the calls of birds and melting snow that plops down from branches, it's quiet. And awkward. I cradle my tin mug, beseeching the coffee to spark some conversation. Clearing my throat, I prepare to break the silence, when Rachel speaks first. "That was really great of you to come last night. You did a wonderful job lighting the tree."

I swallow a sip of coffee and try not to laugh at how generous that compliment is. It doesn't take an expert to plug in some lights. But she did compliment me, so naturally, my face transforms into Death Valley. "When did you start playing guitar in public?"

She studies her coffee. "I don't very often. When Tanner took over the bar a few years ago, he wanted some new acts for the weekend crowd—for tourists from the city and stuff. Adam started playing, and he invites me along sometimes."

Ah, Tanner. Right. He is her type. Like some of the celebrities she crushed on in high school. My cheeks prickle. She plays music for him like she used to play for me.

I'll never forget when she came out to me, sophomore year in her hayloft, our old hangout spot, while she strummed her guitar. "I'm bisexual," she said, a C chord still humming. She didn't look up to read my reaction.

"Cool," was my only response. She was still the same Rachel. She may as well have told me her favorite color was purple.

As I thumbed through my gossip mag, her confession gained weight in my chest, until I couldn't hold back any longer. "I am, too." The words rushed out, taking all my air with them.

Her fingers paused for the briefest second. Strummed another chord. "Cool," she said back, the corner of her mouth sliding up.

I bit my lip and grinned as big as my face allowed as I stared at glossy images of celebrities, not seeing them at all. From the corner of my vision, Rachel beamed so big, it shot straight to my heart.

I can't stop myself. "Are, um, you and Tanner close?"

She looks up at the horizon, and soft peach sunrise lights her face, setting embers in her dark eyes. "He's a friend." She takes a sip of her coffee, then pins that sunlit gaze straight on me. "We're not together, if that's what you mean."

Warmth cascades down my neck, pools in my chest. "Oh." That's exactly what I meant. And, like an emotional avalanche, I can't stop there. "So, do you have a partner?" I bury my nose in my mug. I shouldn't care about this. Not with how she ghosted me after our falling out. All my calls that went unanswered, visits to her house she avoided until that final time when I gave up completely, realized she was done with me. I shouldn't care at all. Yet here I am, holding my breath for her answer, blushing into a tin cup with tiny black bears on the rim while tree bark bites me in the butt.

"Do you start all your business meetings with that question?"

I snort and snap my gaze to her. A teasing smile plays on her lips. I give her a look that says, *Well? Do you?*

"No." She shakes her head, and I become a human balloon, ready to float off into this sunrise.

"What about you?" she asks quietly.

My balloon pops. I cough on my coffee, swipe at my chin. "What about me?"

"Are you with anyone?" Her voice is soft, almost timid. She runs a thumb back and forth over an enameled bear cub, examines it thoroughly.

Maybe this coffee is a conversation stopper, because I can't speak. How's it going to sound that I've never kept anyone around? That I only fail at relationships? I open my mouth to reply several times before finally landing on, "No." No one since Josh. He was good, too. A head caterer I worked with who quickly worked his way into my heart with his dark brown eyes and hair, brown skin, bold laugh, hilarious jokes. If I wouldn't have broken up with him, he would have proposed. But I'm really good at breaking things before they break me. Like Christy broke Dad.

Rachel clears her throat. "So, you're here. You really chose to stay. Is there . . . anything more than the fundraiser that you're staying for?"

Her eyes are so open and sincere. I want to tell her so much, ask her so much. Apologize for hurting her after my graduation party. Ask why she didn't hear me out when I tried to apologize, why she didn't give us a second chance. Why I wasn't good for her anymore. Like Dad and I weren't good enough for Christy . . . and I was no longer sufficient for Dad.

My mind scrambles beneath buried questions and settles on what it knows best, its life vest: business.

I swallow hard and settle on the truth—part of it, at least. I sweep my hand across the landscape before us. "For Fern Falls. This will be my first event focused on results beyond it. With weddings and parties and seminars, I don't have to think about them once they're done. But this, it matters. Your business matters. I see what it means to the town, and last night proved that even more. What you do here, it gives people hope. I want that to continue for you and Fern Falls." And I want to simultaneously bury Christy Vaughn and Miles Knocks.

Rachel is silent, but her eyes soften, like I paid her the greatest compliment. It makes me feel connected to her in a way I haven't in years, and I fidget on the log to add more space between us. "So, you want to save the farm?" I ask, forcing the spotlight off me.

She's quiet for a long time.

Just when I think she's not going to speak at all, she says, "Suddenly, I'm hopeful, too."

She says it so softly that it must mean something big for her to share it. And from the blank look on her face, she's offered all she can right now.

"Okay, then." I stand up and steel my breath as her eyes meet mine. I reach out. "To hope."

A small smile spreads Rachel's lips as she rises. She takes my hand. Her fingers brush my wrist before her palm presses against mine, sending sparks through my veins. I stiffen to not let her see how her touch affects me. How I want her to keep right on doing it.

"To hope," she says. Her eyes bore into mine, and the air between us turns taut, like if I were to move a fraction of an inch, we'd crash together. How does she do this? She steals the air, scrambles my senses, draws all the wrong questions to the tip of my tongue: *Why did you stop talking to me, only to message me years later? Aren't you thinking about these things, too? Are we going to talk about them? Did you ever like me at all?*

When she pulls her hand away, the loss of her touch hits like a cold front. I shake my head, returning to myself. I almost caved and completely let my guard down. Jesus. No more handshakes. Apparently, Rachel's are made of a very dark magic.

"So, what would be the first step in planning this thing?" she asks, scooping some snow into her cup and swirling it around to wash it out.

"Well . . ." I squeeze my eyes and blink back to the present. Get a grip, Morgan. "We have to decide on a theme. What best represents your mission and message. Then we align every detail with that. And, you know, you'd have to officially decide to work with me."

"Mmm-hmm," she says, placing the clean mug into my tote bag. "But it's not really fair for me to make the call yet, when I haven't had a turn to choose a spot for our tour."

My lips turn up as she heads back down the path. Of course, she won't make this easy. She pauses before she rounds the corner, glancing back. "I'll pick you up at eight tomorrow? At a decent hour, because I'm a decent person."

Pick me up? "How do you know where I—" Oh. Of course, Ben told her.

She smirks before disappearing down the hill.

I grab my bag and follow, grateful for the space alone and the chance to let my giddy fool of a smile commandeer my face. I survived Fern Falls Peak with Rachel Reed. Surely, whatever she has planned for tomorrow won't weaken my resolve to resist her. No matter how the damn sun glows in her eyes.

CHAPTER 9

Eight a.m. is way too late. I've been up since five, and that was after I forced myself to sleep and got maybe four hours total. The cold creeps in, and I pull my jacket collar high up my neck, adjusting my stance on the front porch. I want this event, and I want it to be perfect. I need to show Johanna I can come back even better. On my own. That's what all the nerves are for.

My stomach mocks me with anxiety gymnastics when Rachel's red truck pulls up. I should have met her . . . wherever she's taking me. What are we going to talk about for the whole ride? How long is the drive? Am I dressed appropriately?

I shove my hands as deep as they'll go into my jacket pockets and worry at the keys to the rental cabin, rub the metal between my fingers, and try to redirect some frazzled thoughts there.

When I hop onto the passenger seat, I feel slightly better.

"Morning," Rachel says, smiling. The rising sun highlights her freckles, that dimple is out in full force, and I want to throw these keys out the goddamn door.

She is vibrant, and I must look like I only got four hours of sleep. My whole face is tight. It smells like coffee in here, though, and I find the source. Two cups with Peak Perk's mountaintop logo on the sleeves are cradled in the console. "You. Did. Not."

"Mocha was the special today." She hands one to me, and I hold it like precious treasure, close my eyes, breathe in the heavenly chocolate scent.

"You had to show up my thermos coffee."

Rachel snorts as she puts the truck in drive. "It wouldn't take much to show that up."

I let out a squee and playfully pat her arm. She looks at my hand, then quickly back at the road. The shift in the atmosphere is instant. Spontaneously touching crossed the line, and I single-handedly killed any guise of ease between us. I reached for her so naturally. Like old times.

Rachel keeps both hands on the wheel, staring straight ahead.

We pass rows of cozy cabins, the sparkling main street, and turn onto the two-lane highway that cuts through the center of town. There's a snow-covered golf course to the right that's now filled with children on neon sleds, and beyond that . . . our high school.

The campus has the same bungalows, spread out across a snowy field. The forest lines the back, and that's where Rachel and I would eat lunch with Ben. Two years older than the three of us, Adam ate with our group there, too, before he graduated.

Truthfully, this was the large part of what kept me up last night: wondering if we'd go by our old school or another place that's been waiting to gut-punch me. I don't want to get angry or cry in front of her. I don't want to feel any of those things. Just driving past is too much.

I clear my throat and let my useless tongue savor some coffee. One sip gives me the courage to say something, anything. "Where are we headed?" My body braces for her answer.

A small smile creeps across her face. I remember that mischievous look, and something in me sparks. That look meant good things when we were young. Surprise sledding trips, the best snacks for a sleepover, the moment before she kissed me. I focus hard on my mocha.

"So, you remember that garden we made as kids?"

"The one for fairies?" I ask, surprised that she remembers it. She nods.

I'd never forget. It was the most fun I had in that eight-year-old summer. We took every craft supply and whatever trinkets we could sneak out of our respective houses and made an entire fairy village that wound through her farm.

"That's your hint."

"Oh," I bark nervously. "So you're not actually going to disclose where you're taking me?"

Rachel grins with closed lips, then drinks her coffee. A sealed vault.

I sip my own mocha, and some liquid courage spurs me on. "How do I know your intentions are pure, Reed?" What the hell just came out of my mouth?

Rachel's brows hike up her forehead. She coughs and sets her cup back in the console.

What has this mocha done to me? Too much caffeinated confidence. Way too much. Retreat. Flirting with Rachel Reed is on the list of forbidden things.

Before I can open the door and hurl my body into a snowbank, the truck slows to a stop. Rachel unbuckles and opens her door. Thank god for the icy air to break up all my shame that clogs this cab. I fill my greedy lungs with it.

Before she leaves, she looks me directly in the eyes, her gaze heavy. Tingles dance up my arms. "When I have impure intentions, you'll know, Ross. And I'll ask permission."

Then she closes her door, and I forget how to breathe at all.

We're parked in front of a charming building that the sign hanging over the double doors proclaims as FOREST FAIRY'S. Pastel flowers are painted along the base of the wooden siding, so it looks like they spring straight up from the snow.

After taking a second to collect myself (and leaving my lethal mocha in the truck), I run to catch up with Rachel.

Rachel . . . who flirted with me? I didn't imagine that, right? Rachel, who is cool and calm, unlike me, hands in my pockets, clutching my keys for dear life.

"Hi, Morgan!"

Oh, she's with Whitney, the same employee from the tree farm.

Rachel steps aside and makes room for me. "Whit works here when she's not at the farm."

"Hi, Whitney," I say, grateful for a distraction from my blazing cheeks.

"You can call me by my fairy name, Daisy Wildflower," she says with a smile that rivals the twinkle lights strung across the windows behind her. She has on a bright purple sweatshirt with the same swoopy-lettered logo as the business, and her Colgate toothpaste-blue hair peeks out beneath a glittery silver beanie. "So glad you're here! Petunia Pie and I will take you inside and get you all set up."

Rachel turns as red as her truck. Whitney walks ahead, practically skipping. Two little fairy wings are printed on the back of her sweatshirt.

"You first, Petunia Pie," I say, ushering Rachel forward, and she marches on like this is a crucible.

"You're gonna be assigned one, too, ya know." Her voice is low, but there's laughter in it.

"What? An alter ego from My Little Pony?"

Rachel snorts as we enter the shop, and I slow my steps, taking in the wonder of it all.

It's a magical paradise. If I were about seventeen years younger, I'd have dreamed of hiding in here past closing and taking up permanent residence. Hell, as a grown woman, I'm tempted.

Gorgeous oak trees grow straight through the floorboards,

hazily lit by skylights. Their branches drip with soft lights and flower garlands, and all along the trunks are living things. Or, things made to look living, and lived in. Tiny, handcrafted, backlit windows shine, showing peeks of micro-sized living rooms, bedrooms, and potion bottles lined up on shelves. Little fairy dolls with translucent wings flit throughout the branches, blown by ceiling fans. There are porch lights that flicker, and mossy outcrops, and a Celtic soundscape plays.

The place is empty, but clearly ready for visitors under the age of ten. Small workstations are placed just so around the room, close to each of the three oaks. In the center of every table is a lazy Susan brimming with crafts supplies, charms, and figurines reminiscent of the ones on the trees.

I stop short of bumping into Rachel.

"Whoa, hey there, Fluttershy," she says, stepping aside, making space for me at the counter.

I laugh at her MLP reference and blush that she remembers Fluttershy was my fave, thank you very much. A jar of starry pins sits beside the cash register, along with a stack of what looks like filigreed certificates. "Okay, let's do this," I say. "Give me my fairy name."

"We love an eager one!" Whitney claps, puts on a pair of purple-rimmed glasses, and pulls out a chart that resembles an ancient tome.

She splays the faux-aged paper across the counter and peers above her violet rims. "Now. What is the first letter of your first name and the second letter of your last name?"

I laugh. "M and O."

Whitney runs her pointer finger down the page twice, then types into a tablet beneath the glass in the counter. A very good balance of archaic fairy lore and modern technology. "What month were you born?"

"September," Rachel says at the same time as me.

We meet eyes, then flinch away.

Whitney does the tome-tablet thing again, and I brace for

another question. "What is the first letter of the first name of the person you love most?"

I stare at the top of her silver-glitter beanie as she waits, finger poised on the chart. My throat goes dry.

I scramble for a name. Sonia? She's a good friend, but we've never done more than random weeknights out together. There was Josh, before I broke up with him. Johanna and I were close when I first moved to LA, but then I nudged her strictly into the *Boss* category. Pushed her away, too.

I suck in air like a dying vacuum.

Whitney's gaze settles on me, and sweat beads on my upper lip. Rachel looks up as I swipe it off.

The room is too hot.

Dad, there's Dad. But we hardly talk anymore, and by the time I left home, we never really did.

There are my succulents. There was Ben when we were young; I loved him as a friend.

Mostly, there was Rachel.

Now, there is no one.

I stare at some loose glitter on the counter and try to stop my eyes from blurring with fresh tears.

"Hey, we can do this later, okay?" Rachel gently touches my arm, and Whitney nods.

"N," I blurt out.

Rachel lets her arm fall back to her side. I shake off an urge to reach for her hand, place it back where it was.

Whitney references her chart with a little less vigor, and I stand there, trying to keep all my pieces together.

N for no one. N for nothing.

Spitting out a letter gave some relief, but these tears are stubborn.

Rachel glances at me, then says, "Hey, I'm gonna show Morgan the back patio, okay? Can you let us know when her certificate is ready?"

"Of course, Petunia!" Whitney waggles her fingers.

Rachel guides me through two French doors draped in strands of ivy. We're outside on a cobblestone patio, and I can breathe, thank god.

I stand in the middle of the space as she goes to a little mint-green hutch in the corner.

I clench and unclench my fists, breathe some more, focus on the space around me. A pastel-littered table set for a tea party. The pine trees that wall the perimeter in green, the jasmine hanging from the patio cover. The trickling of a fountain in the corner.

Rachel returns and hands me a steaming sky blue mug. The ceramic is warm, and I take a sip. Hot cocoa. Vanilla. I breathe in and out, focusing on how each breath feels in my body.

She stands beside me and waits, and it's not heavy like inside, under Whitney's gaze. It's the kind of company that isn't demanding. The kind that's just there, comfortable, supportive.

Once my breathing returns to normal and my nerves stop jumping across my skin, I offer a weak smile. "Thank you."

"I'm sorry," she says.

"For what?" I keep my tone light. I don't want to be a burden. I don't want to be too much.

"For all that." She waves a hand at the door. "That must have felt like an interrogation and put you on the spot. I'm sorry it made you uncomfortable."

I shake my head and focus on my cocoa. "You didn't do anything."

"Whitney gets really into the theme, but this patio is the real reason I brought you here."

I take in the tea party again. "I, um, think we might need bigger chairs?"

Rachel laughs. "They're hosting a birthday today and are closed to the public, so Whit let me come in beforehand. More specifically, these are why I brought you here." She points at the border of deep green pines.

I move closer, cradling my mug. The shelter of greenery

makes this space warm, and there are heat lamps strewn about, and the hot ceramic feels good in my hands, and the fact that Rachel gave it to me, to comfort me, feels good all over.

I peer closer at a tree, and behind the twinkle lights and fairy-shaped ornaments, glitter-dusted pinecones, and crystal prisms, there is a silver, oval medallion affixed to the trunk that reads: REED FAMILY TREE FARM. "You donated these trees?"

Rachel shoves her hands in her pockets, bites her lip, then says, "When this place opened about five years ago and my parents moved, I donated some saplings." She gazes at the trees softly, like they're her babies. "It's been so rewarding to watch them grow and contribute to this space, and I thought that might lend some inspiration for the event planning, if that's how it works?" She scrubs at the back of her neck.

She was made to take on a lot at a really young age. Kind of like me. "You took over the whole farm when you were twenty?"

She shuffles. "Yeah, well, it was Adam and I back then, so we took it on together. Mom and Dad's dream for the place faded, and then Adam stuck it out with me until his dream changed, too."

"Is it your dream? Do you ever resent them moving on, not having any help?" I'm pushing, but I can't help it. Is this really what she wants?

"I . . . do love the trees and doing things like this." She motions around her. "I have lots of dreams, and I've had to face the fact they'll never be more than that." She looks at her feet, then up, straight at me. "And I'd never want anyone to stay here for me when they don't want to. I deserve more than that."

I'm pinned to the spot, knowing full well she's not just talking about her family. Knowing I left. I left *her*. My gut roils. How dare she? She may have stayed here, but she left me long before I moved away. I'm about to tell her as much when Whitney bursts through the doors, arms filled with sparkling things. "It's official! Welcome to the Forest Fairy's family, Morning Dew Pickle Pop!"

I snort and try not to laugh out loud for her sake. She beams as she hands me a glittery certificate and star pin.

Rachel slaps a hand over her mouth. Her face turns red, like she's stifling laughter, too. I smile and tuck my trinkets into my jacket pocket.

"Thank you, Whi— I mean, Daisy Wildflower."

"Have a magical day!" She waltzes back through the door, then pops her head out and whisper-yells to Rachel, "The party starts in ten minutes."

Rachel nods. "Thanks so much, Whit."

Then it's just the two of us again.

Some Celtic music keys up with a crackle, and more lights blink on. Pinks and violets and blues sparkle to life among the branches.

The colors, the music, the magic . . . "I've got it." I turn to her, eyes wide. "I know exactly what kind of fundraiser we're going to host at the farm."

"Yeah?" Her eyes light up.

"The start of it. I'm going to meet with Ben to sort out the details, then I'll tell you everything."

I set my mug on the hutch and head back through the door, holding it open for Rachel.

We walk through the space and out the front as Whitney calls, "See you soon, Pickle Pop and Petunia!"

I wave. "Why do I get called by my last name and you by your first?"

"Because it's the most flattering," she says on a laugh.

I try my hardest not to smile too big, to stay guarded still. We may be older now, but Rachel's tone on the patio revealed she resents me for leaving, like I resent her for never speaking to me again after I tried to resolve things.

We reach the truck, and I stop. "Wait. So does this mean I can officially run the fundraiser?"

Rachel gives me an angled look from beneath her lashes. "You were always going to run the fundraiser, Ross." Her dimple makes a reappearance as she pulls the passenger door open for me.

I force my weak limbs to climb up into the truck and shut the door as she walks around the hood to her side.

I'm going to stay on the surface with her. If I have any ounce of self-preservation, I won't let the games, fairy names, harmless flirting, and her comfortable company dislodge that stone in my gut.

The mocha she treated me to scents the whole space, and tingles run through me. If she already planned on giving me the fundraiser, then these past two mornings must have been excuses to spend time together.

The cab sways as she hops in. Pine tinges the chocolate.

And that stone in my stomach moves dangerously close to churning into gravel.

CHAPTER 10

The back entrance of Peak Perk is just as adorable as the front. A cold-fogged window offers a glimpse of the kitchen, and gorgeous hand-lettered script swoops across the glass in a pale pink.

"Oh my god, Ben," I snort as I read the words, and he jiggles a key in the lock. "Is this the welcome sign for your vendors?"

THIS BAKERY DOOR DON'T WANT NONE UNLESS YOU'VE GOT BUNS, HON covers the whole pane.

Ben peers at the glass like he forgot all about the Sir Mix-a-Lot lyric mashup displayed there. "Ha, yeah. Gotta keep the people smiling."

I laugh and shake my head. Fern Falls is full of so many surprises. Library bars, fairy gardens, happy signs. So many things slowly dismantling the dark memories I have of this town. I snap a photo of the window and send it to Johanna. She'll get a kick out of it.

The door springs open with a squeal, and Ben and I rush inside, grateful for the warmth of the kitchen, both of us eager to sketch out ideas for the fundraiser. I can't wait to walk away from here today with everything in place, all vendors confirmed. Unfortunately, it's not warm. Not at all. The bakery is as cold as the early morning air outside. Ben flicks on the lights, then strips off his jacket to his gray T-shirt beneath.

"Aren't you freezing?" I ask, clinging to my down coat.

"You really lost that tough mountain skin, didn't you?" He snickers and goes to crank up the wall heater. "Don't worry. It'll be toasty in no time."

Moving about his kitchen like a master, he turns on double ovens, and they glow to life. Then he pulls bags and bowls off metal shelves and spreads out his ingredients on the giant stainless island.

Despite all the steel in this place, it's cozy. The overhead lights gleam off every spotless surface. A big basket of holiday cookies sits on the counter: meticulously decorated snowmen, menorahs, Stars of David, candy canes.

Ben slips on his apron, then hands a matching one to me.

I cock an eyebrow.

"C'mon." He holds it out farther and smirks.

I sigh, place my notebook on a stool, and take off my jacket, too, because it really is warming up fast, and then I slip on the white apron.

He rounds the island to work opposite me. "Bread first, so the fresh dough batches can rise, then we need to pan the risen dough I started yesterday morning, and then we'll move on to scones." He measures yeast into a bowl, then pours in warm water.

"Are we going to discuss the fundraiser at all, or did you just need free help?"

But I'd help out even if he hadn't aproned me into it. My limbs loosen just being in a kitchen with Ben again. When we were younger, his mom, Laura, always had a tray of pastries waiting for us after school. Then, as we got older, we'd bake together. Rachel and Adam would join when chores on the tree farm were less demanding, and Laura always sent us home with leftovers. I hid those extra scones in the freezer, and they stayed fresh for months. I pulled them out when Dad worked late, which, after Christy left, was always, and I'd be a little less lonely.

I haven't thought of that in years.

"Help is subjective in this case," Ben teases. "Plus, I pay in coffee." He reaches across the counter and sets a steaming mug of vanilla-scented heaven before me, along with a fresh ball of dough. "You remember how to knead it?"

I nod as an ache stabs my chest. I remember kneading bread with Rachel, the two of us side by side, taking instructions from Laura. How we'd sneak chocolate chips from the prep bowls when she turned her back to us. How things were so simple back then. I sip my drink, then lightly flour my workspace and begin pressing the sides of the roughly shaped ball, down and away, with the heel of my palm. "How's your mom, Ben?" I ask, my throat tight as the taste of her scones comes back to me. Lemon and rosemary.

He smiles, but it doesn't reach his eyes. "She's been at the coast, actually. For the past six months or so. With my grandma."

Ben spent most school breaks at his grandma's beach house and she would often call while we were baking. She was so spunky and feisty, always taunting Laura about under-seasoning. During the holidays, she'd bring all of us gifts when she visited, little handmade suncatchers with driftwood and sea glass, like we were family, too. "How's your grandma doing?"

He pauses. "She had a stroke back in June."

My heart clenches. "Ben, I'm so sorry. Is she okay?"

He nods sharply, like he's reassuring himself. "She's tough. Her recovery has gone well, surpassing all the milestones the doctors set earlier than expected."

My shoulders relax as I knead the dough. "I'm so glad to hear that."

"Yeah, thanks. It's good my mom can be with her. She's gotten used to it out there. She never liked the cold winters, and I think that's why she keeps prolonging her stay. Grandma calls and tells me to take her back so she can have peace and quiet again."

I laugh. That's exactly something his grandma would say. "What about your mom's shop?"

I picture the front room of Ben's house, which they converted into her business, Mountaintop Mystic. It was filled with gemstones and herbs, teas, elixirs, and all kinds of apothecary items.

He turns and checks on the ovens. "She cut business hours when she helped me start up the bakery. Now that she's gone, I don't have the time to keep it running like she used to. In my spare time, I use her existing inventory to fill the online orders she still gets from loyal customers. Besides that, it's closed to the public."

How does Ben run this bakery and his mom's business, and still have time to save tree farms? "Seems like you're saving everyone's businesses around here," I say, as I fold the dough back toward me.

A blush creeps across his cheeks. I won't tease him about Adam. I'm happy he shared that with me at the bar, like I was worth trusting.

"Only those worth saving." He smiles.

"That reminds me," I say, unease settling in my stomach. "How are we paying for the fundraiser? We need to discuss the budget." This is the first time I've choked on those words. The Barnes's clients have such high budgets, if they exist at all. This is different, and I don't want to make him feel bad or inadequate. I don't want to make him feel like I did when Christy made it clear Dad and I didn't measure up.

Ben blushes. "Have you ever been to my grandmother's, Morgan?"

I shake my head. He shared a bit about her place, his trips there, but I was never able to go. Especially after we grew apart.

"She owns a beachfront mansion and has more money than she knows what to do with."

I loose a startled laugh. "Seriously?"

"Yeah. And not to brag, but I'm her favorite grandchild." He grins so sweetly, I can practically see a halo appear above his blond locks.

"And you asked her for this?"

He pulls at the strap of his apron. "She sends me checks every month because she wants to. I tell her not to, and she says she's seventy-nine and wants to see me use it while she's alive. She one hundred percent knows how to work the grandma guilt."

I laugh, wishing I had a grandma as wonderful as his. Any grandparent would have been a gift. Both Dad's and Mom's parents were gone before I came along. It would have been amazing to know that extension of Mom, to have a piece of her still.

"So, after I got ahead with payments on this place, I wanted to help out other businesses," Ben continues, pulling me out of those dark hallways in my mind. "But I thought throwing a fundraiser would make the money go farther."

"And Rachel is okay with it?"

He flashes a grin that lifts his glasses up his nose. "I have a very sweet way of making people accept things."

I squint at him. "More blind business date shenanigans, huh?"

He shrugs. "I served her coffee and pastries and told her I'm doing this for her. It's not my fault her mouth was so full of sticky buns that she couldn't argue."

I chuckle at the image and grab my notebook, hold it up in salute. "Well, then. Ready to get to work?"

He wipes his hands on his apron and nods enthusiastically. "I love the enchanted forest theme, Morgan. I already have ideas for what kinds of pastries and cakes to sell, and a stack of business cards from local vendors who'd be happy to get involved with this. I'll go grab them."

I open the notebook I found in the rental cabin and browse the ideas I scribbled down yesterday. I haven't been this excited

about an event since, well, ever? The lights on the trees at Forest
Fairy's sparked an idea to turn the farm into a light show on a
grand scale. "Hey, Ben, do you think Adam could help with the
mechanics for the tree lights? Or the music?"

A clatter sounds from behind the door of his office, and I
laugh. He seriously needs to get a grip over that boy. "Two
birds, one stone," I say.

He emerges with a stack of cards in hand, face full-on red.
"If your plan is to get me talking to Adam by the end of this—"

"Oh, no"—I smile devilishly—"my plan is to have you sharing much more than conversation with Adam once this is over."

His face shifts from mortified to malicious. "All right, then."
He crosses his arms. "I'll make you a deal."

I sip my coffee. This isn't going anywhere good.

"I talk"—he clears his throat—"or . . . more with Adam,
and you talk, or more, with Rachel."

I nearly spew my drink across the counter. "I have you beat
on the talking, but I guarantee Rachel wouldn't want more than
that with me." Even as I say it, I remember the way she looked
at me yesterday, her dark, promising stare. *When I have impure
intentions, you'll know.* She didn't say if; she said *when.* I sup-
press a shiver.

"So you're not denying you want to." His look is liquid evil.

"Ben. This is so off-topic." I bury my face in my notebook
and will my cheeks to stay cool. "I'm just here to do this event,
strictly professional. Not dig up old flames."

"M'kay, Morgan. Lie to yourself about your own feelings,
but if you think Rachel hasn't stayed madly in love with you
all these years, you've lost as much sense as cold weather toler-
ance."

I snap my gaze up to him. His face is deadpan. "What are you
talking about? Rachel hates me."

"Why do you think she hasn't had a real relationship all this
time? Why do you think she chose a design school in LA rather

than one of the several that accepted her all across the country? I mean, sure, her family needed her close, but I know that wasn't the only reason."

The memory of her Instagram message hits me, taking my breath away. *Hi, Morgan. I'm in the Los Angeles area and heard you were, too. Would you like to meet up sometime? Maybe for coffee? I hope you're well.* —Rachel Reed

She said she was in LA, not that she was attending school there, not that she'd moved there. How long had she been so close without me knowing? An ache eats at my core. I never even wrote her back. "I didn't know she moved away from here." My voice is monotone.

Ben nods. "Yeah. All the sign lettering around town is done by Rachel. It became her side hobby when she had to move back."

"What? All the gorgeous signs like The Stacks, Forest Fairy's, yours? That's her work?"

"Yeah. Pretty great, right?"

I put her into such a careful box, and now it's cracking wide open. She left Fern Falls to pursue a career she's super talented at, and she chose to stay in LA. Near her family. Near me? Even though I never replied to her. There is so much I don't know. "Why would her parents move, then? Why would they make her give up on her schooling? Couldn't they have stayed a bit longer so she could finish?"

But before Ben can answer, a knock echoes from the front of the bakery.

His face screws up. "We don't open for an hour." He sets down the business cards and whooshes through the double doors of the kitchen.

I follow like a strung-along puppet, incapable of forming my own words or finding my own voice. I can only picture what Rachel wrote me all those years ago. The message I read hundreds of times. It was so casual. Like it didn't matter if I wrote back or not. So I hadn't. It had been too long to tear open that wound. Did it matter to her?

My focus snaps right back to the present when I realize who's knocking.

Even through the foggy glass, Christy Vaughn's teeth gleam.

Ben unlocks the door, and she strides in.

"Good morning, Ben. I wanted to ask if—"

"He doesn't open for an hour," I cut in, finding my voice. It's sharper than I intended. Oh well.

Christy stops and stares. "Morgan. What a pleasure to see you." Her tone has an edge that conveys it's about as pleasurable as combing knots through her hair.

I square my shoulders.

"How can I help you, Christy?" Ben asks, saving us all from me inevitably cussing her out.

"I wanted to see if you're planning on holding a booth at the Fern Falls Holiday Festival this year, and if so, could you display a flyer in your window?"

He takes the paper she hands him, studies it. "Isn't Tanner heading this up?"

I peer at her. There has to be some underlying reason for why she's involved in this.

She straightens, as if she can't contain her own self-satisfaction. "Vaughn Enterprises is fully sponsoring the festival this year." Her smile is brighter than the early sunlight glinting off snow out the window.

Ben looks at me.

I clear my throat. "Out of the goodness of your heart, right?" I say.

"We're invested in the future of Fern Falls, like I told you at the inn."

"Our investments lead to very different futures." I cross my arms.

Her smile wavers. "So you're still planning on holding your fundraiser?"

"Absolutely."

She folds her hands together. "You know, Morgan, I've met

with all the vendors here. A word of advice? You'll want to stick with planning the weddings and city events you're best at. You may have a hard time finding people who are willing to place their businesses, their livelihoods, in the hands of someone who was caught up in a scandal not weeks ago. Just a friendly tip. I wouldn't want you or anyone involved in your fundraiser to suffer any further humiliation or damage to their reputations if paparazzi were to show up. Fern Falls can't weather these things the same way Los Angeles can."

I try to speak. Nothing comes out. What can I say in response to what is clearly an intimidation tactic? That paparazzi won't come to Fern Falls? I know very well that they could.

Ben pulls open the front door. "Thanks so much for your visit, Christy. We look forward to seeing you at the holiday festival as well as at our fundraiser, which is very much still on track."

Christy puffs out her chest. Nods. "Wishing you luck, then."

"Thanks," he says, without a touch of sarcasm, "but we don't need luck. We have Morgan." Then he closes and locks the door before she can reply.

I stare at her through the glass. This woman who once acted like a part of my family is now stooping to the lowest level to sabotage me and my hometown.

Ben walks briskly toward the kitchen, and I follow, shell-shocked, grateful that he could come up with something to say, that he could have so much faith in me, while I stood there like a gaping fish.

"You really think we can do this? What if no one will work with me?" I ask.

"If she's trying so hard to turn people against us, that only proves what a threat we are to her plans." He holds up my journal. "Let's get to work."

We both sit down at the counter, and I flip through my sketches and notes, as if some whimsical ideas could actually stand a chance against a corporation.

"You can take my commission off the budget," I say, not looking up.

"No, Morgan, that's not fair to you."

I shake my head. "You already covered my lodging, and we're going to need to pull together all the funds we can to make this work." I have a good amount of savings, and knowing what's at stake, it wouldn't feel right to take pay for this, especially when everyone else is sacrificing so much.

"You're sure?"

"Absolutely." I nod.

If only I could be so certain of the future. I'm supposed to tell Rachel my plan for the fundraiser by tomorrow morning, and now I don't know if I can pull one off at all.

CHAPTER 11

Ben and I call every vendor in town and encounter a lot of mumbles and "unavailability due to the holidays," and I can't provide my LA go-tos, thanks to Chad the Cheater.

Now, here I am, wringing the life out of my steering wheel, staring at that red kiosk like it's a fire-breathing dragon, ready or not to break the bad news to Rachel. *Hey, Rach, no one in town will work with me, but don't worry, I'll win them over with my sign-smashing grace and snow-slipping charm!*

FML.

I force myself from my car and plaster on a smile as I approach the booth.

Whitney focuses on her ever-present notebook, the bill of her black ball cap emblazoned with ALL PRONOUNS WELCOME tipped low. And she's not alone. Tanner from The Stacks stands in front of the counter with two steaming mugs—and, seriously? He's still only in a white T-shirt and jeans, despite the fact that we're outside. In the snow.

"Are you going on the camping trip next Friday?" I overhear him ask Whitney.

A look of pure malice crosses her face. "Did Ben invite you? I swear to god . . ."

Their conversation sparks my memory. Ben, Adam, Rachel, and I used to go camping every year around this time. I swallow hard. Maybe they still do.

"Oh, hey there," Tanner says, saluting me with his cup and crooked grin.

I give a small wave. Whitney's expression brightens when she sees me. "Hi, Morning Dew Pi—"

"Hello, you two," I reply before she can finish saying my whole fairy name.

"Did you visit Forest Fairy's?" Tanner asks. "I'm Pine Tree Perfect!" He beams like he just shared his biggest life accomplishment.

Whitney glares at him. "That reminds me. You came for more firewood? For the second time this week?"

He clears his throat and slides the mug toward her. "And to bring you coffee, of course."

She sighs. "I only drink tea."

"Okay, okay." He holds up his hands. "I also wanted to talk to you about the holiday festival."

Whitney crosses her arms. "There's no way we're taking part in some commercialized, corporate-backed bullshit."

"Yeah," Tanner says, scrubbing his neck and eyeing me. "So have you also heard about Vaughn Enterprises being our donor, Morgan?"

I ignore Tanner and lock eyes with Whitney. "Wait a minute, Whit," I say, inspiration tingling through me, "this could be an opportunity for us to show we won't back down. And we could use it as a way to promote Enchanted Evenings."

"Enchanted what?" she asks.

"Ben and I brainstormed yesterday, and that's the name we

came up with for the fundraiser." I pass over my notebook that's full of our ideas.

Whitney's eyes light up as she takes it all in, and some confidence returns to my soul. Maybe I've still got the touch after all and won't completely ruin this.

Tanner peeks at it, too. "Wow, this is awesome," he says.

Whitney slides the notebook back to me with a smirk. "So using the Vaughn Enterprises festival to promote a fundraiser to stand against them, is actually pretty punk and badass, and I'm in."

My shoulders sag in relief as I tuck the notebook into my coat. "That makes"—I count my fingers—"six of us."

"Three Musketeers squared!" Tanner cheers.

Whitney glares at him as she rounds the counter. "C'mon, Pine Tree. Let's get your logs before you freeze to death in that T-shirt."

I snort. What a legend.

"Hey, Whit," I call after her as she leads Tanner to a small shed beside the kiosk. "I'm here for my meeting with Rachel. Is she around?" Thankfully, my voice stays steady at the mention of our appointment. You know, the one where I'll break it to her that no one's gonna touch this fundraiser with a ten-foot tree, thanks to me.

"She may be back near the old barn? I saw her clearing some logs when I got in, and she usually takes the wood there."

"Thanks, I'll head that way," I reply, with the most realistic smile I can muster. The barn was our old hang back in the day. I guess I'll have to face it sooner or later because of how we'll use it during the fundraiser. I was just hoping it'd be later. As in 2099.

Maybe I can find her around the farm somewhere and avoid the barn completely.

Beyond the tree-cutting portion, the forest has matured so much over the years. The pines are lush and full, and I let myself wander.

After at least five decades of being hit by sappy branches, I can't find Rachel anywhere. Nor can I hear the *thwack* of her ax.

I don't know how far I've gone or in what direction, when something presses up beneath the sole of my shoe.

I lift my foot to find a fairy—a doll, obviously—and pick it up. It's one that Rachel and I made gardens for when we were young.

On the ground beneath where it was are small blue specks. The trees are so dense that the snow cover is sparse, and the gems peek out from the loam. They've lost their luster, but I follow the trail, fairy doll clenched in my hand, and walk along until I stop dead in my tracks.

The one thing that could drag me into the undertow of History With Rachel Reed stands before me.

The barn.

It seemed bigger when I was young, but it's the size of a small suburban house. Its red paint is more of a rust color now, and a pine wreath hangs on each of the open double doors.

I set the doll back beneath a tree and move forward, like my feet are making this terrible decision and not me, until I'm eye-level with the wreaths.

Until I can see inside.

My heart halts to a stop.

Fresh pine needles squish beneath my boots as I step in.

I remember Rachel's mom, Tanya, would talk about wanting goats and pigs, but Rachel's dad only wanted to raise children and trees, so the barn was used by the latter. Rows of logs stacked high as my head, labeled by wood type and chop date. The piles farther back are dried and cured, ready to sell as firewood. The ones toward the front are a saturated brown and smell like Christmas. I run a finger along the open heart of a log, tracing the growth rings.

All of Rachel's hard work, beneath my fingertips. Years and years of her labor piled here. Years of her doing this alone.

Who knows how long ago she chopped that wood in the back. Was it when she still spoke to me? Before or after she moved to LA?

My rebellious eyes drift to the hayloft.

The wooden banister is looped with strings of tiny white lights that just barely twinkle. She never took them down? What else did she leave untouched? Before I can talk my feet out of it, they're scaling the old stairs.

I crawl into the wide-open space, canopied by arched beams.

My breath catches.

The whole area is a time capsule.

Beaded rainbow garlands span the ceiling, crossing over posters of Paramore and the *Glee* cast. An old boom box sits in the corner with CDs stacked beside it, Taylor Swift still on top. Moth-eaten blankets and cushions are piled upon an old hand-braided rug.

The wooden box we disguised as a faux-fur pillow to hold our secret letters is still in the very center. I scribbled so many never-delivered notes to my junior high crushes, and Rachel wrote to Ashton Kutcher and Mila Kunis.

I crawl across the rug and open the box, fingers gentle, shaky.

The lid falls back. My hand flies to my mouth.

There's a paper on top that's white, brand-new, tri-folded. Labeled with my name, in Rachel's handwriting.

My stomach drops as I pick it up. Unfold it.

It's dated a few days ago and only has one line: *I'm sorry I never told you the truth before you left.*

My eyes sting. The last real conversation we had before I moved away was the most cruel I've ever been. It was a couple days after my graduation party. The shock of Christy's rejection fueled a corrosive, simmering rage inside my chest, waiting to spew upon anyone who cracked me open. Unfortunately, that person was Rachel. She came by to check on me, and I stepped out onto the porch instead of inviting her in.

"Are you okay?" Her voice was soft as she squeezed my hand,

a warm late spring breeze weaving between us, stoking that fire in my chest.

I shook my head, but the world didn't keep up with the movement, like all my parts were detached. It made me woozy.

She pulled me in for a hug, but no matter how much I needed her stability and comfort, I drew back. There were too many sharp feelings inside me, waiting to jab through my skin at the slightest prod.

Her brows knit together. "Hey, it's gonna be okay," she said soothingly, running her hand down my arm. "You and your dad will be fine. You've always been strong, the two of you."

Her words hit like a blow, breaking free everything putrid and rotting. "How can you say that? He's the one who caused all this, who changed everything between us. If he could have just been happy with it being the two of us, if he could have been happy with me, none of this would have happened." I'd still have my dad, and not this hollow listless version of him who sulked around the house the rare hours he was there and not looking for excuses to stay late at the office, to stay away from me.

She cleared her throat. Tucked her hand into her pocket. "You have every right to be upset."

A sour chuckle escaped my throat. *Upset*. Like my pain was in line with a failed math exam or ruined recipe. "You don't understand, Rach." But she should. She, of all people, should get it. She was my best friend. She was more than that.

Instead of elaborating, she didn't say a thing, just stood there with her hands in her pockets. That silence gnawed an ache into my lungs until I had to speak just to breathe again. "Dad wanted more with Christy, more financial stability for our life or something, and now that she's gone, his dreams for us are, too. He doesn't even care about what we had before her or what we have now." There. Now she'd understand.

Her brow creased. "Is that really what you think?" she asked. "That he wanted to be with Christy for her money?"

What wasn't she getting? Why was this so hard to compre-hend? "Why else would he have picked someone so different from my mom, Rach? Someone who would do this to us—lead us on for months, and then run as soon as the commitment turned real? Christy's money is obviously what mattered to him, because she didn't have any character. And now, the life we have isn't what he wants. I'm no longer enough."

"That's not true." She reached for me, and I jerked away, still too sharp to be touched.

Hurt flashed across her features, but I couldn't comfort her. I couldn't even comfort myself. I wanted to burn something down.

"Of course you're enough, Morgan," she said, curling her fingers in protectively. "I'm sure he's just going through a heart-break of his own. I'm sorry it hurts. It will get better."

Pain seared through me like a physical assault. This still didn't make sense to her. The very foundation of my family was severed. The only parent I had left wanted nothing to do with me. What we once were was gone. There was no normal to re-turn to. "I should be enough for him now, like I was before," I shrieked, each word tearing at my throat. "But I'm not, and I'm not enough for Christy either. How am I ever going to be good enough for the rest of the world when I finally get out of here? For leaders and successful, productive people? For people who actually matter?"

Rachel's jaw went slack, and the atmosphere shifted. "Is that what you want? To get out of here? Because you think we don't matter?" Her voice was hushed. She wrapped her arms around herself.

God, why was she making this about her? "I didn't say you don't matter. Of course you do. I just don't think you can un-derstand. You have two parents who adore you no matter what. You have a perfect little life up here." I moved toward her, but she backed up.

She shook her head and laughed bitterly. "That's what you think? Have you really been that self-absorbed?"

I drew back. "What are you talking about?"

She glared at the treeline. "You're not the only one going through hard things."

The corners of my rage softened. "Tell me what's going on. You haven't opened up to me about this at all."

Her shoulders curled forward, and it broke my heart. I hated seeing her feel so small. "You've been so busy with the party prep and with Christy that I didn't want to rain on your parade or bring this up at a bad time, make things harder on you. And now, I can't, Mor. I can't tell you about all this when you're just going to up and leave, too." Her voice was barely a whisper, but my body reacted as if she'd screamed each word.

"Who is leaving? I didn't mean that I wanted to leave you. I just need to leave this town. Is that not what you want? You don't want to see more of the world?"

Rachel swiped at her eyes. I wanted to comfort her, reach out, but there was something between us, a cold new space.

"Your meaning was clear, Morgan. And this is how we're different, I guess. I'm not going to leave just because things are hard. I'm not going to take off when people need me most."

"Rach, I'm sorry," I whispered, voice failing.

She shook her head. "You can't apologize for your view of the world. I'm just glad I found out now that I don't belong in it. And I'll never be someone who holds people here against their will."

I reached out. "No, that's not—"

"Please don't follow me." Her voice broke off as she spun around so fast that the only thing within my grasp was air.

I was pinned to the spot, helpless, horrible, as she walked off the porch and down the road, leaving me alone. With only myself to blame.

I stare at the note for five minutes or five years until I remember I'm in my own body. I gasp like I haven't breathed in days and shove the letter into my pocket.

If Rachel still has things she wants to explain, I'm ready to let her. I'm ready to listen. It's the least I can do for the careless things I said.

Suddenly, I'm on my feet, climbing down the steps, through the trees, back to the kiosk, before I change my mind.

Whitney greets me with a smile.

"I wasn't able to find Rachel," I say, throat dry. "Is there any way I could get her number?" I don't know if it's still the same.

She shoves a purple Post-it into my hand.

A phone number is already scrawled on it with hot-pink gel pen.

"She's actually leaving right now, some family thing, and asked if I could give you her new number."

My heart leaps. "Has she left yet?"

As if in answer, an engine starts in the parking lot.

I turn to find Rachel's truck, tailpipe huffing.

Before Whitney can reply, I'm running at the vehicle like an Olympian.

I reach the driver's side as Rachel starts to take off, and she startles so hard, the cab jolts.

She rolls down the window. "Morgan? Are you okay?"

No. Your letter is burning a hole through my heart. "Can I come with you?"

She looks like I asked her to drink mud.

"I, uh, I'm headed to Snow Hill."

"Great!" I say, rounding the front of the truck. I open the passenger side and climb in.

"Morgan," she says, her tone reserved, "this is sort of a personal matter."

I press my nails into my palms. I have to try to speak with her. Find a way to broach this. "Oh, it is for me, too."

She narrows her eyes.

"What?" I say. "Have you not been to the general store lately? They're completely out of tampons, and so am I."

"I have a box you can have . . ."

"Please?" I'll beg if I have to.

She gives her head a little shake. "Okay. But plan on this being boring."

I buckle up and settle into the seat with a full body sigh, as Rachel backs the truck out.

Her letter gnaws at my hip, and I hope and pray to the goddess above that this trip will be boring . . . and not a repeat of my self-destructing the fragile relationship we've only just begun to rebuild.

I can't lose what little I have of her all over again.

CHAPTER 12

By the time we reach Snow Hill, the tension in this truck is thick enough to, I don't know, whack with an ax.

Something soft has played on the radio for the entire hour of our drive, and I wish it was loud and fast to keep time with my heart.

I clench my hands in my lap, as if reaching for my pocket would set off an alarm that screams: *Morgan has Rachel's letter!* At least if that did happen, I'd actually say something instead of imagining a million ways to ask her about the note and then not bring it up at all. But I have to talk to her about it. I have to know what happened between us, what it was that I missed. I squeeze my eyes shut and open my mouth to say her name, say anything, as my hand wanders to my pocket, reaches for the piece of paper—

"There it is," Rachel says.

My eyelids fly open. "There's nothing," I blurt, jamming my guilty hand beneath my thigh.

Rachel's brow furrows. "My dad's place? We're here." She pulls to a stop along the side of the road.

"Oh," I huff out. "Right." I don't miss that she referred to this home as just her dad's. But one glance at the tight set of Rachel's jaw tells me this isn't the right time to pry.

Out the window, Jim's condo is nestled into a quaint little building, each unit framed out in dark beams, windows flanked with beige shutters. Rachel stares at the gray door of the bottom unit like it's the most offensive thing she's ever seen. Then, with a rushed exhale, she shifts into park and jumps out of the truck.

I open my door to follow.

She holds up a hand. "No, Morgan. You can stay here. It'll just be a minute."

My legs dangle over the side of my seat into the frigid air. All I hear is *No, Morgan,* and flinch, the memory of her sharp tone piercing my mind: *No, Morgan, I can't hear you out. Please. Go.*

It was the final time I tried to apologize for the awful things I said after my party. She gripped her doorjamb for a full minute after she spoke, and I held my breath, praying she might change her mind. She closed her front door instead.

I swallow hard, lean back in the seat. I won't force my way into this, into her life.

She shrugs. "Unless you really want to come."

I hop down into the slushy gravel and close my door before she even finishes talking.

Rachel sighs and walks forward. I follow right behind and bury my chin into the collar of my coat to hide my smile. She gave me a chance.

She knocks on the door, and the silence that follows as we stand on the porch paints lines on her face. Her brows meet, forming deep creases above the narrow slant of her nose, and I have this urge to reach over and smooth them out, put her freckles back where they belong. I clench my fist instead. "Are you okay? This is just a little hello, right?"

Her second forceful knock gives me my answer.

I take a step back. Shit. Why did I force my way into this? She obviously wants to be alone.

But before I can turn to the truck, the door bursts open, and Jim Reed sweeps his daughter up into more of a whir of frantic energy than an actual hug. I stumble back and step off the porch.

Jim's hair is gray now, long and shaggy with hints of black peeking through like memories of yesteryear. Lines crease every corner of his features, from his bushy gray brows to the silver stubble down his neck. His cheeks and nose are a deep rosy red.

"Hey, Dad," Rach says, her voice muffled against his solid frame.

"Oh, Bean. I missed you." His voice cracks, along with something in my heart.

My greeting with my own father was so cold compared to this. So broken.

"You doing okay?" Rachel asks, pulling back and scanning his face.

"You know it," he says, sounding more confident than a congressman.

"Is it okay if we come in for a minute?" She starts to walk into his condo, when Jim looks over, and his eyes go wide. "Morgan Ann Ross, how the hell are ya?"

He strides forward and gathers me up in his sphere of happy chaos. His overwhelming energy cancels out my nerves, and I sink into his hug. "So good to see you, Jim," I say as he squeezes my ribs.

He pulls back, gripping my shoulders. "How long are you in town for?"

"A few weeks." I shrug.

"Wow, it's been some time since you've been back, yeah? Your old man must be thrilled. I love when my kids come visit." He gives my back a hearty pat.

I nod and swallow hard. My dad and I can hardly manage texting, and Rachel drives an hour one-way to see hers on a regular basis.

"Adam was here last week," he continues, then his attention snaps to his daughter. "Hey, how'd that charity show go? The one at the bar?"

She stiffens at that last word. "Yeah, good, Dad. Is it okay if we come in for a bit?" She tries to head inside again, but Jim shakes his head.

"Nah, no way," he replies. "This is a celebration! It's not every day we have your high school crush visiting. We're going out!"

"Dad." Her cheeks turn a Rudolph's-nose shade of red that makes me smile way too big. To my amazement, she grins back at me in that crooked way that hooks my heart.

"Let's go." Then he practically runs to Rachel's truck.

"Sorry," she says. "I guess this will be more than a minute." She sweeps her arm in the air, offering for me to follow her dad first.

I hop in the back, while Jim buckles into the front passenger seat and Rachel pulls out.

"Where to, Dad?" she asks flatly.

"The Country Club!" He hollers as he rolls the window down, dowsing us all with freezing air.

"Okay," Rachel responds in the same dull tone, "whatever you want."

My hair whips across my face, wrestling with mountain wind. Even through my obstructed vision, Rachel's eyes are dark in the rearview mirror. Those deep lines on her brow haven't eased a bit.

The Country Club turns out to be a western-themed sandwich shop at the edge of town.

Jim orders a Braying Brisket with extra Sal's Spicy Sauce, while I opt for the Waddle Ya Gobble turkey club, and Rach gets a Wranglin' Wrap with avocado and bacon.

I pull out my wallet to pay.

"It's on me," she says, staying my hand with hers.

"Are you sure? I really don't mind."

"I've got this." She offers a small smile.

"Thank you so much." I put my wallet back in my coat and can't help but notice how Jim doesn't offer to pitch in at all, doesn't look up from his phone.

Except for the country music radio station blasting overhead, we wait for our food in such a tight silence that I relax with relief when our number is called. Then we grab our trays and settle into a booth in the corner, benches covered in red gingham, table made of distressed barnwood. I grab a bandanna-printed napkin and unwrap my club. Despite the questionable name, it's toasted to perfection and smells so good I want to devour it in one bite.

Rachel sits beside her father, across from me, and fixates on opening her mustard packet like she's trying to decipher a cryptex.

"So," Jim says, catching surplus brisket from the side of his bun with his finger, "how's your dad doing? It's been a while since I've seen Warren. Man, he could really bring in the fish." He laughs, shaking his head. "Never forget the time he caught a twenty-pounder. What a legend."

I take a hearty bite of my sandwich so I'll have more time to rifle through any information I could share. He texts about the weather sometimes, baseball scores. Leaves messages that say he hopes I'm doing well. I should have picked up his calls more often. Maybe then I'd have some kind of answer. My throat constricts. I also should have taken a bigger bite.

Rachel glances up from her condiment conundrum and something like understanding passes over her face. "How's the RC club, Dad?" She smoothly changes the subject.

God, I could kiss her. I— Oh. Okay . . .

"Ya know," Jim replies around a mouthful. "Haven't seen the guys too much since the weather turned."

"So what have you been doing to keep busy?" Her tone is flat.

I can't help but think of Rachel's mom again, notice how they don't bring her up. It sounds like she's been away, maybe for a while.

He clears his throat and raises a hand toward the server passing by.

The young kid comes over, can't be older than sixteen, and looks absolutely thrilled to be wearing a cowboy hat that's twice the diameter of his head.

"Hey there, bud," Jim says. "Any way I could get this topped off?"

The teen glances pointedly at the self-serve soda machine. Jim smiles, and the server shrugs, taking his cup.

"How's the farm doing, Rach?" Jim asks, laying into his sandwich.

"It's fine." Her mouth forms a tight line.

Clearly, that's all she plans on saying, because she stuffs her wrap into her mouth.

I take the opportunity to elaborate. "Actually, Rachel's doing so much to keep the place current, getting involved with local charities and businesses. The holiday festival is coming up, and—"

The server returns and plops Jim's drink down in the center of our table. Coke sloshes, leaving brown droplets on the surface that quickly soak into the wood. "Here ya go," he says, with all the inflection of a robot, as he pulls a slip of paper from his pocket and places it beside the soda.

"What's this?" Jim's brows pinch together as he scans it.

"A big howdy half off for our going out of business sale." He grimaces on the *howdy*.

"Wait, what?" Rachel asks. "The Country Club has been here for at least six years."

"Seven," he drones. "But Sal can't hang onto the place with the resort restaurants and cafés opening up. Our last day is at the end of the month."

"What's happening to Sal?" Jim asks, voice fraught with concern.

He shrugs. "I think she's moving down the mountain. Can't afford to stay here with prices rising."

My gut hollows out. This is what Christy will do to Fern Falls if she gets an inch of ground there.

From the way Rachel peers out the window, it's clear she's considering the same thing.

After the server sulks off, we finish our meals in a stony silence.

Now that I'm paying attention, the drive back through town shows further evidence of the damage Vaughn Enterprises has caused to small businesses. So many shops with quirky names have boards on their windows, LIQUIDATION SALE banners strung up like decor.

We all stare sullenly out the windows. Any stab at conversation never goes beyond the weather. When we reach Jim's apartment, he hops out like his seat's on fire. "Welp, thanks a million for the visit, Bean. Mor, I hope to see you around again soon." He turns on his heel.

"Actually, Dad," Rachel says, her words rushed, "mind if I use the restroom? It's a long drive back."

Jim looks at the condo like he's debating this. "You didn't use it there? At The Country Club?"

What the hell? Why would he care?

She shakes her head.

Rubbing at his shoulder, he says, "Okay. Don't mind the mess, though. Sorry. Been busy."

"No worries. Thanks." She gets out and goes inside, and it's just Jim and me.

I hop down and close my door, lean against it.

He puts his hands in his pockets. "So . . . how's LA going for you?"

I try not to fidget. "Yeah, good, thanks. You enjoying Snow Hill?"

He glances nervously at the condo, like he might bolt inside at any second.

"Ah, quiet without Tanya." He scratches his stubble with his knuckles. "I'm sure Rach told ya about the split. Once we left Fern Falls, Tanya wanted a change from mountain life. I've put her through a lot over the years." He presses his hand to his cheek.

There's the answer to why he lives alone, why Rachel's mom isn't around. God, Rachel. I hope she's okay.

"So, she found happiness in Miami, and I'm glad she's enjoying life now. No matter how much I miss her, she deserves to be happy." He nods like this is the billionth time he's said this and is still reminding himself it's true.

"I'm sorry, Jim." I don't know what else to say, what comfort I could possibly give.

"Thanks. And it's good you're back, because my daughter deserves happiness, too."

I almost swallow my tongue.

Rachel rushes outside with a determination that says I should get back in the truck as fast as humanly possible.

"Bye, Bean," her dad calls as she hurricanes past him.

She doesn't reply.

Jim's cheeks turn crimson, and he shakes his head, looking at the ground as I climb into the passenger seat.

Rachel starts the engine without a word, and we pull away.

Out the window, Jim hangs his head and covers his face with his hands before he turns around and trudges to his place, not sparing us a second glance.

"Are you okay?" I ask quietly.

She gives a quick shake of her head, lips pulled in, and turns the radio back on. This time, it's grunge metal. Then she fixates on the road like it's a mission to conquer. Headlights illuminate her face in oscillating patches. The smooth sweep of her freckled nose. The soft arc of her brows. The thick brush of her lashes. The tear that falls and glistens down her cheek.

CHAPTER 13

It takes everything in me not to wipe that tear away with my thumb.

"Do you need to talk?" I ask, voice as tight as my muscles.

Rachel half shakes her head, half nods.

"Do you want to—"

She pulls over before I say the words.

As soon as we come to a stop off the side of the road, Rachel rushes out.

I sit frozen as she paces back and forth in front of the truck, high beams catching on specks of dust in the air. They fall around her like glitter.

I don't know whether to get out or give her privacy.

She lets out a guttural yell. The forest beyond her soaks up the sound as a car whooshes past on the opposite side of us, erasing any audible trace of her pain. I've never seen her like this, so utterly broken. Something in me breaks in response. Then she kicks the tire, and before I can convince myself not to, I jump out and round the front bumper.

My heart lurches.

Strong, tough, impenetrable Rachel is slumped against the driver's side door with her arms wrapped around her knees, head down, like she's trying to keep from tearing in two. Her shoulders jolt with each sob that rasps from her throat.

I crouch down. "I'm here. If you want me to be," I say calmly, placing a hand on hers, half expecting her to pull away. She doesn't flinch at my touch.

It happens so fast—she unfurls into me, buries her face in the crook of my neck. I move onto my knees to keep taller than her, support her. Wrap my arms around her shaking shoulders as tight as I possibly can. "It's going to be okay," I say, over and over into her pine-sweet hair. "It'll be okay."

Slushy snow soaks through my jeans, making my knees numb. Let them freeze.

Little by little, her breaths slow and steady. She leans back on her heels, covers her face with her hands. "I'm sorry," she says, shaking her head. Shaking all over.

"Please. Don't say that. You have nothing to be sorry for, and you don't owe me an explanation. I'm just here for you. If you need me." *If you want me.*

She lets her hands fall to her sides and looks at me openly. Her eyes are so broken and bright at the same time: light glinting off shattered amber. I clench my fists to keep grounded.

She releases a shaky breath, then peers down at the snow. "Morgan. My dad is an alcoholic." Her voice is jagged.

Everything I know about Jim Reed flashes through my mind: When he drove us in doughnuts around the farm, while we slid along the back bench seat of his truck and squealed with joy. Jim, pulling out the telescope on warm summer nights, to show us the craters on the moon. The bonfires he built so we could have s'mores during our sleepovers. The tree he brought Dad and me one Christmas Eve, when we couldn't afford to buy one.

By the way Rachel's face is pained, I must have missed a hell of a lot. "Is he doing better now? He seemed okay today, yeah?"

Her expression makes me wish I could swallow every word I just said.

"He was in rehab. He's been in and out of one in Snow Hill for years now, since my mom left. Between the facility fees when he needs services, and paying for his living expenses because he can't hold a job, it costs Adam and me a fortune." Her eyes are questioning, like she's asking if I can handle something so heavy.

It takes everything in me not to tear up. "What about your mom? Does she help out?"

She grunts, shakes her head. "When I moved to LA for design school, she left him for Miami. I think she's still there. We don't hear from her often. Adam dealt with their split and the worst of Dad's spiral while I was gone. I moved back to help transition him into rehab, and Adam started mechanic work to help us stay afloat."

I burn with anger at how unfair this is. How Jim and Tanya could do this to their kids, no matter how old. I rub her arms. "Rachel, I'm so sorry."

"And the worst part is," she continues, "I really thought he was doing better. But when I went inside his condo, there were whiskey bottles in the usual places. Beneath the bathroom sink, in the linen closet and his nightstand drawer. All half empty."

I wince. Wish I could help. "I'm so, so sorry." What else can I say? I want to take this pain, make it my own. Save her from it. But all I can do is be here.

Her chest heaves. "I'm tired, Morgan. I hate having to check up on him. Just once, I want to go see him and have it be that, a visit. It would be so much easier to sell the farm to Christy. I don't know what I can do. He's going to need rehab again, but the farm won't survive another slow season, and Adam's income can't cover it all. I don't know how else I'll afford it."

"Is that what you want? To sell the farm? Because you could. That is an option for you." I don't want her to feel like she owes the community anything if she needs to focus on herself, on surviving.

Her eyes find mine, and I steel against the intensity of her stare.

She shakes her head, holding my gaze. "I want to try to help the farm," she whispers. Her breath brushes my lips and my eyelids shutter at the pure pleasure of her nearness. "Mor, when you came back, it was like a lifeline. A sign that things could work out. That this whole mess might be saved. I want to believe that could still happen. I don't want to let anyone down. I . . . don't want you to think less of me."

Without pausing to consider it, I catch a fresh tear as it falls down her cheek. Smooth it away with my thumb until only her freckles are left. "You're taking care of your family. You're doing what needs to be done. I would never think less of you. I'm here to support you however I can. With this event, or . . . any way you need." Heat from her skin shivers up my arm, and I swallow past a lump in my throat.

She closes her eyes and presses her hand over mine, leans into my palm.

A semi whips by, blaring its horn, startling us apart.

I take a breath and take her in. Her eyes are so tired and weary, like the day I broke her heart. The words I said that day will forever echo in my mind, stab my chest: *For people who actually matter.* I only want to comfort her now. However I can.

"How about you let me drive?" I ask, standing, brushing snow and dirt off my jeans.

She shoots me a skeptical look as she rises. "With your track record?"

Oh, thank god she's well enough to crack jokes again. "C'mon," I laugh, holding out my hand. "Just into town. Let's sit down for a bit, relax in someplace warm. Caffeinate before the drive home?"

She raises her brow and plops the keys in my palm.

When we get back in the truck, there's a new gravity between us. Her presence is a tangible thing, seeping beneath my skin.

I walk myself through adjusting the seat, the rearview mirror, starting the engine.

Rachel turns on the radio, and some cheesy carols play while we drive into the center of town. The melody loosens me up a bit. "There was this little café my dad and I used to visit when he'd bring me here to ride the ski lift," I say. My chest warms at the memory. That was well before Christy. Dad would squeeze me into water-resistant layers, bribing me with hot cocoa. We'd get up early to meet his old friend Sam, who still operated the lift, at the slopes. Sam would let us on a chair, and we'd ride the loop all through the sunrise, sipping on cocoa, Dad telling me memories of when he and Mom skied together. We would laugh, and I'd snuggle against his shoulder. We didn't need a ton of money to make memories. It was just the two of us, and that was perfect. I was enough.

I clear my throat, shove down the memory. Things haven't been like that for a long time.

Rachel scans the landscape. "I don't know if it'll still be around. Everything looks like it was built yesterday."

I take my eyes off the road for a second, and even in that short amount of time, it's obvious she's right. Snow Hill is a conglomerate of stucco and slate. Nothing like the little pieced-together, multicolored buildings that used to live here.

We pull into a strip mall parking lot, where we find The Café at Snow Hill.

"This will have to do, yeah?"

She nods in agreement.

After we exit the truck, I swing the café door open and sigh in relief when she actually lets me hold it for her.

At least the temperature in this place is warm, because everything about the aesthetic is sleek and cold. Nothing like the charm of Ben's place.

We get in line and place our order. Rachel lets me pay— a holiday miracle—then we settle for a corner table. There aren't any cozy chairs or fireplaces here. No photos on the walls, just abstract paintings of espresso beans against an entire mono- chrome color palette.

We sit in awkward silence until I can't hold in my feelings any longer. "Thank you for sharing all you did with me."

Rachel offers a small smile. "Thank you for making me feel like I could."

The weight of confession sits on my chest. She shared some- thing so deep, so vulnerable. Can I be brave, too? I hope she won't hate me, that I won't make her life worse.

"There's something I need to tell you, too. And it's kind of terrible."

She snorts, and my heart lights on fire. "I highly doubt it's worse than what I shared."

"It's . . . not great."

Her brows lift. "Spill it, Ross. I promise I won't judge you."

Something in me unravels, because I know that's true.

"No one in Fern Falls will work with me." I hold my breath. What did I just do?

She crosses her arms and feigns surprise. "What did you do, run naked through the mayor's office?"

I make some startled bark. "Like that would be so terrible?"

She lets out a booming laugh, and my heart melts, making my next confession seem like a low-stakes punch line. "No. Christy, she—"

"What did she do?" Rachel leans forward, jokes forgotten.

Her protective stance turns my already melted heart to goo. "Well, it's more like what I did." I take a deep breath and con- tinue, stare down at the steel tabletop. "Back in LA, I sort of . . . messed up."

Rachel leans back, crossing her arms. "Welcome to Fern Falls, where we make mistakes, too."

I laugh, despite everything. "Yeah, well, in LA, we accidentally kiss our clients' fiancés, who dance in disguise in dive bars and ruin weddings while bringing down businesses."

Her eyes go wide. "Shit."

I sigh. "Yeah. And Christy knows about what I did and is using it against me so no vendors in Fern Falls will risk their reputations. I don't know if I'll be able to get any vendors to agree to work with me for the fundraiser. I don't know if I can pull one off at all."

It's quiet for a beat, and I stare at my laced fingers, white knuckles.

"Fuck her. Fuck them." The force of her tone makes me jump in my seat.

Her face is strained with anger. "How dare she blackmail you."

"Yeah?"

"Obviously, what you did was unintentional, and that fiancé was the actual asshole. And now Christy is the asshole, too. And I'm really sorry you have to deal with this. But you don't have to do it alone." She places her hand on mine.

Her touch is warm and grounding, reassuring every cell in my body that I matter. Not to be dramatic, but the planet shifts on its axis, and I'm lightheaded from the force of it.

The calluses on her palms brush my knuckles and steal my breath. I expected her to be mad. To be ashamed of me. Maybe I'm the only one who feels that way. Maybe that needs to change.

I swallow hard and hold her gaze. Run my thumb over her fingers.

A muscle twitches in her jaw and her cheeks redden—

A barista sets our drinks down.

"Peppermint mocha and a drip?"

I never thought there'd be a time when I didn't want to reach for coffee, but here we are.

Rachel takes her mocha, and I grab my cup, the warmth of it doing nothing to replace her touch.

I didn't trust this place to make anything more than plain black coffee. This isn't Ben's. And from the look on Rachel's face when she takes a sip of her drink, I made the right call.

"That your truck out front?" the barista asks.

"Yeah," Rachel says on a cough, wincing at her cup like it wounded her.

"Oh, man," he says, brushing a hand through his bright red hair, "I'd recognize the logo on your door anywhere. My mom used to take me to the Reed Farm every year to get a tree. Great memories." He shakes his head and grins, and warmth spreads through my chest—until I notice Rachel's expression.

Her smile is small and sad, and it shatters my heart. I have to pull off Enchanted Evenings, no matter what Christy throws my way. "Well," I say, finding my voice. "We're going to have a wonderful event on December seventeenth, and you should come."

Rachel grins as the boy's whole face lights up. "Really?" His voice pitches high with excitement. "I'm so glad Vaughn Enterprises hasn't devoured Fern Falls. I heard they want to build an outlet mall in a neighboring town, and I got so scared it was yours."

"An outlet mall?" Rachel asks, taking the words from my mouth.

He grabs a flyer off a bulletin board to the side of our table, then hands it to me.

In bold letters, it clearly states: *Vaughn Outlets coming soon to a mountain near you!*

My stomach sinks.

Rachel peers over, and her tone is firm when she says, "We'll never let this happen in our town."

I can't stop my cheeks from heating. Can't stop my gaze from drifting up to meet hers. I clench the paper between my fingers.

Despite everything we've been through and how long I've been gone, she called it our town. *Ours.*

CHAPTER 14

The warmth from the coffee wears off by the time we make it to the truck.

I rub my hands together like I'm starting a fire with a stick. "How are you feeling?" I ask before we hop in.

"Like we'd better get in that truck and crank the heat before you scrub your palms off."

I laugh as she heads to the driver's side.

Life is back in her eyes. Thank goodness. I jump in and buckle up.

She adjusts the seat and starts the engine as a smile plays at the corner of her lip.

"What's that look for?" I ask.

She shakes her head. "Just you, that's all."

I clear my throat, trying not to burst into a full-on grin. "Me, what?"

She sighs something that sounds like relief as we pull out onto the main street. Lights hit her face in warm splashes, making her eyes dance while soft music plays on some twenty-four-seven holiday music station. "You coming back and bringing this all together. You literally crashing into my life at the most unexpected time. If you hadn't come with me today, we wouldn't have heard about Christy's plans. And I would have driven home miserable and alone." She meets my gaze. "I'm glad I'm not alone."

Her words hit my heart, pushing tears to my eyes. "I'm glad, too."

I lean back into the seat, letting the heat from the vents cover me like a blanket. The music soothes my nerves that are shot from being so close to her. From things left unsaid.

Maybe they don't have to be unspoken anymore.

I've wanted to apologize to her for years. Ran over the scenario thousands of times. How maybe I'd pull up that IG message and finally reply, or make it a point to see her the next time I drove up to Fern Falls.

After our falling out, the words played over and over in my mind until they became a mantra. A monologue that turned and soured in my gut when she couldn't accept my apologies, accept me anymore.

But here we are. Here's my chance.

I push the words through my dry throat. "Rach . . ." I lick my lips. "I'm sorry. For everything." My heart races. She doesn't look over, but at least she's letting me try to talk my way through this. "When we were young, I was an idiot. I was angry and cruel and terribly wrong for the things I said to you. I'm so sorry."

It wasn't perfect, like the elegant speech I had planned years ago, but it was honest and sincere.

She still won't look at me. I hold my breath and bite my lip to keep my eyes from stinging.

Rachel's knuckles whiten around the steering wheel. Then she nods. "I'm sorry, too, Morgan. For not giving you another chance when you tried to reach out. For cutting you out of my life."

She looks over, and her eyes strike like a lit match. I couldn't blink, couldn't move, if I tried.

"It all coincided with when my dad got worse, when my mom was so over it, they'd fight all the time. Throw shit. It was bad."

I lean forward. "Did they hurt you?"

She shakes her head sharply. "No. Nothing like that. It was just a hostile environment, and I couldn't really compartmentalize it, you know? Everything felt awful."

"I'm so sorry, Rachel. Is . . . that why you wrote me this letter?" My voice cracks as I pull the paper from my pocket and set it on the bench between us.

She takes it in, and her cheeks turn red. "I— Yeah." Her gaze cuts back to the road. "Yeah, it is."

We're quiet as a melody hums on the radio.

"You saw the hayloft," she whispers.

"Yes," I breathe. "When I was looking for you earlier today. You . . . left it the same."

I keep my eyes straight ahead, but from the corner of my vision, I see her glance over. "I don't get much time to go up there and clean things out." Her words are clipped, like this is something she doesn't want to discuss. Maybe she's given me all she can tonight, and it's time to stop pushing. We're doing okay, and I don't want that to end. I don't want to mess this up again.

"It looks good," I say, refocusing on the view out my window as my lips tilt into a relentless smile.

I finally told Rachel I'm sorry. Relief dislodges something bitter and deep inside me, letting hope flood in.

She goes quiet. Neither of us speaks for a long time. The road winds, the heater warms the space, and the music soothes. My eyes grow too heavy to keep open, and my head lolls to the side, against the soft leather of the seat. The world turns silent and dark as I fall asleep, smiling.

It was warm the night we celebrated graduating high school and definitely not cold enough to snow.

And yet, there I stood as flecks of white flurried past the green spring leaves of the overhanging branches on the side of the inn. Snow that should be nowhere near mid-June.

I wished Rachel was there to see it.

I blinked hard, yet there they stayed. Magical little flakes, piling up between the cobblestones.

Someone giggled, and I snapped my gaze to the balcony above. "What—? Oh my god. What are you two doing?"

Ben and Adam beamed down.

"Shhhh," Ben said, tossing more sparkly white flakes into the air.

I laughed and brushed them from my hair.

"Hey," came a different voice, low and soft.

My breath hitched. There she was. Rachel. Glitter fluttered past her dark hair, dark suit, dark red lips.

"Hi," I croaked. "I . . . was worried you wouldn't come." My cheeks tingled.

Something flickered in her gaze, like she was hurt I'd think she would miss this celebration of our senior year, before she winked up at Ben and Adam. They rushed inside.

Then it was just her and me, alone in the dark. Shivers ran up my arms. "You planned this?"

My lungs swelled as she stepped close enough to touch. "I know you've always wanted your first kiss to be in the snow."

Oh. My. God. I swallowed hard. What was she saying? She couldn't mean . . .

I bunched my dress in my fists. "Bridget Jones and Mark Darcy are something to aspire to, you know?"

The air charged as she moved in. Closed her hand over mine.

I— *Holy shit.* Rachel Reed was holding my hand. Every cell in my body awakened. *Palms, please don't sweat.*

"It's not snowing for real yet, but we only graduate high school once, and I want to give this to you. If you'll have me?" She brushed some fake snow from my temple, her fingertips made of heat.

I forced my breaths even.

A muscle in her jaw twitched, like she hung on my reply.

"I'm in love with you." I gasped once the words were out. Relief. Fear. Hope.

Her face split into a giant grin that gave me the courage to squeeze her hand and press on. "All I wanted tonight was to tell you. It's all I've wanted for a long time now, and I know we've been friends for forever, and I didn't know I liked girls until you, well, until like maybe a couple years ago? But you, always you, and—"

Rachel swept me up, her arms tight around my waist, the world a swirl of emerald leaves and fake snow and her big, full laugh. I buried my face into her pine-sweet hair.

When she stopped spinning, I slid down, keeping my hands on her arms.

My breath caught as she leaned in and pressed her lips to my cheek, lighting me on fire.

With all the courage in my bones, I clutched her lapels, pulled her close, and whispered, "Kiss me like you mean it, Reed."

The shocked, low growl that rumbled deep in her throat turned me to Jell-O, and I grasped her coat harder to keep from melting at her feet.

Time slowed, noise faded. I moved my mouth toward hers.

Rachel's lips brushed mine, and my body charged like lighting-struck steel. Her kiss was tentative, slow, exploring. I slipped my tongue between her lips, and she responded by deepening the kiss, opening herself to me. My soul sang with each stroke of our tongues, grasp of her fingers in my hair, press of her palm to the small of my back.

With every movement, each give and take, my heart was remade into something bigger, brighter, and always belonging to Rachel Reed.

A small jerk wakes me up, and I find the Airbnb outside the truck window. I rub my eyes, coming back to the present. The way Rachel looked at me back then, so vivid in my mind . . . My eyes burn. The way she kissed me. I touch my lips.

"Morning, Sunshine."

I startle at her voice. "Did I sleep the whole time?" I croak, using the excuse to wipe my eyes, cover my flushed cheeks. "I'm sorry I didn't help keep you awake during the drive."

Rachel's gaze is soft. Like it was in my dream. "And miss the sight of you passed out with your mouth gaping open? I don't think so."

We both laugh, and I come back to myself, this moment reassuring me of how far we've come.

Every part of me is comfortable and warm, and I find Rachel's thick brown jacket draped over me. It smells like her. Like pine and fresh winter nights, woodsmoke through darkened branches. I wish I could wear this forever. Keep her this close forever.

The radio music is soft, weaving between us like velvet.

It would only require the smallest reach to tuck that everrogue wisp of hair behind her ear. Brush her cheek.

"I lied," she blurts out.

"What do you mean?" I pull my stare from her lips, meet her eyes.

"About the hayloft." Her gaze bores into me.

I don't speak, don't move. I want to cling to every word, draw each one out with all of my will. Keep talking. Please.

She takes a deep breath, leans the side of her head against the seat, and keeps those molten eyes fixed on me. "It makes me happy to go up there and remember the good times we had. It makes me happy to think of you. It makes me happy that you're here." Her voice cuts off, jagged and slicing through my heart.

She's so close that her breath shivers down my neck. "I'm happy I'm here, too," I confess, voice hushed.

She reaches for her coat, and her fingers brush my collarbone. Without thinking, I press my hand to hers.

She gasps, a barely-there pull of air between her teeth. I stop breathing entirely as her fingers freeze. She holds them against my skin, as if savoring my touch, as hers burns pleasure into every one of my far-flung cells.

She searches my eyes, my face. Her gaze lingers on my lips and tingles like a touch itself.

Warmth floods my veins like sweet mulled wine.

She leans in and presses her forehead to mine. The tip of her nose skates down the bridge of mine, achingly slow, as she whispers, "You give me hope, Morgan. You always have."

I make a charming whimper-grunt as my heart swells bigger than my chest. My lips part of their own accord. Everything in me reaches for her, needs her, begs to drink her in.

I tilt my chin up. Do you want this again? Me? Us?

She nuzzles my cheek, and each nerve hitches to that point where we're connected.

Her mouth hovers above mine. Cinnamon-sweet on the tip of my tongue.

This is everything I've wanted for so long. Ran from. Feared. Needed.

Rachel cups the back of my head, weaves her fingers through my hair.

I grip the collar of her flannel.

"Have holiday feasts caused you irregularity?"

We startle apart.

I glare at the radio like it's a demon.

"Head over to Fern Falls General Store and browse our wide selection of herbal teas that are sure to get you back to your groove in time for those New Year's celebrations."

Rachel huffs out a breath and flicks off the radio from hell.

I clumsily shoulder out of her jacket. "Thank you."

"So, uh." She clears her throat. "I'll see you soon?"

"Yes," I say in a split second. "I'm going to contact vendors again, and let you know as soon as I make progress."

"Thank you so much, Morgan." Her face and tone are so sincere.

"Of course." I force myself to open the door, exit the truck, walk up the porch, while every muscle in my body screams to turn around and press her hard against that seat, finally let my lips meet hers again.

I turn on the top step and wave. Her answering gesture is small.

Not yet, I almost say aloud. No. If I'm going to kiss Rachel Reed, the moment has to be perfect. I can't risk ruining anything between us.

I enter the dark cabin. Chills run up my arms, but before I mess with the potbelly stove, I press my face against the window.

Only then, when she knows I'm inside, does she pull away.

A flicker of light catches my eye. I look over just as Ms. Holloway snaps her curtains closed.

I'm grateful for the laugh that grants some levity against the want that twists and drags through my gut, and has nothing to do with irregularity, thank you very much.

CHAPTER 15

Norma Lee from Normally Charming Party Rentals looks me square in the eyes, her silver hair bedazzled with rhinestone clips, and says, "I've already spoken to Christy Vaughn, and partnered with her for the holiday festival. She was very clear that the Reed Farm land is taken care of by her company. Plus, I can't just give up the support of Vaughn Enterprises to work with someone who'll be gone at the end of the season."

I grip the counter and try to keep my features smooth, my tone as peppy as the hot-pink balloon bouquets and crepe paper extravaganzas surrounding me. Of course Christy is telling people the land is secure. She needs it for her fucking outlet mall.

"Thank you so much for your time," I grate out.

Norma Lee is clearly not sparing me anymore of her attention, because she turns to the yellow fabric napkins piled on the counter and gets back to work folding them into pineapples.

I muster enough dignity to exit beneath the rainbow balloon arch over the doorway. When I plop into my car, I let my head fall against the seat. That attempt to secure vendors for the fundraiser went as well as the past five stops I've made.

No matter the flyer about the outlets, no matter what I said about what Vaughn Enterprises could do to this town, no one wants to work with the girl who sabotages relationships and brands. Especially when they're already in Christy's pocket.

I drive back to my cottage and don't spare Ms. Holloway a full glance as I stomp up the steps.

"You okay there, neighbor?"

I halt, house key held midair. Ms. Holloway rocks back and forth, staring, awaiting an answer.

"Um, yes. Thank you," I reply, voice quiet. It's . . . nice that she cared?

"So great what you're doing for this town." She looks down at her lap, stroking that ball of tortie fur.

My stomach sinks. "I don't know that they want my help, truthfully." I focus on the WELCOME TO FERN FALLS keychain in my hand. Yeah. Welcome to everyone but this pariah.

I shove the key in the door as the shop owners' words echo through my head.

"The truth is, you left, Morgan. Christy has been here all these years, proving her support."

"We've already lost so much; we can't risk our reputation, too. Not when Christy is so eager to invest in restoring our business. You understand, right, dear?"

The worst part is, I do.

I don't blame any of them for not working with me, not trusting me, and buying whatever honey Christy poured in their ears about how she's going to bring tourism back.

"Give them time," Ms. Holloway continues. "Some folks don't know what's good for them if it hit 'em in the face."

I chuckle as an unexpected warmth fills me. "Thank you, Ms. Holloway."

"You're welcome, Morgan Ross."

She goes about her rocking and petting, and I smile and shake my head as I step inside, hang my coat and keys on a peg, pull off my boots. Of course, she knows my name. Like I know hers, even though we haven't been formally introduced. Welcome to Fern Falls, indeed.

I pull the Vaughn Enterprises Outlets flyer from my pocket and smooth it out on the tile countertop. Then I throw a kettle on the stove and stare at the paper like it might spring up and wield a knife, while I wait for the water to boil.

Christy is besting me at everything. Is there any way out of this? Maybe, no matter how far I move, how much I do, I'll never succeed. Never make the right amount of money, work with big enough names to matter.

Maybe Miles really is the one who deserves the New York promotion. Maybe I'm going to let Rachel down. Again.

I wrap my arms around my stomach, trying to hold myself together.

The kettle screams, so I grab a bag of lavender tea and fill up a mug, savoring the gentle steam on my face.

If I can't do anything else productive, I might as well set up a text message photo shoot for Johanna.

I head to the living room, set my cup on the coffee table. There's a stack of old newspapers on the hearth beside a pile of dried logs, and in no time, I find matches and actually get a small fire burning in the potbelly stove.

Wow, this one thing feels good. So satisfying to start a task and complete it.

I turn on the sappiest holiday movie I can find on cable, nestle into the couch, and prop my wool-shrouded feet on the table, firelight dancing across the glossy pine surface.

It's an acrobatic anomaly to angle my phone in one hand, balance my tea in the other, and capture the whole scene with the fire, the film, and a glimpse of winter white out the bay window. But somehow, I do, and send the image to Johanna captioned with:

Footloose and fancy tea.

She texts back almost instantly with:

Love to see it!

This second accomplishment helps me relax.

I tuck my phone into the farthest reaches of the sofa and wrap my hands around my mug.

It's soothing. Like the cocoa that Rachel gave me at Forest Fairy's. That same sense of warmth, of being cared for in such a simple way, seeps into my limbs.

The heat of the fire, the soft music in this movie, the breathtaking view of the green and white and blue landscape out the ceiling-high window.

I rest my head on the soft, checkered cushion.

Last night.

Rachel.

Our almost-kiss.

She was so close, so *there*. I didn't imagine it. The way she stared at my lips, licked her own with the slightest flick of her tongue. The way her fingers lingered on my skin.

My thighs clench together so tightly it should count as cardio.

I huff out a breath and set my tea on the table, cradle my head in my hands.

That girl.

She left the hayloft the same. Opened up to me in ways she hasn't in years, maybe never has.

I fall back onto the throw pillows, flustered, and my traitorous brain only makes things worse.

Images of Rachel at the chopping stump flash across my mind. Her glistening, bare skin. God, I wanted to see all of it, all of her.

My fingers snake beneath my leggings, press firmly toward that intense pressure building between my legs, pulsing with every thought of her, every memory.

Her heady, intoxicating scent wrapping me up, surrounding me in the cab of her truck.

The infinite depth of her dark brown eyes.

Her hands. What they'd feel like against my skin. Holding, touching, stroking.

I shove my hand lower. Press against that sweetly rising ache, and *god*. I'm swollen and wet for her, wanting, *wanting*—

I want Rachel Reed. The truth of it spreads sparklers through my core, making me moan.

I want her, and even if I can't have her, I can have this moment. I can have her in my mind.

My fingers slide and stroke along my opening, circling my clit. My chest, neck, cheeks heat. My mouth waters.

I press back into the pillows and touch and touch and touch.

Her nearness. Her gaze. Her warmth. The gentle scratch of her work-worn calluses. Her full, glistening lips.

Every thought of Rachel drives me to the edge, and I come so hard I rock into the couch, panting, groaning, absolutely fucking high.

It takes a full scene of some hetero couple making sugar cookies to regain control of my limbs.

To have the strength to sit up.

I walk to the kitchen sink on blessedly loose legs. Rinse out my mug, wash my hands.

I brace against the edge of the counter. I'm going to have to face Rachel again. After images of her just made me come as if it were the very first time.

I shake my head, and my gaze catches on that flyer.

Whether it's from my mind being a bit unburdened now, or the pure tension relief of masturbating, I gasp. There may be something that could make a difference in this fundraiser clusterfuck.

Mrs. Hart had a meeting with Christy.

A meeting that might give me something to use if I can get info from my old boss.

I close the door to the fireplace, grab my keys, and slip into my jacket and boots like a brand-new person.

Getting off can do that to a girl.

* * *

The lobby is quiet, and I take a moment to smile at the image that greets me: Mrs. Hart reading what is clearly a romance novel and stroking a cat that lounges across the counter like a furry black table runner.

The floor creaks as I approach. She looks up, and I love that she doesn't hide her book. Romance novels should be flaunted with pride.

"Hi, Mrs. Hart." I wave.

"Morgan! So happy to see you! I could get used to this again."

I beam bigger than I have in a while. Well, since last night. In Rachel's truck.

She places her book down so it's splayed open to hold her place. The author, Becca Rae, is a name I don't recognize. The cover features snow-capped mountains and a couple who should probably be wearing warmer clothing, and I'd like to live in it, thanks.

The cat gets up and strolls across the counter, jumping down and padding into the library like it's strung on a wire.

"How can I help you, dear?" she asks.

Right. My mission. "I wanted to ask about the meeting you had with Christy the other day."

"Ah." She leans back and stands up. "This is a conversation for the fireplace."

She nods toward where we sat before, and I follow her over until we're settled in our armchairs.

"Now," she says, leaning forward, "I want you to hear this from me."

My muscles brace.

"I am considering selling the B and B."

My heart stutters. "Oh, Mrs. Hart, please, no—"

She raises a hand. "Bill and I aren't getting any younger, and the inn needs upkeep we can't do on our own, and help we can't cover the cost of anymore. It's time for us to retire. To move on and spend time together."

Despite my disappointment, everything she says makes sense, and I want the best for her. "Are you going to sell to Christy?"

She sighs. "I don't want to, but her offer is generous. I don't know if I can get the same amount another way; I don't know how I'd sell so quickly otherwise. I just don't know how much time we have left. Bill's hypertension has gotten worse, and the unexpected work that comes with maintaining this place isn't helping. I can't wait another season to sell. I can't."

"I understand," I say, and mean it. "But could you wait another couple weeks for me to pull off this fundraiser? If we raise enough, we could help the inn, too. And if you'd like, we could run a special room rate for the festival, work together to draw tourists to the event and to stay at the inn. Let's go out with a bang, and hopefully make it so you can sell to someone else other than Christy."

Her brow creases. "That wouldn't be too complicated or draw too much of a crowd? I wouldn't want to turn anyone away."

"You could run the rate for that weekend only, and advertise it on your website, where you can also announce when it's booked up. It could be great for the inn, if you and Mr. Hart are okay with it?"

She twists her lips, contemplating, then breaks out into a big grin. "You know I like to make a splash." She smiles. "Plus, Bill will have such an audience for his readings. Let's do it."

We stand and shake hands, and I make a silent wish that the fundraiser brings in enough to help the hotel, to get rid of Christy Vaughn. The thought of her talking to my old boss chews at me. "Mrs. Hart . . . did Christy say anything about me or my dad while she was here?" It's shameless, but if she's trying anything else, I need the leg up.

She shakes her head. "I wouldn't let her get a word in edgewise besides the offer she wanted to make. You don't give the devil an ear, my dear."

I laugh and give her a hug.

When I step onto the porch, the sun peeks through the clouds and winks off the snowy ground, and I'm lighter inside with at least one person, one wonderful person on my team.

Now, the only way to get more on my side is to prove that Christy doesn't have this town's best interests at heart. To prove that she's lying.

And the only person I know who can do that is the one I've been avoiding since I got here.

I take a deep breath and charge toward my car.

Time to rip off the Dad Band-Aid.

CHAPTER 16

My phone buzzes when I park, and I'm grateful for the distraction. Maybe I'll sit here and scroll social media for the rest of my life. Maybe I'll drink the gasoline from my tank instead of walking up to that door.

A notification makes my thumb freeze over my screen. It's from Rachel.

I blink fast. The first text from her . . . since high school. I should screenshot this. Frame it.

Our nearness from last night still tingles my skin, along with the closeness I conjured on my own, not even an hour ago. My face heats as I pull up her message.

Come by this afternoon? There's something I'd like to talk about.

Wow, vague much? Maybe she's uncomfortable about last night? Maybe she wants to try that kiss again. My anxiety will have a bash with this until I find out.

Best not to allow too much time to decipher the possibilities. I write back:

Be there asap

It gives me the jolt I need to get my ass out of my car and up the wooden steps.

But when I reach the door, I freeze. The bold blue font of ROSS REAL ESTATE stares at me like an omen from the past. Dad never added his first name, because he wanted me to join the firm, be a father-daughter house-selling duo. But he didn't put up a fight when I left for LA. Maybe that dream of his left with Christy.

I shake my head and shove through the door as if smearing the letters off a foggy mirror.

Great. Another place that sits like it hasn't been touched since I was a teen.

Dad's desk still faces the front half of the office, his printer setup behind it.

I cross the hardwood floor to the two leather armchairs closer to the entrance. They face each other, a coffee table between them littered with magazines of local homes for sale and vacation properties for rent—but then I halt. There's a collection of publications that feature articles from events I've done: *California Wedding Day, The Knot, LA Bridal, LA Mag, Ceremony Magazine*. I run a finger over the first, an art deco–style engagement party in Palm Springs. The first real event that made much buzz before the *LA Times* feature. Heat rushes to my face. He saved all these. He cared.

All the questions from Jim Reed flood back. I don't know what Dad's been up to. I should. I want to.

"Be right with you," Dad's voice calls from the hallway that branches off at the back of the office.

I drop the magazine and jam my hands in my coat pockets, like I've been caught snooping through his mail. Very cool. Very casual.

He enters the room, arms piled with manila folders.

When he balances them on his desk, he spots me, and the look on his face puts another lump in my throat. Like he's thrilled I'm here but trying not to let it show too much. So different from the way he watched me from the porch when I left home seven years ago. The way his eyes glimmered with unshed tears, and his wrists turned white from shoving his hands in his pockets, like it took everything in him to not run after me. How I wanted him to, just to see that he cared. It took all my strength not to turn my car around.

"Sorry," I croak, "I should have called."

He rounds his desk and heads over. "No, Morgan. You're always welcome." His smile is genuine, and the surprising warmth of it settles into me, quelling my nerves.

"Thanks, Dad," I say as I take a seat.

He heads to the coffee bar, a wide shelf on the wall beside us. "Cinnamon roll or peppermint bark?" he asks, holding up two coffee pods.

"Surprise me? You made some updates around here, huh? No more big pot?"

"Eh, trying to cut back on caffeine, and since it's just me, the coffee always goes stale."

That warmth I felt curdles in my gut. Hello, Guilt, old friend.

He gets the coffee brewing and sits across from me. "How are you doing? It's really good to see you."

His tone is so genuine that I uncross my legs and relax into the seat.

"Yeah, you, too." I glance down at the magazines involuntarily.

"I hope you don't mind that I've been keeping up with you?" he asks.

Mind? I blink and barely keep from blurting out how I want him to call more, visit LA, invite me up for more than special occasions, want me around.

"I mean, what you do, Mor. It's great. You're incredibly talented. I always knew you were."

I meet his eyes. "Thank you."

"Yeah." He nods, and the coffee maker clicks off.

He shoves off his chair and grabs the cups, giving me a chance to breathe. Gather courage to find out the answers to Jim's questions.

"So, how have you been?" I start, voice scratchy.

He pauses from putting the lids on the cups and looks over.

"Oh, you know. Hanging in there. The job is slow, but thanks to a busy summer, I'll be okay, thank goodness."

"That's great. You still fishing a lot?"

He hands me the coffee and sits opposite me, sipping his.

I take a deep breath. Cinnamon roll. Of course. Like the breakfast he makes on Christmas mornings.

"I meant to send you the photo of my last catch. They put the picture up in the tackle shop. Smallest of the year at half a pound."

I laugh. "That's great, Dad."

"Real proud." He chuckles.

Apologies perch on my tongue. I want to say sorry I haven't called in a while, that I just ... didn't know what to say? Wanted him to be the one to put forth the most effort, prove he still loved me? I clear my throat in an attempt to wipe the words from my brain. This isn't the time.

He shifts in his chair. "So, tell me about the Reed fundraiser. It's great you're doing that for Rachel."

And there's that lump in my throat again. "Honestly? It's not going well."

His brows knit with concern. "What's up?"

"Well, Christy Vaughn"—I search his face, make sure it's okay that I continue, that this isn't triggering bad memories for him, but it's smooth and open, so I press on—"she's bent on keeping all of Fern Falls from working with me. And there's no way I can pull this off without vendors."

He shakes his head. "Wow. I'm sorry. I had no idea you were dealing with this."

"It's okay."

"No, it's not. What happened with her and me is in the past, and I don't want her impacting the present or your future, or Rachel's. Is there anything I can do to help?"

"Actually"—I lean forward, the issue that brought me here in the first place moving to the front of my mind—"there might be."

He holds out a hand, ushering me to continue.

"Christy swears that if she gains land here, she'll preserve it, but that has not been the case in Snow Hill. People have lost their private businesses, and others are being pushed out because they can't compete."

"You're right. It'd be the end of Fern Falls if Vaughn Enterprises took over. Christy has always wanted to please her father and prove herself. She won't hesitate to take down Fern Falls to finally show him she deserves to run their company."

His validation gives me a boost, and my words rush out: "I think she wants to turn the land the inn and farm share into an outlet mall, but I don't know how to prove it, to get people to believe me. I've tried, and they don't want to hear it."

"Hmm." He stands and heads to his desk. "I could pull up MLS listings of businesses sold in Snow Hill, show how many went to Vaughn Enterprises, prove they've been changed completely?"

"But that would just show what everyone already knows. They don't believe that will happen here."

He scrubs his hands together. Then he freezes, eyes widening. "I know. Give me a few minutes, okay?"

He goes into the back, and after a short time, it's an effort to keep my mind from drifting to Rachel's text. To what she could possibly want to discuss, or what could change between us.

One thing at a time, Brain. Geez.

Dad walks out, and his expression gives me something I haven't felt in way too long: hope.

"So, I called my buddy Michael. You remember? From Building and Safety?"

"Okay?" I have no idea who Michael is.

"Yeah, the one with the goats? He just started this side business, goat yoga. Building a whole studio for it, but the goats keep eating the mats, and—"

My insides might burst. "Dad? What did Michael say?"

"Right. He said he was gonna call me, too, because a rep from Vaughn Enterprises contacted him the other day, asking to pull public records on the Reed Family Tree Farm."

Anticipation grips my chest. "What does that mean?"

"Well, they asked about any geological surveys or ground mapping done on the land, and if there were building regulations on the property. And get this, the kicker is that Vaughn Enterprises offered to pay him to keep the call quiet. Of course, Michael wouldn't take that BS. He'd feed it to his goats."

The hairs on my arms raise. "So all this shows that they have intent to build on the land?"

"Yes." He nods enthusiastically. "And that they don't want anyone to know about it."

"Wow, okay. So the outlet mall could actually happen if they get the property?"

"This certainly suggests something like that. I'm sorry it's not hard proof."

"No, it's something. It's a lot more than I had before."

"A good place to start digging, for sure. Can I do anything else?"

"You've been amazing, Dad." Without thinking, I give him a big hug.

It's more comfortable this time, warmer than when we ran into each other in front of The Stacks. He rubs my back. I hold onto him a little longer, this moment a little longer. I hope we have more of them.

"Don't be a stranger, okay?"

I pull back and head toward the exit. "I won't," I say, and mean it.

"Actually . . ."

"Yeah?" I pause, hand on the door.

"I plan on going to Mom's bench next weekend, if you'd like to join?"

My throat tightens at the memory of the spot where we used to go to feel close to her. I haven't been there since I left home. Guilt eats at my core.

"That sounds great, Dad," I say quietly, ashamed I didn't mention visiting her first.

He smiles, and I step outside, the whole world a little bit brighter.

I only hope my talk with Rachel ends as surprisingly well as this one.

CHAPTER 17

When I pull up to the farm, no one is out front. Like, no one. The kiosk is closed and locked, so it looks like a big red wooden box. Maybe Rachel wanted me to meet her somewhere else? I check my phone, but of course, zero bars. The spot where the once-intact sign used to be taunts me. I still need to find a way to make her let me pay for that.

I park, exit my car, glance around. Still, no one. Not even a vehicle— *Oh*. Except for that red truck, up through the trees and parked . . . that's right. In front of the barn.

The barn with the hayloft. The hayloft that hasn't changed because Rachel . . . wanted to think of me.

How I thought of her earlier this afternoon . . .

Squeezing my thighs together and trying to trudge through snow is not a good look on me. But, here we are.

I take a deep breath before entering the barn, like the crisp air might substitute as a cold shower.

My feet crunch dried needles.

Then my libido nearly sets this place on fire.

Rachel stacks logs at the back of the barn, and not only is she in that damn white tank top, but it's tied up to her ribs in a cute little knot, and her hair is pulled up, wisps trailing down her neck. With each move, her lean muscles ripple beneath her skin, her smooth, glistening skin—

"Morgan!"

It takes her greeting me for my gaze to actually meet her face. I could have been a lot more respectful with my looking. *Jesus.*

Keep my eyes on her eyes.

But even her eyes make me combust.

And not far below those eyes are those lips.

They're moving as she walks toward me, but all I can picture is that perfect pout trailing down my chest, blowing across my skin, biting my panties down until she licks—

"Hey, you okay? You've got, you're . . ."

She points to my lips, and I reach up, tasting a faint bloom of blood.

Great. I'm so thirsty for this girl, I'm chewing off my own damn mouth.

That'll do nothing to help my situation.

I suck on my lip until the taste subsides. "Sorry, yeah, I'm fine."

"So, do you want to see them?"

I startle, meeting her eyes. Could I have been any more obvious about checking out her cleavage? Morgan, you are better than a horny teenage boy, dammit.

I clear my throat. "Um, I, okay?"

She beams, and I melt at the relief of having answered correctly.

She goes back to where she was working, and it takes all my strength to keep my gaze from following her ass as she bends down.

Her hips, swaying as she returns to me.

The muscles that move with each stride.

She holds out a stack of cards, and I take it as it dawns on my sex-starved mind what she's done.

They are covered with the most beautiful typography I've ever seen—have seen before on the signs at The Stacks and Peak Perk. In filigreed swirls, each flyer boldly and whimsically states the details of Enchanted Evenings at the Reed Family Tree Farm. A silhouetted forest lines the bottom, sending swirls up past each letter to connect at the top.

Oh my god. She has so much faith that I'm going to pull this off, so much faith in me . . . Emotion wells in my chest.

"Rachel," I say quietly. "You're so talented."

Her expression says it all, how flattered she is. Her gaze goes soft, taking in my raw appreciation of her work. "I took the initiative to make something for the event. I thought we could pass them out at the festival next Saturday? I also took the liberty of posting it on social. Facebook, Twitter, Instagram. Thought it was time to bring the farm into the digital age. I wanted to surprise you. I hope it's a good one?" She searches my face.

"They're stunning," I breathe. "Truly. These are beautiful."

She takes the cards and carefully sets them on a nearby log. Her smile could burst my heart.

"Thank you so much for making them."

"Yeah, of course." She rubs her neck. "But, are you sure you like them?"

"Absolutely. Why?"

"You just seem . . . a little tense." She strokes my arm.

If I was tense before, her touch, the warmth of it seeping through my coat, shocks me into another tense dimension.

God. I want her hands all over me so damn badly.

"To be honest," I blurt, "I thought you wanted to talk about last night and our moment in the truck. I was worried it may not have been okay for you, and I'm sorry, and I—"

"I'm glad you brought it up. I've been thinking about that, too." Her voice deepens. So does her gaze.

"Yeah?" I swallow.

"Yeah." She stares at my mouth. Unabashedly.

My blood flames.

"What were you thinking?" I somehow ask with words from the English language.

She rubs her thumb along my shoulder. "That I should have asked if I could kiss you."

"Hell, yes." Fuck being cool or coy. I could not be chill if I tried.

She sighs. Her scent surrounds me, and her breath warms my lips. Cinnamon, pine, winter, smoke. Such a fragrant way to die.

"Are you sure about this?" she asks. "It's okay that I'm your client?"

I bark out a laugh. "Apparently, clients are my top choice lately."

It's an awful joke. I ruined the moment. My self-made disaster smacks my chest, lungs tightening.

But amusement dances in her eyes. Her lip curls at the corner. "Perfect timing, then."

She moves in, and on a gust of relief, I throw my arms around her neck. "Let's try this almost-kiss thing again and get it right this time," I whisper.

"Deal." She smirks and traces the backs of her fingers down my cheek.

I crush my lips to hers.

She stiffens for the slightest second, then melts. Forms to me, wraps her arms around my body, holds my neck, my head, grasping the roots of my hair like I might disappear.

She tilts me back and explores my mouth with her tongue, each stroke making me drunk. This was worth the wait.

Her lips are sweet, firm, warm, urgent.

I hold her, cling to her, prove this is real. Each sway, touch, shiver.

The ache between my legs pools with heat, reaffirming how very real this is. "Is this okay?" I pant into her mouth.

Her chest heaves against mine. "This is the most okay I've ever been with anything in my entire life." Her voice is husky and raw and so full of want—want for me—that I almost lose it. Then she bites my bottom lip and pulls it between her teeth. Her fingers clutch my hips, and I finally let mine hold hers. Her bare skin fills my fingers. What if all of her was bare, my hands free to roam and please every inch of her? I clutch her close and whimper.

She smiles against my lips.

The sound of earth crunching beneath tires makes us freeze. NO.

An engine cuts off. A car door slams.

No, no.

"Rachel? You here?" Ben's voice calls.

As much as I love that man, I am not above murdering him this very second.

"I've never wished for a superpower more," Rachel says, catching her breath.

"Invisibility or death-ray vision?"

She laughs. "Both."

We barely manage to create a sliver of space between us before Ben enters the barn.

"Oh, hey!" he says.

As he takes us in, a sly grin creeps across his face. "Ooooh. Heeeeeeeeey," he repeats.

We must look like two horny teens.

I cast him a death stare, and he raises his hands. "I see I've interrupted." He winces. "And it's about to get worse."

"What are you talking about?" I say through clenched teeth, while Rachel snorts.

"Weeeell." He stuffs his hands in his jean pockets, and before he can finish answering, another car pulls up, followed by voices, followed by Adam and Whitney and Tanner, bursting into the barn and stopping cold at the sight of us.

"So, are you guys ready to go?" Adam asks, after too many beats of awkward silence.

"Oh. Oh, shit." Rachel says, looking between all of us.

"Rach?" My tone is slow and cautious. "What are they talking about?"

"I forgot what date it is." She grimaces in apology.

I scrunch my brows together. "Date?"

"December third? Remember what we'd always do together on this day? And now that you're back . . ."

It dawns on me just as Ben hollers, "Get in, lovers! We're going camping!"

Everyone laughs and smiles, and oh, hell no. "Absolutely not. I can't handle the cold like I used to. I don't think—"

"It's okay, Ross," Adam says. "We have all the stuff you need. Hop in the truck with Rach, and we'll go. What else do you have going on?"

I try not to chuckle as Rachel shifts on her feet, both of us knowing full well what we just had going on.

Wait. Tingles race through me. I could go camping. With Rachel. All. Night. Long.

She comes close, pulling shivers to the surface of my skin, where her breath grazes my ear in a whisper, "I'd love to keep you warm."

I clap my hands together and announce way too loudly, "Let's go camping!"

Everyone whoops and cheers and heads toward the cars.

Rachel grabs some firewood. Then she bites her lip and winks.

Fuck. Me.

Tonight, I hope.

CHAPTER 18

I deserve a gold medal for carrying on a coherent conversation on this drive to the campground.

After packing up the truck and stopping by my place to don every layer of clothing I own, and the General Store to pick up s'mores essentials, we've talked about everything but that kiss. We pulled off the main highway and into the forest a while ago, and it's obvious our make-out session (our hot-as-hell make-out session) is the one thing on Rachel's mind, too. She keeps glancing over, biting her lip, and gripping the steering wheel like it physically attacked her.

"Mike and Ikes," I say on a sexually frustrated breath.

"Huh?" Her voice sounds dazed.

"The best candy to bring camping."

She smiles. "I stand by M&M's."

"Can we have both?"

"A candy compromise." She grins again, and that dimple, those freckles, my heart, my *god*.

The fire road opens into a clearing, where we pull to a stop.

Rachel hops out but pauses before closing the door. "Hey," she says, "would you check the glove compartment for me? I think I packed something in there."

I lean forward and open it with a click. Staring back are two boxes of candy: Mike and Ikes, M&M's.

She winks. "Like I'd forget your favorites from the General Store."

Then she closes the door and walks toward the back of the truck, and apparently, just the sight of these sweets is an aphrodisiac.

I shake my head as I grab the goods and follow her out.

Everyone else pulls in and parks around the little campsite I remember from my youth. There's a rust-rimmed firepit beside a worn, wooden picnic table and a steel bear box. I put the candy in the metal bin and return to the truck to help Rachel unpack.

Of course, she has everything laid out and perfectly organized on her tailgate.

"What can I do?" I ask, observing the mini recreational equipment store.

"Set up the tent with me?" She holds up a green bag.

I clear my throat. There . . . is only one tent.

"Oh," she says hurriedly, pink rushing into her cheeks, "nothing like that. I plan on sleeping in the truck. I brought the tent and blow-up mattress for you. I figured it'd be more comfortable, but if you'd prefer something different, that's good, too."

She's completely flustered, and if the candy was an aphrodisiac, then this is porn.

"You keep spoiling me, Reed," I say, cursing the way my skin flushes. You know what? Let her see. I've already laid it all out there with that kiss. Why stop now? "And, no pressure," I continue before I completely lose my nerve, "but maybe we could share it?" I point to the bag slung over her shoulder. "The tent."

Her cheeks turn positively fluorescent. "Yeah?"

I smile teasingly. "I can't have your frostbitten death on my conscience."

Her lips tilt up into that crooked grin that makes my toes curl. "I'd hate to cause you guilt from the grave."

We laugh and pick a spot to set up in. Okay, Rachel sets up the tent, and I offer moral support and stay out of the way.

After she's done the hard work, and I've barely succeeded at keeping myself warm, we all huddle around the iron pit, where Tanner has a huge bonfire going, orange flames lapping at the dusky sky.

"Here, all, drink up. Warm the insides," he says, passing around blue metal cups that smell like drunken apple juice.

"So great to have a bartender around," Rachel says. She laughs and taps her cup against mine.

I take a sip and let the spiked cider do its job, heating me from the inside out.

Everyone else sets out camping chairs, and Rach and I settle onto the bench. Like we always pair up together. A pleasurable heat seeps down to my toes.

"How did this tradition start?" Whitney asks as she leans closer to the fire.

Ben grins. "You wanna tell 'em, man?" He looks at Adam.

Adam rolls his eyes. "It's basically a country-western song that started when I was sixteen, Ben was fourteen, and I got my heart broken."

Ben chimes in. "He was so upset over Massie Green dumping him via text that we drove out here, smashed some glass bottles in the firepit, and ended up passing out in a tent." He blushes as he says the last part.

Adam picks up, "We woke up to the first snow of the season, with the tent caved in around us."

Ben laughs, leaning back into the red canvas of his chair. "We froze our asses off and got terrible colds."

"And that made you want to repeat it annually?" Whitney asks, squinting between them.

"Didn't say we were smart." Adam chuckles.

"They brought us along the next year," I say, pointing between Rachel and me, "and it became a tradition. Getting away during a busy time."

"Remembering the hard stuff doesn't keep us down if we have good people in our lives," Adam says quietly and glances at Ben.

"The best people," Rachel says, placing her hand on my thigh.

Her skin glows golden in the firelight. From her gray beanie, her dark, unruly hair goes out in all directions just past her shoulders. Bright sparks reflect in those molten eyes, and her perfect pouty lips tilt up on one side as she smiles.

I set my hand atop hers and squeeze right back, the warmth of our touch working ten times stronger than the drink. "The best," I say, my voice barely a breath.

The sun is set now, and the night chill has us inching closer until our legs press up against each other.

The moment becomes something more. This is me and Rachel like we've never been. Something tugs at my center. After this night, spending it together, what comes next? What if this changes everything in a way that breaks us?

I clutch the cold edge of the wooden bench. I need to say something, talk to her about this. "Rach, I—"

The fire flares, sending a flash of heat our way. I gasp and lean back just as she pulls me close, wrapping her arm around my shoulders. "Oh no, Mor," she says, laughing, "you don't remember Ben's fire tricks?"

Ben smiles. "Want to try?" He holds up a mason jar full of powdered coffee creamer.

I grin back, remembering the wishes we used to make on the flares it would set off with each toss.

"Sure, why not," I reply. I could use a wish or ten.

He passes the jar my way, and I pour a handful of white powder into my palm. Close my eyes.

I want this. I want her. I want us. I don't want to mess this up.

I toss the powder at the fire, sending a plume of gold into the air.

Even though I know it's coming, I still startle and lean into Rach.

She squeezes my shoulder. "That's a wish earner, for sure."

"You want to give it a go?" I ask, holding out the jar.

"Of course." She takes the creamer and does the same; a big flare flashes past the rim of the firepit, then disappears.

She passes the jar to Whitney and puts her arm back around me.

The way she keeps holding me close, like this is something we always do, makes me hope my wish will come true.

But could staying here tonight, with her, change all that? What happens tomorrow? The next day? What do we look like beyond this? I don't want to push us into unchartered territory only to lose us completely. I couldn't take losing her again. Not even for New York.

I clear my throat and hug her back.

At least I can hold onto this moment. Tomorrows and promotions can wait . . . for a moment.

After the hot dogs that Adam cooks and the s'mores fixings Whitney assembles, we are sticky and full, and the moment I held onto is over.

I don't know if I can step into the next one, into the tent with Rach.

"Morgan, can you help me put this stuff away?" Ben calls.

I get up and help him carry the grocery bags filled with the remaining food to the bear bin.

The crackle of the fire is behind us, and cold creeps into me the farther I move from Rachel.

"I know what you're doing," he says, shooting me a slanted stare.

I tuck my hair behind my ear. "I don't know what you're talking about."

He shoves the bags inside the bin, and they scrape along the metal bottom. When he stands, the moon and firelight glint off his glasses. "Stop overthinking things."

I fold my arms across my chest, like I could somehow hold my emotions inside for once, not have them painted across my face. "I'm not."

He glances at Rachel. "Do you want this? With her? For real?"

I sigh and try to avoid the heaviness of his stare, the truth it'll pull from me. Stars glitter down like they never could in the city. Up here, they don't stand alone. They blend from brighter spots of silver-white into messy, miraculous splatters. Gorgeous, expansive spheres that take your breath and know your soul. "More than anything."

"Then trust that. One step at a time. Just be here, now. Tomorrow will take care of itself, and you'll both take care of each other."

I grin up at those stars and then over at my smart-ass friend. "What if I screw things up again?"

"What if you always wonder what could have been between you two?"

I huff a breath and nod. "Touché."

Ben smiles. "My mom always says the universe knows exactly what it's doing, even when we don't."

I laugh. "Thank god something knows what's going on."

"Seriously." He shakes his head.

Adam looks our way, holding up his guitar. "You two coming back or what?" he calls as Rachel catches my eye and smiles.

I wouldn't be surprised if Ben and I spontaneously combust.

"Those Reeds will be the death of us," he says.

And with the way my heart tries to strangle me, I know he's not wrong.

I grab mine and Rachel's candies, and he locks up the bear box.

"You gonna talk to him tonight?" I ask as we head back, pine needles crunching beneath our feet.

He shakes his head. "And take my own advice? Absurd."

I laugh and nudge into him with my shoulder. "Thanks for being such a good friend."

"You too, Mor."

We both settle back into our spots as Adam strums.

I smile their way, and Rachel's warm fingers gently guide my chin to face her.

Her touch grounds me, sets a fire beneath my skin. A tantalizing contradiction.

"You okay?" she asks, tone soft as she searches my eyes.

I nod, and with a burst of bravery from my talk with Ben, from her touch, I lean in. "More than." I nudge her nose with mine and place a gentle kiss on her perfect mouth.

She grins beneath my lips. Clutches my hand. "I'm so happy, Morgan. You make me so happy."

I nestle into the crook of her neck and pull her close. "You deserve to be happy."

"We both do," she whispers, her breath warm and sweet on my cheek.

"Okay, lovebirds," Adam calls, "we need you for the chorus."

We laugh and join in, our voices mingling close in the cold, in our little shelter of pines.

I pass her the M&M's and open my Mike and Ikes, and cling to this moment, this girl beside me, her words.

No matter what comes next, she's right. We both deserve happiness.

I can only hope on the stars that I don't let her down.

CHAPTER 19

Our songs turn from a barely in-tune cacophony to something truly garish as we all grow tired.

"I'm ready to turn in, y'all," Tanner says, as he takes up a bag and rounds the circle, gathering trash to place in the bear bin.

Rachel tosses our candy boxes inside as he passes us, and this is it: tent time.

My heart hammers.

Whitney stands and stretches. "Night, all. Don't forget to put your toiletries in the bin, too."

"Have you seen bears lately? Aren't they hibernating?" I ask, knowing full well they could still be out, but searching for some distraction from me messing this up with Rach.

Whit snorts. "Do black bears ever really hibernate in California?"

"Even this late in the year, Gus still hangs out by the back door of the bakery waiting for me to forget a delivery in my car," Ben says.

"That bear is gonna outlive us all on nothing but waiting for cinnamon rolls," Adam adds, standing.

We all brush our teeth with water bottles, and a few of us scatter to different pines to take care of business before following Whit's instructions and locking everything up.

Adam, Whitney, and Tanner retreat to their respective tents with calls of *sleep tight*, and Ben looks at Rachel and me and says, "I'll stay up and make sure the fire goes out. You two can uh, head to bed, if you want?"

Rachel has been quiet until now. Worry lodges in my core. Maybe she wants to sleep in the truck after all?

She smiles. "Whatever you're comfortable with, Morgan. Are you ready?"

What a question. She holds my gaze as if she intended it as more, like she's offering me a way out if I want it.

I take a deep breath and don't blink. One moment at a time. And I want nothing more than to spend every one of them with her. "I'm ready. You?"

Her answering, beaming smile turns my insides to lava. "Absolutely."

"'Night, you two," Ben says as we stand, and I owe him everything in the world for not making this awkward.

Rachel's nearness is warmer than the fire. As we make our way to the tent, I edge as close to her as I can.

We kick off our shoes and step onto the tarp as she unzips the door and climbs in, holding the flap open for me.

The space behind her is dark, and the gravity of this precipice pulls on me, the knowledge that entering this tent means starting a new chapter together, no matter what we do or don't do tonight.

Her gaze is warm as she waits, not rushing me at all.

I trust her. That's all that matters.

I step inside.

As she rezips the door, I take in the space, and my heart warms at how perfect she made it.

The mattress is in the center and made up with fluffy pillows and a big down comforter.

"I kept the sleeping bags separate underneath the blankets," she says, kneeling beside me.

I'm not exactly surprised by how my stomach drops at her announcement. "Do you want to sleep separately?" I ask.

"I don't want you to feel pressured. Not at all. Tonight can be whatever you want." Her expression is so open and sincere, reassuring.

Whatever I want . . .

I reach for what I want, brush my fingers on hers, take her hand. "I want you. But I don't want to let you down. Not tonight, or tomorrow, or ever." The confession wrenches from my chest, and I want to take it back. It was too much. Too soon.

She lets out a soft laugh and twines our fingers together, grounding me here. "You're not going to let me down. I'm not an event. You don't have to plan this out or make sure every detail is perfect. To me—this, here, you—it's all flawless."

Her words hit straight in my center, and my eyes go wide. "Shit. You're right. I was over-planning, overthinking this."

The corner of her mouth kicks up as she moves closer. "So why don't you let me take care of the details? Let someone take care of you for once?"

I struggle to form words. No one has ever said that to me. I never knew how good it would feel.

She strokes my cheek. I lean into her palm and close my eyes. "What if this changes what we have?"

She draws near. Mint on her breath, campfire in her hair. "I hope it does. Because I'm so ready to be more with you. If you are." Her hand stays, gentle on my cheek, waiting.

It takes me all of a split second to decide.

I close the gap between us and press my lips to hers.

She welcomes me in on a moan. Our tongues brush, and it's peppermint sweetness scorching my nerves, igniting my deepest parts. Her low growl rumbles down my spine. Flashes of the past: glitter in her hair, on cobblestones. Her arms around me, covered in mud. Sunrise reflected in her eyes. Her tears beneath my fingertips. That dreamy expression she wore as we broke from our kiss in the barn. Everything that brought us here. I'd do it all a million times over.

We move in until our jackets become barriers.

I ungracefully unzip mine and shrug it off, refusing to move my lips from hers, and when I reach back, she's down to her shirt, too.

Her arms cinch around my waist, hoisting me against her body. I savor every supple curve, mold to her length. She's hot and soft and hard, all at the same time. The swell of her breasts and hips. The lean corded muscle down her arms, planes of her stomach and back. Every ridge and contour is a valley I want to get lost in.

Heat pools between my thighs. My muscles clench. I dig my fingers into her hips, and she gasps.

"Is this too fast?" she asks, hot against my mouth.

"Hell, no." My voice is husky and raw. "Nothing is too fast. Or too much."

Her head tilts as her mouth curves up at the corner, moonlight gleaming off her swollen lips. "Nothing?"

I lean in. Slow, slow, and nip the curve of her ear. She groans. I smile against her neck. "Nothing at all."

She pulls me into her lap and lets out a surprised *oh* when I straddle her waist. God, this girl. How she's opening to me, letting me past each stoic layer, trusting me with her vulnerable parts. She fucking chops wood for a living and kisses me with so much tenderness it hurts. Rachel Reed is unraveling before my eyes, beneath my touch, and I want every unguarded piece of her. The deepest parts of me burn to be closer to her than my own damn skin, and I clench my legs, tightening my hold on her waist.

Her hands cup my ass, solid and steady, and I'd be lying if I said I haven't imagined this from the moment she caught me in the snow. She kisses a trail down my neck, along the collar of my shirt. Sparks ignite wherever her lips touch, lighting me up between my legs, in that tense bunch of nerves begging for release. I need her. Now. "Rach." I pull back, breathless. "Mattress?"

Her eyes widen before she tips back her head and breathes, "Holy fuck, Morgan." Then she's lifting me, carrying me across the tent floor on her knees, each movement of my center against her waist drawing me that much closer to climax. "Hurry," I pant in her ear, nuzzling her with my nose.

She responds with an urgent kiss, searching my mouth with her tongue, before placing me down on the mattress—which squeals in protest. We freeze, eyes wide, cheeks filled with held-in laughter.

The soft glow from the fire emanates undisturbed, and I add this to the list of things I owe Ben for.

I inch up the soft blanket and wince as each movement sounds like a freight truck in desperate need of a brake job.

Rachel snorts. "So much for letting me plan the details, huh?"

I shake my head and let the bed have one final say as I yank the comforter off and pile it on the ground. "See, you thought of everything."

Rachel smiles. The soft light casts her in an ethereal glow, and this is the only image I want in my mind for the rest of time.

I pull off her beanie, cast it aside, trail my fingers through her wild, silky waves. Her gaze darkens and turns wild, too, and I could live wild in the woods with Rachel Reed forever.

I loose a breath, and all my inhibitions leave along with it. I crash into her like I'm connecting to my missing piece. Both of us on our knees: thighs, hips, entire bodies melding.

I grab the hem of my top and tug it up and off—freeze at the shock of cold against bare skin. "Fuck," I hiss, "it's freezing."

She wraps her arms around me, drawing me back onto her lap. Surrounding me with the warmth of her body, she pulls the blanket around us. The sexiest pillow-fort ever.

I lean into her touch as she pulls slightly back, lips red, eyes bright, and brushes my hair behind my ear. She gazes down so tenderly . . . like I'm something treasured. "I never thought this could happen. Not in a million years," she whispers.

It hits me all at once, squeezing my center. What if I'm not what she envisioned? What if I fall short of the fantasy in her mind? What if I'm terrible at this? "Rach, I . . ."

She is so focused that I shudder. All of Rachel's attention on me is something else. Warm, grounding. Good.

"You can tell me," she says, rubbing her hands along my arms.

It's Rachel. I can tell her anything. "I've . . . never done this. With a girl."

Her gaze holds me as her hands slow along my arms, stay steady on my elbows.

I rush to get the rest out. "Not that I haven't been with girls; there were some in LA over the years, nothing serious, but I never went all the way with any of them. Do people still say that?" My voice breaks, and I cover my face with my hands.

Rachel gently lowers my wrists. Holds my hands in hers. "You couldn't be bad at this if you tried."

"What if I am?"

"It's just you and me, here and now, okay? Nothing else."

She brings my hands to her lips, kisses each knuckle.

"Okay," I breathe.

"Plus, I'm taking care of you, remember?" She flashes a crooked smile before placing another kiss on the inside of my wrist.

All my nerves must be located in that single spot, because it catches fire.

But then she kisses my other wrist, and that ignites, too.

Then, binding both wrists in her hands, she gently guides my arms above my head and lays me back until I'm flat against the blanket, its edges soft around me, Rachel over me as she trails her fingertips down my raised arms, wraps her hands around my ribs, and presses her lips along my throat, my collarbone, sending ripples of pleasure wherever they caress. Her touch trails up the sides of my stomach, and then her thumbs are on my nipples, already hard through the thin fabric of my bralette. I gasp and arch up.

"This okay?" she asks.

"God, yes," I sigh as her thumbs circle in a euphoric rhythm.

I run my fingers through her hair, gripping gently at the roots, as she moves down my body with that perfect mouth, those magic hands.

Before I can catch my breath, she presses a kiss to my hip. Unbuttons my jeans.

I gasp—her tongue meets my navel and licks its way down.

Rachel Reed is kissing my body. The thought alone puts me at the brink of ecstasy, and I drag my fingers through her hair again and clutch.

Sensing my need, she slips her hand between my jeans and stupid cotton thermals and presses exactly where I need her to.

I bow into the feel of her, and she rises, kissing my exposed throat.

"Rach—god. The way you touch me. It's better than I imagined."

"You imagined me touching you?" She pulls back so moonlight dances in her eyes, and highlights all her wily freckles.

I can't believe I said that out loud. My cheeks turn hot as I bite my lip and nod.

She smiles something sexy, erotic, wild. "That's hot as hell."

I grin and relax into her touch, which pauses as she speaks. "So," she starts, her voice low and melodic, "when you imagined me touching you . . ." She hooks the waist of my jeans and tugs them down in one smooth motion. Then her fingers splay over my thermal-covered thighs until her thumbs meet at the crest of my sex, coaxing that swollen, aching bud with firm strokes. "Did you imagine it like this?"

"Fuck." I must be soaking.

"How about this?" she asks as she wraps her fingers around the elastic and pulls, increasing the pressure with her thumbs.

"Oh my god, Rachel. Please."

She does exactly what I want and frees me from these goddamn long johns, stripping them off.

I sigh in relief.

Her hands on my bare skin feel so amazing, I could come from a single stroke. Her touch tingles up my legs until she grips my ass, kneading it— Holy *fuck*.

I raise onto my elbows, move to my knees.

She pulls me forward, still clutching my ass, and draws me against her.

I kiss her deeply, beckoning her tongue, as her hand finds its way to my front. She caresses the wet length of my opening. I am drunk on her, high on her, motherfucking gone for her. I whimper into her mouth. "Rachel."

My hands grow greedy and snake beneath her shirt. She raises her arms, and I pull her free, tossing her top and bra to the corner of the tent. Her skin is smooth and sculpted, and her bare nipples bead for me. Somehow, I live, despite the heart-stopping sight of her.

I cup her breasts. They fill my hands perfectly. "Is this okay?"

Her eyes are glassy, and she clears her throat. "I— Yes. Anything."

I go weak. Pinch her nipples between my fingers and relish the sound my touch pulls from her throat, the goosebumps it casts across her skin.

She buries her face into my neck, painting it with the pleasure of her lips, as her fingers find me again. Her touch is urgent and firm between my thighs, and I lose all sense of myself, every cell warm and languid and bright and merry fucking Christmas to me.

I grip her hips and writhe on her fingers as I work my own along the clasp of her jeans.

She nips my ear, and I almost shatter.

Pushing down her pants, I let my hands have their fill of her perfect ass, finally making that denim share.

"I love how you touch me," she pants into my mouth. In the same breath, her fingers move to my opening. "You feel amazing."

I moan and grip her tight. I wanted to last, to please her first, but I can't take it, I— "Rach—god, I can't hold on—"

"You don't have to," she breathes on my neck. "Let go for me. Please."

I sink into her touch.

She thrusts inside me. Again. Again. Again.

My brain turns to a blank, blissful space as she leans onto her heels, the new angle intensifying my pleasure. I grip her arms, fold against her, bury my face in her hair.

She holds me steady with a hand on my ass, the other coaxing my most sensitive spot. Euphoric pressure from every side drives me to the edge. I scream into her shoulder. Break apart in her arms.

She gently braces my pulsing sex, the small of my back, soothing me with gentle strokes as I come back together.

I pull her to me and she presses her lips to mine, drawing out each kiss as my body calms.

My hands grow hungry and I move my fingers down her waist, finding where I want to touch most. "I also imagined this," I breathe into her ear. "Pleasuring you."

"Morgan." She leans back, and I take the opportunity to deepen my touch until my fingers play along her opening, and oh my god—

"You're so wet. You're so hot," I rasp.

She moans, humming along my skin. "I'm so going to come in two seconds."

A shiver runs through me at the challenge, and I slip my fingers inside her, relishing the soft melting warmth, this luscious, intimate space.

She gasps and pulls me close, and I follow her lead with each pulse, each stroke of her clit.

Her panting breaths set me on fire, and she finds me again, caresses me again, until her fingers are inside me again, and we're sharing this bliss.

"Morgan," she breathes, and that's the end of me.

I press into her palm as she rides mine. "I've got you," I say.

Her fingers dig into my back, and she whimpers against my neck. Her thighs clench around my hand.

This is all I want. This girl. Right here. Right now.

We both shatter.

Joy cascades through my wasted limbs as Rachel sighs and breathes a whispered, *"oh my god."*

Clutching each other close, we fall atop the blanket, tangled together.

I stroke the corner of her smile with my thumb and gaze into her sparkling eyes until mine won't stay open anymore.

CHAPTER 20

How am I supposed to talk to these customers when I can only think of you?

I shift into park and smile at my screen. Messages from Rachel have gotten me through another week of vendors still refusing to work with me.

I reply:

How am I supposed to type back when my hands only want to please you, like they did last night?

Okay, sleeping with her at my place has also sustained me.

GET YOUR HOT ASS OVER HERE, ROSS. I MISS IT.

I giggle like a teenager and step out of my car onto a transformed Main Street. If I could whistle, I'd let out a long, low one. It's a wonder I found a parking spot. People must have come from all over to attend the Fern Falls Holiday Festival.

The whole space is now an outdoor market, with a stage at the front where local musicians play holiday pop songs. A large banner spans the entrance that clearly notes, Sponsored by Vaughn Enterprises. I worry at my coat pocket as I walk beneath the sign and edge my way through the crowd, peering atop heads to find the tree farm's booth.

Along the way, I spot Ben at Peak Perk Café's table, with a line at least four stalls long. He's smiling and in his element, handing out small pink boxes the perfect size for cupcakes. And alongside him is Adam, doing the same. They both talk up the crowd while stealing glances at each other, and my heart might explode.

Just as I nudge past a group of teens, a pair of flannel-clad arms wrap around my waist, and that low voice I love whispers in my ear, "You took too long."

I nuzzle into Rachel's cheek. "It's been an hour, bossy."

She turns me around, her fingers hooked into the belt loops of my jeans. "Like I said, too long." She grins and leans in, taps my nose with hers.

"You know everyone is gonna see us, right?"

"Good." Then she kisses me soft and long and sweet, and I completely forget where I am.

We slowly pull apart as Whitney's voice cuts through the crowd. "Actually, sir, Christmas trees were originally a pagan tradition to pay homage to nature, and we don't adhere to any specific religion at our farm. All are welcome."

We approach the booth, hand in hand, just as an old white guy huffs off muttering something about what the world has come to.

"So, how's it going?" Rachel asks, dragging out the *so*.

"Smashing the patriarchy one Christmas tree at a time." Whitney bats her lashes.

"Your service is greatly appreciated," I say, stepping into the booth. "You two set this all up?" I take in our table with a red skirt and drape, REED FAMILY TREE FARM proudly displayed on the front. Planting kits with tiny saplings are lined up in rows. "Rach, did you put these together?" I ask, picking up a little red bag with potted soil and an instruction card inside, a green sprig popping out the top.

She smiles. "You like it?"

"Such a great idea." I set the bag down, lining it back up with the others.

"Thanks, and it was practically free; we just combed through the lot and found little sprouts we'd have to move anyway."

"You and Whit?"

Whitney rolls her eyes as Tanner approaches. "Hey, look how amazing our giveaways turned out!" He picks one up and hands it to a passerby, smiling that Tanner smile. "Whitney," he says, turning back, "the Forest Fairy's booth is all set. Karina has the kids painting ceramic fungi. You need any help here?"

Whitney holds up a hand. "No, that's—"

"Actually," Rachel says, "we could use an extra hand, because Morgan and I need to pass out these flyers, see if other booths can distribute them, too." She holds up a stack of the gorgeous handouts she made for Enchanted Evenings.

Whitney glares at Tanner and folds her arms, but steps over to make room in the booth. "Hurry back," she says.

"I appreciate your faith that we're still going to pull this off," I say to Rachel as we walk away.

"Not to bring up that graduation party, but remember how amazing it was? How you set everything up?"

"I had support from Christy then." I shake my head. "She paid for the whole thing, organized all the suppliers. I don't have that backing now." I don't even have the professional support from vendors, something I worked years to build.

Rachel takes my hand. "You have me, Adam, Ben, Whitney, Tanner. No matter what happens, we're going to figure this out together, okay? We're not giving up."

I take a deep breath, take in her words. "Even if it's not as grand as I'd like it to be, you're right. There will be Enchanted Evenings." I smile for Rachel, but my stomach falls. This has to be over-the-top grand to raise enough money to save the farm and aid the inn. And the six of us can't do it all alone.

"There will be." She squeezes my hand as we walk through the crowd.

After a few minutes, though, she scans the faces, brows creased.

"Are you okay?" I ask. "Is it about the fundraiser?"

She shakes her head. "No, it's just . . . I invited my dad." She gives the crowd another glance. "He hasn't shown up yet."

My throat tightens. "I bet he will," I offer. "It's still early."

She gives a small smile and nods. "Yeah. I'm sure you're right."

I squeeze her hand and hope he doesn't let her down.

Rachel shares that Adam already brought Ben a huge stack of flyers, so our first stop is Rainbow Reading, Fern Falls' indie bookstore with Pride flair. "Thanks so much, Marcus," Rachel says, as the shop's employee places our flyers on the counter beside a book I definitely recognize: *Winter's Warm Embrace*, by Becca Rae. The same book Mrs. Hart was reading at the inn the other day. Marcus hands Rachel a couple of Rainbow Reading bookmarks. "One for you, one for your girlfriend," he says, pushing his black-framed glasses up his dark nose.

Rachel's face turns as red as mine feels. "Thanks." She hands one to me with a shy smile.

We walk to the next booth quietly, very much not mentioning the title Marcus gave us, and stop before a sign that says: Tea and Tarot.

Three women huddle together. Blond, red, and black hairstyles smashed close with no clear intention of looking up.

"I heard it's a shotgun wedding," one says.

"Whatever the reason, I doubt they'll be faithful with their track record."

The tea part of this booth is crystal-ball clear.

Rachel clears her throat. "Hello."

One of the women eyes us atop her glasses.

Rachel steps forward. "Would you be so kind as to pass out some flyers for our fundraiser?"

The red-headed white lady takes the stack that Rachel holds out. "This sounds delightful," she says.

My chest swells with pride. I'm assuming it's hard to come by a compliment from this trio.

"Thank you for your time," Rachel says, taking my hand.

"Wait," the woman with black hair and brown skin says before we escape.

She holds a finger toward us, eyes clenched shut. Then her lids fly open, and she nods decisively. "You two have good energy. I feel it."

Rachel and I face each other, smiling.

"We do," she says, with her eyes on me.

"Please send some of those good vibes for our event, okay?" I ask, looking back at the group.

They all waggle their fingers at us as we walk away.

"I forgot how many characters there are up here," I say.

"All of them," Rachel says. "Hermits, gossips, nature lovers, corporate hounds."

I take a deep breath and slow my steps. "Girlfriends?" My voice is quiet among the crowd, but she stops and turns to me, smiling wide.

She tugs me closer and cups my face, opening her mouth to reply—

"Hello!"

We startle to find Christy beside us.

"So glad the Reed Family Tree Farm could participate in the festival!" she says. "We wanted to bring out every business, make sure everyone is represented."

I stifle a grimace at her words. She sounds like she's already in charge of Fern Falls.

"It's a great turnout," Rachel replies, her tone flat. She lowers her arms.

"Rachel Reed!" An older woman with light brown skin comes up and gives her a hug. "Are things getting better at the farm?"

"Trying our best, Mrs. Hernandez. We're having a special event next Saturday, and we'd love for you to come." She hands Mrs. Hernandez a flyer.

Christy eyes the literature I'm holding.

I give her one.

"Charming," she says with a thin smile. "You're forging ahead after all."

I try to feign the confidence I sure as hell don't feel. "Absolutely."

"What vendors did you get to work with you?" she hollers over the chatter and music.

Acid churns my gut. I scan the booths to find the businesses I approached in-store, all of them too afraid to work with me, to go against Vaughn Enterprises. I try to come up with some reply, when thankfully, the mayor buys me time.

"Everyone, I'd like to have your attention, please." Mayor Natashia Park takes the stage in a gray skirt suit, her black bob tucked behind her ears, bright smile against her warm, light brown skin.

My chest swells with pride.

I haven't been home since she was elected, and to see the town's first trans and Asian woman mayor is history made, even though it should have happened long ago.

"I'd like to take a moment to thank the Fern Falls Children's Choir for their lovely medley of Winter Around the World," she says.

Claps and cheers sound as the kids bow and their director ushers them off stage in a surprisingly organized manner.

Rachel steps close and takes my hand as Mayor Park continues. "I'd also like to thank Vaughn Enterprises for sponsoring this year's festival. The turnout is almost as big as our annual Pride Parade!"

More claps sound.

"Christy Vaughn, vice president of Vaughn Enterprises, is with us today." She searches the crowd. "Ms. Vaughn, would you like to speak?"

"Excuse me," Christy says as she nudges past us, shoving the flyer back into my hand.

I grip it as she takes the stage and the mic.

"I want to thank you all for welcoming me into Fern Falls with open arms," she says, smiling way too big. "Because of your open hearts, and my company's open wallet," she says with a laugh, "we've been able to put on the best Fern Falls Holiday Festival ever, yes?" Her arms spread wide, as though she constructed each booth herself.

Everyone claps. I cringe, clutching onto Rachel. She runs her thumb over my knuckles.

"Vaughn Enterprises has much more in store for Fern Falls, and this is only a taste of the progress to come!" More applause as she steps aside and offers the mic back to the mayor.

It can't be like this. She can't trick everyone into trusting her by throwing money around. It's on me to show them what her true intentions are. And if they won't work with me, maybe I can at least make them listen.

I swallow hard, give Rachel's hand a squeeze, and make my way to the stage.

"Morgan, what—" she says behind me. I don't let myself turn around.

I can do this.

I make my way up the steps with every muscle begging me to stop.

When I reach the mayor, I force my words through a tight throat. "Mayor Park, I'm sorry to interrupt. I'm Morgan Ross, Warren Ross's daughter. Is there any way I could speak for a moment?"

"Oh, um—" She scans the crowd as if questioning, then nods. "Okay, Morgan. Go ahead."

I take the mic, and it squeals, the feedback making everyone flinch.

Clearing my throat, I fix my eyes on Rachel. She gives me a smile and nods. Complete faith in me, even though she has no idea what I have planned.

Her support gives me the courage to speak. "Hi, everyone."

The crowd is quiet.

"I have, um, met with some of you over the past couple weeks, visited your stores. Others I haven't seen in a long time. So, hi. Hello." I raise my hand.

A few people wave back, while most keep their arms crossed.

I swallow. Charge ahead. "I haven't been home in a while, and now that I made it back, I have to say, I've missed it so much. Something I've always loved about Fern Falls is the way the community comes together to help one another."

Some murmur in agreement.

"I'm heading a fundraiser for the Reed Family Tree Farm. A place that's brought so much joy to this town, a place we'd feel the loss of deeply if Vaughn Enterprises took over its land. Rachel Reed donates a lot to this town, and I'm asking you, if you can't bring yourself to work with me, please, think of her."

When no one moves or responds, I reach for my last resort. "We already know what happened to Snow Hill once Vaughn Enterprises took over. Small businesses have been forced to sell, unable to compete with the resort."

Christy's gaze feels heavy on my back as I continue. "And there have been rumors of an outlet mall being built in a nearby town, a town I have every reason to suspect is Fern Falls, if Vaughn Enterprises acquires the tree farm's acreage. There have already been calls to the city office, requesting building regulations for the land. Vaughn Enterprises has clear intent to take down the farm, and your small businesses won't be able to compete with chain stores and food courts—"

"Wait a minute," Christy says, swiping the mic. "This is unsubstantiated. I am here to offer you financial backing. To keep what you love about Fern Falls and restore the tourist appeal so it can thrive as much as Snow Hill. Are you willing to give that up based on rumors?"

"I am," Rachel says. She steps onto the stage and stands beside me, her presence steadying and solid.

"Me, too," says Ben, coming up next.

Adam follows, then Whitney and Tanner, as they make their way through the crowd.

"Everyone is entitled to their assumptions," Christy says, "but I assure you, Vaughn Enterprises is heavily invested in maintaining the integrity of—"

"I stand with Morgan, too."

I glance over, and there's Dad, now standing on the stage with the rest of us. Emotion floods me. I didn't even know he was at the festival.

"Warren," is all Christy can say.

I freeze. This is most likely the first time they've seen each other in years, and here we are in front of the whole town. Just like the night he proposed. Murmurs ripple through the crowd. My muscles brace, ready to lunge to Dad's defense, recalling how Christy replied after he proposed: *"I can't, Warren. I'm sorry. I'm so sorry,"* she said, her voice jagged. Then she turned and ran, leaving Dad alone on his knees.

My heart shattered as I stared at him from the crowd that night.

Dad rose, tucking the ring back into his pocket, not looking up. I wanted to run to him, comfort him. He ran after Christy instead.

Today, though, he's standing up for me. A swell of gratitude makes me blink hard. He steps beside Rachel and addresses the crowd, projecting without the mic, "I've lived here a long time and don't want to see us change into something we're not. If you're with me"—he glances at our group—"if you're with *us*, show your solidarity, your support, by a simple wave. Show Vaughn Enterprises we won't give in."

There is movement and chattering, but no one raises a finger, let alone a hand. Everyone looks between us and Christy like their livelihoods depend on it. Which to be fair, they do.

Someone yells out, breaking the silence, "So, if we go with or without Vaughn Enterprises, we're screwed?"

Another voice sounds, "I can't keep on with how things are. Tourism falls every year, and this has been the slowest by far."

Mayor Park takes the mic. "Listen, everyone. We will get to the bottom of this. I will investigate, and I assure you, we won't allow our mountain to become a strip mall." She peers at Christy. "I will personally work with Ms. Vaughn to ensure that any possible arrangement is in the best interest of this town and its people."

Everyone cheers, and Christy shakes hands with the mayor. "There's nothing else I'd appreciate more," she says.

Great. Instead of helping Fern Falls, I facilitated a mayoral endorsement for Christy. I might be sick.

We all dismount the stage, and Rachel pulls me in for a hug, keeping Christy at my back as she rushes past us wordlessly. "Thank you for trying."

I choke up. I let everyone down.

She pulls back, and the tears fall just as Dad comes up.

"Sunshine. I'm proud of you," he says, making it a group hug. "And Mom would be, too."

Rachel rubs my back.

The way he stood up for me eases some of the pain. We need to talk. I'm ready to fix things between us. "Hey," I say, voice thick, "any way we could head to Mom's spot?"

"Of course. When would you like to go?" he asks.

"Now?" I question. "Are you guys okay with the booth here, Rach?"

"Absolutely," she and Whitney say in unison.

Tanner, Ben, and Adam all give me a giant unified hug I don't deserve.

Then it's me and Dad walking toward the parking lot, off to talk to Mom and hope for a holiday miracle.

CHAPTER 21

Late afternoon sun glints off the lake, and all is still and peaceful and calm, unlike the storm brewing in my chest.

Even though I know exactly where to go, I let Dad lead the way.

There were pictures in our house of when we'd come here as a family. Me, a tow-headed toddler; Mom, crouching down next to me, demonstrating how to skip stones across the water. Dad beside us, fishing.

We pass rushes and reeds, all a winter-muted brown, and find the little bench Dad and I used to visit whenever we wanted to talk to Mom.

It's immaculate, the white wooden slats crisply painted, iron frame oiled. The memorial plaque is spotless and shiny with the inscription that might as well be engraved on my heart: *In Loving Memory of Wendy Ross, devoted mother and wife.*

I clear my throat and take a seat, letting my body settle into the place it remembers from when I came here with and without Dad. He stands at the edge of the lake, hands in his pockets.

Moments pass through my mind of when I'd visit alone to feel a connection to Mom, something to claim as a memory of my own besides the pictures on our walls.

Dad comes and sits with me, and the bench doesn't even creak.

"You've maintained this so well," I say.

"Keeps me connected, you know?" He doesn't take his eyes off the lake.

"I do." I feel closer to her just by being at the spot she loved. It's the only real way I can. I envy Dad for having had so much time with her. "What was she like, really?" A duck lands on the water, and another. They paddle in a little circle. "Did she ever mess up like me?" My voice is quiet.

"Oh, Sunshine." He pulls me close. Kisses the top of my head. "You know how I met your mom?"

"Of course. Skiing in Snow Hill."

He smiles and shakes his head. "Yes, but the story is more than that."

"You've never told me."

"I went on a road trip." He leans forward and laces his fingers together, staring at the lake like he's watching the World Series. "I had time off work, between sales, and passed through the mountains on my way to Vegas. Took the long route to blow off steam, and stopped in Snow Hill. There was a village of family-owned shops along the slopes. Thought I'd get a sandwich or something, when, out of nowhere, this woman barrels into me with her skis, knocking me to the ground."

I laugh so hard I have to grab my side. "Seriously?"

"Your mom literally swept me off my feet," he says between laughs.

"But I thought she was great at the sport?"

He sits back, folds his hands in his lap. "After she apologized profusely, I offered to give her lessons. All the hotels in Snow Hill were booked, so I stayed in Fern Falls and drove an hour each way for the remainder of my break, teaching her on the bunny slopes."

I blink hard. "That's the sweetest story."

He smiles. "Way better than Vegas."

"So you dated then? After the lessons?" I'm not ready for this story to end.

"Not exactly." He gets a glint in his eye that tells me this will be good.

"What happened?"

"I had to go back to LA for business. Mom was in Snow Hill for the season, working remotely. I sat in that big city office, thinking of her every day. So, after Christmas, I called and asked her out on a proper date. I didn't care that it would take five hours to go back up just to take her to dinner."

I picture this younger version of my father so caught up on Wendy Ross that he would drive ten hours round trip all to have a meal with her. What a love. "Where did you go?"

"Snow Hill was so crowded that we couldn't get a reservation, so we came to Fern Falls and ended up spending the night and the rest of the week through New Year's here."

"And that's how you fell in love with the town?"

"And each other. Yeah."

I stare at the water, emotions washing over me in waves. Gratitude, grief, joy. "I love that story, Dad. Thank you for sharing it with me," I say, voice hoarse.

He squints against the sun. "The point of it being, it all started with a mistake, you know? I would have never met her if she was good at skiing. Sometimes, mistakes are the beginning of something wonderful."

I reflect on the Chad-tastrophe. If I hadn't messed up like that, I would have never come back or reconciled with Rachel, reconnected with Dad. With Mom. A lump forms in my throat. "I wish I had stories like that to remember Mom by."

Dad squeezes my shoulder. "You have this place. She loved it so much that she left her corporate job for this simpler way of life."

Simpler. The word slashes at me, and I can't hold the questions back anymore, they've been pushed down for far too long. "Was that simplicity not enough for you, then? When you proposed to Christy, did you want more than what we already had?"

He squeezes me. "Me proposing to Christy never had to do with her money."

"Really?"

He shakes his head. "Believe it or not, she was a really good person. Deep down, I think she still is. When I first met her in Fern Falls, when she was considering settling in the area, it was before Vaughn Enterprises monopolized Snow Hill. She was down-to-earth and loved spending time with you. But as time went on, and her family's company grew, she felt all this pressure to appease her father, to run the business. Ultimately, that's what she chose over us. I think she regrets it every day."

Each moment with Christy from the day I returned replays in my mind. "That makes a lot of sense, actually."

"She's not a happy person. She's set on proving herself to someone who only counts profits as success."

I swallow hard, seeing too much of myself here. "Yeah, well, now I've failed, and she probably will succeed."

"I wouldn't be so sure. Look at what you have going for you."

"What do you mean?"

"The group that came up and stood with you on that stage."

My heart warms, picturing the faces of those who mean so much to me. "They're pretty great."

"And just as talented as every vendor here in Fern Falls."

Ben and his baking and motivation. Adam and his mechanic and music skills. Tanner's drinks and way of mobilizing people. Whitney's drive and understanding of local business. Rachel and her graphic design skills, and big, caring heart.

"You're right. It was in front of me all along." Rachel even said as much at the festival, but I was only thinking of their support instead of their individual skill sets. We might actually have enough talent between us to make this happen.

He nods at the lake. "Sometimes we just need some perspective."

I hug him tight. "I love you."

He holds me, clears his throat, and says, "I love you, too."

I pull back, wiping my eyes. "And I'm so sorry I didn't make more of an effort to keep in touch. That I didn't call more and—"

"No." He leans forward. "I'm the one who's sorry." He runs a hand down his face.

I swallow hard.

His eyes crease together. "It's my fault we were in a bad place when you moved away, and I wanted to let you have your space. I should have tried harder, stayed involved. Said the hard things. I miss you."

I try to keep my voice steady. "Let's find a way together? I want you to be in my life. I miss you, too. I miss this. Talking with you." The admission is a weight off my chest.

He smiles bigger than I've seen in years. Like old times. "I'd love that," he says, voice soft. "Thank you for this."

We sit, staring at the lake, until the sun's belly grazes the water. After everything we said, there's this new presence of something bigger than us, something beyond words. I run my fingers along Mom's bench as the gentle light of the sunset warms my face. She's here, in this moment. That's the feeling. It feels whole. It feels like home.

And I will never let Christy destroy the place that Mom loved so much.

I stand, stronger than I've been in years, ready to spring into action. "Do you mind if I go gather my group?" I ask, facing Dad. "We've got a fundraiser to put on." I can't contain my smile.

"I want you to," he grins back. "I'm going to hang out with Mom a little longer. I'll see you back in town?"

"Absolutely." I give him one last hug.

He beams. "Go get 'em."

I head back to my car and text Rachel, asking her to gather everyone and meet me at The Stacks as soon as possible.

Before I pull away, I take in the lake one last time. "Thank you, Mom."

CHAPTER 22

The Stacks is bursting with townspeople and tourists, thirsty after a long day at the festival.

"Okay, I have a minute, but that's probably it." Tanner flings a towel over his shoulder and squeezes between Adam and Rach as we all squish around a table.

"We can do this," I say, huddling in. "We can pull off this fundraiser. The six of us. It won't be easy, but if we commit, we have the skills to pull it off."

"What's your plan?" asks Whitney.

Ben presses into Adam's shoulder, and I smile as I continue. "I want to do a synchronized light show with the trees. We're going to decorate them in different themes and auction them off, and the big draw will be that all the lights are timed to music. Adam, that's where you come in. With your musical and mechanical experience, could you take on something like that?"

Even as I say the words, I worry that he won't want to work with me. Things have warmed between us, but I can't shake off that cold reception he gave when I first arrived.

He nods without hesitation. "For sure. Sounds like a blast, and the shop is slower right now anyway, so I'll have the time."

"Great, thank you." I smile at him, and something passes between us. Like an agreement to move forward.

Then I turn to the man beside him. "Ben?"

There's a pause as he shifts his attention from Adam to me. "Hmm?"

"I want to turn the barn into a space for food and desserts. I think a cake auction could raise more funds."

"That sounds great," he says. "And it wouldn't hurt to help bring more business to the bakery, too."

"Wonderful. And Tanner, this is where you come in. Could we have drink tickets?"

"Yeah," Tanner replies. "I have my liquor license, so it'd be no problem to set up a small bar. I could even create an Enchanted Evenings signature cocktail."

I grin at the thrill of this finally coming together. "I need to figure out decorations. My boss in LA might be able to help us out with that. And Whitney and Rach, the three of us will need to run everything else. The kiosk, the crowd, the auction, the whole event. Are you up for it?"

Rachel leans into me and squeezes my hand, as Whitney raises her glass and says, "Sticking it to the man with a grand party sounds like my kind of night."

"Cheers!" we yell in unison, clinking our glasses and bottles together.

Tanner heads back to the bar, and the others fall into conversation. I take a sip of something cold that tastes like pumpkin pie while Rachel slips her arm around me. "I'm so glad you and your dad are doing better."

I meet her eyes. "Oh, Rach, I'm sorry, I didn't even ask. Did your father show up?"

Disappointment pinches her features before her expression goes smooth again. "No, he didn't. But I'm okay, really. I knew he probably wouldn't make it."

I rub her back and wish I could take away the hurt she's feeling, even though she puts on such a brave face. "You deserve to have him show up for you. I'm sorry he didn't."

Her smile is soft, but then it shifts to wily, as she angles her gaze and whispers in my ear, "Well. You are amazing. And seeing you in action like this?" She squeezes my upper thigh with her free hand. "Damn, it's hot."

"Yeah?" I grip her leg right back. "Then brace for me to take charge later tonight when it's just the two of us at my place."

My girl practically growls. "It's convenient for me that I can't get a visible boner, because everything you do turns me on."

I laugh low in her ear. "Wait until I get you home."

She flicks her gaze at the hallway that leads to the restrooms. "Maybe we don't have to wait that long?"

My cheeks positively boil as I grip higher up her thigh.

But then a voice comes out of nowhere. "Excuse me?"

I startle from my lusty haze and turn to find one of the vendors I visited last week right behind us. Izzy from Mountain Florals is in a cute pinup-style dress with leggings, and her bright red hair is in victory rolls, berry lips vibrant against her pale skin.

Last we met, I was leaving her shop after she turned down the offer to work with me.

"Hi, Iz," Rachel says, clearing her throat and swiveling around. "Good to see you."

"Yeah," she replies, with her hand on her full hip. A rainbow-colored vine of roses trails up her forearm before disappearing beneath the rolled sleeve of her sweater. "I wanted to come by and let you know I'd be happy to partner with you for the fundraiser."

I look between her and Rachel. "I— Really?"

"Yes," she says, nodding decisively, hair staying in perfect place. "We Fern Falls folk stick together. I should have listened to you before. I'm not willing to take the chance on the outlet mall, on losing our town, our businesses, and our way of life."

"I really appreciate that," Rachel says.

"I do, too." I hold out my hand.

She gives it a firm shake and steps aside to reveal a line of others behind her. The first group being the three women from Tea and Tarot.

"Aunties!" Ben jumps up and rounds the table, and we all gape as the salty coven embraces him in a chorus of *squees*.

"What's this," says one, her long purple nails in his hair. "Growing it shaggy now?"

"Eh, a little more warmth for the winter." He blushes as they pinch and prod.

Ben finally gains enough ground to spin around. "Everyone, these are my mom's really good friends and customers—"

"What? That's all we get?" asks the woman with a jet-black pixie cut. "After all the late-night readings?"

"They've become like family over the past couple years," he says as one of them pinches his cheek.

"And family sticks together, which is why we're here. I'm Mari," says the woman with dark hair and brown skin.

"And I'm Adelaide," voices the one with long blond hair and a pale complexion. "We have an entire attic filled with antiques and decorations we'd like to contribute to the cause." Her voice is so chipper and her smile so perky, I would accept a twig if she wanted to donate it. And I'm also thankful I won't need to ask Johanna for help, show her I can still handle this on my own.

"I'm Florence," says the redhead with white skin and freckles, "and I'm sorry we weren't vocal at the festival. During cleanup, we had time to talk, and decided that no matter what Vaughn Enterprises offers, we won't risk the soul of our town, its heritage, its legacy."

"Woo! We've got the coven on it!" Whitney yells.

We all cheer.

One by one, more people approach, talking about the fundraiser and offering to get involved now that they're out from beneath Christy's gaze.

"Attention, everyone!" Tanner yells from behind the bar. "In the spirit of things, and in light of all she's done for this town, ten percent of tonight's proceeds will be donated to help save Rachel Reed's tree farm!"

Everyone hollers and shouts, glasses clink, and the warm ambience grows cozier as people embrace.

Rachel takes my hand and pulls me gently toward the bar, where Tanner places two craft brews before us. She nips on my ear and whispers, "Meet me in the restroom? I can't wait any longer to taste your sweet pussy." Then she winks and doesn't even give me time to scrape my jaw off the floor before sauntering away. This girl I've gotten myself into. She's fucking amazing.

After a few minutes and sips of my beer, I follow, nerves already tingling, anticipating her touch.

But just as I pass by them, the front doors burst open on a gust of cold air, and I freeze in my tracks, face-to-face with Christy Vaughn.

Voices hush as she walks in and approaches me.

I cross my arms. "Hi, Christy. What are you having?" I ask, nodding at the bar.

"A chat with you? Outside?" she replies.

I glance down the hall to where Rachel is waiting for me. Seriously? Now Christy's a corporate shark *and* a cockblock?

"I only have a few minutes," I snap.

"I'll make this fast." She pushes through the door.

Tanner eyes me from behind the bar. "You good?" he asks.

"If I'm not back in ten minutes, send the hounds."

He nods. "You got it."

Leaving all joyous energy behind, I step through the door into the icy dark.

I take in the street, the people still cleaning up booths and the stage from the festival, and refuse to meet the stare of the woman beside me. It's quiet for too long, then Christy finally speaks. "I get what it's like having others depend on you," she says, fixing her gaze on the street. "It's easy to look at Snow Hill and assume that people lost so much. But between the shops, the restaurants, and the resort, we employ over five hundred locals with steady, reliable incomes. Wages they used to hope and pray they'd make in a good season. Now, it's guaranteed. We give them peace of mind."

I take her in. The frown lines on her cheeks, between her brows. She stands rigid, as if fighting the cold. Does she know how much she hurt Dad and me? Did she even care? "Taking away people's choice is nothing to be proud of, Christy. They have no other option except to work for you. Snow Hill used to be filled with individuality." I point to the sign across the street, PEAK PERK CAFÉ, and picture the funny one around the back. "Now it's lost its soul, along with any hope of private businesses thriving. I can't let that happen here."

She turns to me, arms crossed. "So you're staying, then? You're moving to Fern Falls permanently, since you're so committed to it now?"

Her question gives me whiplash. "What do you mean?" My voice cracks.

"I mean, you're fighting so hard for this place to stay the same, so are you going to stay, too?"

I picture the New York promotion and how much I wanted it. But now there is something—*someone*—I might want more. That thought makes my limbs shaky, like I've come untethered, the future uncertain. "I . . . don't know."

She squints. "That's because you have vision, Morgan. You want more, like I want to bring more to this town. I've seen promise in you since you were young, and you're lucky you've been able to pursue it."

Her mention of the past makes me bristle. "You obviously didn't see enough in me to become a part of my family." I want to shove the words back in. There's no reason to bring this up. It won't do any good.

Christy flinches. She stares at the trees. "Family is something you and your dad figured out right." Her tone is softer, introspective. "Mine always felt like a business transaction. You can understand wanting to prove yourself, can't you?"

The conversation I shared with Dad today echoes through my mind. The apologies we held in for far too long soothe my heart, beginning to soften the hardened parts. I nod. "Yeah. I can, actually."

"If I close the deal on the Reed Farm, I'll have finally done that. My father will relinquish the company to me. I'll be CEO. You can appreciate the value, the satisfaction of success, right? Look at all you've done in LA." Her voice is desperate now, words rushed.

"That's not the same," I snap defensively.

"No? You don't make dreams come true like I do in Snow Hill?"

"Christy, I'm here to protect a dream. To protect people's livelihoods, the soul of this town. This is more than a fundraiser. This is a fight for Fern Falls."

She widens her stance as she faces me. "Well, then. The line is drawn."

I cross my arms and hold her gaze. "It is."

Christy pulls her gloves on. "I think, Morgan Ann, you'll find yourself wishing you chose the other side."

I square my shoulders. "And I hope you see you've been on the wrong one all along."

Christy shakes her head and walks off.

I stare after her until a strong, steady arm wraps around my shoulders.

"You okay out here?" Rachel asks, voice low and even.

"I was just about to come in."

She pulls me close. "Come in here first." Her arms hold me, tight and warm, and she kisses me until I forget all about Christy and her threats. There is only right now. With Rachel. It's almost enough to make tomorrow and all the days to come feel like they're not closing in.

Almost.

CHAPTER 23

December fourteenth, the Wednesday before the fundraiser, comes surprisingly fast. The past few days were consumed by a whirlwind of event prep and wrangling the coven . . . *er*, Ben's mom's friends . . . and all the volunteers they corralled to clear the barn and help install decorations throughout the farm. It's been busy enough that I've only spent every other minute wishing I could steal Rachel away into a mistletoe-adorned corner.

I run my thumb over the backs of her fingers, and she squeezes my hand, which does something wild to my already jittery insides.

We still haven't talked about what was brought up at the festival, that title: Girlfriends.

That conversation means making decisions about the future. Decisions between my dream promotion . . . and my dream girl.

Decisions I don't have the strength to face yet.

I clear my throat and adjust. Sitting cross-legged for so long has made my ass go numb.

"Ahem." Florence, one third of Tea and Tarot, sits across

from us on the now-open floor of the barn, sunlight glinting off her bright red hair and gray roots. "Close your eyes, Morgan," she says, hers still shut.

Rachel snorts beside me, and I give her hand a little shake, trying not to laugh.

I straighten my spine like I've been caught texting in class and lower my lids, allowing a sliver of vision.

Florence waves a bundle of dried herbs back and forth, smoke wafting from the tip.

It smells like weed, but she insists it'll set us up for a flawless event, so weed away, Florence.

"Envision any negative energy leaving this space," she says, her tone hypnotic. "In your mind's eye, picture this smoke pushing out the bad. Now watch it flee."

"Just like her last husband."

My eyes fling wide to find Mari with a devilish grin, her lipstick as black as her pixie cut.

Adelaide, with her blond hair pooled around her, gasps and stares at Mari, horrified.

All eyes open, and Ben and Rachel and I gape at Florence, her cleansing bundle frozen midair. "Yes, Mari," she says in a chilling tone. "Richard was negative."

"Oh, dear." Adelaide worries at the hem of her paisley shawl. I hold my breath.

An impish grin creeps across Florence's face. "A negative ten in bed."

"Ah!" Mari shrieks, throwing her head back.

Then sweet Adelaide swipes the bundle from Florence and thwacks her and Mari on the shoulders with it, platinum hair swinging. "You two never take rituals seriously! Out! Out, out!" She smacks them on their behinds with sage until all three women scatter through the open doors, laughing heartily.

Ben is red with laughter as I help him to his feet. "Your pseudo aunts are something else," I say.

He shrugs, eyes bright. "They've been such a great support

since Mom's been gone." He smiles affectionately at their silhouettes, growing smaller down the snow-paved path.

"They're the best, Ben," Rachel says, smiling. She goes out the front of the barn to meet Whitney, who's heading our way.

My heart squeezes. Could I have had a whole community of family-like friends if I'd stuck around? I look between Ben and Rachel. Could I still have that now? Christy's words from the other night echo in my mind: *So you're staying, then? You're moving to Fern Falls permanently, since you're so committed to it now?* I shake my head like I can cast off this sick feeling I've had since that question arose. Every day spent up here makes Los Angeles and the dreams it holds seem farther and farther away, new dreams easing closer to my heart than an NYC version of me. I don't know how I'm ever going to choose, or if moving back here could even be an option. "They're wonderful," I say, voice small. "Goals, honestly."

"They sure helped us reach ours, yeah? This place looks freaking fantastic." He scans the space, hands on his hips.

He's not wrong. Thanks to his adopted aunts' decor contributions, and all the vendors who volunteered to work with us, the barn has transformed, and now it's down to finishing touches for Saturday's big event.

Tables span the perimeter, draped with cream linens and vintage lace overlays. Antique accents like old skeleton keys, books, and a one-hundred-year-old typewriter are placed just so among the fabric. Cake platters, stands, and domes were brought from the bakery and set at varying heights among the objects. Cascading arrangements of eucalyptus, pine, and holly berries add texture and winter charm to the display. And above each table, blue, green, and clear jars of every shape and size are filled with twinkle lights and strung at different lengths.

"I think you'll be able to get top bid on each cake with this setup, Ben."

He nods in agreement. "The auction was such a great idea. And the vintage aesthetic is sure to make guests nostalgic and want to bring this feeling to their holiday tables. You brought everyone's ideas together in a cohesive way, Morgan. We couldn't have done this without you."

I take in a shaky breath, willing the emotion down. What is wrong with me? I never get choked up over events.

"Hey!" Whitney bounds in through the door, arms looped with twine. Rachel follows her with more in her arms.

I clear my throat, grateful for the distraction. "Hi, Whit. How did the photo sessions go?" I was thrilled when she offered to handle this project and can't wait to see how it turned out. She unspools the strings to reveal small square images tied along every few inches.

"Oh, these are gorgeous." Rachel takes the words right out of my mouth.

Each photo is of a different place or person in town, making a garland of Fern Falls moments, frozen in time. The idea is to remind everyone of what this farm means to them, what stands to be lost if Christy wins. The final result is better than I could have imagined. And the style is so similar to the photos mounted behind glass in Ben's café, and on the wall of the tree farm kiosk. "Are those your photos around town, Whitney?" I ask.

Her cheeks pinken. "Just something I love to do in my free time. There's so much inspiration in the mountains."

I smile. These people never cease to surprise me. "Let's hang these among the lantern jars, okay? Have each photo double-sided, so when they spin, the photos revolve." I hand Ben a handful of strings and take some for myself.

Rachel and I move to a ladder beside the table, and I thank the hardware-store gods that I get to hold it as she climbs up. Her sweet ass in those tight jeans, taunting me to bury my face—

"Can you hand me a strand?" she asks.

I shake my head to rejoin the moment and disentangle a garland of photos. As I hand it up to her, my gaze catches on one: Rachel and me, laughing and hugging at The Stacks. It's just our profiles, and it's candid, the room around us a blur of unfocused lights and bright glints off glasses, and we're at the center of it all. I tug it off and move another photo up the string, slip this one into my pocket before handing the twine her way.

"Hey, you two, we're heading to the kiosk to check on progress up there," Whitney calls.

"Sounds good," I reply as she and Ben head out of the barn.

Rachel reaches up to hang the top of the string, and her flannel lifts to reveal the small of her back, the two perfect dimples there.

"Hey," I say, my voice coming out hoarse. "It's just the two of us in here." It could be the right time to talk about that official title for us. Words stick in my throat. I don't know how to bring it up. Maybe there's a reason she hasn't yet, and I don't want to push her if she doesn't want this . . . doesn't want us. Plus, it's not something I have the right to push. Not when I'm going back to LA. Pain grips my chest. The same one that comes whenever I think about leaving Fern Falls, leaving Rachel.

She looks around and steps down the ladder, pulling me against her. "You're absolutely right, baby. We are alone." Her lips meet mine, and all that swims through my mind is what she called me: Baby. I want to hear her call me that every minute of every day.

When we finally pull away, I lean my head against the warmth of her chest, and she wraps her arms around my back.

We stand like this for a while, swaying slightly, back and forth. Maybe it could always be this way. Maybe, somehow, LA and Fern Falls and whatever possibility there is with New York could all coexist. This is such an amazing space. I could talk to Johanna and see if she'd be interested in running events up here—

"Uh-oh. You're doing that thing," she says, her face angled down at me.

"What?" I ask, leaning back. My mouth goes dry. I'm not ready to tell her about the possibility of my move to New York.

She already has so much on her plate with the fundraiser and her dad, I don't want to taint whatever time we have left.

She smiles. "That thing where you quirk your lips to the side and stare off. You're planning something, aren't you?"

I laugh, the tension in my limbs easing. "Well," I say, taking in the space, "I was thinking you could do big events here. It's so polished now and large enough for fire codes, you could host full-on weddings at the farm, or anything you wanted. If I were getting married, this is what I would want. A place like this." The words slip out, followed by a heavy silence. I hold my breath for dear life.

"Is it?" she asks.

I nod, tapping her chin with the top of my head. "Yeah."

"And what kind of wedding would you have in here?"

My fingers cling to her instinctively, the mention of the future reminding me this is temporary. Like she's already slipping through my fingers like Santa Monica sand. "Honestly?" I say, trying to keep my tone light, "I would want something sweet and simple, a day I wouldn't have to plan myself."

She tucks my hair behind my ear. "Really? You, the planner, not wanting to plan anything?"

"Really." I laugh. "I guess if I'm marrying someone, I would want to be caught up in enjoying every minute with them, not worrying over an event. Details wouldn't matter as much as the person beside me." I hide in her hug as my cheeks grow hot. I can't even try to pretend that when I talk about who I'll marry, the only face in my mind isn't hers.

I don't know what that means. All I know is that I don't want to lose her.

I look up and stare into her dark brown eyes. I want to live in her gaze. "You could do so much here. And maybe I could come up and help, you know? If we plan it right, I could make trips up here?"

She sighs, nods. "I've been thinking about this, too. About the future."

Just like that, the thing I've been avoiding is on the table, and all I can say is, "Nothing is going to be the same without you." Because it's the truth. Returning to LA will be a much less hopeful thing. It was where I ran to when I needed to get away from Fern Falls, but so much is changing now. The New York promotion will only bring me farther away from this new, fragile thing with Rachel. This thing I want to protect and cherish and try for.

I take a deep breath and motion toward the stairs. "How about a good, old-fashioned Ross and Reed heart-to-heart in the hayloft?"

"Absolutely." She smiles.

My heart leaps into my throat. I want to talk about this, even if it means making hard decisions about my career, about us.

She grabs a lantern at the bottom of the stairs and a packet of matches off a beam. It lights with a hiss. I follow her up to the hayloft, taking tight breaths. Each swing of the lamp illuminates the wood grain on the walls in bouncy golden orbs.

She sets it down at the top of the stairs, and we settle into our old spots at the banister like we didn't take a years-long break from doing this.

Through the arched windows, the trees are a patchwork of snow-dappled green. The sun slings low in the sky, blurring the farthest point of forest into a honeyed haze. The world is ripe with possibility up here, simple and clear. I wish it could always be this way.

"You first," she says, reaching behind her for a blanket. She wraps it around our shoulders, and the warmth is so comforting. She is so comforting.

I take a deep breath. I can do this. I need to be honest and not hide, even if it means she might resent me, if it means I take up space. I can do hard things. "I broke up with a guy I was seriously dating, Josh, shortly after you messaged me a couple years ago. When you were in LA. After I left here, I could never pull it together to keep a relationship going." Great, my cheeks are wet. "I can't handle waiting for everyone to leave or tell me how they really feel. I can't handle the idea of being rejected again, like Christy rejected my dad and me. So I leave first, before anyone can show me I'm not enough." I meet her eyes and speak through my thinning voice, "But I don't want to leave or hide or make myself small. Not now. Not this time."

Rachel's eyes shine with welled tears. Soft light from the lantern wavers across her skin. Her face is filled with so much emotion, I can barely handle having it all focused on me. I wrap a loose thread from the blanket around my finger, clench tight.

"I'm so sorry I didn't understand the pain you were going through back then. I'm sorry I wouldn't hear you out," she says, voice cracking.

"No." Panic seizes my stomach. "That's not why I brought it up. I forgive you. I know why you acted that way, why you didn't want to hear my apologies. You had your own pain, and I'm sorry for that. I said some awful things I didn't mean. We were young. We're different now. Which is why . . ."

"This is so big and scary."

"Yes." I swallow. "I don't want to mess this up, Rach."

She takes my hand and runs her thumb along my fingers. "Love never stops being scary. People choose to keep being brave." She takes a deep breath. "Which is what I promise I'll do. I won't push you away ever again." She moves closer, and our legs press against each other. "I want to be brave enough to believe I deserve what I truly want."

Her words are weighted with meaning. The air charges.

I squeeze her hand and brace for what I'm about to say, however she'll respond. I turn her face toward mine, my fingers gentle and steady against her cheek. "I don't know all the details yet, how we'll arrange our jobs and lives, but Rachel, what I want, what I've always wanted, is for you to be my girlfriend."

Girlfriend. It's only a word. A single word that consumes my entire being, hanging for her reply.

"I want you to be my girlfriend, too," she says, her voice soft, words slow, like she's savoring each one.

"Yeah?" My skin tingles all over.

She laughs, this little self-conscious thing of disbelief that melts my already molten insides. She cups my face in her palms. "Yeah."

We're so close that it takes no time at all to sling my leg across her thighs, lean in, and press my lips to hers.

A kiss filled with promises for a future we want to face together.

She wraps her arms around my hips and draws me onto her lap.

I surround her with my body, my hair, this blanket around us.

Her lips are glistening, eyes bright, as she brushes my hair behind my ear. I lean into her touch.

"I have a confession," she whispers.

"Tell me." I press my forehead to hers.

"The night we went camping and made wishes on the fire?"

My throat grows thick. "Yeah?"

"This is what I wished for."

My eyes sting, and I say as much to myself as to her, "We deserve this, you know. This second chance."

Our scarred hearts deserve a different story, a better one.

My mouth meets hers, and I pour my whole beat-up soul into our kiss. Tell her everything I feel with each touch of my tongue, press of my fingers, letting go of all the other decisions that await me as I cling to her.

She lies back, and I roll to the side so we face each other.

"I have to tell you something else," she says, voice quiet.

I nod for her to go on, ready to treasure another part of herself that she wants to share.

"I'm so proud of everything you've done in LA, Morgan, of your amazing success, but I'd be lying if I said I didn't hope every day that you might come back. It's why I never sold the farm sooner, why I played guitar at The Stacks sometimes, hoping you might be among the visitors from the city. When you crashed into my sign, I could barely speak for how happy I was to have you home, to hold you in my arms. Mud and all."

I close my eyes and breathe in the smoky scent of the barn wood, the warmth of her nearness, the fresh pine air. LA is a world away. A world that, despite the sun, seems very cold without Rachel in it. "There is nowhere else I would rather be. Mud and all." I mean it with my whole heart.

She leans in and smiles against my lips, runs a hand down my throat, my chest, my side. Grips my hip and draws a finger along the waist of my jeans. Lingers over the clasp.

I suck in a hiss through my teeth.

"Well then, Ms. Ross," she says in a husky voice that raises goosebumps along my skin, "allow me to demonstrate some perks of mountain life."

She rolls on top of me and kisses me long and deep and slow.

Before I can catch my breath, she presses her lips to my neck, unbuttons my jeans.

"Yeah," I rasp, clutching her shoulders, "this would be hard to do from LA."

Rachel peers down through her lashes. "You think I'd pass on the chance to see my girlfriend on the beach in a bikini? Winter doesn't last forever. We're doing this in LA, too."

I smile, picturing that future, and tuck her hair behind her ear. "We'll figure it out. Take care of all the details."

"We will." Her grin grows wicked. "But first, all I want to do is take care of you."

I laugh—then gasp—as she pulls up my jacket and presses her mouth to my navel, then licks her way down.

Rachel Reed is my girlfriend. I moan at the thought. It courses pleasure through my veins.

Sensing my need, she doesn't wait another second. She plunges her hand beneath my clothes and presses exactly where I need her to.

I arch into her kiss, her lips hot against my skin as her fingers pay special, pleasure-mounting attention to my clit.

I can't help but groan and grip her hair.

Her touch grows firm and moves close, so close, to my opening as she works the sensitive skin along my hips with her warm, wet mouth.

"Rach . . . oh my god."

I feel her smile against my skin as her fingers find their way inside me, stroking, pulsing, casting sparks through every last cell.

She moves her lips back up to mine as I dig my nails into the denim of her jeans.

"Come for me, baby," she growls in my ear. *Baby*. There's that word again. I am helpless to resist.

Her touch, her words, cast me over the edge, and I shatter in her arms.

She holds me steady as I fall apart, presses sweet kisses to my cheeks, my neck.

I trace my fingers along her waist, seeking the closure of her jeans. Taking my hand, she entwines her fingers with mine, kisses each knuckle. "We'll have so much time for that, baby girl. Right now, I just want to hold you."

I swallow against building emotion as she pulls me close and hugs me tight. I nestle into her chest, clutch her close. Never let her go.

Her breath is sweet and warm against my cheek when she says, "I want to let this all sink in. You, here, in my arms. My girlfriend."

"My girlfriend," I say into the hollow of her neck, and kiss there, forcing down the lump in my throat that wants to scream about the possibility of New York. About what all the details might look like . . . but maybe all those details mean nothing compared to her arms around me.

I need to talk to her about this, though. Tell her of my plans for this promotion. Let her know what the future might hold. "Rach, I—"

But before I can get another word out, the barn doors fly open. "Morgan? Rachel?" Ben calls from down below.

Fuck, he really has some timing with this barn. Note to self: Do not get intimate with Rach in here while Ben is anywhere near the premises.

"Maybe, if we don't move, he'll go away," she says, holding me tighter.

I laugh into her arm, and that turns into a snort, and there goes our cover.

"Are you two up there? Oh my god, can't leave you alone for five minutes."

We both roll our eyes and peer over the banister.

"What do you need, Ben?" I ask, forcing some irritation into my voice despite my smile.

"We need you two at the front, actually. We have some company."

From his tone, I can tell it's not the welcome kind.

"Is everything okay?" Rachel asks him as I pull myself together.

"Not really? Someone from some department is here, and they want to talk with the event organizer."

My stomach clenches as we snuff out the lantern, climb down from the hayloft, exit the barn. Christy's words come back to me: *I think, Morgan Ann, you'll find yourself wishing you chose the other side.*

We make our way through the trees, where people from all around the community are putting up decorations and lights, and setting up the auction booths. Each volunteer is working so hard to pull this off.

I hope I don't let them all down.

I reach the kiosk, where a man in a gray suit stands with a clipboard.

Immediately noted: His feet slip on the icy ground.

I smirk. That was me, not three weeks ago.

"Hi, how can I help you?" I say, voice light.

The man turns, sharp pale nose, dark hair slicked to the side of his forehead. "Are you the organizer, Morgan Ross?" His voice is strained, thin lips rigid as if fighting the cold.

"I am. Would you like a warm drink?" I offer, pointing toward the cocoa thermos at the kiosk.

"No, thank you. I'm Herbert Insled with the mountain council. Here to run through some safety regulations with you."

Rachel steps closer to me, her presence reassuring. I can handle this. *We* can handle this.

"Arrangements have already been made with the mayor's office. Who are you with? What is the mountain council?" I speak firmer than before.

He clears his throat, shifts on his feet, narrowly avoids falling. "We work closely with the city. An invested group of lawyers."

"You work with Fern Falls?" I ask, tone sharpening. "Because we've already secured our permits." I pull out my phone to pull up the PDFs.

"I specifically want to address the fire codes for the barn, and accessibility issues for the, um, avenues you have here," he says, pointing at the tree pathways.

"Oh, absolutely. We are still setting up and will be combing the pathways so they are completely level, lit up, and fully accessible. We'll also be placing warning signs about the flashing lights, and making overhead announcements before each show. The barn meets all fire codes, and there will be monitored lines and ticketed access, so no more than fifty people can be in the building at the same time. If I could show you my permits—"

He steps forward. "I'd like to take a look at the grounds myself."

"I'll escort you," Rachel says in an icy tone. "You'll find that everything on your checklist there is sound and secure. We're not cutting any corners, nor would we want to for the safety of our guests."

"Doubtful," he replies. "I already see safety violations with the electrical setup. They aren't to code." He marks his notepad.

I meet Rachel's eyes. Her gaze is stony, determined, which soothes some of the nerves tightening my chest. I take a breath. "Who did you say you work for?"

"The mountain council. A firm that protects mountain businesses."

I squint at him. "Do you mean corporations? And do you mean Vaughn Enterprises?"

His pen stutters on his clipboard. "I'll take that tour now."

"Right this way," Rachel says, ushering him forward.

"One second there," comes a voice from behind us.

We turn to find Mayor Natashia Park walking up from the parking lot in a blue pantsuit and a full-on stride.

Herbert stops and actually shivers. "Mayor."

"Insled." Natashia nods. "I received word you were in town and had an idea of where you'd be."

"Clients first." His voice pitches high.

"Yes, well, Fern Falls is first for me, and Rachel Reed's tree farm is part of that. So I'm here to put a stop to this charade. I know you're a lawyer, that Vaughn Enterprises is your client, and that you are here in their interest, upstanding or not. And I'm here in the interest of my town."

"How do you mean?" Herbert mumbles.

I smirk. Natashia Park is a badass.

She flashes me a smile. "Well, Morgan here so inspired me with her speech the other day that I've decided to offer my full support in backing this event. Since Vaughn Enterprises so generously covered our holiday festival this year, we have freed up funds to bring in more resources for Enchanted Evenings." Natashia holds her palm open, motioning for his clipboard.

Herbert sighs and hands it over.

"Let's see here," she continues. "Yep, we'll bring in more portable restrooms. The nice kind, like the honey wagons they use on movie sets. More wheelchair ramps, heating lamps, enclosed party tents." She hands the clipboard back, and Herbert's face is even paler than before.

"So please give our thanks to Vaughn Enterprises for making all this possible." Her smile is as sweet as an arsenic-iced cake.

The lawyer looks between us and opens his mouth a few times, but no words come out. Then he huffs, shoves his notes beneath his arm, and stomp-slides back to his car.

"Thank you so much, Mayor," Rachel says, beaming.

"Mayor Park, I don't know what to say. Thank you," I echo, feeling wholly inadequate.

"Nope. No problem at all. We're in this together. You have my full support." She hands Rachel her card. "My assistant will be on site the next couple days to help with whatever you need, and you call me directly if there's anything specific I can do." Then she turns to me. "Seeing you stand up to Vaughn Enterprises like that, Morgan, it reminded me why I love the spirit of this town so much. We're united, and I thank you for reminding me of that."

Rachel puts her arm around me as we watch Natashia leave.

"You're amazing, you know," she says into my ear.

"I only spoke up for what I believe in." I turn to her. "And I believe in you."

She pulls me up by the collar of my coat and kisses me hard as a light snow begins to fall.

"Oh my god, you two," Ben says from somewhere nearby. "Let's get set up as much as we can before this snow comes down harder," he hollers, clapping his hands at everyone around.

We laugh and pull away.

"See you in a bit," Rachel says, nudging my nose with hers. "Girlfriend."

I straight-up giggle, which makes her beam. "Will you stay over tonight?" she asks.

"Please," I reply, not caring how desperate I sound.

She grins wickedly. "Good. Because once I get you alone, my entire goal will be to make you scream that."

She pats my ass and turns, walks into the trees, looks back with a wink that makes that light imprint of her hand on my jeans spread heat to every Rachel Reed-wasted part of me.

I bite my lip and smile. A promise to repay her for that hayloft moment as soon as humanly possible.

I turn to the kiosk just as my phone buzzes.

"Really?" I laugh. Service in this one spot?

I pull out my phone to a text from Sonia:

Hey, girl! I'm back from the UK, and look who's with me!

A photo of her and Bridget is attached.

OMG, SONIA! CONGRATS! Can't wait to hear all about it. SO happy you two are okay.

I can't wait to tell her about how very okay I am, too.

THANKS! Also though . . . there's this . . .

Another image comes through, a screenshot of a headline featured in *BuzzWhir News*, an outlet that borders on tabloid level:

BARNES EVENTS CO. MAKES A CHRISTMAS COMEBACK WITH HOLIDAY CHARITY

Miles Knocks stands front and center at a toy drive gala.

He's in plaid capris.

I could crush this phone with my fist.

Sonia writes:

This wasn't on the main schedule. Looks like Knocks kept this one all for himself and BuzzWhir.

My stomach sinks. I can't even form a reply.

I stuff my phone into my pocket and walk the festive rows of trees, trying to keep busy, distract myself from all the new feelings mingling in my core.

The disappointment of possibly losing a promotion I've worked years for. The reminder that losing that new position won't just impact me, it'll make things harder for Sonia, too.

Up ahead, Rachel disappears into the barn, and I brace against some knee-jerk instinct to chase after her.

Because despite every logical reason I should fight tooth and nail for my job, losing her for New York just might kill me.

It's becoming clear that there may be no real way to win.

CHAPTER 24

We barely beat the weather before finishing the day's tasks. Now, it's just me and my cold ass, sitting on Rachel's covered porch, trying to forget Sonia's texts and anything associated with my job. The landscape is a worthy distraction. Snow covers our hard work in layers of white, and lights glow beneath the wintry veil, making the sprawling forest seem touched by magic.

"You could have waited inside, you know." Rachel comes out from her cabin with two steaming mugs.

She's awash in buttery light, and it takes me a minute to form words. "It's actually nice to remember what it feels like to be cold and watch the snow fall," I say, inching over to make room for her on the step.

She sits, warming my whole right side. I take the mug she hands me, and heat runs up my arms. "Oh my god, this smells amazing. What's in it?"

She glances at her own red mug. "Whiskey, honey, a squeeze of fresh orange, and this juniper berry simple syrup I make."

"Step aside, Tanner!"

Rachel chuckles. My worries ease a bit as I sink into this moment with her, by her side.

I take a sip and savor the taste of Christmas on my tongue, let it warm me up as it goes down, burning in the best way. "Are you trying to get me drunk, Reed?"

She nuzzles into me. "Only if you want to be."

I lean in right back. "It feels good to be away from the city. To take time off like this." I shove work from my mind. It's too complicated to unravel right now, and I don't even know if I want New York anymore. There's no sense in bringing it up with Rachel yet, when it's all too foggy to see clearly. I can sit on this. I can tell her later.

"Funny that I'd have to come to the city to get a break." She laughs and angles in closer, cold air framing our little bubble of warmth. I take her hand without a breath of hesitation, and we weave our fingers together, cling tight. "I don't remember the last time I took time off." She smiles. "I'd love to do that with you."

I trace my thumb over hers and smile, remembering how Johanna wanted me to take a vacation so badly. I never dreamed it would turn out like this. "Rach, you should. I don't even remember you taking a break in high school. You were always so busy with the farm."

"I think that was partly why I picked a school in LA. It felt like a vacation, but it was close enough that I didn't need a plane ticket to get home last-minute."

I squeeze her hand. "I'm sorry I didn't see you when you were there."

She shakes her head. "I don't think we would have been ready for that, you know?"

I nod. "Things worked out at the right time."

"They really did." She nudges me with her shoulder. "Plus, you may not have liked me back then. I was . . . a bit of a player."

I lean back, my eyebrows shooting up my forehead. "Rachel Dawn Reed."

Her cheeks turn crimson. "It's true. I never dated anyone for more than a week. And my weeks were booked. One after the other."

I snort. "I mean, I get it. When I first moved to the city, I burned through three dating apps before settling down as single. It was a novelty, all the new people."

She opens her mouth to speak, then stops, shakes her head.

"What?" I ask.

"No, I don't . . ."

"You can tell me."

She takes a deep breath, then lets her words spill out: "I thought they'd all help me get over you. They didn't. No one's laugh warmed me from the inside like yours. No one looked at me in that gentle way you do that instantly reassures me everything will be okay. No one's voice was as sweet as yours, presence as easy as yours. They made me miss you more." She stops and takes a shuddering breath, and the corner of her eye glimmers. "And I know you'll have to leave, Mor. I know you have to go back to the city. I just . . . however we can do this, I want to make it work."

Before I can process her words, respond at all, she puts her mug down beside mine, leans in, and kisses me hard, cradling the back of my head in her palms. She tastes like the honey from her drink and the salt from her tears, and I try to comfort her with my wordless lips. I never want her to hurt again.

After a while, our kisses slow and we pull back, touching foreheads. I draw her head into the crook of my neck and let her rest there as long as she needs.

My words perch on the tip of my tongue until I can't hold them back any longer. "So, what's next?" I ask, voice hoarse. "I mean, now that we're saving the town and all?" I try to play it off. Big, life-uprooting decisions can wait. Just long enough to sort them out for myself.

Rachel lets out a small laugh, and it's music to hear. Then she sighs like she's relieved I asked first. She sits upright and squeezes my hand. "I . . . hope you don't disappear?" Her tone is teasing, but her eyes crinkle with a concern that grips my chest.

"I never want to disappear from you," I say. Surprise trickles through me at how easily the truth slipped off my tongue. How I almost said, *I never want to leave you.*

She clutches my hand and stares down at our fingers. "When I was in high school, my mom wanted to leave my dad. I begged her not to. Cried for days straight. I couldn't bear the thought of being without her. So when I left for LA, it was like she took my move as the permission she needed to leave, too. And I wonder, if I didn't ask her to stay when I was younger, could their separation have been smoother? Would she have at least chosen to live on the same coast as us?"

I reach up and wipe her cheek with the pad of my thumb. "Rachel, you can't do that to yourself. It's not right, and it's not fair."

She nods, eyes still downcast. "I know that, I do, but it's why I'll never ask you or anyone to stay for me again. It has to be your choice, or there will always be a part of me that hates myself for asking."

I swallow hard. "Is that what you want? For me to stay here?"

She sighs. "I just want you to be happy. All I want is you, whatever that looks like."

Emotion floods my chest with suffocating pressure. I don't know what I can live with giving up: my career, or Rachel. It's impossible to choose. I can't right now. No matter how much I want to ease her mind, give my heart instant gratification. "Whatever comes next, I'll talk to you about it first, okay?"

Rachel nods, and I wish I could give her more answers now, but this is the best I can do until I can think everything through.

We kiss again, a firm promise between our lips. We're in this together.

"There is something really serious I need to mention, though," she says, rubbing a hand down my back.

I tense for bad news. Hope we can turn it around. I'm so glad she's opening up to me like this. I never want it to stop.

She gets an evil glint in her eye. "It's been way too long since you've had a snowball fight."

Before I can prepare, she runs her hand along the step and crushes a ball of snow on my shoulder, flecks of ice spraying my cheek.

"Oh yeah?" I laugh and jump to my feet, run down the steps into open snow. "Muscle memory is a thing." I scoop up a handful, press the powder until it compacts, and let it fly. It bursts against her thigh, and her look of shock makes my heart soar.

She descends the steps in one stride, flinging another snowball that erupts at my hip, and oh, it is on.

Each one of our laughs softens the nudge of the future.

I wish the present could last forever.

All I want to do is be here, with her, pretend like nothing else exists.

A fire comes over me, and I rush at her so fast, we fall into the snow, laughing.

She brushes my hair from my face and kisses me softly. But I don't want soft. I want to feel this. I want this to make a mark. To last.

I pull her up by her collar, straddle her, crush my lips to hers, and bite as I pull away.

Rachel growls in a way that makes my fingers claw through the roots of her hair.

In a flash, she wraps her arms around my ass and stands, carrying me as I cinch my legs around her waist, devouring her mouth with mine.

"I'm gonna tear these wet jeans off you," she says in a rough, scratchy voice I want to memorize.

"I'm wet underneath, too," I moan into her ear.

"Fuck," she says, struggling to get the door open.

We're inside, and I vaguely register the honeyed light, the

crackle of a fire, the pine and woodsmoke scent of her space, as we kick off our boots by the door, rip off our snow-damp socks.

Rachel bumps backwards into the sofa, and I work my legs around her so I'm kneeling on the arm of the couch, pinning her between my thighs.

Her hands roam the length of my back, and I wrench off my coat, not caring to unbutton it. Let it tear apart, I don't give a single fuck.

In one swift motion, her warm hands slip beneath my shirt and pull it over my head to land on the floor.

She cups my breasts, running her thumbs over the edge of my bra, her firm touch tracing a sweet heat on my bare skin. I throw my head back, savoring the pleasure. "More," I rasp.

When I look down her eyes turn hooded, and she wastes no time in pleasing me. My bra is cast off in a blink, and Rachel's perfect mouth is on my tits, hot and tantalizing. She flicks her tongue over a nipple, sucks with the slightest scrape of teeth that makes me tremble and clench my thighs around her.

My patience is worn. I need her now.

I slide off her lap, the pressure against my center making my core tighten.

Taking her hand, I pull her toward the hallway. "Guessing the bed's this way?" I ask, leading her along.

"It is," she says, voice husky. Her free fingertips graze the small of my back, like she can't stand to not be touching me.

We enter her room, and I didn't think anything could distract me from her hands on my skin, but *holy shit*. "Rach," I say, completely awestruck. I let my arms fall to my sides as my bare toes sink into the plush rug. "These are stunning." I approach the nearest wall and run my fingers along the edge of one of the hundreds of sketches that cover the surface. Moonlight filters in through a window, and strings of fairy lights illuminate each work of art.

This one is of a pinecone she's somehow made into a minuscule world, each scale drenched with detail. I scan the room, my body humming with a new kind of desire. This is Rachel. Every thought and emotion displayed across these walls. There are landscapes and portraits, watercolors and sketches, still lifes and miniatures, covering every inch of space.

"You are so talented. You could make a killing selling these in LA."

"They're just for me, really," she whispers. "An outlet."

I turn in a circle, not wanting to miss a thing, to soak her in. Then one image makes my breath catch. I walk toward it in a daze, fingers pressed to my lips.

"Morgan . . ." Her voice is soft as I near the portrait. The portrait of me.

The paper is crisp and white, and the sketch isn't faded. I remember this. When I stared into my coffee mug, sitting on that log at Fern Falls Peak. The first official meeting we had about the fundraiser. She caught a soft expression, my lip turned up at the corner. My profile is softly lit by the sunrise. I imagine her looking at me in that moment and clutch my hands to my aching chest.

Rachel's breath caresses my neck. "I'm sorry if this is too much. If seeing this makes you uncomfortable."

Her face is mere inches from mine. I reach up and smooth the worry lines above her cheek with my thumb.

"I just—" She takes a deep breath and takes me in, the intensity of her gaze making my skin heat. "I've cared about you for so long, Morgan. I don't know how to show you that without overwhelming you."

I cup her face with my palm as the edges of my vision blur. "For the first time in my life, I feel nothing but cherished." The words tear a sob from my throat.

She pulls me in. "You are cherished. You always have been." She presses kisses to my forehead, my temples.

"I've wanted this for so long, too," I continue, voice bolder now, "to know what you feel." I look up and drown in the depth of her eyes, their complete openness. "I want to be over-whelmed by you. All of you."

No sooner are the words out of my mouth than Rachel backs me up to the bed, and we fall upon the cloud-soft white com-forter.

She peppers kisses along my hairline, my cheeks, my neck, whispering lovely things into my skin. "You're beautiful." *Kiss.* "In every way." *Kiss.* "You deserve—" *Kiss.* "every wonderful thing."

All the pieces of my shattered heart I've tried so hard to hold together are laid bare before her, and somehow, with each press of her lips, murmur of her voice, I let go. She can have all of me. I don't want to hold back anymore.

I take her beautiful face in my hands.

Her gaze softens, then turns hungry. Chills race over me, peaking my nipples.

She crushes her lips to mine.

This kiss isn't tentative or exploratory; it devours. It's hun-ger and passion and heat. Her tongue strokes mine in demand-ing, greedy pressure. I take her bottom lip between my teeth and pull, ushering a low growl from deep in her throat, before molding my mouth to hers. Then she's on top, her knee braced between my legs, pressing where I need her most.

My pants are too tight, too constricting, a barrier between us I suddenly despise. "Get me naked," I pant into her mouth. She smiles against my lips, then backs up so I can sit.

I raise my hips and she tugs down my jeans, my panties. Her fingertips trace sparks along my thighs.

She stands, her gaze falling steady on my bare body. "God, you are so fucking beautiful, Morgan."

Pleasure courses through me at her words, at her pure appre-ciation. The way she drinks me in, makes me feel. *Cherished.*

I wrap my hands around her hips, press my lips above the waist of her pants. She smells so good. Earthy and sweet. When she takes in a sharp breath, I smile, pausing just long enough that she takes over again. Back in control, she bends down and kisses me hard, pressing me into the mattress, until I lie flat, held in her embrace and feather-filled blankets.

I gasp as she crawls up the length of my body, moves her mouth down my neck, my chest, kisses along the curves of my swelling breasts. My nipples bead harder, and the ache between my legs pulses with desire. "Rach," I breathe. "I want you." I claw at her back, snaking my reach beneath her top. "Now."

She smirks and shakes her head, staying my hand with a touch. "I want you first." Then she drags her fingers up my arms and raises them above my head, pinning me gently as she nuzzles into my neck and whispers, "I'm going to make you come so hard you see stars."

Holy fuck. Rachel Reed will be the death of me.

Her words shoot straight to my center, sparking the deepest parts of me with pleasure.

I become something wild. Moving my arms from beneath her hands, I kiss her so fiercely, so hard, I don't know where I end. I try to shift, to get on top, let my mouth have what it wants, all of her, but she presses against me and crawls backwards, her kisses making me shiver as she moves down, down.

Then she stops and tilts her head up. Her gaze is hot and dark beneath angled brows.

The shift sends a thrill through my core. I lunge at her again, but she holds up a finger. I don't dare defy that finger. I lean back on my elbows, and a wicked smile pulls at her lips. She hovers above me, then moves her attention to my breasts, taking each nipple in her mouth, one by one, painfully slow, circling and flicking with her tongue.

My breaths come hard and fast, and my whole body clenches with need. "Oh my god," I gasp, as I let my head fall back.

"I could kiss your body forever," she says, voice raw. She lightly traces the outline of my stomach and hips, nearly making me come with her touch alone.

I gasp for air. For more. "Rach—"

She smiles as her fingers reach the crest of my sex.

"Please," I moan, not caring how I beg.

She strokes my entrance with increasing pressure, driving me dangerously close to the edge. "Oh my god, yes."

Her fingers slide right where I need them, working the base of my clit so good, I nearly scream. Heat flushes my face.

Then she moves so fast, my breath catches. In a blink, she's kneeling before me at the edge of the bed. She tugs me down like I weigh nothing, firmly cradling my ass as she covers me with her mouth.

The instant pleasure is so intense I scream her name. She grins against my thighs. Then her fingers slip inside me. Slow at first, then pulsing. She circles my apex with her tongue and licks me up and down and in and out, in perfect sync with her touch. Blissful warmth seeps into every inch of my body.

"I love the way you taste," she moans.

I grip the comforter so hard, I might tear it.

Without warning, she pulls back, and cool air floods the heat between my legs.

There's that devilish smile again. My sex pulses so hard, my body begs for her. "Oh my god," I breathe, and reach out, but she gently presses a hand to my chest, letting it drag between my breasts, down the center of my torso, until her palm comes to rest on my pelvis. That one stroke makes me fly. I would commit crimes for this girl.

Then her mouth is between my legs again, urgent and hard. That pause she forced heightened my senses. Every part of me screams with desire.

I grip her arms, digging in, as her tongue works in magical ways. Euphoria fills my veins, making me hot and liquid, seizing my core while the rest of my body succumbs.

She slips her fingers inside me, beckoning my most sensitive spot. The tip of her tongue circles outside, and I can't hold back.

The lights along her wall blink in and out like tiny shimmering stars as my orgasm crashes through me, flooding me with pleasure so intense, my whole body is alight, every nerve its own orbit of ecstasy.

Rachel holds my hips as the bliss lingers, dragging out long and sweet.

Once I still, she lies beside me, tracing her fingers up and down my arm, as my breaths return to normal.

"You're gorgeous when you come," she says, her voice gravelly.

I turn onto my side to face her, insatiable need returning to my core. She kisses me soft and slow as my hands and body grow eager for her.

Savoring every inch of her bare skin, I run my fingers beneath her shirt.

Her lips break from mine, and she pants, eyes clenched shut. "I nearly came when I brought you into this room." She bites her lip like she's trying to hold back and presses her forehead to mine. "I'm so gone over you, sweetheart, you'll push me over the edge in an instant."

I flash my own wicked smile and flip her onto the mattress in a single motion, crawl on top, inch her back until she's pressed against the pillows.

Her eyes widen with anticipation and I feel like a damn god, solely dedicated to pleasuring this beautiful woman.

"I'm not letting you off that easily." I peel down her jeans, kissing the insides of her thighs as they're revealed, soft and sweet, and toss the pants to the floor. "Or, should I say, getting you off."

"Morgan," she gasps, head pressing back.

This thrill could turn me feral. I want to make her scream my name.

Being with Rachel fills me with a confidence I've never known. Each time teaches me something new about her, and about me. How if I kiss right here, this spot just inside her right thigh— There. She rewards my work by arching against my mouth and crying out.

Hungrily, I run my palms up the length of her until my fingers are splayed beneath her top. I kiss her navel as she braces up on her elbows, and the fabric strips away before me as I pull it above her head, each arm, off.

I'm wet all over again at the sight of her.

Rachel Reed lies naked beneath me, bathed in moonlight.

I bend low and ghost my lips over her collarbones, her gorgeous breasts. "You're perfect," I whisper as I brush my fingers over the points of her nipples, gently squeeze. She hisses through her teeth, and I respond by kissing a line down her stomach.

Her thighs clench around my hips. I don't have much time to draw this out for her, so I make it the best I can give.

I race my hand down her sex—holy fuck, drenched and ready for me—and press my fingers to her clit, circling back and forth in firm, demanding strokes.

She grips the pillows and moans, like words are beyond her reach. I pulse my fingers right where they are as I command, "Come for me, Rachel." Then I plunge my mouth between her legs. She grips the roots of my hair and cries out louder, quelling any nerves I have about my inexperience.

I run my tongue along her entry, tasting her. Savory and sweet. I did this to her body. This is how I affect her. The thrill of it undoes me. Urgently, I wrap my free arm around her ass, bracing her, and pulse my fingers along the length of her wetness, letting my tongue explore and stroke and circle, soaking in the perfect flavor of her.

She whimpers, and I pause. Smile against her thighs.

"Oh my god, oh my god," she pants, and all my nerves spike with want.

Then I press my tongue against the swollen bud of her desire and push my fingers deep inside her.

She grips my shoulders like I'm the only thing tethering her down. Her muscles tense, and her body wracks beneath mine as she screams my name. It's the sweetest thing I've heard in my life.

I lift up and take in the stunning sight of her. Her breasts heave, thighs tremble. Sweat glistens her glorious curves, that majestic swollen pussy. My sweet girl came like a legend. She trusted me to do this, to take her to this most vulnerable place.

And god, I trust her right back. With every part of me.

I soothe her with my hands as her orgasm subsides, caressing her hips with firm pressure. "I've got you," I say.

A tear falls into her hair.

"Rach . . ." I whisper, leaning in, my own eyes brimming.

"And I've got you." She tugs me down and kisses me savoringly, letting our lips linger together.

We close in as tight as we can, and wrap the blankets around us, while those soft lights sparkle above.

I'm so safe, so utterly home in her arms, that there's no boundary to where I end and she starts. There's only warmth and joy and . . .

In that fragile hazy space before sleep, there's a whispered, *I love you.*

And I can't tell if it's Rachel's voice or mine.

CHAPTER 25

Light eases in through the curtains, and I blink against the glint of snow dripping from a pine outside Rachel's window.

I love being in her room, her bed, her sheets. I pull the linens to my chest as I sit up.

Her artwork is even more beautiful in daylight.

Most of the sketches are filled in with soft watercolors, and that's the whole aesthetic of her work: whimsical and dreamy. It brings a smile to my lips, because it's a whole other part of her. Something so different from her wood-chopping, snow-stomping moods. I love all of her sides.

Clanging sounds from the kitchen, announcing exactly where she is and what she must be doing. Then a waft of smoke and a rasped *"Shit"* confirm it.

I laugh and grab a flannel shirt from her bedpost. A green-hued pattern that reaches to my thighs when I wrap it around me and pad barefoot down the hall.

Separate from the main house she grew up in farther up the farm, this guest home is where we used to have sleepovers when we got older. I force a deep breath. This must have been where she went to get away from her parents' fighting, her dad's drinking. No wonder she didn't want to live in the main house anymore.

Her living room is airy and simple. The log walls are mostly bare, except for her guitar in the corner and a trio of art above the sofa: a clean-lined sketch of a pine-crested mountain range that spans three frames, definitely her style. She must have painted these.

On my way to the kitchen, I pass a potbelly stove that glows with a low-burning flame, but this isn't the source of the smoke.

Precious Rachel stands at the sink, steam hissing as running water hits a hot pan. Wisps of dark hair hang loose from her ponytail. Flowy gray pants sling low on her hips, and I swallow at the bare skin peeking from where the hem of her tank top crawls up the small of her back. This is the first time I've seen her in pajamas since we've been together like this, and something about it is more intimate than anything. This is the Rachel the rest of the world doesn't get to see, yet here I am. Warmth floods my chest, and I lean against the wall, crossing my arms. I want to wake up to this view every single day.

My throat tightens.

How many more days do I have with her? How much more time do I have in this town . . . on this coast?

She turns around, smiling in that crooked way that replaces the weight on my mind with a smile on my lips. Her voice is soft when she says, "I wanted this morning to be perfect when you woke up, so I tried cooking." She winces at the scene, dishes piled across the counters. "Obviously, I failed miserably, but . . ." She rushes to the coffee maker, where two steaming cups wait. "I did succeed at the most important thing." Rachel comes to me and hands me my mug. I take it in my hands and breathe in the rich sweet scent. "Oh my god, did you add vanilla to this? And cinnamon?"

She nods. "To the coffee grounds. I thought you'd like it."

"You always know exactly what I like."

Her eyes roam the length of me, making it apparent how very

bare my legs are. "You do, too," she says, her husky tone raising goosebumps along my skin. She leans in and presses a kiss to my neck, and those tingles turn to a maelstrom of want.

Setting my coffee on the counter, I kiss her back greedily. Chills race up my arms as I run my fingers along the small of her back. "Listen," I pant, "you're so thoughtful and went to so much trouble"—I reach for her hand—"and I'm really looking forward to enjoying this coffee, but truly . . ." I kiss each of her knuckles one by one, then press my lips against the inside of her wrist. "Right now, all I want is you."

I have a split second to witness Rachel's lips tip into a slanted smile before her mouth is on mine, hot and firm. Our tongues explore each other's mouths with desperate, seeking strokes.

This is all I want when I wake up. Forever. For always. The need to hold on to her—to us—makes me pull her in close.

We trip to the couch we scandalized last night and fall back onto the soft cushions. I catch a quick glimpse of the painting above us. "Wait, Rach," I say, hating to stop this even for a second, but I'll forget to ask if I don't now.

"Hmm?" Her gaze is hazy, lips red.

"These paintings, you made them?"

"Yeah." She sits up, brushing some hair from her face, and her cheeks pinken. "Do you like them?"

"I love them. And I know a lot of other people would, too."

"I don't know."

"Do you have any you'd be willing to sell?"

"Maybe? I have some in my closet, if you want to take a look? Maybe I'll get to it one day."

"Don't doubt yourself, Reed. You're amazing."

"Yeah?" She smiles, getting that evil glint in her eye that promises ultimate pleasure.

"Oh god," I say, laughing, "don't you dare—"

But before I can feign protest, her lips meet my thighs, and I fall back into the couch, clutch a throw pillow, and don't care if my coffee goes cold.

CHAPTER 26

My stomach is made of sparklers. Each time I think of to-night's fundraiser, my nerves zing.

At least I've got my armor on: the black power slacks I wear to each event. I run my hands down the waist-high cotton. Paired with my ankle boots, jade-green blouse, and thick, hi-low lavender cardigan, I stand tall and confident. Not even Christy can mess with me tonight. There go those sparks again. I fiddle with the ends of my hair and focus on the soft music lilting among the scenery. Every branch is aglow with dreamy light.

From where I stand at the kiosk, each themed pathway fans out before me. My eyes roam over the beautiful signs that Rachel painted, strung from pine-draped arbors, leading to trees overflowing with decorations. There's Hallmas (a mix of Halloween and Christmas) and Wizards and Witches for magic fans. Superheroes and Sci-Fi claim another; then Shared Joy, with trees decorated for families who celebrate multiple holidays: Hanukkah and Kwanzaa, to name a couple. There's Rustic Charm for nature lovers. Colors of Us boasts trees decorated with the colors of Pride flags. Rope lights border each snowy path we combed and widened for added accessibility.

Every tree is marked with a numbered plaque for auction, and a few small podiums are at the front, where volunteers stand ready to take bids. After the fundraiser, winners will be called and arrangements made for them to collect their fully decorated trees.

There's a fundraising meter on a board that, thanks to Tanner's contribution from bar proceeds the night of last Saturday's festival, is already off to a great start. A red arrow points to a painted evergreen trunk, marking twenty percent.

I swallow as I take in the grounds and hope the surprise I have for Rachel goes over well.

I check my watch, then the parking lot. Twenty minutes until opening, and the only cars here belong to those of us running Enchanted Evenings.

What if no one comes? My gut clenches. I can't let this flop. I can't let Rachel down.

Following the flat, well-lit path that leads to the barn, I head up to make sure the final touches are set, to busy my mind.

Maybe the select media Johanna invited is running late, navigating the mountain roads. The press announcement went out, so I have to trust in their love of a scandal and hope my complete humiliation with Chad McTannum will count for something.

Nearing the glow of the barn pulls me into the present a little more.

"I knew you'd pull this off." Adam greets me at the doors with the biggest smile. He's dressed completely in black, and every ounce of his natural charm. I swear his teeth sparkle. The Reeds are electric.

"I couldn't have done any of this without you," I say.

"Nah, it was nothing. I loved messing with the music and mechanics."

Ben is across the space, placing finishing touches on the tables. Every surface is adorned with sugary delights for the cake auction. Crystal-white, triple-tiered confections stun with candy glass snow globe toppers. Smaller cakes with sheer frosting have trails carved into the sides like a mountain, complete with layers of handcrafted chocolate pine trees. Among the larger offerings are tons of cookies, brownies, and savory treats to satisfy all appetites. His eyes dance when he places his hands on his hips, taking in his work.

"And I definitely couldn't have done this without him." I nod in Ben's direction.

Adam follows my gaze, and I don't imagine that his cheeks glow pink. Something in me warms. Like pride and hope. "He's amazing, you know."

Adam glances down at his shoes, and the corner of his lips tip up. "I know I didn't give you the warmest welcome when you arrived, but thank you for helping my sister. This has meant the world to her."

My heart lurches. "It's been good to be back," I reply, and mean it.

"We all hope you stay." He looks at me pointedly. "Especially my sister."

Forget sparklers. My stomach sets off a damn firework finale. "Do you think she'll like the surprise we have planned? I can't thank you enough for helping me with it."

He rubs the back of his neck and winces. "It couldn't have come at a better time, honestly."

"Wait, is she okay?" I ask, concern tightening my throat.

"Yeah, yeah." He nods. "Sorry to worry you; she's fine. It's just that our dad isn't going to make it tonight. He took a turn for the worse, and we're going to have to have another intervention. It's hard on her. I know she told you about it, I'm glad she did. Glad she doesn't have to shoulder it alone."

"Oh, god, Adam. I'm so sorry. Is there anything I can do for you? For Rachel?"

Adam's gaze catches over my shoulder as Rachel's voice sounds behind me. "There are plenty of things you could do for me, Ross, but none that I'd like to discuss in front of my brother."

I laugh as her arms wrap around my waist. She's acting normal, and that's reassuring. It also quells my nerves about tonight. I wish she knew how comforting her touch was, how she keeps me together at the seams. I turn and hold her arms, her biceps firm beneath my touch. "Are you doing okay? Adam just told me about your dad. I'm so sorry."

Her brows pinch together, but her eyes stay soft and bright. "I knew it was coming, so I was prepared. I'm okay, and Dad will be, too. But that can wait for another time. Tonight is for celebrating, yeah?"

She pulls me in close, and I rub my hands down her back.

"Speaking of celebrating," Adam says. "Now's as good a time as any. Right, Morgan?"

I smile, fighting back negative thoughts. She'll love this. She will. "C'mon," I say, stepping back. My jaw drops as I take her in. Her hair is long and loose, hanging past the breast pockets of her black leather coat. A white blouse peeks out from beneath, tracing the hem of her perfectly fitted, dark-washed jeans. She shifts her black boots in the snow and tucks her loose hair behind her ear, her cheeks blushing beneath those freckles.

"You're stunning," I breathe.

Her eyes glisten as she looks at me. "You are, always." She places a sweet, soft kiss on my forehead.

I run my hand down her arm, twine our fingers together, and gently pull her to the outdoor tent beside the barn, a large white canopy that the city brought in. Adam follows close behind, and it takes everything in me to not let Rachel feel my hand shake.

"What are you both up to?" she asks, following without hesitation.

We stop at the closed opening of the tent, where soft yellow light seeps through the panels.

"We wanted this to be a surprise." Adam smiles beside me.

I take her hands. "This is something I know you may need a

little push to do, but I really wanted to show you how much I believe in you. Like you have believed in me."

She cocks her head. "Mor, what did you—"

Adam sweeps the tent open, and a room filled with Rachel's artwork is revealed.

Her hands fall to her sides as she enters the space.

I follow, tethered to every move she makes. She doesn't even blink, just scans the walls, the easels. What did I do? Why did I push like this? "You told me these were ones you weren't particularly attached to, and I thought you could price them verbally as people come through. If this was too much, if I overstepped, we can keep the tent closed off to the public."

She presses a hand to her cheek, not tearing her gaze from the walls.

"Rach, I—"

"I'm sorry," she says, finally turning to me. "I don't have words."

"Okay," I say cautiously, "I can have all these taken back to the house right now. Adam?"

He nods sharply and goes to remove the first.

"No, wait," Rachel blurts.

Adam halts, places his hands in his pockets.

Rachel takes a deep breath, and I stop breathing all together.

"Morgan. No one has ever done anything like this for me."

"I'm sorry. I understand if you aren't ready." Tears sting my eyes.

"No." She shakes her head. "No one has ever thought enough of me, been so proud of me, to show me off in this way."

My sigh of relief comes out jagged and broken. I swipe at my eyes.

"I don't know how to accept it, how to be in the spotlight." Her voice is soft.

I pull her in close. It's a challenge to be the comforting one when we're standing, because she's a whole head taller. But she nuzzles her cheek into my hair, and maybe that's as reassuring to her as snuggling into her shoulder is to me. "You deserve to be admired for all your talents."

"I love you," she says. It's so soft. A breath in my ear that almost brings me to my knees.

I whimper into her neck, "I love you, too."

We hold each other as if the night has nothing more to demand of us. Nothing else matters. Rachel . . . loves me.

"Ahem," Adam clears his throat, making us pull apart just the slightest amount.

He swipes at the corner of his eye. "Sounds like they're ready for you two out there."

Rachel takes a deep breath and holds out her hand. "Ready?"

"As I'll ever be." I weave our fingers together and clutch tight.

We exit the tent, and . . . oh my god. A long line is forming at the kiosk, and more cars pull into the lot. I let out a small shriek. Take that, Vaughn Enterprises.

Whitney waves from behind the counter, and Tanner is beside her, accepting donations and handing out tickets. He's taken a break from overseeing the bar he constructed beside the entryway, a warm, sleek welcome of a pine counter decked out in string lights and draped in fresh greenery. Even from here, his employees and volunteers can be seen passing out glasses filled with a sparkling, deep red concoction he named after Enchanted Evenings.

Closer to the trees, several volunteers staff the auction podiums, and others monitor the line into the barn.

"Where are you most comfortable?" I ask, turning to Rachel.

"Honestly, I was anxious to be in the crowd, but everything is running so smoothly, and you've given me a space I can feel at home in through all this."

I grin, peeking back into the tent one last time. Guests are already making their way toward us. "I'll check in with you in a bit?"

She smiles, squeezes my hand. "Sounds amazing."

She kisses me softly, her lips lingering on mine. "Thank you for this. Are you sure you're okay?"

"Please." I smile, thrilled that I can give something back to her for all she's done for me. "This is what I do."

"And you're so fucking good at it, and I'm so fucking proud of you and so grateful, no matter the financial outcome, okay?" she says, grinning simply, as if she doesn't know how much confidence she just bolstered me with. Then she heads back into the tent as people follow. Their praises hit my ears. Rachel thanks them with the same mouth that just professed her love for me not moments ago, and my heart soars. No matter what happens tonight, I've already won.

Now, to make sure the farm wins, too.

I spend the next hour or so walking the grounds. Children's laughter echoes among the trees, spiking when the lights pulse in time to a rock cover of "Have Yourself a Merry Little Christmas." Rainbows sparkle off every ornament and hold a steady beam for the lyrics of *make the yuletide gay*. I throw my head back, laughing as joy bubbles through me. Adam freaking nailed it.

The crowd grows fast. Families mill through the paths, taking photos at the booth we set up with *Enchanted Evenings at the Reed Family Tree Farm* on a step-and-repeat, a table with festive props laid out beside it. People fill the barn, and the line at the kiosk stretches as more cars enter the parking lot.

Suddenly, a familiar face pops out from the crowd, and I might cry all over again. "Morgan, this looks incredible," Dad says when he reaches me, dressed in jeans and boots and . . . oh my god. A bright green sweater that says, FOLLOW ME TO ENCHANTED EVENINGS AT THE REED FAMILY TREE FARM.

"Dad, you had this made? It's amazing!" I say as I hug him. This is the first of my professional events he's been to and his support means everything, and calms my nerves.

A smile splits his face. "Nothing but hype for the best planner in the biz! I knew you'd pull this off in a big way."

My chest swells, especially at his very Dad-like phrasing. I've wanted him to be proud of me for so long. But the magazines in his office, the articles he shared with Mrs. Hart. Maybe he has been. This whole time.

His grin broadens. "And you should know, I swung by the inn for some of Mrs. Hart's famous eggnog, and that place was poppin'."

"Poppin'?" I snort.

"They had to open up their overflow rooms to accommodate all the folks here for the fundraiser."

I glance up the hill, where the lights of the inn glimmer down, and I smile as if I'm there. "Dad, that's amazing."

"This place is important. It means a lot to our town. You've made it shine and reminded me of that." He looks around. "You've reminded all of us."

Emotion springs to my eyes, and I clear my throat. "That's all I could hope for."

"Welp, that barn is calling to my stomach." He says, rubbing his ribs. "Can I bring you back anything? Did you get to eat yet?"

Warmth floods me at his care. "I'd love a snack," I say. "Whatever you pick out."

He smiles and turns toward the barn. "Be right back, Sunshine."

I smile after him.

But as he passes by the fundraising meter, I catch a glimpse of that red arrow, and my optimism wavers. We're only halfway up the tree, and the night is half over.

"Excuse me, are you Morgan Ross?" I turn to find a man in a crisp suit with a camera slung over his neck.

"I am."

"I'm Ky Bryant from the *LA Times*. May I take a photo of you and ask a few questions about this event?" He has dark brown skin and a bright smile that lifts his glasses.

My heart leaps. Johanna always comes through. "Nice to meet you. Yes, that would be great."

He pulls out a notepad. "May I ask what inspired such a cinematic event? With the synchronization of the lights and music, it's not something you'd expect to find in a tucked-away town like this, and has drawn a crowd most wouldn't anticipate, either."

My heart expands in my chest as I look around. Adam grooves behind the switchboard, hands cupping his headphones as he mixes different holiday songs together; Whitney and Tanner are engaged in conversation with customers at the kiosk; Ben is just visible through the doors of the barn; and a line stretches from the art tent, where I know Rachel is in her element with tons of new clients. Fern Falls is not what I expected it to be. They didn't need some hotshot event planner to come in and save them; they had the resources all along. I swallow hard. Maybe I was the one who needed them to save me.

I focus on Ky. "This town is what inspired everything. The resiliency of the people, their unique talents and visions—Enchanted Evenings is something homemade and truly speaks to the heart of Fern Falls. It's bright, united, progressive, and dynamic."

My gaze shifts from Ky's notetaking as I spot another reporter behind him. Sweat beads on his pale lip, he glances around skittishly, and the placard around his neck is from a tabloid. My heart races. The paparazzi arrived after all, and they definitely weren't invited by Johanna.

"And how can I help you?" I call past Ky.

"I, uh, Ms. Ross? I'm Richard with *BuzzWhir*, and I have a few questions for you about your relationship with Chad McTannum."

I freeze.

Not far behind him is Christy, arms folded, squinting at us from the Hallmas path.

I hold her gaze, that courage from my girlfriend and my dad bracing me.

Nodding sharply at Richard, I address Ky again. "Mr. Bryant? I'd also like to add that Fern Falls is worth saving. Vaughn Enterprises, the corporation that has monopolized Snow Hill, the next town over, is looking to do the same here. Maybe that is something you could add to your article?"

"Oh, absolutely. Especially at this time of year, folks are looking to preserve wholesome and meaningful efforts."

"Thank you." I shake Ky's hand. "And Richard?" I say, fixing him with a glare, "Why don't you and Mr. Bryant here head up to the tent beside the barn." I point to the canopy that houses Rachel's artwork. "You'll both find lots of material to report on a promising new artist from this wonderful town. Like Ky pointed out, wholesome and meaningful is what people actually care about."

Richard reluctantly follows the *Times* reporter, and I smirk at Christy as I head to the kiosk to help sell tickets. She stares at me but seems unaffected, just cinches her white fur coat around her waist.

I can only hope she doesn't have any more sabotages planned.

But an hour later, we tally up the earnings, and the way my stomach drops feels like an attack itself.

Even after the amazing bids Rachel's artwork brought in, and the tree and cake auction, ticket sales, and food and drink efforts, we're still short of our goal, and not by a little.

I spare a glance at Christy, who lingers at the edge of the crowd.

My throat constricts.

I failed. After everything, it doesn't matter. I'm still the girl with nothing who can't hold her own against those with more. I failed Rachel, and I have no idea how I'll tell her without falling apart.

Before I can form a plan, a familiar face appears in my path. It's my neighbor, Ms. Holloway. Her silver hair is long and freed from its perpetual bun, hanging to the hem of a royal purple shawl.

"Ms. Holloway?" I blurt. "How are you?"

My quirky neighbor holds a giant bag at her side, covered in the pink, purple, and blue stripes of the bi pride flag.

"Fine, fine," she says, digging into her tote. "There's actually something I came to give you." She produces a thick envelope and hands it out to me. "Please. Take it."

I do what she says and open it to find a stack of cash inside. "Oh my god, Ms. Holloway, I can't—"

"You know," she says with a sly grin and twinkle in her eye, "most of the world knows me by my pseudonym, Becca Rae, the romance writer."

The cover of Mrs. Hart's book pops in my mind: Becca Rae's name emblazoned beneath the embracing couple. I smile as big as my face allows.

"Listen," she continues, "I'll admit that you and your girl-friend have provided me with lots of front porch inspiration over the past few weeks. This is my way of paying you back."

I laugh nervously.

"The world needs more queer holiday romances, don't you think?"

I smile big and true. "Absolutely."

"Well, then, you'd better keep this tree farm going. You know, to fuel the inspiration." She winks and nods at the donation.

"Thank you so much," I say, giving her a big hug.

She clears her throat and adjusts her purse on her shoulder. "There, there. It's my pleasure. Now let's see if it helped you meet your goal?"

I hand the envelope to Whitney, who mouths, "Becca Rae, oh my god," then counts the contents of the envelope.

When she's done, her expression is bright, but not the full-fledged joy I hoped to see. "We almost did it," she says, voice cracking. "We're so close."

I swallow my disappointment and turn to Ms. Holloway. I wouldn't want her to feel like her donation wasn't valuable, even though we didn't meet the goal. "Will you do us the honors?"

Heading to the fundraising meter, I wave Rachel over as she exits the tent.

When she reaches me, she's beaming. "We did it, didn't we?"

My smile wobbles, vision blurring as my cheeks turn wet. "Almost, Rach."

She squeezes my hand. "We couldn't have even gotten this far without you. We did our best; it's all we can do."

And it's all I can do to keep myself together as Ms. Holloway moves the fundraising meter just below full. Almost the right amount of funds to help the farm and Mrs. Hart fix up the inn to draw a different buyer. Almost successful. Almost enough.

I hate that I search out Christy, but some masochistic part of me wonders if she's gloating. But no matter where I look, she's nowhere to be found.

"I think this might be useful about now." Her voice sounds behind me.

Rachel and I turn to find Christy holding out a slip of paper.

Rachel takes it, and her eyes go wide. "Christy, what? Why would you . . ."

My blood boils. "You can't be satisfied with calling the paparazzi? Now you have to slap us with some bullshit fees? What's next? Are you going to confiscate puppies from this town? Ban donuts? Outlaw smiling?"

"No, Mor—" Rachel starts.

Christy holds up her hands. "I can't blame you for thinking the worst of me. It's all I've shown you since you returned, and since you were young, if I'm being honest. But here's the truth: You've inspired me, Morgan. Our conversation outside of The Stacks the other night, you saw right through me. Everything about pursuing this land has felt desperate to me, small. One last attempt to prove myself to my father. Well, I've decided I care more about what I think of myself than what he does. I'm not asking for forgiveness; I know it's too late for that. But please take this donation."

I stand staring at this woman like I finally see her for who she is. Insecure, trying to figure herself out in a world that expects her to know who she is already, that constantly demands she prove herself.

Not unlike me.

Before I can reply, Rachel wraps her in a hug.

Christy's eyes fling wide, but then she smiles, loosens.

"This means everything," Rachel says, stepping back.

I clear my throat. "How about we move that marker?"

Christy bursts into a smile, big and genuine, as she raises the meter to full.

Rachel takes my hands.

Everyone cheers, phones flash, but all I see is Rachel's sparkling smile and the tears of joy that trail down her cheeks.

Then the girl I love kisses me in the snow, before trees bedazzled with lights, and cameras and crowds and a whole wide world we made together.

CHAPTER 27

The atmosphere is so warm and bright, I hardly notice the cold. Families whoop and holler when their names are called for the tree auctions, and Whitney arranges pickups at the kiosk. Even after the bar closes, the lines into the barn and artwork tent weave through the trees. Volunteers at each end kindly let guests know the lines have been capped to accommodate our closing time and adhere to our permits. The tree lights gently fade in and out to soft music as patrons head to the parking lot.

"Gosh," Dad says, wrapping me into a hug, his sweater warm against my cheek. "I'm so proud of you." He pulls back, holding my gaze. "And Mom would be, too."

"Dad. Thank you." I hug him back. For all the times I've missed over the years.

Another voice sounds behind us. "It really was something, Morgan."

I freeze. It's Christy.

Dad and I part and stand side by side, taking her in.

She's bundled up, so just her face is visible through layers of white, furry fabric.

"You definitely surprised us all," Dad says quietly.

I want to thank her, but there is something that's bothering me. "Christy, if you planned on making a donation tonight, turning things around, then why invite the paparazzi?"

She shakes her head and takes a step forward. "I admit I've stooped low, but even I can't stand the bottom feeders of the media. It wasn't me who called them."

I think back on who else would have. Could it have just been a coincidence? Wait. Sonia's text about Miles and his toy drive. It was in *BuzzWhir News*. The same outlet that Richard was from.

Goddamn Miles Knocks.

I let out a long-suffering sigh.

Christy sweeps a hand at the scenery. "You did a fantastic job."

I can only gape at her words as Dad squeezes my shoulder and says, "She sure did."

I give my head a shake. "So, what now? What's Vaughn Enterprises' next move? What's yours?"

She smiles, her bright pink lips spreading wide. "Oh, Vaughn Enterprises will be fine. Snow Hill is thriving, and I'm sure my father will find other towns somewhere else to suck the souls out of." She winks, repeating my words from our icy reunion at the inn.

I squint at her. "What are you saying? Don't you want to build franchises, too?"

"Listen." She clears her throat. "I sacrificed happiness once." She glances at Dad. "I won't do it again, not to meet my family's impossible standards."

"What will you do?" he asks.

"Honestly?" She says with a laugh, "I'm moving somewhere warm. Somewhere I can maybe, I don't know, broker real estate deals for people seeking some ocean therapy and sunshine."

I bark out a shocked sound. "So you're quitting?"

She smiles. "I'm finally doing what I want. And it's all thanks to you, Morgan. All the effort you put into this fundraiser, into helping a whole town, into finding your own happiness. It made me want to do the same. So, thank you."

I shake my head as she turns and walks off toward the parking lot.

"That's one for the books," Dad says, patting my back.

"I don't know if I'm relieved or shocked? Both?"

"One thing's for certain, you saved this place, honey. You did it, and I'm so proud of you."

"Thank you, Dad." I hug him tight. "I'll see you . . ." I don't know when I'll return to Fern Falls after this. Rachel and I still need to sort it out, face the future we've been avoiding. Now that the fundraiser is over, the next thing on the schedule is to go back to LA. I swallow past a lump in my throat.

"I'll see you, too, Sunshine." Then he pats my back and heads to his car.

Before I can go to the tent to be with Rachel, my phone buzzes. I laugh. Of course, during such a special night, I find that one magical cell service spot.

My thumb freezes over the screen as it displays the name *Johanna Barnes*.

"Hello?" I say, fighting to keep my voice from jumping.

"Morgan?"

"Hi, Johanna."

"I am getting so many calls. You hit this event out of the park. Chad McTannum *who* is what I'm saying!"

Her voice lilts through the cold air like a summer breeze.

My breath catches at her words, at the hope they hold. "I'm so glad."

"The New York promotion is yours. It always was, and I couldn't wait another minute to make it official."

I grip my phone so hard, it might crack. Her voice rings in my ears like a winner's celebration. It's mine. The promotion is all mine. Oh my god. "Oh my god."

"So I'm taking that as a yes? You want to spearhead the new site?"

The thrill of triumph overcomes me. Sonia and I are finally getting what we deserve, what we've worked our asses off for. Miles Knocks can take his paparazzi stunt and shove it. "Yes!" I yell victoriously. "Yes, yes, yes!"

Johanna's bright laugh fills the air. "Good, then, it's settled. Take your break now, and once you're done, say, after Christmas, let's talk logistics about the move. I'll set you up with a relocation package."

"Thank you so much" is all I can seem to say.

"No, thank *you*, Morgan. Now go enjoy the rest of your night."

"You, too," I reply, tucking my cell into my pocket with a shaking hand.

I turn toward the barn, and my celebration is trampled by fear. Fear of what comes next with Rach. Fear of what I stand to lose.

I can't wait any longer. Now that it's official, I need to tell her.

My boots crunch through the snow as I approach the art tent.

Attendees surround the entrance, no one quite ready to stop staring at her beautiful work. I can't blame them.

"There she is! The planner of the hour!" Mayor Park comes up beside me, tote bag loaded with prints.

"Mayor, I can't thank you enough for everything. We couldn't have pulled this off without your support."

Her dark brown eyes shine. "Good news. I'm going to keep supporting this."

"What do you mean?"

"I just spoke with Rachel, and we want to make Enchanted Evenings into a city event held every weekend in December. And, thanks to your friend with the *LA Times* over there, I think we're about to have a huge increase in tourism." She nods to Ky Bryant, who smiles and waves from across the room, like he and the mayor are old friends.

My chest swells with joy. "That's fantastic!"

"It's brought in so much business for everyone, Morgan. The inn, the local shops, and especially the tree farm."

"Who knew that one event could help a whole town in this way," I say, my voice quiet.

"You did." She smiles. "And I thank you for sticking it out. We're lucky to have you."

I blush. "Happy holidays, Mayor Park."

The edges of her black bob sway forward as she nods. "And to you, Ms. Ross."

She heads toward the parking lot, smiling and stopping to chat with people along the path.

I make my own way through huddles of onlookers gathered to appreciate Rachel's art.

There's a line to approach her, and I happily take my place behind one of the newest members of the Rachel Reed fan club.

"Ms. Reed. Do you plan on expanding your business so people outside of Fern Falls can purchase your work? Online, perhaps?"

"I don't know yet," she replies. "I think a large part of the draw is the environment. And keeping it here lets people appreciate where it comes from. I'm not saying no, I'm just saying I don't know yet."

"Thank you for your time," the man says, turning to look at another portrait.

I step forward, and she instantly sweeps me up into a huge hug. "We did it, babe."

I smile against her shoulder. "We sure did," I say, pausing the news about the promotion. It can wait a moment. I can keep this one moment.

We stand side by side as Rachel thanks everyone for coming and shakes hands until the tent fully clears.

It's just the two of us now, and my time has run out. I can't stall this any longer. "Hey, Rach. Do you have a minute to talk?" My voice is so small. Scared.

"Of course. What's going on?"

I take a deep breath and get straight to the point. "I got a promotion at work."

"Morgan! That's amazing!" She pulls me into an embrace that makes the next part even harder.

"It's . . . in New York," I say quietly. "An opportunity to expand The Barnes Events Company on the East Coast."

She loosens her grip and steps back. "Okay," she says, searching my face. "Um, how long have you known about it?"

I clear my throat. "I knew where it was, but I didn't know if I'd get it—"

"Wait, what?" She looks as if I just slapped her. "So this whole time you knew you'd be moving across the country? The whole time we talked about the possibility of driving back and forth from here to LA?"

It occurs to me, it doesn't have to be either-or. This could all coexist, like I'd hoped. "It was never a sure thing until my boss called just now. After the past few weeks up here, I was questioning if I even wanted it anymore. But this could actually be a huge opportunity for both of us."

"How?" she asks, taking another step back.

I open my arms, gesturing at everything around. "Look at all the options you have now. The farm is taken care of. Whitney could run it, fully caught up on payments. You could come with me and take your chance at that vacation, you know? Regain that adventure you never fully got in LA? You could practice your art in New York and have the time to do what you love." The words make sense in my head, in theory, but even as I say them, my hope wavers. That image doesn't quite fit with the Rachel before me. She's strong and steady on this ground, in this community. But couldn't she be with me, too, if she gave it a chance? Why should I have to be the one to uproot and give up something I've worked so hard for? "Johanna is giving me a relocation package, and I could cover everything until you—"

"You think that's what I want?" Her voice is so quiet I have to strain to hear it.

My chest heaves. "Do you want us? Could you be flexible? Try this for me?"

"Of course I do. I—" She grips her hair at the roots. "How could you not tell me about this, Morgan? You could have. So many times. I thought we were being honest with each other. This just feels like something you intentionally hid. This whole time I was open with you, you planned on leaving. Like you did before. Like my mom."

My skin prickles in defense. I did this for *her*. "I didn't want to worry you. I didn't know that I'd get this promotion for sure until I pulled off this fundraiser."

Her face falls and I immediately know it was the wrong thing to say, but it's too late to take it back.

"So that was the only reason you offered to help with the farm? To get your promotion? And then you waited until I'd completely fallen for you to let me know that I could either change my entire life or see my girlfriend when I have the time and money for a five-hour flight? Morgan, this was real to me. More than anything. Was any of it real to you?"

I step back at her words. At how she could question me so easily, after everything we've shared. "Of course, god. Everything I told you was true. I want the best for you and this town, but I also love my career. I get that this is a big deal, and I didn't mean to blindside you, I'm sorry. I got excited thinking this could work, my dreams and yours together. Especially after everything you said on your porch the other night about wanting adventures. I thought you might want to take one with me. I thought you'd be happy for me."

She shakes her head. "I am. This just isn't what I pictured. You said we'd talk about everything, that we'd figure this out together. I want you to be fulfilled in your work, and I'm proud of you, but I feel whiplashed. New York is so far away. I just need a minute. This is a lot to take in."

I wince. Why would she need any time at all? The answer should be easy. Everything could work out if she wanted it to . . . if I was enough for her. My skin burns hot, and my body turns restless, like angry things want to claw out. "So, what? How does this work then? You expect me to give everything up? Everything I've worked seven years for? I know my city job is different for you, but it's given me so much. It gave me a place to belong when I needed it most. And now, am I just supposed to give that up? You want me to move back here? To this little town to do little things, make no money, and limit myself again?"

Rachel's eyes fling wide. "No. I honestly thought we'd go between here and LA for a while until we figured out a more permanent situation. But is that really how you see this place, so small and limiting still? After all we've built these past weeks? Do you see my life as something constricting? You said you cared about the farm. About Fern Falls."

"Rachel." My voice pitches high, rage pressing up against my chest. Can't she see that this is for her, too? "This could be an opportunity for you to pursue your passions, like you said you wanted to. To travel and visit places where a little tree festival isn't the biggest event of the year."

Rachel nods, tucks her hands into her pockets. Backs away.

Over her shoulder, people stare. When did a crowd gather? My cheeks flame as I try to angle away from them. That's when I spot Ben. He shakes his head and exits the tent, followed by Whitney and Tanner. Before they disappear, they all look at me like I'm a stranger.

Lead pummels my gut.

Here it is. The horror spurred by my high school graduation party, repeating. I ruined this all over again. Like I knew I would. Instantly, anger is replaced by something all too familiar: hollowness. "I—I'm sorry."

Rachel sighs. "You don't need to be sorry for how you feel about Fern Falls, for wanting to chase something bigger. I just . . ." She grips the back of her neck. "We're not on the same page. I love this place, this community. I don't want to leave it right now, like I don't want to sell my artwork outside of town, but you're pushing and—"

I step forward, raise on my heels to get closer to her face. "I love it here, too. But that doesn't mean it's the only place we have to love. There is so much more to the world, and I want you to do more for yourself. Pursue your own dreams instead of letting this place hold you down, letting your dad suck you dry."

Her whole body stiffens. "What the hell, Morgan? That's my family. I won't be someone who just leaves my family."

It's a blow. A final gutting. She won't leave her father like her mom did . . . and like I left mine.

I shake my head. "It's the truth, and you need to hear it." My voice is flat, gone.

"And what's the truth for you?" she says hoarsely. "You go to New York and live it up, and what makes you happy then? You came here completely miserable, with a life you claim you loved. But really, I never saw you happier than in the simple times we had together, reconnecting with everyone. Your friends, your dad. With me."

I swallow hard. "You never saw how successful I was in LA. How I had everything together."

"Did it make you happy, though?" Her voice is scratchy, tired.

"It made me feel like enough."

She sighs. "That's the thing. You've always been enough. But this"—she motions between us—"will never work if you don't see it, too."

A vise grips my heart. "You don't understand. You don't see what I need."

Her eyes search mine. Then she clenches hers tight and shakes her head. "Neither do you." Then she nudges past me, parting the crowd.

I reach for her. "Rachel, please, wait—"

The air leaves my lungs as she disappears beyond the tent doors.

Adam crosses my path, his face a wall of stone, brows pinched together. "Let her go, Morgan." He shakes his head. "God. When will you just let her go? Stop hurting her like this. This is the last time I'll let you."

He's out the door before I can reply. Not that I could. My lungs are empty. I'm empty.

I thought I made a difference here. I thought things could change. I—I don't belong. I never did.

Cold air assaults me as I exit the tent.

Ben stands before me, cheeks wet.

I swallow rising bile and step around him, not able to meet his eyes.

"Morgan, wait," he calls, following me down the path.

"I'm so sorry, Ben. I just . . ." Any excuse dies on my lips. "I'm sorry."

He catches up to me. "Please stay. Let her cool off. We'll get through this together. You have me, too."

The pain in his eyes is piercing, pain I put there. "I have to go."

He reaches for me. I step back.

Hurt flashes across his face. "You didn't just leave her that first time. And you're not just leaving her now." His voice cracks.

"Ben, that's not . . ." Not what? The truth? What is the truth, then? I took off the first time because I didn't belong here. I'm leaving now for the same reason. Nothing has changed. I haven't changed, no matter how much I've tried to.

His expression hardens over. "Fine. Just please don't let it take another seven years before I see you again."

He turns and walks away before I can speak.

I don't have anything left to say. All that comes out now is sobs.

Trudging down the pathway, cheery lights attack my steps, flash off the wet gravel of the parking lot.

I get into my car and pull away. The destruction I caused blinks bright in my rearview, burning through my heart.

CHAPTER 28

After leaving my rental cabin in a whir of tears and grocery bags used for extra suitcases, the grind of traffic and my nearly dead succulents welcome me home.

I give my favorite little haworthia a drink, then toss my belongings on the couch and curl up beside them.

All the sappy holiday movies are streaming, and because I'm leaning into this whole disaster form of myself, I watch four variations of people finding everlasting love beneath mistletoe until the sun is well and risen, and my eyes are gritty from lack of sleep and refuse to stay open any longer.

When I wake, it's that time of day that's either early evening or early morning. One look at my phone says it's the six p.m. kind of gray out, and I can't live like this, sleeping through entire days, lying on my couch in a perpetual fog.

I pick up my cell and pull up my text thread with Johanna.

How soon can I get back to work?

She replies in an instant:

Speak of the devil! I had an unexpected event come up, a

new client Miles booked on his own before he quit today. Sonia is busy. You're available? Are you sure you're ready to come back?

The current demise of my life is littered across my apartment. Dishes I left in my rush to get to Fern Falls are piled in my sink. Dying plants wilt in the window. Dust scurries in the sunbeams sulking through the blinds. *Are you still watching?* is frozen on my TV screen.

I go back to my messages. The last one from Rachel stabs afresh:

Last night was perfect. Just like you.

I can't believe how badly I fucked everything up, how badly it all ended in general. I let her down, just like I feared I would. But she let me down, too. I was never trying to up and leave her, and everything I said to her was genuine. My feelings are too much, too big to even pull apart right now. The only thing I can do is somehow try to function, distract myself.

I swallow hard, pull up Johanna's text, and hammer out:

I'm definitely ready to come back. As soon as possible.

She responds:

Okay! Pacific Park at 3:00 pm tomorrow. Can't wait to see you!

In few other places could a holiday event be held on a pier a week before Christmas. In other places, it's snowing. In other places, people are cuddled up by a fire, listening to their girl-friend strum her guitar. I shake the thought from my head and stop my arm from reaching for my phone, fighting the urge to text Rachel for the millionth time since I've been home. She hasn't written me, and I should respect her space. Even if it means she cuts me out of her life again. I wouldn't blame her this time.

The boardwalk creaks beneath the ladder as I string lights above the tables placed at the end of the pier. One last stretch, and the final strand is hooked on the pole we secured in a planter filled with poinsettias, wrapped with garland. The same garland that trims the carousel. The same that reminds me of evergreen branches. The scent of pine and woodsmoke. The taste of cinnamon.

"Morgan, this is our client, Marissa May." Johanna introduces me to a young white woman in a black, wide-brimmed hat, then walks away to fix something on the other side of the space. Garland, probably.

"Hi," I say, stepping down from the ladder, trying to at least appear alive.

I shake Marissa's hand. Her grip is limp and careless, and her other hand is busy texting. She doesn't look up from her cell. "Yeah, fine, but can we have like, more of a modern minimalist vibe?"

I peer around the space. No, I didn't imagine that we're on a goddamn pier. No, it's not made of brushed metal accents and marble countertops. "I, um, how do you mean?"

"Could we remove all these?" She waves her hand at the greenery she specifically requested in the event notes I glimpsed.

"I—these were all brought in by local florists you wanted to work with. We pulled a lot of strings to have them delivered on time. You don't like them?"

"Ugh, you know what, fine. This is too much of a hassle for a content session." She turns on her heel.

"A photo shoot?" I ask.

"Yeah. For social. Whatever." She waves a hand over her shoulder and picks up a call with the other. "Jared. You're late with the merch. Get here now."

Something in me hollows out as she walks away.

All of this is fake. For social media. Nothing in this has soul or community. There's no heart.

And there hasn't been for a long time. Not since the beginning of my work in LA, when I viewed the smaller, sincere clients as a stepping-stone to build a portfolio to reach the success

I wanted: working with A-list celebrities, public figures, and high-profile executives.

People who send their assistants to plan special events for them. How special could those events really be?

The person who must be Jared runs toward us, a white scarf looped up to his pale chin, arms laden with bags. He dumps everything out onto an empty table.

Marissa unpacks the first burlap tote and arranges the product in a line. Protein shakes flavored with peppermint, eggnog, and gingerbread.

I might be sick. I lean against the railing, letting the sea breeze hit my face. If not for the briny scent, it might pass for mountain wind.

"You doing okay?" Johanna asks, coming up beside me.

I sigh. "How did you decide you wanted to be here in the city? What makes you stay?"

She leans on the worn-smooth railing and looks out to sea. "It's been a while since we've done this, had a heart-to-heart," she says. "I'm sorry for that."

I clear my throat to keep from tearing up. I've missed this connection with her. I don't remember the last time we talked like this. "I'm sorry, too," I reply as I stare at the horizon.

"Want to tell me what happened up there?" Her voice is soft and caring.

I hardly wait for her to finish asking before I spill the whole story.

Johanna listens to all of it, then fixes her gaze on me. "Love is scary," she says.

I nod. Understatement of the century.

"For me, being a mom is scary. With Brynn getting older, I thought my fear would lessen, but there's even more to worry about now. Watching her enter new situations and relationships that grow farther out of my control."

She adopted Brynn around the time I moved to LA, and it's

been a while since I last saw her. I can still picture her pigtails. "Is she about ten now?"

"Fourteen." Johanna holds up her phone.

I do a double take at the photo on her home screen. Instead of pigtails, long, thick hair curls past her shoulders. Makeup highlights her brown skin. I'm not looking at a little girl anymore. "I—how could I have missed all this?"

Johanna's eyes hold so much kindness it hurts. She places a hand on my shoulder. "Can I say something pretty direct?" She gives my back a pat, then folds her hands on the railing.

I take her in. This woman who has been a mother figure to me for seven years. "Of course. You don't need to ask."

She leans forward, and I brace for whatever is coming.

"In the past, anytime we had a deeper conversation, you'd pull back by not calling for a couple weeks, not sharing anything more than work stuff. I wanted to respect your space, but I see now that I should have been more open with you about what I saw." She looks into my eyes like she sees my entire broken heart. "I'm sorry I let you go that easily."

"No, Johanna . . ." I choke up.

She raises a hand. "The thing is, I see you use work as a safety net, throwing yourself into everyone else's celebrations while avoiding personal connections of your own. I'm afraid every day of my love for Brynn. But that love makes life worth living, you know?"

Her words hit every jagged edge of my soul. I wrap my arms around her and cry.

She's right. Sonia always tried to be a closer friend to me, but I held her off with surface conversations and canceled plans, like I did with Ben years ago. I changed my relationship with Johanna to only be about work, filtering out personal connections along the way. I avoided speaking to Dad in favor of telling him how I really felt. And instead of fighting for Rachel, it was easier to leave, so I could shelter whatever part of my heart that was still intact. Easier to blame my actions on a promotion, a beefed-up version of LA, than own up to the fear that still beats through my heart: *Not. Good. Enough.*

Johanna holds me until I breathe evenly.

"What now?" I croak, wiping my cheeks. "How do I live with this fear? How do I try again?"

She rubs my arm and smiles. "The answers will come when you're ready. It's okay to let yourself feel this pain before you know how to move forward."

She's right. Maybe uncomfortable feelings are just a part of existing, period.

She grins. "If you don't have plans, come to my family's Christmas Eve celebration with me on Saturday night. Then you can see why I stay here, why I do what I do."

It's the first time I truly smile in what feels like five advent calendars.

CHAPTER 29

I knock on the door of a charming little sage-green craftsman home in one of the tucked-away parts of Pasadena. A menorah shines in the window, eight candles lit, plus the shamash. Joyful voices drift through the door, making me grin.

"Morgan Ross!" A woman I've never met pulls me into her bosom and her home as if I were one of her own.

"I'm Regina," she says, "and my sister has told me everything about you." Regina is a rounder, shorter version of Johanna, and her dark skin glows beneath the holiday lights strung along the doorframe. Eight reindeer adorn her sweater, cascading down her torso along reins of blinking LED lights.

I love her already.

"Good things, I hope," I reply.

"I am so happy you came." She beams, teeth a pearly white. "Come in, come in."

"Thank you for having me." I hand her a bottle of cabernet.

"Aw, thanks, hun." She takes the wine and ushers me to a table that is positively covered with food, nestling my gift into the center. I'm amazed she found a spot. Even the spaces between plates have trays on risers filled with more food.

"Are you hungry?" Her eyes are wide and eager.

"I—"

"Good! I made you a plate." She hands me not a plate, but a platter laden with every holiday treat imaginable.

"Here," she says, reaching across the buffet, "the latkes. You need to try those with sour cream." She plops a spoonful onto my plate. "Then the sufganiyot. My husband makes them from scratch. His grandmother's recipe." She points to the center of my plate/platter at what is the most delicious-looking donut I've ever seen. My mouth waters.

A tall man with cropped white hair puts his arm around Regina. "And I make special ones filled with Nutella for my love here." His pale cheeks are rosy, and his eyes squint with the biggest smile as he looks at her. Then he holds out his hand to me. "Morgan? I'm Larry, Regina's husband. Such a pleasure to meet you."

"Nice to meet you, too," I say, balancing my food on one hand to shake his. "Thank you for having me."

"Oh gosh, it's our joy. We've heard so much about you over the years. And you joined us on one of our favorite nights."

Warmth flutters through me.

"So," Regina says, a grin stretching across her face, "when Larry and I started dating and celebrating December holidays together, we combined our favorite traditions."

Larry beams down at her. "On the eighth night of Hanukkah, my family had a feast of our favorite foods after we lit the candles and said our blessings."

Regina smiles up at him. "And around this time each year, my family walked the best streets to see Christmas lights."

"So now, we do both," they say in unison, then laugh.

"Zayde! Are we leaving soon?" An adorable little girl with brown skin and a curly dark bun hugs Larry's leg.

"We are, sugarplum." He pats her head.

"Morgan," Regina says, "you load up at the cocoa bar"—she swings a hand toward the kitchen counter—"and we'll meet you in the foyer in ten minutes. Bring a warm drink along for the light walk."

"Thank you, Regina and Larry," I say, wondering how I'll make a respectable dent in any of this delicious food in that time frame.

They smile, placing their arms around each other, and cross the room to greet family members.

I laugh to myself as I find a corner of the table to put my plate on, making sure to take a bite of every item before I leave it for later. Each thing is better than the last.

The cocoa bar is a slightly scaled-down version of the buffet. Jars and bowls hold everything from marshmallows and candy canes to sprinkles and cookie straws.

It's amazing, but nothing beats Ben's drinks. I swallow hard, forcing the image of his face from my mind, the pain in his eyes before I left.

"Morgan, oh my god!" I have one second to set my cup down before I'm wrapped in a warm embrace. Soft dark curls that smell like coconut shampoo press against my cheek.

"Sonia!" I pull back. "It's so good to see you!"

"You too!" She beams. "And I'd love for you to meet Bridget."

Sonia steps aside to reveal her girlfriend. Bridget is wearing a gorgeous rose-gold hijab paired with a creamy cashmere sweater that hugs her full curves. Her eyes are big and dark and positively shine against her warm brown skin as she smiles and takes my hand in both of hers. "Morgan!" She says in the warmest British accent. "It's so lovely to finally meet you!"

"Bridget, you too!" I say, squeezing back.

She goes to fill up her cup, and I rub Sonia's shoulder. "I'm so happy for you."

"She's the best," Sonia says, gazing lovingly at her girlfriend. "We had to work it out. I couldn't let her go."

"So how are you doing that?" My stomach sinks. I failed at a bicoastal relationship, and here Sonia and Bridget are making it work across continents.

"For now, we're going back and forth. Bridget's here on a visa for a while, working remotely, and if I can coordinate it with Johanna, I plan to go to London next, giving us more time to decide something final."

That's what Rachel wanted to do. Give us more time before settling on a permanent situation. Now, thanks to the way I mishandled everything, I permanently don't have her.

Thankfully, a commotion pulls our attention to the front door and off my watering eyes.

"Sorry we're late, everyone!" Johanna enters and waves heartily when she spots me and Sonia.

She strides over, radiant in a gray sweater with glittery threads woven throughout, Brynn by her side.

"It's so good to see you again, Brynn," I say.

Johanna's daughter gives me a big hug. She's almost as tall as me now. "You too, Auntie Mor!" Then she heads to the coffee table in front of the Christmas tree, where a group of kids are locked in what appears to be a fiercely competitive game of dreidel. They all cheer when she approaches.

Brynn's warm greeting fills me with sudden joy. I grin at Johanna. "Auntie? What did I do to deserve such an esteemed title?"

"You think she'd forget who gave her AirPods last Christmas?" She laughs, her loose hair swaying at her shoulders.

"She deserves the best," I say past the lump in my throat. I only bought something so nice and gave it to Johanna to pass along to Brynn to cover my guilt for not seeing her in so long. But I'm here now. And that's a start.

She winks. "You spoil her."

"Johanna!" Sonia pulls our boss into a hug, and they laugh and chat with Bridget while I snag a few sips of cocoa.

"Okay, everyone," Regina says above the crowd. "Now that we're all here"—she slides Johanna a pointed stare—"we're ready to walk!" She claps her hands as we cram through the door and spill into the street.

After a block, we round the corner onto a cul-de-sac that swarms with people. Our crew falls into a rambunctious line along the sidewalk, beneath strands of lights that crisscross overhead, attached to neighboring roofs, creating a ceiling of sparkles.

Kids run ahead. Larry and Regina follow with their arms around each other, affectionately yelling the occasional, "Don't lick the fake candy canes, Christopher!" Johanna and Brynn stroll with their arms linked at the elbows, laughing in unison, as Christopher does indeed taste multiple plastic candy canes. Sonia points out different light features with full-body hand gestures, as Bridget beams.

I shove my hands in my pockets and force a smile. Joy surrounds me, but it only penetrates so deep. Like my very core is ice now, a jagged shard that only Rachel can thaw. I clear my throat. Keep moving forward.

We pass yards bedazzled in purple and gold lights, and white and blue ones—for the Lakers and Dodgers, respectively. Penguins skating on roofs. Inflatable Grinches popping out of chimneys. Every set decorator from the studios must live on this street, because some displays look like a Disneyland ride.

Rachel would love this.

I swipe at my eyes as we stop at one house with a gingerbread cottage on the lawn, complete with animatronic elves on a track passing in and out of the doorway.

The middle-aged-man band playing in the garage rocks a version of "Deck the Halls."

"Aw, look!" says a stranger beside me. Lights flash and people holler, and I trail my gaze to where they all point to find Bridget and Sonia beneath a candy-cane gazebo.

Sonia is on one knee, slipping a ring onto Bridget's finger.

Bridget pulls her up into her arms, and they both laugh and cry, lights glittering around them.

My cheeks are wet, and I press my hand to my chest.

Johanna's arm wraps around me.

"Now you see why I choose to live here. I wanted to show you. To answer your question."

"What do I do, Johanna? I love her. I really love her."

"Then you make it work. However you can. And I'll be behind you. Sonia is back right now, and Brynn is on winter break and wanting to get in some intern time with me to put on her future college applications." She gives my shoulder a squeeze. "Go figure this out and let me know what you need. I'll see you after New Year's, okay? That was the original plan, anyway."

I hug her tight. "I can't thank you enough."

She pulls back and winks. "Go."

Before I lose time, I follow orders and run to my car.

After cursing every traffic jam and stoplight, I finally make it back to my apartment—to find there's already a vehicle parked in my spot. One I'd recognize anywhere. I pull up behind the station wagon, eyes blurring.

"Dad?" I choke out, exiting my car.

He tucks his phone away, straightens. "Oh, honey. After everything, I didn't want to spend the holiday apart. Not again. I hope it's okay that I came."

My heart expands, filling my whole body with warmth. I hug him, bury my face into his brown canvas jacket, and force myself not to sob. "Of course it is. I'm so glad you did." He didn't let me go again.

I pull back. "But, um, how do you feel about heading back to Fern Falls?"

He laughs, eyes crinkling at the corners. "Yeah?"

"There's nowhere else I'd rather be, if you're okay with the drive? I just need to grab my bags."

He smiles. "If we leave in a bit, we'll make it by Christmas morning."

Joy tingles through my limbs.

He gets in his car, and I run upstairs as fast as I can, throw essentials in a bag, and grab a cold brew from the fridge for each of us.

And this time, I bring my haworthia.

CHAPTER 30

Dad's house is dark by the time we pull up. A simple string of white lights illuminates the porch.

My tires crunch gravel as I pull in behind him and park in the driveway.

I step out, breath fogging, and grab my haworthia in its little pink pot, and my bag from the passenger seat.

Dad hustles up the steps and unlocks the door. The lights reflect off his glasses, the streaks of silver in his hair, and his teeth when he smiles so big that it makes my heart burst.

"You sure it's no imposition?" I ask as we step inside.

"You and your plant are always welcome home." His voice is soft and warm.

Okay, I've cried enough for one day.

He shuts the door, and the clock on the wall reads two a.m. Despite the cold brew, my eyes are heavy, but I manage to take in details of my childhood home that still make me warm inside.

The same painting of a pine-rimmed lake hangs above the

stone mantel. The wall behind it is the pale green we picked together.

Looking pretty tired himself, Dad gives me an extra set of towels for the morning and walks me to the second bedroom.

I hold my breath. Will my old room be the same?

He opens the door.

It's Teen Morgan Lite. The walls are bare, stripped of my emo band posters and magazine collages, but still painted that light blue. The furniture is in the same arrangement, but a white rug is in place of my purple one, and a new white-framed mirror hangs over the dresser.

I set my bath towels and bags on the fluffy white bed linens, and place my plant on the nightstand, when I stop, hands hovering. There's a photo of Dad and me in that aluminum fishing boat we used to rent at the lake every summer. In a frame beside that, a picture of Mom, smiling at the top of Fern Falls Peak, sunlight glinting off her dark glasses, her blond hair. Before she had me, before she got sick. "Thank you. This is perfect," I manage without losing it.

Dad comes up beside me and picks up the image of Mom. "That was the day we decided to move here. She loved this place so much. Look how big it made her smile." He holds out the frame, examining it from different angles like a new memory might appear if he tilts it just right. "I would have moved to the moon to see her light up like that every day."

A tear slides down my cheek and I swipe it away.

He places the photo down and turns to me. "Truth is, I haven't found the words to apologize to you. Words that are enough to fix all the wrong I did."

I swallow hard. "For what?"

His eyes crease together. "For failing you."

"Dad," I choke out.

He shakes his head. "I had a chance to give you a mom with Christy, to help fill that void in your life, and I couldn't make it happen. I hated myself for that, for letting you down. I still can't forgive myself. I'm so sorry, Morgan." His voice cracks.

His confession takes fifty pounds off my shoulders, but I never knew how much he carried himself. "Dad, I never felt a void before Christy. Our life was always complete. I never needed her. I only needed you. And I wanted to be enough for you."

"Oh, honey." He reaches over and places a hand on my arm. "You were always enough for me. I'm sorry I became so wrapped up in my failure that I didn't show you that."

I hug him, and we cry. For all the years we didn't. For all the time we lost to unspoken words. "You never failed me."

He runs a hand over my hair. "You were always enough, Morgan." He pulls back and looks me in the eyes, his glistening. "You will always be enough, just as you are."

His words touch the deepest parts of my soul, stitching me back together.

"Thank you for that," I manage to say. He'll never know how thankful I am.

His eyes are red and bright. "Merry Christmas, Sunshine. You were the little light summertime gifted us twenty-five years ago. That's why Mom and I always called you that."

I smile through my tears, glance over at the picture of Mom and smile at her, too. "Merry Christmas."

"Sleep well." He kisses my head and walks to the door. When it clicks closed, I plop onto the bed and sink into the blankets, relieved to be alone, to be home—a place that isn't painful anymore.

I reach to turn off the lamp when a magazine rack beneath the table catches my eye. Several spines I recognize.

A quick thumb over them confirms it, and has me tearing up all over again. Dad saved every magazine and newspaper my work has ever been featured in.

Across the room, old photos are pinned to the bulletin board above the antique secretary desk: Ben, me, Adam, and Rachel, laughing over a box of half-eaten pizza. Rachel and me in high school, arms around each other, trees at our back. I clear my throat and pull the photo I saved from my purse. The one Whitney took of the two of us at The Stacks. I get up and pin it among the ones from years ago.

Everything I'm proud of, and everything I want, gathered in one small space.

The scent of buttery cinnamon wakes me. I savor it before opening my eyes, feeling six years old again, expecting Santa. It's Christmas. The first Christmas I've woken up at home for in years, and anticipation sparkles through me, like anything could happen.

I pull an oversized beige sweater over my tank top and leggings, wrangle my hair into a pony, and head down the hall. The house is warm, and a fire crackles from the living room. Dad isn't in the kitchen, but I find the source of that nostalgic cinnamon scent. He made sticky buns. The pan is full, so I grab two dishes and forks (still where I remember them to be) and plate servings. Two each, to start with.

I carry the brown sugar and cinnamon treasures into the living room, where Dad squats before the fireplace, sparks sizzling as he nudges a log with a poker.

"Merry Christmas, Dad." It's so good to say that again.

"Morgan." He closes the fireplace screen, sets the poker in its stand. Brushes his plaid pajamas off. "Merry Christmas." He looks at me like I might dissipate into thin air.

I move in and set the plates on the coffee table, settle onto the couch. "I love that you made these."

"Mom's recipe," he says, leaning forward to grab his dish. "The best."

I smile. The only treat Ben's can't touch. I bite into the chewy, sweet, spicy perfection that made Christmas mornings so special. He always baked these when I was young to keep her around during the holidays. Mom's presence must have been sweet and warm like this. "I'm glad you made them today," I say around a bite.

"I'm glad you're here."

"Me, too." Good thing I didn't put on mascara yet.

We sit back and take in the tree. Rainbow lights sparkle, and the fire reflects off the sparse ornaments.

"I love that you got a tree."

"I haven't in years. Not since you left. It was a gift," he says, sipping from a coffee mug.

My chest tightens. I don't need to ask who gave it to him. "When did she drop it off?"

He eyes me knowingly. "Rachel brought it by yesterday. It even had an ornament on it already."

Yesterday. Not last week, when things were good. Yesterday, within the time she's hated me again.

I move closer, kneel before the branches. Some ornaments are from my childhood. A fishing rod, a tiara, Baby's First Christmas. The whimsical fairies and angels we put up for Mom.

Dad reaches beneath the tree and pulls out a red envelope, hands it to me.

"No, Dad, you don't have to give me anything."

"Honey," he says, eyes shining, "I've been holding onto this for a very long time." He holds the gift out farther. "And it isn't from me."

I take the envelope, fingers shaking, and turn it over to reveal what I suspected. My hand flies to my mouth. On the front, penned in soft, swooping letters, are the words:

To: Morgan
Love: Mom

I open it up, barely keeping myself together, and pull out a piece of paper. Unfold it as the words blur together.

My Dearest Daughter,

What do I say to the one whose smile makes every moment a joy? From the minute you came into our lives, sweet Morgan Ann, you lit up our world. Our little Sunshine.

And I want to leave you something that will help me stay a part of yours.

I'm asking your daddy to hold onto this, for when you're ready to receive it. For a time in your life when you'll need to make a big decision, like I had to make years ago. Use it wisely, use it well, but most of all, use it with all your heart.

I never regret following mine. It led me to your father, it gave us you. I love you every moment, every day. I'm never far away.

All my love forever,
Mommy

I clutch her words to my aching chest. "Dad? What's going on? What did she mean?"

He places his hand on my back. "Honey, your mom, she left you a gift. And like her letter says, she wanted me to give it to you when you found your heart's desire. When it would help you achieve it." He leans forward and pulls another envelope from beneath the tree.

"I thought of passing it on to you when you moved to LA, but you needed to make your own way then. And gosh, you did, phenomenally." He holds out the green envelope. "So this is to help set you up for the rest of your life. For what will bring you the most joy."

I take the new gift. My tears splash onto the paper as I pull out a white slip.

As soon as I read the amount on the cashier's check, I drop it. Bawl into my palms.

Dad hugs me.

I shake my head. "This is too much."

"Not for her little girl, it isn't. She wanted you to have it."

Rachel was always right. My dad's love for Christy was never about the money. We already had enough. I was enough.

I rest my chin against his shoulder, the lights and colors on the tree blending into one.

Once my tears slow, I notice something on a low branch. It's a new ornament of two small fairies sitting in a pine, a heart above their heads, engraved with the names *Petunia Pie and Pickle Pop.*

I cry even harder. Rachel must have had this made weeks ago. And she still gave it to me.

Suddenly, I know exactly what to do with some of the small fortune Mom left me. And how I might win back Rachel's heart, one last time.

CHAPTER 31

The scent of fresh pancakes and powdered sugar wafts through the lobby of Hart's Home B&B.

Any worry about intruding on personal holiday celebrations vanishes, replaced by all the joy of Christmas Day. Guests huddle around the fire in the sitting room, while others heap plates full of delicacies from the breakfast buffet. On the other side of the lobby, the library tables are full of families, laughing and talking over steaming mugs.

"A very Merry Christmas to you, Morgan Ann." Mrs. Hart beams from behind the front desk.

My whole body lightens. Her presence does that to people. "Oh, Mrs. Hart"—my voice cracks, and I clutch the envelope in my jacket pocket and clear my throat—"Merry Christmas."

She comes around and gives me a giant hug. "Knew you'd be back."

I laugh. "Yeah?"

"Absolutely. I saw it in your eyes this time."

I tilt my head in question. "Saw what?"

Her smile is so genuine and thoughtful as she takes me in. "That same look your mama had when she told me she was moving here."

My heart stutters, and I rub the paper in my pocket.

"I'm the reason they got married, you know?" She winks and heads to the breakfast bar, ushering for me to follow.

"I—" A million questions perch on my tongue as she hands me a mug. Clearly, this is a conversation that calls for cocoa. Are there any that don't?

We get in line behind two children in plaid pajamas. One clutches a toy microscope, and the other, a boxed Lego set. I grin at their excellent choices.

Once our red mugs are heaped with marshmallows and whipped cream, we head across the lobby and settle into the last open table in the library, a fresh pine and poinsettia arrangement between us.

"Tell me everything," I blurt before I take a sip.

Mrs. Hart lets out a hearty laugh, ushering smiles from those around us. "Well," she says, wiping her eyes, "this is where your mom and dad stayed when they were first dating. And shortly after, your dad talked to me about ideas on how to propose to your mom."

"And what did you do?"

She leans forward, eyes twinkling. "Your mama loved this little library, so when your dad came to me, I told him to slip that ring inside a book and have her find it."

I can't contain my smile as my eyes roam over the shelves, the rainbow of spines bringing me closer to her. "So they were reading when she found the ring?"

"Well, no." She shakes her head, pressing her palm against her cheek. "The book got lost."

I gasp. "No!"

"Yep. He hid it in a copy of *The Nutcracker*, and we turned the place upside down looking for it."

"How did you find it?" Guests around us grow quiet, hanging on each word of her story.

She leans back in her chair. "Turns out, a little five-year-old guest tucked the book into her backpack. When she told her parents that it came with a real-life princess ring, they turned around and drove right back to the inn."

"Oh my gosh." I laugh along with others, who now crowd the entrance to the room, lean against the walls.

"So"—Mrs. Hart's voice grows louder—"when little Aisley returned the book in the lobby, your mom and dad were there. Your dad got on one knee, the girl held out the book, and your mom took it. It was the second happiest day here at the inn."

Everyone claps and lets out soft sighs of adoration.

I wish I could remember details about Mom like Mrs. Hart does, like Dad does. But hearing these stories makes her feel close, makes me feel like I own memories, too.

I lean in. "What was the first happiest day? When you and Bill purchased it?"

She grins. "Why don't you tell me why you're here."

I clear my throat. "I have a proposal of my own for you."

"Why, Morgan, I'm honored."

I laugh. "My dad gave me this today." I hand over the letter.

Mrs. Hart takes it and presses her hands to her lips. Without a word, she gets up and grabs a book from a top shelf draped with fresh garland.

She touches the cover for a long moment before coming back. When she sits down, she pulls a piece of paper from between the pages and slides it across the table to me.

My vision blurs as my mom's handwriting stares up at me again.

Take care of Morgan. If she gets lost, help her find her way home.

My cheeks grow wet for the millionth time today. "Mrs. Hart," I say through the thickness in my throat, "I want to ask you about buying the inn."

"I know."

I snap my gaze to hers. "You do?"

Her eyes glisten. "Of course. Why do you think I held out on selling all this time?"

"Did you know about the money my mom put aside?"

"Morgan, you are family." Her voice is quiet. "You belong here. It just took you time to see it. You're the only person I was ever going to sell to."

I swipe at my eyes. "What if I wouldn't have figured this out?"

"It was only a matter of time. I had faith." She reaches over and covers my hand with hers.

"Mrs. Hart, I'd like to use the money my mom left me and partner with Rachel's land to hold events, sharing the business to support the farm, and in turn, the inn."

She stands, and I follow; then, she sweeps me up in a giant hug. "This is it. The happiest day the inn has ever had."

Everyone around us claps as I smile and laugh, peering over her shoulder at the book she pulled my mother's note from.

A worn, pastel-pink copy of *The Nutcracker*.

CHAPTER 32

Morning light dances off the ivy and cobblestones on the back patio of Forest Fairy's, but no amount of charm can quell the nerves churning my gut.

"Here you go, hun." Whitney walks out with a cup of chamomile tea.

"Thank you." I clutch it like a flotation device and drain half in one gulp.

"It's going to be okay." She smiles with all the skill of someone used to calming small children.

"I hope so, Whit. I can't thank you enough for meeting me here."

I texted the others, too, but I don't know if they'll come. If they ever want to see me again.

So it's just me and Whitney and a giant cloud of nervous energy—

"Hey, hey, sorry I'm late." A blond bartender breezes through the doors.

"I hope it's okay I texted him?" Whitney says under her

breath. "He was so involved with everything, I thought he should be here, too."

I shake my head. "No, of course. I'm glad you did."

"Aaaaand"—Tanner holds out two steaming to-go cups— "tea this time."

I place my own empty mug on the table and accept its replacement. "I will never turn down more warm beverages. Thank you, Tanner." His smile is genuine. I hope the others can welcome me back this easily. Even if I don't deserve it.

Whitney eyes the cup like it might bite.

Tanner's brow creases. "It's, um, a wintry peppermint thing. Had Ron whip it up in the bar's kitchen. If you don't like it, I can—"

She takes the cup, and he appears to shrink two inches from relief.

"Thank you, Tanner." She says the words slowly, like she's trying out a new language.

He grins, pulling in his lips. They whiten against his crimson cheeks. "Welcome."

Both of them take a seat at the table, and the only sound between them is the sporadic sip of tea.

If I sit, I'll probably vibrate off the chair. I check my phone. No new messages, and it's almost ten.

"If they don't come," Whitney says from her spot at a stool around the table set for a tea party, "it'll be their loss."

I love her for trying to make me feel better. "No matter what happens, you are the absolute best." I squeeze my cup. Mint and vanilla waft into the air and make my mouth water, but I can't drink it. I can't do anything except stare at the French doors to the patio like they might explode.

Ten a.m. comes and goes, and the doors stay closed. I take a deep breath. If I've hurt them too much, I'll need to give them more time, but I will try again. I won't disappear. Not this time.

Whitney and Tanner look at me like I'm the last puppy in the adoption pen.

"It's okay," I say, trying to keep my voice from warbling. "Thank you. So much." I set down my tea and gather up my purse along with any last shred of my dignity, then make my way to the French doors—and stumble back as they burst open.

"Sorry we're late," Ben says. "He had to have coffee." He juts a thumb over his shoulder as Adam follows with a coffee traveler full of something that smells rich and hazelnutty. I almost melt. Whitney and Tanner pin their high-beam smiles on me as Ben and Adam cram into chairs.

Suddenly, I'm standing at the head of a very tiny table with four sets of eyes trained on me.

Ben and Adam stare like I'm in the witness seat, but it's okay. They're here. They're giving me a chance.

I don't have a speech prepared, so I start with what's on my heart, and apparently, it's nothing eloquent, because I blurt out, "I fucked up."

There's a pause, and Ben says, "Amen," followed by a "Hallelujah" from Adam and a chorus of laughs from everyone.

The ice is broken, and I sag onto a stool. "I'm really, really sorry," I continue, making eye contact with them all, one by one, holding Adam's gaze the longest. It's the truth. And they deserve to know all of it. "I ruined everything for a version of myself I didn't love. New York me would have been the same as Los Angeles me. Chasing success to feel like enough." I press my hand to my chest. "But you all helped me to see I'm okay, just as I am. I love Fern Falls for that. I love you all." I clear my throat. "And I'm in love with Rachel. I know I don't deserve it, but if you give me another chance, I will give it my all. I won't run away. And I know it's more than I should ask for, but if you could help me make things right with her, or try to, I would be really, really grateful." Their collective attention is so heavy that I have to breathe in deep.

All eyes land on the only Reed representative present.

Adam clears his throat. "This will ultimately be Rachel's call, but all I know is that I've never seen my sister happier than when she's with you. And she's never been more miserable than during these days you've been gone. And miserable Rachel is a pain in my ass. So if you have a plan to fix that, I'm all in."

I let out a truly mortifying whimper. "Thank you, Adam. If she gives me the chance to make things right, I won't hurt her again. I promise."

He smiles. "I know. Plus, this isn't all for her. I really like having you around, Morgan. You're good people."

My eyes water just as Ben bursts into tears and practically knocks over every pastel place setting to get to me. He throws his arms around my neck, and I don't even try to hold back my sobs.

"I would have forgiven you over the phone, you idiot," he cries.

"I love you, Ben."

He pulls back, braces my shoulders, holds my gaze. "And I love you just as much as I love grand gestures. Let's do this."

"A toast!" Whitney shouts.

"With the good stuff," says Adam, eliciting an eye roll from Whit as he pours steaming coffee into four mini tea cups.

Whitney clutches her tea, and Tanner beams.

The rest of us take our drinks and hold them up, pinkies out.

"To better days ahead," Tanner says, raising his cup.

"To true love!" says Whitney.

"To mad, mad plans." Adam winks.

Ben laughs and salutes us all. "We're all mad here."

"To the best friends I've ever had." I smile and sip to keep more tears from falling.

Then we all lean across the table like a truly mad tea party, and I spill my plan to earn back Rachel's heart.

CHAPTER 33

My breath blurs the trees, and it's a wonder I can breathe at all. This is it. The night we planned. Everything is set and ready to go, and now I have to face what's next: either Rachel will forgive me and take me back, or she won't, and I'll need to live with this pain. Either way, I have to try. I'm not running from the hurt this time. I'm facing it head on. Because I deserve a happy ending, too. I'm worth this. Rachel and I are worth this.

Shoving my hands into my down jacket, I fill my lungs with chilly mountain air.

From farther down the row of trees, past clusters of families enjoying the last night of Enchanted Evenings before New Year's, Ben hops out and gives me a thumbs-up, and suddenly, I'm not cold at all, but burning with panic and dread and anticipation and all the hope my chest can hold. Adam peeks out next. He's more discreet, a quick finger gun from behind a pine branch closer to me.

I huff out a breath and walk past them to the podium, now

empty since no more trees are being auctioned, to where a mic is set up.

Rachel and the city have done an amazing job keeping Enchanted Evenings running through December, and this is the last one. The final Saturday of the month. I wasn't even here to see more of the event I helped create, and the guilt of that collides with the anxiety already storming in my chest.

Whitney's voice cuts through the crowd as she approaches with Rachel. I press my feet into the ground and try to keep myself from crying or straight-up combusting.

"This will only take a minute," she says, just like we planned. "There's a question I have about the electrical dismantle for tomorrow."

Somehow, with every thread of self-preservation I have left, I keep myself together as Rachel nears.

She's in that red flannel she loves, those denim jeans.

"Okay, Whit, I only have a few minutes to—" She stops cold when she sees me standing at the front of the Hallmas path. I clutch the sides of the podium.

Even though we arranged this, Whitney gasps and looks between Rachel and me, like we'll either start kissing or killing each other.

"Hi," I say into the announcer's mic, breathy and flushed like an idiot.

"Morgan." Her eyes widen, and I can't tell if it's an excited or angry shock, exasperated or murderous, but I won't let any one of those things stop me. Not this time. I'm here, and no matter how scary this is, I'm not going to leave until I've given my all.

Whitney backs up and slips into the crowd, beside Tanner, who gives me a very cheery thumbs-up.

I swallow hard as visions of Christy rejecting my dad, rejecting me in front of the whole town, attack my brain. Make me want to haul ass out of here.

But the crowd doesn't matter.

It's just Rachel and me and a handful of minutes to save our future.

I grab the mic, and step around the front of the podium. "I know I'm the last person you want to see right now, and I'll leave if you want me to. I got your Christmas gift, the ornament. I'm sorry it's late, but I'd like to give you one of my own?"

Rachel glances at the sides of the path as if some hidden prank camera might pop out. Then she approaches slowly, as if I'm a wild animal, which is fair, because I basically acted like one the last time we spoke. When she reaches me, she takes a breath and says, "Okay."

She may as well have proposed, I am so happy. "Okay."

People start to notice us now, and they crowd around, forming a messy circle.

My heart pounds in my ears as I usher Rachel up the path to the first marker: a small purple ribbon tied to a tree branch.

"I want to tell you a story," my voice booms through the speakers. As soon as I say the words, the tree lights up, and music plays.

Rachel startles, then her lips twitch. "Is this an Irish drinking song?"

Back down the path, whispers rush from the trees. A second later, the music changes to something Celtic and ethereal, like the music at Forest Fairy's. I smile and walk toward the tree, sticking to the script. "Once, there were two fairies." Surprisingly, my voice doesn't crack. A large white bulb illuminates two fairy ornaments on a middle branch, and I want to give Ben a big gold star. Adam taught him the lighting so well. "They met in the forest and became instant friends, and life was wonderful."

Then another pine lights up farther down the path. As we approach, the music turning slow and sad. "But as they grew up, things turned complicated, including their feelings for each other. They got scared. And flew away." I can't look at Rachel as I say this part. She's quiet, and I don't want to see the pain in her eyes. I need to be able to keep speaking.

We walk to the next lit tree, a few steps away. "And just when they thought they might never see each other again, they did. And they fell in love."

Rachel sort of jerks at that, and I still can't meet her eyes, so I lead her to the fourth evergreen. "But again, they were afraid, and one fairy thought it would be safer if she left a second time. If she could go make herself into something more, something worthy of love." I clear my throat and lead her to the fifth and final stop.

The path lets out to the front entrance, to the same place where the sign I crushed used to stand. Now, it's covered in a white cloth. Rachel must be concealing the damage until she can get a new sign made. I shove past that guilt, pull a red envelope from my pocket, and hold it in my gloved hand until I can finally speak. People crowd around us, waiting. Although I ran through this a hundred times, all the fairy-story stuff leaves my brain, and I let my heart do the talking. "I am so sorry I made you feel like you weren't enough. I'm sorry I pushed you to do something you weren't ready for, that I didn't tell you about the New York promotion sooner." I stop and swallow hard as people murmur. "It took leaving for me to realize that here, with you, is where I want to be. Here, with you, makes me realize I'm enough." I take a deep breath, and speak my decision for the first time. "I bought Hart's Home B and B, Rach. I am all in. And if you'll have me as a business partner, please consider this money I owe you for your sign, plus more, as an investment. A partnership for events on your land for our hotel guests, if that's something you might be interested in?" I step forward and hold it out. "And although I don't deserve a second chance, please take my heart, too." I meet her eyes. My chest might burst. "Because I am hopelessly in love with you, and I always will be."

The noise of the crowd fades away as Rachel moves closer.

Her eyes search my face. "What about The Barnes? Wasn't that your dream?"

"Johanna wants me to be happy and said she'd back me up wherever I choose to take the business. I don't have everything worked out yet, but I will. And I have her full support to run events up here. At the hotel or on the farm, if you'd like, starting with fixing your sign."

Rachel smiles, actually smiles. My heart soars.

She reaches forward, but instead of taking the envelope, she grasps the drape that covers the sign.

My hope plummets. I was so stupid to bring it up, to remind her of another awful thing I did.

She takes a deep breath and pulls off the white tarp.

I step back and stare at a brand-new sign. Glossy wood, gorgeous red script engraved in solid pine.

R & R Resort and Events Center
"A magical escape in the heart of the evergreens."

R&R. Reed & Reed. I brace all my muscles to keep my heart from shattering. Here's my answer. Instead of taking me up on my offer, Rachel and Adam will transform this place themselves. I don't know why Adam didn't tell me, but I can't blame him for keeping it a secret. And I can't blame Rachel for not giving me a second chance. I had one. I blew it. At least I tried my hardest. I gather all the strength I have and say, "I'm really happy for you both."

She tilts her head. "Both?"

I swallow. "You and Adam. You'll turn this place into a great events center adjacent to the inn. My money still stands. And I hope you'll consider working with me. When you're ready." I hold out the envelope, trying to keep my hand from shaking as sounds of disappointment ripple through the crowd.

"Morgan." Rachel takes the mic, places it on the ground,

then holds my hands, squeezing the envelope. My whole body anchors to her touch.

She locks her eyes with mine and says, "R&R isn't for Reed and Reed, although that is a good backup plan, I guess. Before I knew you already had, I thought we could work with Mrs. Hart to buy the inn. So my hope is that it will be used for us. Ross and Reed. You and me. I won't take your money, because I want to give this to you as a gift. If you want it. If you'll have me. Which is more than I deserve after how I acted, after I pushed you away. You weren't entirely wrong, you know. I talked with my dad. He's going back to rehab, and I'm slowing my assistance with his bills, and stopping completely once he is out and can get a job. And Morgan, I made a website for my art and am already getting a lot of interest. I had this idea that we could travel back and forth from New York to here, and share it all—but buying the inn yourself. Are you sure you want to give up New York?"

My heart is in my throat, and I can barely get the words out. "I love being here. I love the community, the people; I love it like my mom loved it. Nothing would make me happier than to stay here with you."

She grins and nods at the sign. "You brought life back to this place. To me."

I swallow hard and take in her gorgeous work. "Ross and Reed, huh?"

"Except on days we're bickering. Then I reserve the right to the first R." She grins. "And I hope I can make you laugh, even during the hard days, and make you feel all the love I have for you every day, the love I've had for you my entire life. I love you always, Morgan Ann. Always."

I wrap my arms around her neck and let the tears fall. "I love you, too."

Then Rachel kisses me like the world has just been saved, because for us, it has.

Everyone claps and cheers. When we finally pull apart, we turn to find Ben, Adam, Tanner, and Whitney applauding, too.

She nuzzles my ear. "Maybe one day we can kiss out here and not have an audience."

We both laugh and lean into each other.

"Did you know about this?" I shout up to Adam, motioning to the sign.

"Gotta keep some secrets in a small town." He smiles coyly.

"Double grand gesture!" Ben says, and gives him a giant hug.

Adam looks stunned, then he breaks into the biggest grin and embraces Ben before they all run forward and surround me and Rachel in a giant group hug filled with laughter and tears and more joy than a small mountain town could ever contain.

I'm exactly where I belong, and it's the best celebration of my life.

EPILOGUE

I forgot how breathtaking summer is in the mountains. How the lavender festivals and wildflower blooms of spring blend into fresh blue sky laced with the invigorating scent of pine, promising another season of holiday magic to come.

The inn is sparkling, and people are checking in. A sign identical to the one Rachel unveiled now stands outside. The manual Mrs. Hart left for me already has notes of my own scribbled in the margins, and Johanna is coming this weekend to see the site and make the partnership with The Barnes Events Company official.

She eagerly invested in R&R Resort and Events Center, seeing the potential. During the wedding season, we've touted it as a honeymoon retreat for Los Angelenos who want a romantic escape closer to home. Come winter, we'll run packages that coincide with Enchanted Evenings.

And it worked out great for Sonia, too. Now that she and Bridget are engaged, Sonia took the East Coast position so they could have shorter flights to the UK to visit Bridget's family.

Everyone has been so busy preparing for Johanna's arrival that I haven't seen them all day. Ben hasn't brought the cinnamon rolls yet and isn't answering his phone.

"Hey, babe. Oh. Wow." Rachel's voice materializes beside me, captivating my senses. I turn to her . . . *holy shit.*

She is so fucking hot in a crisp, light blue button-up rolled halfway up her forearms and navy slacks that hug her curves. Her hair is loose and soft-looking, and I want to run my fingers through those waves.

She holds out her hand to me. "Darling, you are stunning." Her eyes are soft and shimmer at the edges. She lifts my arm above my head, spinning me in a circle, making the hem of my white summer dress swirl at my knees.

I keep my eyes on her. "That's a lot of emotion for a website photo shoot, Reed."

She clears her throat. "Everything's ready in the barn. Let's go make this partnership official, yeah?"

I take her hand and . . . is she shaking? "Hun? Are you okay?"

"Never better." She smiles.

We step into the fresh air, and Rachel gulps it in.

I grip her hand tighter, hoping it will help. "Hey, this is all going to be amazing. Johanna will love everything we've done, and the new website and branding is going to look incredible. We've put in all we've got. There's no way we can fail."

She grins. Cups my cheek. "You're absolutely right."

On the way to the barn, we pass by the new greenhouse that Rachel built for me.

This summer, we'll compost the leaves and flowers from the displays around the property for the fall garden we planted this spring. It's full of pumpkins, corn, and sunflowers, and will give even more to the community during harvest time. Turns out my green thumb extends beyond plants that only need watering every two weeks. There's so much to look forward to.

We also pass Rachel's art studio.

With us living in her cabin, we turned the main level of her family's old house into her gallery. Filling it up with new memories.

When we reach the barn, Rachel pulls me close. "Can we stop for a second?" she says, face serious.

"Of course. Is everything okay?"

"I have something for you." Her cheeks redden as she pulls a small notebook from her back pocket, and hands it to me.

I open the leather journal, and my whole body lifts with joy.

Each page is filled with gorgeous typography and drawings of trees, our inn, the barn, all the gorgeous nature around it. Custom material for the entire year. Samples of invitations and announcements we can offer our clients for their special events.

"Rachel, oh my god. These are perfect." I look to her, but she's not there.

She's down on her knee.

My heart consumes me.

"Turn the page, sweetheart." She beams up, her gaze unwavering.

Tears fill my eyes. My hands shake as I do what she says.

There, in the center of the next page is a small square cutout. Tied inside is a diamond ring. A tear falls, landing beside her gorgeous hand lettering that swoops with whimsical precision. Words that take my breath away.

I read them as she says them aloud.

"Morgan Ann Ross, will you marry me?"

I clasp the notebook to my chest and fall into her arms, crying. "Yes. Yes, yes. I'll marry the shit out of you, Rachel Reed."

She takes my face in her hands and kisses away my tears. Then she pulls back and smiles, her own eyes shimmering. She takes the ring out of the journal and slips it onto my finger. It twinkles in the sunlight. "I love you, Morgan."

"I love you," I say past a fresh wave of tears.

We hold each other there, among the pines, for what feels like an eternity and not long enough.

"I, um, have one more surprise that I might be even more nervous about."

I run my thumb over her cheek. "Rach. You never have to be nervous with me. I want everything you do."

"Okay, then," she says on a shaky breath. She stands and pulls me up, leading me to the barn.

With the way she's acting, this is going to be one hell of a website photo shoot. My heart is in my throat as I pull the wooden doors open—and nearly fall back once I do.

The talk we had in this space months ago fills my mind. My hands fly to my mouth as all my loved ones look back, seated on either side of an aisle that leads to a pine-draped arbor.

Twinkle lights swag the ceiling, creating a low, cozy feel. Pine boughs frame the aisle, and glowing lanterns mark every row of seats.

"Rach—" I turn to talk to her, but she's already making her way around the side of the seats to the front of the aisle. She takes her place beneath the arbor and waits for me, smiling, eyes shining.

I beam so big my face can't contain it. My whole heart expands bigger than my body. This is everything I've ever wanted.

My dad comes up beside me; his touch on my shoulder is grounding. "You ready, Sunshine?"

I throw my arms around him.

He rubs my back. "I love you." His voice cracks as he hands me the most gorgeous bouquet of pink, purple, and blue wildflowers. On the ribbon that bounds the stems, there's a silver pin engraved with my parents' monogram: *WRW*.

Dad smiles down at it. "Same one that was on your mom's bouquet, too, the day we married." Then he looks at me, eyes full of tears. "We're both with you today, and couldn't be more proud."

"Dad. I love you." I hold him close and a tear soaks into the shoulder of his coat.

After a minute I take his arm, and we head down the aisle . . . of my wedding.

We pass Whitney and Tanner. They both flash big, teary grins.

Adam is at the front, strumming a beautiful melody on his guitar. He beams, face glowing.

Dad kisses my cheek and takes a seat, right beside Johanna, Brynn, Sonia, and Bridget. Mrs. and Mr. Hart wave from nearby seats. Jim and Tanya Reed are seated in the front row, and both smile, tears in their eyes.

I reach Rachel underneath the arbor, the scent of pine surrounding us.

She takes my hands, and I can't stop the tears from falling. "You did all this?"

She nods. "I just hope it's exactly what you wanted?"

"It's more than I could have ever dreamed of."

Ben steps up between us. "By the power invested in me from the almighty Internet, I say let's do this," he announces to everyone's applause. Then he opens up a book and begins leading us through our vows.

Rachel pulls two wedding bands from her pocket. One gold for her, one platinum to match my engagement ring. We slip them on each other's fingers.

When we kiss, it's different than any other. It's the kind of promise that surpasses words. A promise that says we're always enough.

We raise our hands, and everyone cheers as we head out the barn doors. Rachel leads me up to the inn, around the back, to the courtyard, where the whole space is decorated.

String lights cross above a dance floor and tables. Everything overflows with bright summer colors and flowers and that touch of magic that comes with the profession of love.

Adam has a DJ booth set up and starts playing music.

Ben's dessert station features the most beautiful cake. A triple-tiered pastel rainbow beauty with two brides on top.

Tanner mans the bar, and Whitney already takes photos of our family and friends, directing them into groups. All of Fern Falls is here.

"I can't believe you pulled this off." My voice is barely a breath.

Rachel puts her arm around me and pulls me close. "I'm the luckiest girl in the world." She nuzzles my ear. "Dance with me?"

"Always," I say, taking her hand.

We head onto the dance floor, and everyone we care about surrounds us. I swallow hard. A dance we finally get to have here. I pull her into my arms, bury my face into her long, silky hair, breathe her in. My wife.

Johanna and Dad laugh at some personal joke after being inseparable since the ceremony.

Whitney rolls her eyes as Tanner plucks a daisy from a vase and offers it to her. She tucks it behind her ear when he turns away.

Sonia and Bridget sway together in an embrace.

Behind the DJ booth, Ben offers Adam a cupcake. He accepts with cheeks pink enough to rival the frosting.

"Bouquet toss time!" Whitney calls, her camera at the ready.

Rachel takes my hand and leads me into the middle of the courtyard as the crowd gathers behind us. I laugh, and after affixing my mom's pin to my dress, send my flowers flying through the air. Somehow, I know exactly where they'll land, and my heart leaps when I'm proven right. The bouquet drives right into Ben's hands. His face turns as red as the setting sun, then he looks at Adam, who bobs behind his turntable, pausing when he catches Ben's gaze. Something passes between them. A sort of anticipation and magic sparkles. I can't wait to see their story unfold. I'm so happy I'll be here to see it.

With everyone happy and celebrating, Rachel pulls me toward the edge of the forest.

Hand in hand, we head down the closest tree-lined path until the wedding is a soundscape of joy.

Fresh summer air tingles my skin and the waking stars wink down.

Rachel's intense gaze sends a jolt of heat straight to my center. She smooths her hand along my hip as I take in the sweeping hills, our land, our life. *Ours.*

"I know that look." She cups the side of my face, running her thumb over my cheek. "What are you planning?"

I tug her close, leaning into her warmth. "I was thinking that we're finally alone in these trees."

A knowing smile pulls at the corner of her lips. "We are most definitely alone, my love."

I wrap my fists around her collar. "And from now on, I plan to make love to you beneath the stars whenever I want."

Her head dips low. "That's an event I'll happily and frequently attend." She presses me up against the cool bark of a pine and kisses me so deep, my limbs melt into honey.

My wife's embrace is steady and strong. It's home—and it's more than enough.

Acknowledgments

Writing a book about family and community would not have been possible without my own. The biggest, most heartfelt thanks to:

Claire Friedman. You called this book a "firecracker," and from the start, you've brought immeasurable passion and care into championing me and my work. All those years I dreamed of working with an agent, I dreamed of working with an agent like YOU. Thank you will never be enough. You are a FORCE.

Elizabeth Trout. Your editorial vision for this story clicked in a way every creative hopes for. Thank you for your ever-grounding presence, clarity, and for always knowing how to help me through. Thank you for seeing the heart of this book and for making it shine. The Fern Falls crew and I are the luckiest to have you.

Jane Nutter, Michelle Addo, Carly Sommerstein, and the rock star team at Kensington. Thank you for all the energy you've put into making this story a book.

Scott Heim for the spectacular copyedits.

Hannah Schofield. You have been such an uplifting source throughout everything. THANK YOU for championing this book across the pond and beyond.

Kate Byrne, Sophie Keefe, and the stellar team at Headline Eternal. Your care for this messy main character and her lumberjane fills my heart to overflowing. It's an honor to work with you all.

Olivia Fanaro. Thank you for falling in love with Morgan and Rachel. They are lucky to have you.

Rachel Lynn Solomon for helping me craft ITEOL into what it wanted to be. For all the chats, for all the love, for sharing a brain. I am forever grateful for your friendship.

Team G: My dear Jenny L. Howe and Renée Reynolds. I couldn't be more grateful that our journeys found each other. Thank you for your steadfast, heart-bolstering friendship, and for always believing you'd be in my acknowledgments one day. I love your guts.

Samantha Eaton for being the dearest friend, pointing out truck cab technicalities, and celebrating the 69 percent.

ITEOL's earliest readers: Sonja J. Kaye, Leanne Schwartz, Emily Grey, and London Shah, for being the most supportive, jump-on-a-call or into-a-writing-sprint friends.

RomDom: Maggie North, Regina Black, Nikki Payne, Sarah Burnard, and Ella Synclair. Thank you for making me laugh every damn day.

Viva La Colin: Ash K. Alexander, ReLynn Vaughn, Trysh Thompson, Jen DeLuca, and Helen Hoang. Thank you for all the love and support (and of course, the Hook GIFs).

The wonderful SoCal Crew: Susan Lee, Carlyn Greenwald, Auriane Desombre, Lindsay Grossman, and Marisa Kanter, for all the happy-screaming in DMs and IRL. I can't wait to brunch again soon.

My Pitch Wars Fam and Writing Community: Meryl Wilsner, Ruby Barrett, Sonia Hartl, Annette Christie, Rosie Danan, Monica Gomez-Hira, Heather Van Fleet, Rachel Griffin, Re-becca Sky, Lindsay Landgraf Hess, Kalie Holford, Erin Connor, Claire Laminen, Ashley Herring-Blake, Angela Montoya, Melanie Schubert, Jessica Parra, Kyla Zhao, Anita Kelly, Meredith Ireland, Sarah Glenn Marsh, Jessica James, Briana Morgan, Trisha Kelly, Kimberly VanderHorst, Kara McDowell, Brittany Kelley, Hailey Harlow, Kate Cochrane, Elora Cook, Jenna Miller, Torie Jean, anyone else I have chatted with along the way, and literally ALL of the Pitch Wars 2020 mentees. You have given me more light and strength than you'll ever know.

My agent sibs: Skyla Arndt, M.K. Lobb, Jo Fenning, Ava Wilder, Lacie Waldon, and ALL of #TeamClaire. Thank you for holding my hand during signing, sub, and every day after.

The #HoliGays22: Helena Greer, Alison Cochrun, Timothy Janovsky, and Jake Arlow. I am so happy and honored to be making the holidays gay with you!

#22Debuts. You all inspire me more than I could ever express, and I'm honored to be in your debut class.

My dear friends, Jessica Apperson and Megan Pratchard. Over the past decade, you never stopped asking how the writing was going. I love you. Also, to the Mom Group for fighting over who would receive the first copy.

Mom, thank you for listening for hours while I brainstormed terrible story ideas and always believing I'd get here. To Dad, for being a dreamer, for raising them, and for always knowing my dreams would come true. To Kelsey, whose loyal and tenacious heart is a rock, for being the biggest support, for happy-crying on the phone with me. To Grandma, who most definitely WILL star in any possible movie one day. I love you all more than words can say.

Carol, Brock, Jordan, Julia, and of COURSE my little Edith and Margaret. Thank you for the celebratory dinners, for being proud of my hard work, and for still giving me hugs, even when that work had me skipping showers. You are my biggest champions, and I love you.

Kona. You were the best dog a human could have. Thank

you for being by my side for as long as you could, and for every word that I typed. You're a good boy and I love you.

Aisley. When I look at you, I see two things: a daughter who will forever be much cooler than me, and the meaning of love embodied in one person. I write novels, and I could never find the words to describe my love for you; none are enough. Thank you for your heart, your smile, for saying, "Mom, go write your book." I love you, my darling.

Michael. Your heart is the most beautiful one I know. Thank you for believing in me, for seeing me, and for holding me with the greatest love. When I told you I wanted to be an author, you said, "Then you will." Having you by my side makes me soar. Thank you for keeping up with all the Adulting while I wrote. Thank you for always asking, "Is your book done yet?" because you knew that one day I'd answer with *yes*. The book is done now, and I couldn't have done it without you.

To you, beautiful reader. Thank you for making this book possible. This is for you.

Author's Note

Dear Reader,

Writing to you directly without the veil of story is an incredibly vulnerable feeling and the greatest honor. *Thank you* for spending your time with Morgan, Rachel, and the Fern Falls crew. Thank you for making this possible.

A few years ago, I never could have dreamed I'd be typing this letter today. All I wanted was to see my queer identity reflected in a happy holiday rom-com.

It was the end of 2019, and my town was racked by a terrible tragedy. My family and I spent that season holding each other close on the couch, watching countless holiday movies. The promise of warmth and joy by the time the credits rolled was a comfort we desperately needed; however, I couldn't help but notice that not only was my bisexual identity nowhere to be found, but the queer community as a whole was left out of the narrative almost completely.

I longed for that to change.

So, when a work-worn protagonist popped into my head

and crashed into a tree farm, I knew I had to tell her story. It's said that each character an author writes represents a piece of themselves. At first, that was impossible for me to believe about Morgan, because she was feisty, vibrant, and confident from the first line. As someone struggling with anxiety and depression, I hadn't felt any of those traits in quite a while. As that difficult winter lurched into 2020, it turned out that I needed Morgan's strength more than ever.

At the time, I had amassed several fantasy manuscripts that were never ready to go into the world, and as an avid romance reader, I was scared to fail at this genre I adore. But there was Morgan, barreling her way through my self-doubts and self-rejections, and the more I fell in love with her story, the more I found my writing voice, healed, and hoped. I also gained the courage to seek further care for my mental health.

Drafting *In the Event of Love* was truly a magical experience, like the story came to me when I needed it most. Eager to be in Fern Falls, I would write as the sun rose, and sometimes, if I paused typing and closed my eyes, I could envision threads of the world building up around me. This fictional town became a character of its own, wrapping me in a bright, sheltered space where I could be bold and brave and pour more of myself into a story than I ever had before. Fern Falls was inspired by many different places I've traveled with my family (to name one specifically: Pine Mountain Club, CA, where they have a hiking trail called The Enchanted Forest!), and by places I wished existed, but ultimately, it's my greatest hope that the world within these pages does for you what it did for me: Welcomes you in. Keeps you safe. Reaffirms that you are more than enough.

With all my heart, thank you for visiting.

Love,

Courtney Kae

IN THE EVENT OF LOVE

About This Guide

The suggested questions are included to enhance your group's
reading of Courtney Kae's *In the Event of Love*.

Discussion Questions

1. If you could visit Fern Falls, whom would you bring, where would you go in the town, and what would you do there?

2. What drink would you choose to be the drink of the day at Peak Perk Café?

3. Throughout the book, Morgan feels intense pressure to prove herself and gain external validation. Have you ever felt this way, and how did you work through it?

4. Both Morgan and Rachel experience strained relationships with their fathers, and they each handle them differently. Has there been a time in your life when you needed to make hard decisions about an important relationship?

5. Rachel and Morgan both endure different kinds of loss in their lives, and in the end, they lean on each other and their community and family to heal. Has there been a time in your life when someone has helped you heal?

6. Found family is a big theme in this book. Whom do you consider your found family?

7. What were your favorite holiday and romance tropes used throughout this book?

8. As Morgan settles back into being home, she has many fond memories of her childhood holidays. What is your favorite holiday memory?

9. The events discussed and staged in this book run from glamorous to rustic. If you could organize any event, what

would it be, and would you prefer it to be grand or simple in style?

10. Do you see Morgan and Rachel going on a honeymoon? If so, where do you see them going? What would Rachel pack in her suitcase, and what would Morgan pack in hers? If you don't see them going on a honeymoon, what do you see them doing instead?